Robert Louis Stevenson (13 November 1850 – 3 December 1894) was a Scottish novelist and travel writer, most noted for Treasure Island, Kidnapped, Strange Case of Dr Jekyll and Mr Hyde, and A Child's Garden of Verses. Born and educated in Edinburgh, Stevenson suffered from serious bronchial trouble for much of his life, but continued to write prolifically and travel widely, in defiance of his poor health. As a young man, he mixed in London literary circles, receiving encouragement from Andrew Lang, Edmund Gosse, Leslie Stephen and W. E. Henley, the last of whom may have provided the model for Long John Silver in Treasure Island. His travels took him to France, America and Australia, before he finally settled in Samoa, where he died. A celebrity in his lifetime, Stevenson attracted a more negative critical response for much of the 20th century, though his reputation has been largely restored. He is currently ranked as the 26th most translated author in the world.(Source: Wikipedia)

Literary works:

The Hair Trunk or The Ideal Commonwealth (1877)
Unfinished and unpublished.
Treasure Island (1883)
Prince Otto (1885)
Strange Case of Dr Jekyll and Mr Hyde (1886),
Kidnapped (1886)
The Black Arrow: A Tale of the Two Roses (1888)
The Master of Ballantrae: A Winter's Tale (1889),
The Wrong Box (1889)
The Wrecker (1892); co-written with Lloyd Osbourne.
Catriona (1893)
The Ebb-Tide (1894); co-written with Lloyd Osbourne.
Weir of Hermiston (1896)

THRONE CLASSICS

IN THE SOUTH SEAS, SONGS OF TRAVEL AND OTHER VERSES & EDINBURGH: PICTURESQUE NOTES

Robert Louis Stevenson

THRONE CLASSICS

This is a work of fiction. Names, characters, places, and incidents either are the product of the author's imagination or are used fictitiously. Any resemblance to actual persons, living or dead, events, or locales is entirely coincidental.

First Printing: 2019

ISBN 978-93-5383-954-3 (paperback)

ISBN 978-93-5383-955-0 (Hardcover)

Published by Throne Classics

www.throneclassics.com

Contents

IN THE SOUTH SEAS,
SONGS OF TRAVEL AND OTHER VERSES
&
EDINBURGH: PICTURESQUE NOTES

IN THE SOUTH SEAS

PART 1: THE MARQUESAS

CHAPTER I—AN ISLAND LANDFALL

For nearly ten years my health had been declining; and for some while before I set forth upon my voyage, I believed I was come to the afterpiece of life, and had only the nurse and undertaker to expect. It was suggested that I should try the South Seas; and I was not unwilling to visit like a ghost, and be carried like a bale, among scenes that had attracted me in youth and health. I chartered accordingly Dr. Merrit's schooner yacht, the Casco, seventy-four tons register; sailed from San Francisco towards the end of June 1888, visited the eastern islands, and was left early the next year at Honolulu. Hence, lacking courage to return to my old life of the house and sick-room, I set forth to leeward in a trading schooner, the Equator, of a little over seventy tons, spent four months among the atolls (low coral islands) of the Gilbert group, and reached Samoa towards the close of '89. By that time gratitude and habit were beginning to attach me to the islands; I had gained a competency of strength; I had made friends; I had learned new interests; the time of my voyages had passed like days in fairyland; and I decided to remain. I began to prepare these pages at sea, on a third cruise, in the trading steamer Janet Nicoll. If more days are granted me, they shall be passed where I have found life most pleasant and man most interesting; the axes of my black boys are already clearing the foundations of my future house; and I must learn to address readers from the uttermost parts of the sea.

That I should thus have reversed the verdict of Lord Tennyson's hero is less eccentric than appears. Few men who come to the islands leave them; they grow grey where they alighted; the palm shades and the trade-wind fans them till they die, perhaps cherishing to the last the fancy of a visit home, which is rarely made, more rarely enjoyed, and yet more rarely repeated. No part of the world exerts the same attractive power upon the visitor, and the task before me is to communicate to fireside travellers some sense of its seduction, and to describe the life, at sea and ashore, of many hundred thousand persons, some of our own blood and language, all our contemporaries, and yet as remote in thought and habit as Rob Roy or Barbarossa, the Apostles or the Cæsars.

The first experience can never be repeated. The first love, the first sunrise, the first South Sea island, are memories apart and touched a virginity of sense. On the 28th of July 1888 the moon was an hour down by four in the morning. In the east a radiating centre of brightness told of the day; and beneath, on the skyline, the morning bank was already building, black as ink. We have all read of the swiftness of the day's coming and departure in low latitudes; it is a point on which the scientific and sentimental tourist are at one, and has inspired some tasteful poetry. The period certainly varies with the season; but here is one case exactly noted. Although the dawn was thus preparing by four, the sun was not up till six; and it was half-past five before we could distinguish our expected islands from the clouds on the horizon. Eight degrees south, and the day two hours a-coming. The interval was passed on deck in the silence of expectation, the customary thrill of landfall heightened by the strangeness of the shores that we were then approaching. Slowly they took shape in the attenuating darkness. Ua-huna, piling up to a truncated summit, appeared the first upon the starboard bow; almost abeam arose our destination, Nuka-hiva, whelmed in cloud; and betwixt and to the southward, the first rays of the sun displayed the needles of Ua-pu. These pricked about the line of the horizon; like the pinnacles of some ornate and monstrous church, they stood there, in the sparkling brightness of the morning, the fit signboard of a world of wonders.

Not one soul aboard the Casco had set foot upon the islands, or knew, except by accident, one word of any of the island tongues; and it was with something perhaps of the same anxious pleasure as thrilled the bosom of discoverers that we drew near these problematic shores. The land heaved up in peaks and rising vales; it fell in cliffs and buttresses; its colour ran through fifty modulations in a scale of pearl and rose and olive; and it was crowned above by opalescent clouds. The suffusion of vague hues deceived the eye; the shadows of clouds were confounded with the articulations of the mountains; and the isle and its unsubstantial canopy rose and shimmered before us like a single mass. There was no beacon, no smoke of towns to be expected, no plying pilot. Somewhere, in that pale phantasmagoria of cliff and cloud, our haven lay concealed; and somewhere to the east of it—the only sea-mark given—a certain headland, known indifferently as Cape Adam and Eve, or Cape Jack and Jane, and distinguished by two colossal figures, the gross statuary of nature. These we were to find; for these we craned and stared, focused glasses, and wrangled over charts; and the sun was overhead and the land close ahead before we found them. To a ship approaching, like the Casco, from the north, they proved indeed the least conspicuous features of a striking coast; the surf flying high above its base; strange, austere, and feathered mountains rising behind; and Jack and Jane, or Adam and Eve, impending like a pair of warts above the breakers.

Thence we bore away along shore. On our port beam we might hear the explosions of the surf; a few birds flew fishing under the prow; there was no other sound or mark of life, whether of man or beast, in all that quarter of the island. Winged by her own impetus and the dying breeze, the Casco skimmed under cliffs, opened out a cove, showed us a beach and some green trees, and flitted by again, bowing to the swell. The trees, from our distance, might have been hazel; the beach might have been in Europe; the mountain forms behind modelled in little from the Alps, and the forest which clustered on their ramparts a growth no more considerable than our Scottish heath. Again the cliff yawned, but now with a deeper entry; and the Casco, hauling her wind, began to slide into the bay of Anaho. The cocoa-palm, that giraffe of vegetables, so graceful, so ungainly, to the European eye so foreign, was to be seen crowding on the beach, and climbing and fringing the steep sides of mountains. Rude and bare hills embraced the inlet upon either hand; it was enclosed to the landward by a bulk of shattered mountains. In every crevice of that barrier the forest harboured, roosting and nestling there like birds about a ruin; and far above, it greened and roughened the razor edges of the summit.

Under the eastern shore, our schooner, now bereft of any breeze, continued to creep in: the smart creature, when once under way, appearing motive in herself. From close aboard arose the bleating of young lambs; a bird sang in the hillside; the scent of the land and of a hundred fruits or flowers flowed forth to meet us; and, presently, a house or two appeared, standing high upon the ankles of the hills, and one of these surrounded with what seemed a garden. These conspicuous habitations, that patch of culture, had we but known it, were a mark of the passage of whites; and we might have approached a hundred islands and not found their parallel. It was longer ere we spied the native village, standing (in the universal fashion) close upon a curve of beach, close under a grove of palms; the sea in front growling and whitening on a concave arc of reef. For the cocoa-tree and the island man are both lovers and neighbours of the surf. 'The coral waxes, the palm grows, but man departs,' says the sad Tahitian proverb; but they are all three, so long as they endure, co-haunters of the beach. The mark of anchorage was a blow-hole in the rocks, near the south-easterly corner of the bay. Punctually to our use, the blow-hole spouted; the schooner turned upon her heel; the anchor plunged. It was a small sound, a great event; my soul went down with these moorings whence no windlass may extract nor any diver fish it up; and I, and some part of my ship's company, were from that hour the bondslaves of the isles of Vivien.

Before yet the anchor plunged a canoe was already paddling from the hamlet. It contained two men: one white, one brown and tattooed across the face with bands of blue, both in immaculate white European clothes: the resident trader, Mr. Regler, and the native chief, Taipi-Kikino. 'Captain, is it permitted to come on board?' were the first words we heard among the islands. Canoe followed canoe till the ship swarmed with stalwart, six-foot men in every stage of undress; some in a shirt, some in a loin-cloth, one in a handkerchief imperfectly adjusted; some, and these the more considerable, tattooed from head to foot in awful patterns; some barbarous and knived; one, who sticks in my memory as something bestial, squatting on his hams in a canoe, sucking an orange and spitting it out again to alternate sides with ape-like vivacity—all talking, and we could not understand one word; all trying to trade with us who had no thought of trading, or offering us island curios at prices palpably absurd. There was no word of welcome; no show of civility; no hand extended save that of the chief and Mr. Regler. As we still continued to refuse the proffered articles, complaint ran high and rude; and one, the jester of the party, railed upon our meanness amid jeering laughter. Amongst other angry pleasantries—'Here is a mighty fine ship,' said he, 'to have no money on board!' I own I was inspired with sensible repugnance; even with alarm. The ship was manifestly in their power; we had women on board; I knew nothing of my guests beyond the fact that they were cannibals; the Directory (my only guide) was full of timid cautions; and as for the trader, whose presence might else have reassured me, were not whites in the Pacific the usual instigators and accomplices of native outrage? When he reads this confession, our kind friend, Mr. Regler, can afford to smile.

Later in the day, as I sat writing up my journal, the cabin was filled from end to end with Marquesans: three brown-skinned generations, squatted cross-legged upon the floor, and regarding me in silence with embarrassing eyes. The eyes of all Polynesians are large, luminous, and melting; they are like the eyes of animals and some Italians. A kind of despair came over me, to sit there helpless under all these staring orbs, and be thus blocked in a corner of my cabin by this speechless crowd: and a kind of rage to think they were beyond the reach of articulate communication, like furred animals, or folk born deaf, or the dwellers of some alien planet.

To cross the Channel is, for a boy of twelve, to change heavens; to cross the Atlantic, for a man of twenty-four, is hardly to modify his diet. But I was now escaped out of the shadow of the Roman empire, under whose toppling monuments we were all cradled, whose laws and letters are on every hand of us, constraining and preventing. I was now to see what men might be whose fathers had never studied Virgil, had never been conquered by Cæsar, and never been ruled by the wisdom of Gaius or Papinian. By the same step I had journeyed forth out of that comfortable zone of kindred languages, where the curse of Babel is so easy to be remedied; and my new fellow-creatures sat before me dumb like images. Methought, in my travels, all human relation was to be excluded; and when I returned home (for in those days I still projected my return) I should have but dipped into a picture-book without a text. Nay, and I even questioned if my travels should be much prolonged; perhaps they were destined to a speedy end; perhaps my subsequent friend, Kauanui, whom I remarked there, sitting silent with the rest, for a man of some authority, might leap from his hams with an ear-splitting signal, the ship be carried at a rush, and the ship's company butchered for the table.

There could be nothing more natural than these apprehensions, nor anything more groundless. In my experience of the islands, I had never again so menacing a reception; were I to meet with such to-day, I should be more alarmed and tenfold more surprised. The majority of Polynesians are easy folk to get in touch with, frank, fond of notice, greedy of the least affection, like amiable, fawning dogs; and even with the Marquesans, so recently and so imperfectly redeemed from a blood-boltered barbarism, all were to become our intimates, and one, at least, was to mourn sincerely our departure.

CHAPTER II—MAKING FRIENDS

The impediment of tongues was one that I particularly over-estimated. The languages of Polynesia are easy to smatter, though hard to speak with elegance. And they are extremely similar, so that a person who has a tincture of one or two may risk, not without hope, an attempt upon the others.

And again, not only is Polynesian easy to smatter, but interpreters abound. Missionaries, traders, and broken white folk living on the bounty of the natives, are to be found in almost every isle and hamlet; and even where these are unserviceable, the natives themselves have often scraped up a little English, and in the French zone (though far less commonly) a little French-English, or an efficient pidgin, what is called to the westward 'Beach-la-Mar,' comes easy to the Polynesian; it is now taught, besides, in the schools of Hawaii; and from the multiplicity of British ships, and the nearness of the States on the one hand and the colonies on the other, it may be called, and will almost certainly become, the tongue of the Pacific. I will instance a few examples. I met in Majuro a Marshall Island boy who spoke excellent English; this he had learned in the German firm in Jaluit, yet did not speak one word of German. I heard from a gendarme who had taught school in Rapa-iti that while the children had the utmost difficulty or reluctance to learn French, they picked up English on the wayside, and as if by accident. On one of the most out-of-the-way atolls in the Carolines, my friend Mr. Benjamin Hird was amazed to find the lads playing cricket on the beach and talking English; and it was in English that the crew of the Janet Nicoll, a set of black boys from different Melanesian islands, communicated with other natives throughout the cruise, transmitted orders, and sometimes jested together on the fore-hatch. But what struck me perhaps most of all was a word I heard on the verandah of the Tribunal at Noumea. A case had just been heard—a trial for infanticide against an ape-like native woman; and the audience were smoking cigarettes as they awaited the verdict. An anxious, amiable French lady, not far from tears, was eager for acquittal, and declared she would engage the prisoner to be her children's nurse. The bystanders exclaimed at the proposal; the woman was a savage, said they, and spoke no language. 'Mais, vous savez,' objected the fair sentimentalist; 'ils apprennent si vite l'anglais!'

But to be able to speak to people is not all. And in the first stage of my relations with natives I was helped by two things. To begin with, I was the show-man of the Casco. She, her fine lines, tall spars, and snowy decks, the crimson fittings of the saloon, and the white, the gilt, and the repeating mirrors of the tiny cabin, brought us a hundred visitors. The men fathomed out her dimensions with their arms, as their fathers fathomed out the ships of Cook; the women declared the cabins more lovely than a church; bouncing Junos were never weary of sitting in the chairs and contemplating in the glass their own bland images; and I have seen one lady strip up her dress, and, with cries of wonder and delight, rub herself bare-breeched upon the velvet cushions. Biscuit, jam, and syrup was the entertainment; and, as in European parlours, the photograph album went the round. This sober gallery, their everyday costumes and physiognomies, had become transformed, in three weeks' sailing, into things wonderful and rich and foreign; alien faces, barbaric dresses, they were now beheld and fingered, in the swerving cabin, with innocent excitement and surprise. Her Majesty was often recognised, and I have seen French subjects kiss her photograph; Captain Speedy—in an Abyssinian war-dress, supposed to be the uniform of the British army—met with much acceptance; and the effigies of Mr. Andrew Lang were admired in the Marquesas. There is the place for him to go when he shall be weary of Middlesex and Homer.

It was perhaps yet more important that I had enjoyed in my youth some knowledge of our Scots folk of the Highlands and the Islands. Not much beyond a century has passed since these were in the same convulsive and transitionary state as the Marquesans of to-day. In both cases an alien authority enforced, the clans disarmed, the chiefs deposed, new customs introduced, and chiefly that fashion of regarding money as the means and object of existence. The commercial age, in each, succeeding at a bound to an age of war abroad and patriarchal communism at home. In one the cherished practice of tattooing, in the other a cherished costume, proscribed. In each a main luxury cut off: beef, driven under cloud of night from Lowland pastures, denied to the meat-loving Highlander; long-pig, pirated from the next village, to the man-eating Kanaka. The grumbling, the secret ferment, the fears and resentments, the alarms and sudden councils of Marquesan chiefs, reminded me continually of the days of Lovat and Struan. Hospitality, tact, natural fine manners, and a touchy punctilio, are common to both races: common to both tongues the trick of dropping medial consonants. Here is a table of two widespread Polynesian words:—

	House.	Love. [12]
Tahitian	FARE	AROHA
New Zealand	WHARE	
Samoan	FALE	TALOFA
Manihiki	FALE	ALOHA
Hawaiian	HALE	ALOHA
Marquesan	HA'E	KAOHA

The elision of medial consonants, so marked in these Marquesan instances, is no less common both in Gaelic and the Lowland Scots. Stranger still, that prevalent Polynesian sound, the so-called catch, written with an apostrophe, and often or always the gravestone of a perished consonant, is to be heard in Scotland to this day. When a Scot pronounces water, better, or bottle—wa'er, be'er, or bo'le—the sound is precisely that of the catch; and I think we may go beyond, and say, that if such a population could be isolated, and this mispronunciation should become the rule, it might prove the first stage of transition from t to k, which is the disease of Polynesian languages.

The tendency of the Marquesans, however, is to urge against consonants, or at least on the very common letter l, a war of mere extermination. A hiatus is agreeable to any Polynesian ear; the ear even of the stranger soon grows used to these barbaric voids; but only in the Marquesan will you find such names as Haaii and Paaaeua, when each individual vowel must be separately uttered.

These points of similarity between a South Sea people and some of my own folk at home ran much in my head in the islands; and not only inclined me to view my fresh acquaintances with favour, but continually modified my judgment. A polite Englishman comes to-day to the Marquesans and is amazed to find the men tattooed; polite Italians came not long ago to England and found our fathers stained with woad; and when I paid the return visit as a little boy, I was highly diverted with the backwardness of Italy: so insecure, so much a matter of the day and hour, is the pre-eminence of race. It was so that I hit upon a means of communication which I recommend to travellers. When I desired any detail of savage custom, or of superstitious belief, I cast back in the story of my fathers, and fished for what I wanted with some trait of equal barbarism: Michael Scott, Lord Derwentwater's head, the second-sight, the Water Kelpie,—each of these I have found to be a killing bait; the black bull's head of Stirling procured me the legend of Rahero; and what I knew of the Cluny Macphersons, or the Appin Stewarts, enabled me to learn, and helped me to understand, about the Tevas of Tahiti. The native was no longer ashamed, his sense of kinship grew warmer, and his lips were opened. It is this sense of kinship that the traveller must rouse and share; or he had better content himself with travels from the blue bed to the brown. And the presence of one Cockney titterer will cause a whole party to walk in clouds of darkness.

The hamlet of Anaho stands on a margin of flat land between the west of the beach and the spring of the impending mountains. A grove of palms, perpetually ruffling its green fans, carpets it (as for a triumph) with fallen branches, and shades it like an arbour. A road runs from end to end of the covert among beds of flowers, the milliner's shop of the community; and here and there, in the grateful twilight, in an air filled with a diversity of scents, and still within hearing of the surf upon the reef, the native houses stand in scattered neighbourhood. The same word, as we have seen, represents in many tongues of Polynesia, with scarce a shade of difference, the abode of man. But although the word be the same, the structure itself continually varies; and the Marquesan, among the most backward and barbarous of islanders, is yet the most commodiously lodged. The grass huts of Hawaii, the birdcage houses of Tahiti, or the open shed, with the crazy Venetian blinds, of the polite Samoan—none of these can be compared with the Marquesan paepae-hae, or dwelling platform. The paepae is an oblong terrace built without cement or black volcanic stone, from twenty to fifty feet in length, raised from four to eight feet from the earth, and accessible by a broad stair. Along the back of this, and coming to about half its width, runs the open front of the house, like a covered gallery: the interior sometimes neat and almost elegant in its bareness, the sleeping space divided off by an endlong coaming, some bright raiment perhaps hanging from a nail, and a lamp and one of White's sewing-machines the only marks of civilization. On the outside, at one end of the terrace, burns the cooking-fire under a shed; at the other there is perhaps a pen for pigs; the remainder is the evening lounge and al fresco banquet-hall of the inhabitants. To some houses water is brought down the mountains in bamboo pipes, perforated for the sake of sweetness. With the Highland comparison in my mind, I was struck to remember the sluttish mounds of turf and stone in which I have sat and been entertained in the Hebrides and the North Islands. Two things, I suppose, explain the contrast. In Scotland wood is rare, and with materials so rude as turf and stone the very hope of neatness is excluded. And in Scotland it is cold. Shelter and a hearth are needs so pressing that a man looks not beyond; he is out all day after a bare bellyful, and at night when he saith, 'Aha, it is warm!' he has not appetite for more. Or if for something else, then something higher; a fine school of poetry and song arose in these rough shelters, and an air like 'Lochaber no more' is an evidence of refinement more convincing, as well as more imperishable, than a palace.

To one such dwelling platform a considerable troop of relatives and dependants resort. In the hour of the dusk, when the fire blazes, and the scent of the cooked breadfruit fills the air, and perhaps the lamp glints already between the pillars and the house, you shall behold them silently assemble to this meal, men, women, and children; and the dogs and pigs frisk together up the terrace stairway, switching rival tails. The strangers from the ship were soon equally welcome: welcome to dip their fingers in the wooden dish, to drink cocoanuts, to share the circulating pipe, and to hear and hold high debate about the misdeeds of the French, the Panama Canal, or the geographical position of San Francisco and New Yo'ko. In a Highland hamlet, quite out of reach of any tourist, I have met the same plain and dignified hospitality.

I have mentioned two facts—the distasteful behaviour of our earliest visitors, and the case of the lady who rubbed herself upon the cushions—which would give a very false opinion of Marquesan manners. The great majority of Polynesians are excellently mannered; but the Marquesan stands apart, annoying and attractive, wild, shy, and refined. If you make him a present he affects to forget it, and it must be offered him again at his going: a pretty formality I have found nowhere else. A hint will get rid of any one or any number; they are so fiercely proud and modest; while many of the more lovable but blunter islanders crowd upon a stranger, and can be no more driven off than flies. A slight or an insult the Marquesan seems never to forget. I was one day talking by the wayside with my friend Hoka, when I perceived his eyes suddenly to flash and his stature to swell. A white horseman was coming down the mountain, and as he passed, and while he paused to exchange salutations with myself, Hoka was still staring and ruffling like a gamecock. It was a Corsican who had years before called him cochon sauvage—coçon chauvage, as Hoka mispronounced it. With people so nice and so touchy, it was scarce to be supposed that our company of greenhorns should not blunder into offences. Hoka, on one of his visits, fell suddenly in a brooding silence, and presently after left the ship with cold formality. When he took me back into favour, he adroitly and pointedly explained the nature of my offence: I had asked him to sell cocoa-nuts; and in Hoka's view articles of food were things that a gentleman should give, not sell; or at least that he should not sell to any friend. On another occasion I gave my boat's crew a luncheon of chocolate and biscuits. I had sinned, I could never learn how, against some point of observance; and though I was drily thanked, my offerings were left upon the beach. But our worst mistake was a slight we put on Toma, Hoka's adoptive father, and in his own eyes the rightful chief of Anaho. In the first place, we did not call upon him, as perhaps we should, in his fine new European house, the only one in the hamlet. In the second, when we came ashore upon a visit to his rival, Taipi-Kikino, it was Toma whom we saw standing at the head of the beach, a magnificent figure of a man, magnificently tattooed; and it was of Toma that we asked our question: 'Where is the chief?' 'What chief?' cried Toma, and turned his back on the blasphemers. Nor did he forgive us. Hoka came and went with us daily; but, alone I believe of all the countryside, neither Toma nor his wife set foot on board the Casco. The temptation resisted it is hard for a European to compute. The flying city of Laputa moored for a fortnight in St. James's Park affords but a pale figure of the Casco anchored before Anaho; for the Londoner has still his change of pleasures, but the Marquesan passes to his grave through an unbroken uniformity of days.

On the afternoon before it was intended we should sail, a valedictory party came on board: nine of our particular friends equipped with gifts and dressed as for a festival. Hoka, the chief dancer and singer, the greatest dandy of Anaho, and one of the handsomest young fellows in the world-sullen, showy, dramatic, light as a feather and strong as an ox—it would have been hard, on that occasion, to recognise, as he sat there stooped and silent, his face heavy and grey. It was strange to see the lad so much affected; stranger still to recognise in his last gift one of the curios we had refused on the first day, and to know our friend, so gaily dressed, so plainly moved at our departure, for one of the half-naked crew that had besieged and insulted us on our arrival: strangest of all, perhaps, to find, in that carved handle of a fan, the last of those curiosities of the first day which had now all been given to us by their possessors—their chief merchandise, for which they had sought to ransom us as long as we were strangers, which they pressed on us for nothing as soon as we were friends. The last visit was not long protracted. One after another they shook hands and got down into their canoe; when Hoka turned his back immediately upon the ship, so that we saw his face no more. Taipi, on the other hand, remained standing and facing us with gracious valedictory gestures; and when Captain Otis dipped the ensign, the whole party saluted with their hats. This was the farewell; the episode of our visit to Anaho was held concluded; and though the Casco remained nearly forty hours at her moorings, not one returned on board, and I am inclined to think they avoided appearing on the beach. This reserve and dignity is the finest trait of the Marquesan.

CHAPTER III—THE MAROON

Of the beauties of Anaho books might be written. I remember waking about three, to find the air temperate and scented. The long swell brimmed into the bay, and seemed to fill it full and then subside. Gently, deeply, and silently the Casco rolled; only at times a block piped like a bird. Oceanward, the heaven was bright with stars and the sea with their reflections. If I looked to that side, I might have sung with the Hawaiian poet:

Ua maomao ka lani, ua kahaea luna,

Ua pipi ka maka o ka hoku.

(The heavens were fair, they stretched above,

Many were the eyes of the stars.)

And then I turned shoreward, and high squalls were overhead; the mountains loomed up black; and I could have fancied I had slipped ten thousand miles away and was anchored in a Highland loch; that when the day came, it would show pine, and heather, and green fern, and roofs of turf sending up the smoke of peats; and the alien speech that should next greet my ears must be Gaelic, not Kanaka.

And day, when it came, brought other sights and thoughts. I have watched the morning break in many quarters of the world; it has been certainly one of the chief joys of my existence, and the dawn that I saw with most emotion shone upon the bay of Anaho. The mountains abruptly overhang the port with every variety of surface and of inclination, lawn, and cliff, and forest. Not one of these but wore its proper tint of saffron, of sulphur, of the clove, and of the rose. The lustre was like that of satin; on the lighter hues there seemed to float an efflorescence; a solemn bloom appeared on the more dark. The light itself was the ordinary light of morning, colourless and clean; and on this ground of jewels, pencilled out the least detail of drawing. Meanwhile, around the hamlet, under the palms, where the blue shadow lingered, the red coals of cocoa husk and the light trails of smoke betrayed the awakening business of the day; along the beach men and women, lads and lasses, were returning from the bath in bright raiment, red and blue and green, such as we delighted to see in the coloured little pictures of our childhood; and presently the sun had cleared the eastern hill, and the glow of the day was over all.

The glow continued and increased, the business, from the main part, ceased before it had begun. Twice in the day there was a certain stir of shepherding along the seaward hills. At times a canoe went out to fish. At times a woman or two languidly filled a basket in the cotton patch. At times a pipe would sound out of the shadow of a house, ringing the changes on its three notes, with an effect like Que le jour me dure, repeated endlessly. Or at times, across a corner of the bay, two natives might communicate in the Marquesan manner with conventional whistlings. All else was sleep and silence. The surf broke and shone around the shores; a species of black crane fished in the broken water; the black pigs were continually galloping by on some affair; but the people might never have awaked, or they might all be dead.

My favourite haunt was opposite the hamlet, where was a landing in a cove under a lianaed cliff. The beach was lined with palms and a tree called the purao, something between the fig and mulberry in growth, and bearing a flower like a great yellow poppy with a maroon heart. In places rocks encroached upon the sand; the beach would be all submerged; and the surf would bubble warmly as high as to my knees, and play with cocoa-nut husks as our more homely ocean plays with wreck and wrack and bottles. As the reflux drew down, marvels of colour and design streamed between my feet; which I would grasp at, miss, or seize: now to find them what they promised, shells to grace a cabinet or be set in gold upon a lady's finger; now to catch only maya of coloured sand, pounded fragments and pebbles, that, as soon as they were dry, became as dull and homely as the flints upon a garden path. I have toiled at this childish pleasure for hours in the strong sun, conscious of my incurable ignorance; but too keenly pleased to be ashamed. Meanwhile, the blackbird (or his tropical understudy) would be fluting in the thickets overhead.

A little further, in the turn of the bay, a streamlet trickled in the bottom of a den, thence spilling down a stair of rock into the sea. The draught of air drew down under the foliage in the very bottom of the den, which was a perfect arbour for coolness. In front it stood open on the blue bay and the Casco lying there under her awning and her cheerful colours. Overhead was a thatch of puraos, and over these again palms brandished their bright fans, as I have seen a conjurer make himself a halo out of naked swords. For in this spot, over a neck of low land at the foot of the mountains, the trade-wind streams into Anaho Bay in a flood of almost constant volume and velocity, and of a heavenly coolness.

It chanced one day that I was ashore in the cove, with Mrs. Stevenson and the ship's cook. Except for the Casco lying outside, and a crane or two, and the ever-busy wind and sea, the face of the world was of a prehistoric emptiness; life appeared to stand stock-still, and the sense of isolation was profound and refreshing. On a sudden, the trade-wind, coming in a gust over the isthmus, struck and scattered the fans of the palms above the den; and, behold! in two of the tops there sat a native, motionless as an idol and watching us, you would have said, without a wink. The next moment the tree closed, and the glimpse was gone. This discovery of human presences latent overhead in a place where we had supposed ourselves alone, the immobility of our tree-top spies, and the thought that perhaps at all hours we were similarly supervised, struck us with a chill. Talk languished on the beach. As for the cook (whose conscience was not clear), he never afterwards set foot on shore, and twice, when the Casco appeared to be driving on the rocks, it was amusing to observe that man's alacrity; death, he was persuaded, awaiting him upon the beach. It was more than a year later, in the Gilberts, that the explanation dawned upon myself. The natives were drawing palm-tree wine, a thing forbidden by law; and when the wind thus suddenly revealed them, they were doubtless more troubled than ourselves.

At the top of the den there dwelt an old, melancholy, grizzled man of the name of Tari (Charlie) Coffin. He was a native of Oahu, in the Sandwich Islands; and had gone to sea in his youth in the American whalers; a circumstance to which he owed his name, his English, his down-east twang, and the misfortune of his innocent life. For one captain, sailing out of New Bedford, carried him to Nuka-hiva and marooned him there among the cannibals. The motive for this act was inconceivably small; poor Tari's wages, which were thus economised, would scarce have shook the credit of the New Bedford owners. And the act itself was simply murder. Tari's life must have hung in the beginning by a hair. In the grief and terror of that time, it is not unlikely he went mad, an infirmity to which he was still liable; or perhaps a child may have taken a fancy to him and ordained him to be spared. He escaped at least alive, married in the island, and when I knew him was a widower with a married son and a granddaughter. But the thought of Oahu haunted him; its praise was for ever on his lips; he beheld it, looking back, as a place of ceaseless feasting, song, and dance; and in his dreams I daresay he revisits it with joy. I wonder what he would think if he could be carried there indeed, and see the modern town of Honolulu brisk with traffic, and the palace with its guards, and the great hotel, and Mr. Berger's band with their uniforms and outlandish instruments; or what he would think to see the brown faces grown so few and the white so many; and his father's land sold, for planting sugar, and his father's house quite perished, or perhaps the last of them struck leprous and immured between the surf and the cliffs on Molokai? So simply, even in South Sea Islands, and so sadly, the changes come.

Tari was poor, and poorly lodged. His house was a wooden frame, run up by Europeans; it was indeed his official residence, for Tari was the shepherd of the promontory sheep. I can give a perfect inventory of its contents: three kegs, a tin biscuit-box, an iron saucepan, several cocoa-shell cups, a lantern, and three bottles, probably containing oil; while the clothes of the family and a few mats were thrown across the open rafters. Upon my first meeting with this exile he had conceived for me one of the baseless island friendships, had given me nuts to drink, and carried me up the den 'to see my house'—the only entertainment that he had to offer. He liked the 'Amelican,' he said, and the 'Inglisman,' but the 'Flessman' was his abhorrence; and he was careful to explain that if he had thought us 'Fless,' we should have had none of his nuts, and never a sight of his house. His distaste for the French I can partly understand, but not at all his toleration of the Anglo-Saxon. The next day he brought me a pig, and some days later one of our party going ashore found him in act to bring a second. We were still strange to the islands; we were pained by the poor man's generosity, which he could ill afford, and, by a natural enough but quite unpardonable blunder, we refused the pig. Had Tari been a Marquesan we should have seen him no more; being what he was, the most mild, long-suffering, melancholy man, he took a revenge a hundred times more painful. Scarce had the canoe with the nine villagers put off from their farewell before the Casco was boarded from the other side. It was Tari; coming thus late because he had no canoe of his own, and had found it hard to borrow one; coming thus solitary (as indeed we always saw him), because he was a stranger in the land, and the dreariest of company. The rest of my family basely fled from the encounter. I must receive our injured friend alone; and the interview must have lasted hard upon an hour, for he was loath to tear himself away. 'You go 'way. I see you no more—no, sir!' he lamented; and then looking about him with rueful admiration, 'This goodee ship—no, sir!—goodee ship!' he would exclaim: the 'no, sir,' thrown out sharply through the nose upon a rising inflection, an echo from New Bedford and the fallacious whaler. From these expressions of grief and praise, he would return continually to the case of the rejected pig. 'I like give present all 'e same you,' he complained; 'only got pig: you no take him!' He was a poor man; he had no choice of gifts; he had only a pig, he repeated; and I had refused it. I have rarely been more wretched than to see him sitting there, so old, so grey, so poor, so hardly fortuned, of so rueful a countenance, and to appreciate, with growing keenness, the affront which I had so innocently dealt him; but it was one of those cases in which speech is vain.

Tari's son was smiling and inert; his daughter-in-law, a girl of sixteen, pretty, gentle, and grave, more intelligent than most Anaho women, and with a fair share of French; his grandchild, a mite of a creature at the breast. I went up the den one day when Tari was from home, and found the son making a cotton sack, and madame suckling mademoiselle. When I had sat down with them on the floor, the girl began to question me about England; which I tried to describe, piling the pan and the cocoa shells one upon another to represent the houses, and explaining, as best I was able, and by word and gesture, the over-population, the hunger, and the perpetual toil. 'Pas de cocotiers? pas do popoi?' she asked. I told her it was too cold, and went through an elaborate performance, shutting out draughts, and crouching over an imaginary fire, to make sure she understood. But she understood right well; remarked it must be bad for the health, and sat a while gravely reflecting on that picture of unwonted sorrows. I am sure it roused her pity, for it struck in her another thought always uppermost in the Marquesan bosom; and she began with a smiling sadness, and looking on me out of melancholy eyes, to lament the decease of her own people. 'Ici pas de Kanaques,' said she; and taking the baby from her breast, she held it out to me with both her hands. 'Tenez—a little baby like this; then dead. All the Kanaques die. Then no more.' The smile, and this instancing by the girl-mother of her own tiny flesh and blood, affected me strangely; they spoke of so tranquil a despair. Meanwhile the husband smilingly made his sack; and the unconscious babe struggled to reach a pot of raspberry jam, friendship's offering, which I had just brought up the den; and in a perspective of centuries I saw their case as ours, death coming in like a tide, and the day already numbered when there should be no more Beretani, and no more of any race whatever, and (what oddly touched me) no more literary works and no more readers.

CHAPTER IV—DEATH

The thought of death, I have said, is uppermost in the mind of the Marquesan. It would be strange if it were otherwise. The race is perhaps the handsomest extant. Six feet is about the middle height of males; they are strongly muscled, free from fat, swift in action, graceful in repose; and the women, though fatter and duller, are still comely animals. To judge by the eye, there is no race more viable; and yet death reaps them with both hands. When Bishop Dordillon first came to Tai-o-hae, he reckoned the inhabitants at many thousands; he was but newly dead, and in the same bay Stanislao Moanatini counted on his fingers eight residual natives. Or take the valley of Hapaa, known to readers of Herman Melville under the grotesque misspelling of Hapar. There are but two writers who have touched the South Seas with any genius, both Americans: Melville and Charles Warren Stoddard; and at the christening of the first and greatest, some influential fairy must have been neglected: 'He shall be able to see,' 'He shall be able to tell,' 'He shall be able to charm,' said the friendly godmothers; 'But he shall not be able to hear,' exclaimed the last. The tribe of Hapaa is said to have numbered some four hundred, when the small-pox came and reduced them by one-fourth. Six months later a woman developed tubercular consumption; the disease spread like a fire about the valley, and in less than a year two survivors, a man and a woman, fled from that new-created solitude. A similar Adam and Eve may some day wither among new races, the tragic residue of Britain. When I first heard this story the date staggered me; but I am now inclined to think it possible. Early in the year of my visit, for example, or late the year before, a first case of phthisis appeared in a household of seventeen persons, and by the month of August, when the tale was told me, one soul survived, and that was a boy who had been absent at his schooling. And depopulation works both ways, the doors of death being set wide open, and the door of birth almost closed. Thus, in the half-year ending July 1888 there were twelve deaths and but one birth in the district of the Hatiheu. Seven or eight more deaths were to be looked for in the ordinary course; and M. Aussel, the observant gendarme, knew of but one likely birth. At this rate it is no matter of surprise if the population in that part should have declined in forty years from six thousand to less than four hundred; which are, once more on the authority of M. Aussel, the estimated figures. And the rate of decline must have even accelerated towards the end.

A good way to appreciate the depopulation is to go by land from Anaho to Hatiheu on the adjacent bay. The road is good travelling, but cruelly steep. We seemed scarce to have passed the deserted house which stands highest in Anaho before we were looking dizzily down upon its roof; the Casco well out in the bay, and rolling for a wager, shrank visibly; and presently through the gap of Tari's isthmus, Ua-huna was seen to hang cloudlike on the horizon. Over the summit, where the wind blew really chill, and whistled in the reed-like grass, and tossed the grassy fell of the pandanus, we stepped suddenly, as through a door, into the next vale and bay of Hatiheu. A bowl of mountains encloses it upon three sides. On the fourth this rampart has been bombarded into ruins, runs down to seaward in imminent and shattered crags, and presents the one practicable breach of the blue bay. The interior of this vessel is crowded with lovely and valuable trees,—orange, breadfruit, mummy-apple, cocoa, the island chestnut, and for weeds, the pine and the banana. Four perennial streams water and keep it green; and along the dell, first of one, then of another, of these, the road, for a considerable distance, descends into this fortunate valley. The song of the waters and the familiar disarray of boulders gave us a strong sense of home, which the exotic foliage, the daft-like growth of the pandanus, the buttressed trunk of the banyan, the black pigs galloping in the bush, and the architecture of the native houses dissipated ere it could be enjoyed.

The houses on the Hatiheu side begin high up; higher yet, the more melancholy spectacle of empty paepaes. When a native habitation is deserted, the superstructure—pandanus thatch, wattle, unstable tropical timber—speedily rots, and is speedily scattered by the wind. Only the stones of the terrace endure; nor can any ruin, cairn, or standing stone, or vitrified fort present a more stern appearance of antiquity. We must have passed from six to eight of these now houseless platforms. On the main road of the island, where it crosses the valley of Taipi, Mr. Osbourne tells me they are to be reckoned by the dozen; and as the roads have been made long posterior to their erection, perhaps to their desertion, and must simply be regarded as lines drawn at random through the bush, the forest on either hand must be equally filled with these survivals: the gravestones of whole families. Such ruins are tapu [29] in the strictest sense; no native must approach them; they have become outposts of the kingdom of the grave. It might appear a natural and pious custom in the hundreds who are left, the rearguard of perished thousands, that their feet should leave untrod these hearthstones of their fathers. I believe, in fact, the custom rests on different and more grim conceptions. But the house, the grave, and even the body of the dead, have been always particularly honoured by Marquesans. Until recently the corpse was sometimes kept in the family and daily oiled and sunned, until, by gradual and revolting stages, it dried into a kind of mummy. Offerings are still laid upon the grave. In Traitor's Bay, Mr. Osbourne saw a man buy a looking-glass to lay upon his son's. And the sentiment against the desecration of tombs, thoughtlessly ruffled in the laying down of the new roads, is a chief ingredient in the native hatred for the French.

The Marquesan beholds with dismay the approaching extinction of his race. The thought of death sits down with him to meat, and rises with him from his bed; he lives and breathes under a shadow of mortality awful to support; and he is so inured to the apprehension that he greets the reality with relief. He does not even seek to support a disappointment; at an affront, at a breach of one of his fleeting and communistic love-affairs, he seeks an instant refuge in the grave. Hanging is now the fashion. I heard of three who had hanged themselves in the west end of Hiva-oa during the first half of 1888; but though this be a common form of suicide in other parts of the South Seas, I cannot think it will continue popular in the Marquesas. Far more suitable to Marquesan sentiment is the old form of poisoning with the fruit of the eva, which offers to the native suicide a cruel but deliberate death, and gives time for those decencies of the last hour, to which he attaches such remarkable importance. The coffin can thus be at hand, the pigs killed, the cry of the mourners sounding already through the house; and then it is, and not before, that the Marquesan is conscious of achievement, his life all rounded in, his robes (like Cæsar's) adjusted for the final act. Praise not any man till he is dead, said the ancients; envy not any man till you hear the mourners, might be the Marquesan parody. The coffin, though of late introduction, strangely engages their attention. It is to the mature Marquesan what a watch is to the European schoolboy. For ten years Queen Vaekehu had dunned the fathers; at last, but the other day, they let her have her will, gave her her coffin, and the woman's soul is at rest. I was told a droll instance of the force of this preoccupation. The Polynesians are subject to a disease seemingly rather of the will than of the body. I was told the Tahitians have a word for it, erimatua, but cannot find it in my dictionary. A gendarme, M. Nouveau, has seen men beginning to succumb to this insubstantial malady, has routed them from their houses, turned them on to do their trick upon the roads, and in two days has seen them cured. But this other remedy is more original: a Marquesan, dying of this discouragement—perhaps I should rather say this acquiescence—has been known, at the fulfilment of his crowning wish, on the mere sight of that desired hermitage, his coffin—to revive, recover, shake off the hand of death, and be restored for years to his occupations—carving tikis (idols), let us say, or braiding old men's beards. From all this it may be conceived how easily they meet death when it approaches naturally. I heard one example, grim and picturesque. In the time of the small-pox in Hapaa, an old man was seized with the disease; he had no thought of recovery; had his grave dug by a wayside, and lived in it for near a fortnight, eating, drinking, and smoking with the passers-by, talking mostly of his end, and equally unconcerned for himself and careless of the friends whom he infected.

This proneness to suicide, and loose seat in life, is not peculiar to the Marquesan. What is peculiar is the widespread depression and acceptance of the national end. Pleasures are neglected, the dance languishes, the songs are forgotten. It is true that some, and perhaps too many, of them are proscribed; but many remain, if there were spirit to support or to revive them. At the last feast of the Bastille, Stanislao Moanatini shed tears when he beheld the inanimate performance of the dancers. When the people sang for us in Anaho, they must apologise for the smallness of their repertory. They were only young folk present, they said, and it was only the old that knew the songs. The whole body of Marquesan poetry and music was being suffered to die out with a single dispirited generation. The full import is apparent only to one acquainted with other Polynesian races; who knows how the Samoan coins a fresh song for every trifling incident, or who has heard (on Penrhyn, for instance) a band of little stripling maids from eight to twelve keep up their minstrelsy for hours upon a stretch, one song following another without pause. In like manner, the Marquesan, never industrious, begins now to cease altogether from production. The exports of the group decline out of all proportion even with the death-rate of the islanders. 'The coral waxes, the palm grows, and man departs,' says the Marquesan; and he folds his hands. And surely this is nature. Fond as it may appear, we labour and refrain, not for the rewards of any single life, but with a timid eye upon the lives and memories of our successors; and where no one is to succeed, of his own family, or his own tongue, I doubt whether Rothschilds would make money or Cato practise virtue. It is natural, also, that a temporary stimulus should sometimes rouse the Marquesan from his lethargy. Over all the landward shore of Anaho cotton runs like a wild weed; man or woman, whoever comes to pick it, may earn a dollar in the day; yet when we arrived, the trader's store-house was entirely empty; and before we left it was near full. So long as the circus was there, so long as the Casco was yet anchored in the bay, it behoved every one to make his visit; and to this end every woman must have a new dress, and every man a shirt and trousers. Never before, in Mr. Regler's experience, had they displayed so much activity.

In their despondency there is an element of dread. The fear of ghosts and of the dark is very deeply written in the mind of the Polynesian; not least of the Marquesan. Poor Taipi, the chief of Anaho, was condemned to ride to Hatiheu on a moonless night. He borrowed a lantern, sat a long while nerving himself for the adventure, and when he at last departed, wrung the Cascos by the hand as for a final separation. Certain presences, called Vehinehae, frequent and make terrible the nocturnal roadside; I was told by one they were like so much mist, and as the traveller walked into them dispersed and dissipated; another described them as being shaped like men and having eyes like cats; from none could I obtain the smallest clearness as to what they did, or wherefore they were dreaded. We may be sure at least they represent the dead; for the dead, in the minds of the islanders, are all-pervasive. 'When a native says that he is a man,' writes Dr. Codrington, 'he means that he is a man and not a ghost; not that he is a man and not a beast. The intelligent agents of this world are to his mind the men who are alive, and the ghosts the men who are dead.' Dr. Codrington speaks of Melanesia; from what I have learned his words are equally true of the Polynesian. And yet more. Among cannibal Polynesians a dreadful suspicion rests generally on the dead; and the Marquesans, the greatest cannibals of all, are scarce likely to be free from similar beliefs. I hazard the guess that the Vehinehae are the hungry spirits of the dead, continuing their life's business of the cannibal ambuscade, and lying everywhere unseen, and eager to devour the living. Another superstition I picked up through the troubled medium of Tari Coffin's English. The dead, he told me, came and danced by night around the paepae of their former family; the family were thereupon overcome by some emotion (but whether of pious sorrow or of fear I could not gather), and must 'make a feast,' of which fish, pig, and popoi were indispensable ingredients. So far this is clear enough. But here Tari went on to instance the new house of Toma and the house-warming feast which was just then in preparation as instances in point. Dare we indeed string them together, and add the case of the deserted ruin, as though the dead continually besieged the paepaes of the living: were kept at arm's-length, even from the first foundation, only by propitiatory feasts, and, so soon as the fire of life went out upon the hearth, swarmed back into possession of their ancient seat?

I speak by guess of these Marquesan superstitions. On the cannibal ghost I shall return elsewhere with certainty. And it is enough, for the present purpose, to remark that the men of the Marquesas, from whatever reason, fear and shrink from the presence of ghosts. Conceive how this must tell upon the nerves in islands where the number of the dead already so far exceeds that of the living, and the dead multiply and the living dwindle at so swift a rate. Conceive how the remnant huddles about the embers of the fire of life; even as old Red Indians, deserted on the march and in the snow, the kindly tribe all gone, the last flame expiring, and the night around populous with wolves.

CHAPTER V—DEPOPULATION

Over the whole extent of the South Seas, from one tropic to another, we find traces of a bygone state of over-population, when the resources of even a tropical soil were taxed, and even the improvident Polynesian trembled for the future. We may accept some of the ideas of Mr. Darwin's theory of coral islands, and suppose a rise of the sea, or the subsidence of some former continental area, to have driven into the tops of the mountains multitudes of refugees. Or we may suppose, more soberly, a people of sea-rovers, emigrants from a crowded country, to strike upon and settle island after island, and as time went on to multiply exceedingly in their new seats. In either case the end must be the same; soon or late it must grow apparent that the crew are too numerous, and that famine is at hand. The Polynesians met this emergent danger with various expedients of activity and prevention. A way was found to preserve breadfruit by packing it in artificial pits; pits forty feet in depth and of proportionate bore are still to be seen, I am told, in the Marquesas; and yet even these were insufficient for the teeming people, and the annals of the past are gloomy with famine and cannibalism. Among the Hawaiians—a hardier people, in a more exacting climate—agriculture was carried far; the land was irrigated with canals; and the fish-ponds of Molokai prove the number and diligence of the old inhabitants. Meanwhile, over all the island world, abortion and infanticide prevailed. On coral atolls, where the danger was most plainly obvious, these were enforced by law and sanctioned by punishment. On Vaitupu, in the Ellices, only two children were allowed to a couple; on Nukufetau, but one. On the latter the punishment was by fine; and it is related that the fine was sometimes paid, and the child spared.

This is characteristic. For no people in the world are so fond or so long-suffering with children—children make the mirth and the adornment of their homes, serving them for playthings and for picture-galleries. 'Happy is the man that has his quiver full of them.' The stray bastard is contended for by rival families; and the natural and the adopted children play and grow up together undistinguished. The spoiling, and I may almost say the deification, of the child, is nowhere carried so far as in the eastern islands; and furthest, according to my opportunities of observation, in the Paumotu group, the so-called Low or Dangerous Archipelago. I have seen a Paumotuan native turn from me with embarrassment and disaffection because I suggested that a brat would be the better for a beating. It is a daily matter in some eastern islands to see a child strike or even stone its mother, and the mother, so far from punishing, scarce ventures to resist. In some, when his child was born, a chief was superseded and resigned his name; as though, like a drone, he had then fulfilled the occasion of his being. And in some the lightest words of children had the weight of oracles. Only the other day, in the Marquesas, if a child conceived a distaste to any stranger, I am assured the stranger would be slain. And I shall have to tell in another place an instance of the opposite: how a child in Manihiki having taken a fancy to myself, her adoptive parents at once accepted the situation and loaded me with gifts.

With such sentiments the necessity for child-destruction would not fail to clash, and I believe we find the trace of divided feeling in the Tahitian brotherhood of Oro. At a certain date a new god was added to the Society-Island Olympus, or an old one refurbished and made popular. Oro was his name, and he may be compared with the Bacchus of the ancients. His zealots sailed from bay to bay, and from island to island; they were everywhere received with feasting; wore fine clothes; sang, danced, acted; gave exhibitions of dexterity and strength; and were the artists, the acrobats, the bards, and the harlots of the group. Their life was public and epicurean; their initiation a mystery; and the highest in the land aspired to join the brotherhood. If a couple stood next in line to a high-chieftaincy, they were suffered, on grounds of policy, to spare one child; all other children, who had a father or a mother in the company of Oro, stood condemned from the moment of conception. A freemasonry, an agnostic sect, a company of artists, its members all under oath to spread unchastity, and all forbidden to leave offspring—I do not know how it may appear to others, but to me the design seems obvious. Famine menacing the islands, and the needful remedy repulsive, it was recommended to the native mind by these trappings of mystery, pleasure, and parade. This is the more probable, and the secret, serious purpose of the institution appears the more plainly, if it be true that, after a certain period of life, the obligation of the votary was changed; at first, bound to be profligate: afterwards, expected to be chaste.

Here, then, we have one side of the case. Man-eating among kindly men, child-murder among child-lovers, industry in a race the most idle, invention in a race the least progressive, this grim, pagan salvation-army of the brotherhood of Oro, the report of early voyagers, the widespread vestiges of former habitation, and the universal tradition of the islands, all point to the same fact of former crowding and alarm. And to-day we are face to face with the reverse. To-day in the Marquesas, in the Eight Islands of Hawaii, in Mangareva, in Easter Island, we find the same race perishing like flies. Why this change? Or, grant that the coming of the whites, the change of habits, and the introduction of new maladies and vices, fully explain the depopulation, why is that depopulation not universal? The population of Tahiti, after a period of alarming decrease, has again become stationary. I hear of a similar result among some Maori tribes; in many of the Paumotus a slight increase is to be observed; and the Samoans are to-day as healthy and at least as fruitful as before the change. Grant that the Tahitians, the Maoris, and the Paumotuans have become inured to the new conditions; and what are we to make of the Samoans, who have never suffered?

Those who are acquainted only with a single group are apt to be ready with solutions. Thus I have heard the mortality of the Maoris attributed to their change of residence—from fortified hill-tops to the low, marshy vicinity of their plantations. How plausible! And yet the Marquesans are dying out in the same houses where their fathers multiplied. Or take opium. The Marquesas and Hawaii are the two groups the most infected with this vice; the population of the one is the most civilised, that of the other by far the most barbarous, of Polynesians; and they are two of those that perish the most rapidly. Here is a strong case against opium. But let us take unchastity, and we shall find the Marquesas and Hawaii figuring again upon another count. Thus, Samoans are the most chaste of Polynesians, and they are to this day entirely fertile; Marquesans are the most debauched: we have seen how they are perishing; Hawaiians are notoriously lax, and they begin to be dotted among deserts. So here is a case stronger still against unchastity; and here also we have a correction to apply. Whatever the virtues of the Tahitian, neither friend nor enemy dares call him chaste; and yet he seems to have outlived the time of danger. One last example: syphilis has been plausibly credited with much of the sterility. But the Samoans are, by all accounts, as fruitful as at first; by some accounts more so; and it is not seriously to be argued that the Samoans have escaped syphilis.

These examples show how dangerous it is to reason from any particular cause, or even from many in a single group. I have in my eye an able and amiable pamphlet by the Rev. S. E. Bishop: 'Why are the Hawaiians Dying Out?' Any one interested in the subject ought to read this tract, which contains real information; and yet Mr. Bishop's views would have been changed by an acquaintance with other groups. Samoa is, for the moment, the main and the most instructive exception to the rule. The people are the most chaste and one of the most temperate of island peoples. They have never been tried and depressed with any grave pestilence. Their clothing has scarce been tampered with; at the simple and becoming tabard of the girls, Tartuffe, in many another island, would have cried out; for the cool, healthy, and modest lava-lava or kilt, Tartuffe has managed in many another island to substitute stifling and inconvenient trousers. Lastly, and perhaps chiefly, so far from their amusements having been curtailed, I think they have been, upon the whole, extended. The Polynesian falls easily into despondency: bereavement, disappointment, the fear of novel visitations, the decay or proscription of ancient pleasures, easily incline him to be sad; and sadness detaches him from life. The melancholy of the Hawaiian and the emptiness of his new life are striking; and the remark is yet more apposite to the Marquesas. In Samoa, on the other hand, perpetual song and dance, perpetual games, journeys, and pleasures, make an animated and a smiling picture of the island life. And the Samoans are to-day the gayest and the best entertained inhabitants of our planet. The importance of this can scarcely be exaggerated. In a climate and upon a soil where a livelihood can be had for the stooping, entertainment is a prime necessity. It is otherwise with us, where life presents us with a daily problem, and there is a serious interest, and some of the heat of conflict, in the mere continuing to be. So, in certain atolls, where there is no great gaiety, but man must bestir himself with some vigour for his daily bread, public health and the population are maintained; but in the lotos islands, with the decay of pleasures, life itself decays. It is from this point of view that we may instance, among other causes of depression, the decay of war. We have been so long used in Europe to that dreary business of war on the great scale, trailing epidemics and leaving pestilential corpses in its train, that we have almost forgotten its original, the most healthful, if not the most humane, of all field sports—hedge-warfare. From this, as well as from the rest of his amusements and interests, the islander, upon a hundred islands, has been recently cut off. And to this, as well as to so many others, the Samoan still makes good a special title.

Upon the whole, the problem seems to me to stand thus:—Where there have been fewest changes, important or unimportant, salutary or hurtful, there the race survives. Where there have been most, important or unimportant, salutary or hurtful, there it perishes. Each change, however small, augments the sum of new conditions to which the race has to become inured. There may seem, a priori, no comparison between the change from 'sour toddy' to bad gin, and that from the island kilt to a pair of European trousers. Yet I am far from persuaded that the one is any more hurtful than the other; and the unaccustomed race will sometimes die of pin-pricks. We are here face to face with one of the difficulties of the missionary. In Polynesian islands he easily obtains pre-eminent authority; the king becomes his mairedupalais; he can proscribe, he can command; and the temptation is ever towards too much. Thus (by all accounts) the Catholics in Mangareva, and thus (to my own knowledge) the Protestants in Hawaii, have rendered life in a more or less degree unliveable to their converts. And the mild, uncomplaining creatures (like children in a prison) yawn and await death. It is easy to blame the missionary. But it is his business to make changes. It is surely his business, for example, to prevent war; and yet I have instanced war itself as one of the elements of health. On the other hand, it were, perhaps, easy for the missionary to proceed more gently, and to regard every change as an affair of weight. I take the average missionary; I am sure I do him no more than justice when I suppose that he would hesitate to bombard a village, even in order to convert an archipelago. Experience begins to show us (at least in Polynesian islands) that change of habit is bloodier than a bombardment.

There is one point, ere I have done, where I may go to meet criticism. I have said nothing of faulty hygiene, bathing during fevers, mistaken treatment of children, native doctoring, or abortion—all causes frequently adduced. And I have said nothing of them because they are conditions common to both epochs, and even more efficient in the past than in the present. Was it not the same with unchastity, it may be asked? Was not the Polynesian always unchaste? Doubtless he was so always: doubtless he is more so since the coming of his remarkably chaste visitors from Europe. Take the Hawaiian account of Cook: I have no doubt it is entirely fair. Take Krusenstern's candid, almost innocent, description of a Russian man-of-war at the Marquesas; consider the disgraceful history of missions in Hawaii itself, where (in the war of lust) the American missionaries were once shelled by an English adventurer, and once raided and mishandled by the crew of an American warship; add the practice of whaling fleets to call at the Marquesas, and carry off a complement of women for the cruise; consider, besides, how the whites were at first regarded in the light of demi-gods, as appears plainly in the reception of Cook upon Hawaii; and again, in the story of the discovery of Tutuila, when the really decent women of Samoa prostituted themselves in public to the French; and bear in mind how it was the custom of the adventurers, and we may almost say the business of the missionaries, to deride and infract even the most salutary tapus. Here we see every engine of dissolution directed at once against a virtue never and nowhere very strong or popular; and the result, even in the most degraded islands, has been further degradation. Mr. Lawes, the missionary of Savage Island, told me the standard of female chastity had declined there since the coming of the whites. In heathen time, if a girl gave birth to a bastard, her father or brother would dash the infant down the cliffs; and to-day the scandal would be small. Or take the Marquesas. Stanislao Moanatini told me that in his own recollection, the young were strictly guarded; they were not suffered so much as to look upon one another in the street, but passed (so my informant put it) like dogs; and the other day the whole school-children of Nuka-hiva and Ua-pu escaped in a body to the woods, and lived there for a fortnight in promiscuous liberty. Readers of travels may perhaps exclaim at my authority, and declare themselves better informed. I should prefer the statement of an intelligent native like Stanislao (even if it stood alone, which it is far from doing) to the report of the most honest traveller. A ship of war comes to a haven, anchors, lands a party, receives and returns a visit, and the captain writes a chapter on the manners of the island. It is not considered what class is mostly seen. Yet we should not be pleased if a Lascar foremast hand were to judge England by the ladies who parade Ratcliffe Highway, and the gentlemen who share with them their hire. Stanislao's opinion of a decay of virtue even in these unvirtuous islands has been supported to me by others; his very example, the progress of dissolution amongst the young, is adduced by Mr. Bishop in Hawaii. And so far as Marquesans are concerned, we might have hazarded a guess of some decline in manners. I do not think that any race could ever have prospered or multiplied with such as now obtain; I am sure they would have been never at the pains to count paternal kinship. It is not possible to give details; suffice it that their manners appear to be imitated from the dreams of ignorant and vicious children, and their debauches persevered in until energy, reason, and almost life itself are in abeyance.

CHAPTER VI—CHIEFS AND TAPUS

We used to admire exceedingly the bland and gallant manners of the chief called Taipi-Kikino. An elegant guest at table, skilled in the use of knife and fork, a brave figure when he shouldered a gun and started for the woods after wild chickens, always serviceable, always ingratiating and gay, I would sometimes wonder where he found his cheerfulness. He had enough to sober him, I thought, in his official budget. His expenses—for he was always seen attired in virgin white—must have by far exceeded his income of six dollars in the year, or say two shillings a month. And he was himself a man of no substance; his house the poorest in the village. It was currently supposed that his elder brother, Kauanui, must have helped him out. But how comes it that the elder brother should succeed to the family estate, and be a wealthy commoner, and the younger be a poor man, and yet rule as chief in Anaho? That the one should be wealthy, and the other almost indigent is probably to be explained by some adoption; for comparatively few children are brought up in the house or succeed to the estates of their natural begetters. That the one should be chief instead of the other must be explained (in a very Irish fashion) on the ground that neither of them is a chief at all.

Since the return and the wars of the French, many chiefs have been deposed, and many so-called chiefs appointed. We have seen, in the same house, one such upstart drinking in the company of two such extruded island Bourbons, men, whose word a few years ago was life and death, now sunk to be peasants like their neighbours. So when the French overthrew hereditary tyrants, dubbed the commons of the Marquesas freeborn citizens of the republic, and endowed them with a vote for a conseiller-général at Tahiti, they probably conceived themselves upon the path to popularity; and so far from that, they were revolting public sentiment. The deposition of the chiefs was perhaps sometimes needful; the appointment of others may have been needful also; it was at least a delicate business. The Government of George II. exiled many Highland magnates. It never occurred to them to manufacture substitutes; and if the French have been more bold, we have yet to see with what success.

Our chief at Anaho was always called, he always called himself, Taipi-Kikino; and yet that was not his name, but only the wand of his false position. As soon as he was appointed chief, his name—which signified, if I remember exactly, Prince born among flowers—fell in abeyance, and he was dubbed instead by the expressive byword, Taipi-Kikino—Highwater man-of-no-account—or, Englishing more boldly, Beggar on horseback—a witty and a wicked cut. A nickname in Polynesia destroys almost the memory of the original name. To-day, if we were Polynesians, Gladstone would be no more heard of. We should speak of and address our Nestor as the Grand Old Man, and it is so that himself would sign his correspondence. Not the prevalence, then, but the significancy of the nickname is to be noted here. The new authority began with small prestige. Taipi has now been some time in office; from all I saw he seemed a person very fit. He is not the least unpopular, and yet his power is nothing. He is a chief to the French, and goes to breakfast with the Resident; but for any practical end of chieftaincy a rag doll were equally efficient.

We had been but three days in Anaho when we received the visit of the chief of Hatiheu, a man of weight and fame, late leader of a war upon the French, late prisoner in Tahiti, and the last eater of long-pig in Nuka-hiva. Not many years have elapsed since he was seen striding on the beach of Anaho, a dead man's arm across his shoulder. 'So does Kooamua to his enemies!' he roared to the passers-by, and took a bite from the raw flesh. And now behold this gentleman, very wisely replaced in office by the French, paying us a morning visit in European clothes. He was the man of the most character we had yet seen: his manners genial and decisive, his person tall, his face rugged, astute, formidable, and with a certain similarity to Mr. Gladstone's—only for the brownness of the skin, and the high-chief's tattooing, all one side and much of the other being of an even blue. Further acquaintance increased our opinion of his sense. He viewed the Casco in a manner then quite new to us, examining her lines and the running of the gear; to a piece of knitting on which one of the party was engaged, he must have devoted ten minutes' patient study; nor did he desist before he had divined the principles; and he was interested even to excitement by a type-writer, which he learned to work. When he departed he carried away with him a list of his family, with his own name printed by his own hand at the bottom. I should add that he was plainly much of a humorist, and not a little of a humbug. He told us, for instance, that he was a person of exact sobriety; such being the obligation of his high estate: the commons might be sots, but the chief could not stoop so low. And not many days after he was to be observed in a state of smiling and lop-sided imbecility, the Casco ribbon upside down on his dishonoured hat.

But his business that morning in Anaho is what concerns us here. The devil-fish, it seems, were growing scarce upon the reef; it was judged fit to interpose what we should call a close season; for that end, in Polynesia, a tapu (vulgarly spelt 'taboo') has to be declared, and who was to declare it? Taipi might; he ought; it was a chief part of his duty; but would any one regard the inhibition of a Beggar on Horse-back? He might plant palm branches:

it did not in the least follow that the spot was sacred. He might recite the spell: it was shrewdly supposed the spirits would not hearken. And so the old, legitimate cannibal must ride over the mountains to do it for him; and the respectable official in white clothes could but look on and envy. At about the same time, though in a different manner, Kooamua established a forest law. It was observed the cocoa-palms were suffering, for the plucking of green nuts impoverishes and at last endangers the tree. Now Kooamua could tapu the reef, which was public property, but he could not tapu other people's palms; and the expedient adopted was interesting. He tapu'd his own trees, and his example was imitated over all Hatiheu and Anaho. I fear Taipi might have tapu'd all that he possessed and found none to follow him. So much for the esteem in which the dignity of an appointed chief is held by others; a single circumstance will show what he thinks of it himself. I never met one, but he took an early opportunity to explain his situation. True, he was only an appointed chief when I beheld him; but somewhere else, perhaps upon some other isle, he was a chieftain by descent: upon which ground, he asked me (so to say it) to excuse his mushroom honours.

It will be observed with surprise that both these tapus are for thoroughly sensible ends. With surprise, I say, because the nature of that institution is much misunderstood in Europe. It is taken usually in the sense of a meaningless or wanton prohibition, such as that which to-day prevents women in some countries from smoking, or yesterday prevented any one in Scotland from taking a walk on Sunday. The error is no less natural than it is unjust. The Polynesians have not been trained in the bracing, practical thought of ancient Rome; with them the idea of law has not been disengaged from that of morals or propriety; so that tapu has to cover the whole field, and implies indifferently that an act is criminal, immoral, against sound public policy, unbecoming or (as we say) 'not in good form.' Many tapus were in consequence absurd enough, such as those which deleted words out of the language, and particularly those which related to women. Tapu encircled women upon all hands. Many things were forbidden to men; to women we may say that few were permitted. They must not sit on the paepae; they must not go up to it by the stair; they must not eat pork; they must not approach a boat; they must not cook at a fire which any male had kindled. The other day, after the roads were made, it was observed the women plunged along margin through the bush, and when they came to a bridge waded through the water: roads and bridges were the work of men's hands, and tapu for the foot of women. Even a man's saddle, if the man be native, is a thing no self-respecting lady dares to use. Thus on the Anaho side of the island, only two white men, Mr. Regler and the gendarme, M. Aussel, possess saddles; and when a woman has a journey to make she must borrow from one or other. It will be noticed that these prohibitions tend, most of them, to an increased reserve between the sexes. Regard for female chastity is the usual excuse for these disabilities that men delight to lay upon their wives and mothers. Here the regard is absent; and behold the women still bound hand and foot with meaningless proprieties! The women themselves, who are survivors of the old regimen, admit that in those days life was not worth living. And yet even then there were exceptions. There were female chiefs and (I am assured) priestesses besides; nice customs curtseyed to great dames, and in the most sacred enclosure of a High Place, Father Siméon Delmar was shown a stone, and told it was the throne of some well-descended lady. How exactly parallel is this with European practice, when princesses were suffered to penetrate the strictest cloister, and women could rule over a land in which they were denied the control of their own children.

But the tapu is more often the instrument of wise and needful restrictions. We have seen it as the organ of paternal government. It serves besides to enforce, in the rare case of some one wishing to enforce them, rights of private property. Thus a man, weary of the coming and going of Marquesan visitors, tapus his door; and to this day you may see the palm-branch signal, even as our great-grandfathers saw the peeled wand before a Highland inn. Or take another case. Anaho is known as 'the country without popoi.' The word popoi serves in different islands to indicate the main food of the people: thus, in Hawaii, it implies a preparation of taro; in the Marquesas, of breadfruit. And a Marquesan does not readily conceive life possible without his favourite diet. A few years ago a drought killed the breadfruit trees and the bananas in the district of Anaho; and from this calamity, and the open-handed customs of the island, a singular state of things arose. Well-watered Hatiheu had escaped the drought; every householder of Anaho accordingly crossed the pass, chose some one in Hatiheu, 'gave him his name'—an onerous gift, but one not to be rejected—and from this improvised relative proceeded to draw his supplies, for all the world as though he had paid for them. Hence a continued traffic on the road. Some stalwart fellow, in a loin-cloth, and glistening with sweat, may be seen at all hours of the day, a stick across his bare shoulders, tripping nervously under a double burthen of green fruits. And on the far side of the gap a dozen stone posts on the wayside in the shadow of a grove mark the breathing-space of the popoi-carriers. A little back from the beach, and not half a mile from Anaho, I was the more amazed to find a cluster of well-doing breadfruits heavy with their harvest. 'Why do you not take these?' I asked. 'Tapu,' said Hoka; and I thought to myself (after the manner of dull travellers) what children and fools these people were to toil over the mountain and despoil innocent neighbours when the staff of life was thus growing at their door. I was the more in error. In the general destruction these surviving trees were enough only for the family of the proprietor, and by the simple expedient of declaring a tapu he enforced his right.

The sanction of the tapu is superstitious; and the punishment of infraction either a wasting or a deadly sickness. A slow disease follows on the eating of tapu fish, and can only be cured with the bones of the same fish burned with the due mysteries. The cocoa-nut and breadfruit tapu works more swiftly. Suppose you have eaten tapu fruit at the evening meal, at night your sleep will be uneasy; in the morning, swelling and a dark discoloration will have attacked your neck, whence they spread upward to the face; and in two days, unless the cure be interjected, you must die. This cure is prepared from the rubbed leaves of the tree from which the patient stole; so that he cannot be saved without confessing to the Tahuku the person whom he wronged. In the experience of my informant, almost no tapu had been put in use, except the two described: he had thus no opportunity to learn the nature and operation of the others; and, as the art of making them was jealously guarded amongst the old men, he believed the mystery would soon die out. I should add that he was no Marquesan, but a Chinaman, a resident in the group from boyhood, and a reverent believer in the spells which he described. White men, amongst whom Ah Fu included himself, were exempt; but he had a tale of a Tahitian woman, who had come to the Marquesas, eaten tapu fish, and, although uninformed of her offence and danger, had been afflicted and cured exactly like a native.

Doubtless the belief is strong; doubtless, with this weakly and fanciful race, it is in many cases strong enough to kill; it should be strong indeed in those who tapu their trees secretly, so that they may detect a depredator by his sickness. Or, perhaps, we should understand the idea of the hidden tapu otherwise, as a politic device to spread uneasiness and extort confessions: so that, when a man is ailing, he shall ransack his brain for any possible offence, and send at once for any proprietor whose rights he has invaded. 'Had you hidden a tapu?' we may conceive him asking; and I cannot imagine the proprietor gainsaying it; and this is perhaps the strangest feature of the system—that it should be regarded from without with such a mental and implicit awe, and, when examined from within, should present so many apparent evidences of design.

We read in Dr. Campbell's Poenamo of a New Zealand girl, who was foolishly told that she had eaten a tapu yam, and who instantly sickened, and died in the two days of simple terror. The period is the same as in the Marquesas; doubtless the symptoms were so too. How singular to consider that a superstition of such sway is possibly a manufactured article; and that, even if it were not originally invented, its details have plainly been arranged by the authorities of some Polynesian Scotland Yard. Fitly enough, the belief is to-day—and was probably always—far from universal. Hell at home is a strong deterrent with some; a passing thought with others; with others, again, a theme of public mockery, not always well assured; and so in the Marquesas with the tapu. Mr. Regler has seen the two extremes of scepticism and implicit fear. In the tapu grove he found one fellow stealing breadfruit, cheerful and impudent as a street arab; and it was only on a menace of exposure that he showed himself the least discountenanced. The other case was opposed in every point. Mr. Regler asked a native to accompany him upon a voyage; the man went gladly enough, but suddenly perceiving a dead tapu fish in the bottom of the boat, leaped back with a scream; nor could the promise of a dollar prevail upon him to advance.

The Marquesan, it will be observed, adheres to the old idea of the local circumscription of beliefs and duties. Not only are the whites exempt from consequences; but their transgressions seem to be viewed without horror. It was Mr. Regler who had killed the fish; yet the devout native was not shocked at Mr. Regler—only refused to join him in his boat. A white is a white: the servant (so to speak) of other and more liberal gods; and not to be blamed if he profit by his liberty. The Jews were perhaps the first to interrupt this ancient comity of faiths; and the Jewish virus is still strong in Christianity. All the world must respect our tapus, or we gnash our teeth.

CHAPTER VII—HATIHEU

The bays of Anaho and Hatiheu are divided at their roots by the knife-edge of a single hill—the pass so often mentioned; but this isthmus expands to the seaward in a considerable peninsula: very bare and grassy; haunted by sheep and, at night and morning, by the piercing cries of the shepherds; wandered over by a few wild goats; and on its sea-front indented with long, clamorous caves, and faced with cliffs of the colour and ruinous outline of an old peat-stack. In one of these echoing and sunless gullies we saw, clustered like sea-birds on a splashing ledge, shrill as sea-birds in their salutation to the passing boat, a group of fisherwomen, stripped to their gaudy under-clothes. (The clash of the surf and the thin female voices echo in my memory.) We had that day a native crew and steersman, Kauanui; it was our first experience of Polynesian seamanship, which consists in hugging every point of land. There is no thought in this of saving time, for they will pull a long way in to skirt a point that is embayed. It seems that, as they can never get their houses near enough the surf upon the one side, so they can never get their boats near enough upon the other. The practice in bold water is not so dangerous as it looks—the reflex from the rocks sending the boat off. Near beaches with a heavy run of sea, I continue to think it very hazardous, and find the composure of the natives annoying to behold. We took unmingled pleasure, on the way out, to see so near at hand the beach and the wonderful colours of the surf. On the way back, when the sea had risen and was running strong against us, the fineness of the steersman's aim grew more embarrassing. As we came abreast of the sea-front, where the surf broke highest, Kauanui embraced the occasion to light his pipe, which then made the circuit of the boat—each man taking a whiff or two, and, ere he passed it on, filling his lungs and cheeks with smoke. Their faces were all puffed out like apples as we came abreast of the cliff foot, and the bursting surge fell back into the boat in showers. At the next point 'cocanetti' was the word, and the stroke borrowed my knife, and desisted from his labours to open nuts. These untimely indulgences may be compared to the tot of grog served out before a ship goes into action.

My purpose in this visit led me first to the boys' school, for Hatiheu is the university of the north islands. The hum of the lesson came out to meet us. Close by the door, where the draught blew coolest, sat the lay brother; around him, in a packed half-circle, some sixty high-coloured faces set with staring eyes; and in the background of the barn-like room benches were to be seen, and blackboards with sums on them in chalk. The brother rose to greet us, sensibly humble. Thirty years he had been there, he said, and fingered his white locks as a bashful child pulls out his pinafore. 'Et point de résultats, monsieur, presque pas de résultats.' He pointed to the scholars: 'You see, sir, all the youth of Nuka-hiva and Ua-pu. Between the ages of six and fifteen this is all that remains; and it is but a few years since we had a hundred and twenty from Nuka-hiva alone. Oui, monsieur, cela se dépérit.' Prayers, and reading and writing, prayers again and arithmetic, and more prayers to conclude: such appeared to be the dreary nature of the course. For arithmetic all island people have a natural taste. In Hawaii they make good progress in mathematics. In one of the villages on Majuro, and generally in the Marshall group, the whole population sit about the trader when he is weighing copra, and each on his own slate takes down the figures and computes the total. The trader, finding them so apt, introduced fractions, for which they had been taught no rule. At first they were quite gravelled but ultimately, by sheer hard thinking, reasoned out the result, and came one after another to assure the trader he was right. Not many people in Europe could have done the like. The course at Hatiheu is therefore less dispiriting to Polynesians than a stranger might have guessed; and yet how bald it is at best! I asked the brother if he did not tell them stories, and he stared at me; if he did not teach them history, and he said, 'O yes, they had a little Scripture history—from the New Testament'; and repeated his lamentations over the lack of results. I had not the heart to put more questions; I could but say it must be very discouraging, and resist the impulse to add that it seemed also very natural.

He looked up—'My days are far spent,' he said; 'heaven awaits me.' May that heaven forgive me, but I was angry with the old man and his simple consolation. For think of his opportunity! The youth, from six to fifteen, are taken from their homes by Government, centralised at Hatiheu, where they are supported by a weekly tax of food; and, with the exception of one month in every year, surrendered wholly to the direction of the priests. Since the escapade already mentioned the holiday occurs at a different period for the girls and for the boys; so that a Marquesan brother and sister meet again, after their education is complete, a pair of strangers. It is a harsh law, and highly unpopular; but what a power it places in the hands of the instructors, and how languidly and dully is that power employed by the mission! Too much concern to make the natives pious, a design in which they all confess defeat, is, I suppose, the explanation of their miserable system. But they might see in the girls' school at Tai-o-hae, under the brisk, housewifely sisters, a different picture of efficiency, and a scene of neatness, airiness, and spirited and mirthful occupation that should shame them into cheerier methods. The sisters themselves lament their failure. They complain the annual holiday undoes the whole year's work; they complain particularly of the heartless indifference of the girls. Out of so many pretty and apparently affectionate pupils whom they have taught and reared, only two have ever returned to pay a visit of remembrance to their teachers. These, indeed, come regularly, but the rest, so soon as their school-days are over, disappear into the woods like captive insects. It is hard to imagine anything more discouraging; and yet I do not believe these ladies need despair. For a certain interval they keep the girls alive and innocently busy; and if it be at all possible to save the race, this would be the means. No such praise can be given to the boys' school at Hatiheu. The day is numbered already for them all; alike for the teacher and the scholars death is girt; he is afoot upon the march; and in the frequent interval they sit and yawn. But in life there seems a thread of purpose through the least significant; the drowsiest endeavour is not lost, and even the school at Hatiheu may be more useful than it seems.

Hatiheu is a place of some pretensions. The end of the bay towards Anaho may be called the civil compound, for it boasts the house of Kooamua, and close on the beach, under a great tree, that of the gendarme, M. Armand

Aussel, with his garden, his pictures, his books, and his excellent table, to which strangers are made welcome. No more singular contrast is possible than between the gendarmerie and the priesthood, who are besides in smouldering opposition and full of mutual complaints. A priest's kitchen in the eastern islands is a depressing spot to see; and many, or most of them, make no attempt to keep a garden, sparsely subsisting on their rations. But you will never dine with a gendarme without smacking your lips; and M. Aussel's home-made sausage and the salad from his garden are unforgotten delicacies. Pierre Loti may like to know that he is M. Aussel's favourite author, and that his books are read in the fit scenery of Hatiheu bay.

The other end is all religious. It is here that an overhanging and tip-tilted horn, a good sea-mark for Hatiheu, bursts naked from the verdure of the climbing forest, and breaks down shoreward in steep taluses and cliffs. From the edge of one of the highest, perhaps seven hundred or a thousand feet above the beach, a Virgin looks insignificantly down, like a poor lost doll, forgotten there by a giant child. This laborious symbol of the Catholics is always strange to Protestants; we conceive with wonder that men should think it worth while to toil so many days, and clamber so much about the face of precipices, for an end that makes us smile; and yet I believe it was the wise Bishop Dordillon who chose the place, and I know that those who had a hand in the enterprise look back with pride upon its vanquished dangers. The boys' school is a recent importation; it was at first in Tai-o-hae, beside the girls'; and it was only of late, after their joint escapade, that the width of the island was interposed between the sexes. But Hatiheu must have been a place of missionary importance from before. About midway of the beach no less than three churches stand grouped in a patch of bananas, intermingled with some pine-apples. Two are of wood: the original church, now in disuse; and a second that, for some mysterious reason, has never been used. The new church is of stone, with twin towers, walls flangeing into buttresses, and sculptured front. The design itself is good, simple, and shapely; but the character is all in the detail, where the architect has bloomed into the sculptor. It is impossible to tell in words of the angels (although they are more like winged archbishops) that stand guard upon the door, of the cherubs in the corners, of the scapegoat gargoyles, or the quaint and spirited relief, where St.

Michael (the artist's patron) makes short work of a protesting Lucifer. We were never weary of viewing the imagery, so innocent, sometimes so funny, and yet in the best sense—in the sense of inventive gusto and expression—so artistic. I know not whether it was more strange to find a building of such merit in a corner of a barbarous isle, or to see a building so antique still bright with novelty. The architect, a French lay brother, still alive and well, and meditating fresh foundations, must have surely drawn his descent from a master-builder in the age of the cathedrals; and it was in looking on the church of Hatiheu that I seemed to perceive the secret charm of mediæval sculpture; that combination of the childish courage of the amateur, attempting all things, like the schoolboy on his slate, with the manly perseverance of the artist who does not know when he is conquered.

I had always afterwards a strong wish to meet the architect, Brother Michel; and one day, when I was talking with the Resident in Tai-o-hae (the chief port of the island), there were shown in to us an old, worn, purblind, ascetic-looking priest, and a lay brother, a type of all that is most sound in France, with a broad, clever, honest, humorous countenance, an eye very large and bright, and a strong and healthy body inclining to obesity. But that his blouse was black and his face shaven clean, you might pick such a man to-day, toiling cheerfully in his own patch of vines, from half a dozen provinces of France; and yet he had always for me a haunting resemblance to an old kind friend of my boyhood, whom I name in case any of my readers should share with me that memory—Dr. Paul, of the West Kirk. Almost at the first word I was sure it was my architect, and in a moment we were deep in a discussion of Hatiheu church. Brother Michel spoke always of his labours with a twinkle of humour, underlying which it was possible to spy a serious pride, and the change from one to another was often very human and diverting. 'Et vos gargouilles moyen-âge,' cried I; 'comme elles sont originates!' 'N'est-ce pas? Elles sont bien drôles!' he said, smiling broadly; and the next moment, with a sudden gravity: 'Cependant il y en a une qui a une patte de cassé; il faut que je voie cela.' I asked if he had any model—a point we much discussed. 'Non,' said he simply; 'c'est une église idéale.' The relievo was his favourite performance, and very justly so. The angels at the door, he owned, he would like to destroy and replace. 'Ils n'ont pas de vie, ils manquent de vie. Vous devriez voir mon église à la Dominique; j'ai là une Vierge qui est vraiment gentille.' 'Ah,' I cried, 'they told me you had said you would never build another church, and I wrote in my journal I could not believe it.' 'Oui, j'aimerais bien en fairs une autre,' he confessed, and smiled at the confession. An artist will understand how much I was attracted by this conversation. There is no bond so near as a community in that unaffected interest and slightly shame-faced pride which mark the intelligent man enamoured of an art. He sees the limitations of his aim, the defects of his practice; he smiles to be so employed upon the shores of death, yet sees in his own devotion something worthy. Artists, if they had the same sense of humour with the Augurs, would smile like them on meeting, but the smile would not be scornful.

I had occasion to see much of this excellent man. He sailed with us from Tai-o-hae to Hiva-oa, a dead beat of ninety miles against a heavy sea. It was what is called a good passage, and a feather in the Casco's cap; but among the most miserable forty hours that any one of us had ever passed. We were swung and tossed together all that time like shot in a stage thunder-box. The mate was thrown down and had his head cut open; the captain was sick on deck; the cook sick in the galley. Of all our party only two sat down to dinner. I was one. I own that I felt wretchedly; and I can only say of the other, who professed to feel quite well, that she fled at an early moment from the table. It was in these circumstances that we skirted the windward shore of that indescribable island of Ua-pu; viewing with dizzy eyes the coves, the capes, the breakers, the climbing forests, and the inaccessible stone needles that surmount the mountains. The place persists, in a dark corner of our memories, like a piece of the scenery of nightmares. The end of this distressful passage, where we were to land our passengers, was in a similar vein of roughness. The surf ran high on the beach at Taahauku; the boat broached-to and capsized; and all hands were submerged. Only the brother himself, who was well used to the experience, skipped ashore, by some miracle of agility, with scarce a sprinkling. Thenceforward, during our stay at Hiva-oa, he was our cicerone and patron; introducing us, taking us excursions, serving us in every way, and making himself daily more beloved.

Michel Blanc had been a carpenter by trade; had made money and retired, supposing his active days quite over; and it was only when he found idleness dangerous that he placed his capital and acquirements at the service of the mission. He became their carpenter, mason, architect, and engineer; added sculpture to his accomplishments, and was famous for his skill in gardening. He wore an enviable air of having found a port from life's contentions and lying there strongly anchored; went about his business with a jolly simplicity; complained of no lack of results—perhaps shyly thinking his own statuary result enough; and was altogether a pattern of the missionary layman.

CHAPTER VIII—THE PORT OF ENTRY

The port—the mart, the civil and religious capital of these rude islands—is called Tai-o-hae, and lies strung along the beach of a precipitous green bay in Nuka-hiva. It was midwinter when we came thither, and the weather was sultry, boisterous, and inconstant. Now the wind blew squally from the land down gaps of splintered precipice; now, between the sentinel islets of the entry, it came in gusts from seaward. Heavy and dark clouds impended on the summits; the rain roared and ceased; the scuppers of the mountain gushed; and the next day we would see the sides of the amphitheatre bearded with white falls. Along the beach the town shows a thin file of houses, mostly white, and all ensconced in the foliage of an avenue of green puraos; a pier gives access from the sea across the belt of breakers; to the eastward there stands, on a projecting bushy hill, the old fort which is now the calaboose, or prison; eastward still, alone in a garden, the Residency flies the colours of France. Just off Calaboose Hill, the tiny Government schooner rides almost permanently at anchor, marks eight bells in the morning (there or thereabout) with the unfurling of her flag, and salutes the setting sun with the report of a musket.

Here dwell together, and share the comforts of a club (which may be enumerated as a billiard-board, absinthe, a map of the world on Mercator's projection, and one of the most agreeable verandahs in the tropics), a handful of whites of varying nationality, mostly French officials, German and Scottish merchant clerks, and the agents of the opium monopoly. There are besides three tavern-keepers, the shrewd Scot who runs the cotton gin-mill, two white ladies, and a sprinkling of people 'on the beach'—a South Sea expression for which there is no exact equivalent. It is a pleasant society, and a hospitable. But one man, who was often to be seen seated on the logs at the pier-head, merits a word for the singularity of his history and appearance. Long ago, it seems, he fell in love with a native lady, a High Chiefess in Ua-pu. She, on being approached, declared she could never marry a man who was untattooed; it looked so naked; whereupon, with some greatness of soul, our hero put himself in the hands of the Tahukus, and, with still greater, persevered until the process was complete. He had certainly to bear a great expense, for the Tahuku will not work without reward; and certainly exquisite pain. Kooamua, high chief as he was, and one of the old school, was only part tattooed; he could not, he told us with lively pantomime, endure the torture to an end. Our enamoured countryman was more resolved; he was tattooed from head to foot in the most approved methods of the art; and at last presented himself before his mistress a new man. The fickle fair one could never behold him from that day except with laughter. For my part, I could never see the man without a kind of admiration; of him it might be said, if ever of any, that he had loved not wisely, but too well.

The Residency stands by itself, Calaboose Hill screening it from the fringe of town along the further bay. The house is commodious, with wide verandahs; all day it stands open, back and front, and the trade blows copiously over its bare floors. On a week-day the garden offers a scene of most untropical animation, half a dozen convicts toiling there cheerfully with spade and barrow, and touching hats and smiling to the visitor like old attached family servants. On Sunday these are gone, and nothing to be seen but dogs of all ranks and sizes peacefully slumbering in the shady grounds; for the dogs of Tai-o-hae are very courtly-minded, and make the seat of Government their promenade and place of siesta. In front and beyond, a strip of green down loses itself in a low wood of many species of acacia; and deep in the wood a ruinous wall encloses the cemetery of the Europeans. English and Scottish sleep there, and Scandinavians, and French maîtres de manœuvres and maîtres ouvriers: mingling alien dust. Back in the woods, perhaps, the blackbird, or (as they call him there) the island nightingale, will be singing home strains; and the ceaseless requiem of the surf hangs on the ear. I have never seen a resting-place more quiet; but it was a long thought how far these sleepers had all travelled, and from what diverse homes they had set forth, to lie here in the end together.

On the summit of its promontory hill, the calaboose stands all day with doors and window-shutters open to the trade. On my first visit a dog was the only guardian visible. He, indeed, rose with an attitude so menacing that I was glad to lay hands on an old barrel-hoop; and I think the weapon must have been familiar, for the champion instantly retreated, and as I wandered round the court and through the building, I could see him, with a couple of companions, humbly dodging me about the corners. The prisoners' dormitory was a spacious, airy room, devoid of any furniture; its whitewashed walls covered with inscriptions in Marquesan and rude drawings: one of the pier, not badly done; one of a murder; several of French soldiers in uniform. There was one legend in French: 'Je n'est' (sic) 'pas le sou.' From this noontide quietude it must not be supposed the prison was untenanted; the calaboose at Tai-o-hae does a good business. But some of its occupants were gardening at the Residency, and the rest were probably at work upon the streets, as free as our scavengers at home, although not so industrious. On the approach of evening they would be called in like children from play; and the harbour-master (who is also the jailer) would go through the form of locking them up until six the next morning. Should a prisoner have any call in town, whether of pleasure or affairs, he has but to unhook the window-shutters; and if he is back again, and the shutter decently replaced, by the hour of call on the morrow, he may have met the harbour-master in the avenue, and there will be no complaint, far less any punishment. But this is not all. The charming French Resident, M. Delaruelle, carried me one day to the calaboose on an official visit. In the green court, a very ragged gentleman, his legs deformed with the island elephantiasis, saluted us smiling. 'One of our political prisoners—an insurgent from Raiatea,' said the Resident; and then to the jailer: 'I thought I had ordered him a new pair of trousers.' Meanwhile no other convict was to be seen—'Eh bien,' said the Resident, 'où sont vos prisonniers?' 'Monsieur le Résident,' replied the jailer, saluting with soldierly formality, 'comme c'est jour de fête, je les ai laissé aller à la chasse.' They were all upon the mountains hunting goats! Presently we came to the quarters of the women, likewise deserted—'Où sont vos bonnes femmes?' asked the

Resident; and the jailer cheerfully responded: 'Je crois, Monsieur le Résident, qu'elles sont allées quelquepart faire une visite.' It had been the design of M. Delaruelle, who was much in love with the whimsicalities of his small realm, to elicit something comical; but not even he expected anything so perfect as the last. To complete the picture of convict life in Tai-o-hae, it remains to be added that these criminals draw a salary as regularly as the President of the Republic. Ten sous a day is their hire. Thus they have money, food, shelter, clothing, and, I was about to write, their liberty. The French are certainly a good-natured people, and make easy masters. They are besides inclined to view the Marquesans with an eye of humorous indulgence. 'They are dying, poor devils!' said M. Delaruelle: 'the main thing is to let them die in peace.' And it was not only well said, but I believe expressed the general thought. Yet there is another element to be considered; for these convicts are not merely useful, they are almost essential to the French existence. With a people incurably idle, dispirited by what can only be called endemic pestilence, and inflamed with ill-feeling against their new masters, crime and convict labour are a godsend to the Government.

Theft is practically the sole crime. Originally petty pilferers, the men of Tai-o-hae now begin to force locks and attack strong-boxes. Hundreds of dollars have been taken at a time; though, with that redeeming moderation so common in Polynesian theft, the Marquesan burglar will always take a part and leave a part, sharing (so to speak) with the proprietor. If it be Chilian coin—the island currency—he will escape; if the sum is in gold, French silver, or bank-notes, the police wait until the money begins to come in circulation, and then easily pick out their man. And now comes the shameful part. In plain English, the prisoner is tortured until he confesses and (if that be possible) restores the money. To keep him alone, day and night, in the black hole, is to inflict on the Marquesan torture inexpressible. Even his robberies are carried on in the plain daylight, under the open sky, with the stimulus of enterprise, and the countenance of an accomplice; his terror of the dark is still insurmountable; conceive, then, what he endures in his solitary dungeon; conceive how he longs to confess, become a full-fledged convict, and be allowed to sleep beside his comrades. While we were in Tai-o-hae a thief was under prevention. He had entered a house about eight in the morning, forced a trunk, and stolen eleven hundred francs; and now, under the horrors of darkness, solitude, and a bedevilled cannibal imagination, he was reluctantly confessing and giving up his spoil. From one cache, which he had already pointed out, three hundred francs had been recovered, and it was expected that he would presently disgorge the rest. This would be ugly enough if it were all; but I am bound to say, because it is a matter the French should set at rest, that worse is continually hinted. I heard that one man was kept six days with his arms bound backward round a barrel; and it is the universal report that every gendarme in the South Seas is equipped with something in the nature of a thumbscrew. I do not know this. I never had the face to ask any of the gendarmes—pleasant, intelligent, and kindly fellows—with whom I have been intimate, and whose hospitality I have enjoyed; and perhaps the tale reposes (as I hope it does) on a misconstruction of that ingenious cat's-cradle with which the French agent of police so readily secures a prisoner. But whether physical or moral, torture is certainly employed; and by a barbarous injustice, the state of accusation (in which a man may very well be innocently placed) is positively painful; the state of conviction (in which all are supposed guilty) is comparatively free, and positively pleasant. Perhaps worse still,—not only the accused, but sometimes his wife, his mistress, or his friend, is subjected to the same hardships. I was admiring, in the tapu system, the ingenuity of native methods of detection; there is not much to admire in those of the French, and to lock up a timid child in a dark room, and, if he proved obstinate, lock up his sister in the next, is neither novel nor humane.

The main occasion of these thefts is the new vice of opium-eating. 'Here nobody ever works, and all eat opium,' said a gendarme; and Ah Fu knew a woman who ate a dollar's worth in a day. The successful thief will give a handful of money to each of his friends, a dress to a woman, pass an evening in one of the taverns of Tai-o-hae, during which he treats all comers, produce a big lump of opium, and retire to the bush to eat and sleep it off. A trader, who did not sell opium, confessed to me that he was at his wit's end. 'I do not sell it, but others do,' said he. 'The natives only work to buy it; if they walk over to me to sell their cotton, they have just to walk over to some one else to buy their opium with my money. And why should they be at the bother of two walks? There is no use talking,' he added—'opium is the currency of this country.'

The man under prevention during my stay at Tai-o-hae lost patience while the Chinese opium-seller was being examined in his presence. 'Of course he sold me opium!' he broke out; 'all the Chinese here sell opium. It was only to buy opium that I stole; it is only to buy opium that anybody steals. And what you ought to do is to let no opium come here, and no Chinamen.' This is precisely what is done in Samoa by a native Government; but the French have bound their own hands, and for forty thousand francs sold native subjects to crime and death. This horrid traffic may be said to have sprung up by accident. It was Captain Hart who had the misfortune to be the means of beginning it, at a time when his plantations flourished in the Marquesas, and he found a difficulty in keeping Chinese coolies. To-day the plantations are practically deserted and the Chinese gone; but in the meanwhile the natives have learned the vice, the patent brings in a round sum, and the needy Government at Papeete shut their eyes and open their pockets. Of course, the patentee is supposed to sell to Chinamen alone; equally of course, no one could afford to pay forty thousand francs for the privilege of supplying a scattered handful of Chinese; and every one knows the truth, and all are ashamed of it. French officials shake their heads when opium is mentioned; and the agents of the farmer blush for their employment. Those that live in glass houses should not throw stones; as a subject of the British crown, I am an unwilling shareholder in the largest opium business under heaven. But the British case is highly complicated; it implies the livelihood of millions; and must be reformed, when it can be reformed at all, with prudence. This French business, on the other hand, is a nostrum and a mere excrescence. No native industry was to be encouraged: the poison is solemnly imported. No native habit was to be considered: the vice has been gratuitously introduced. And no creature profits, save the Government at Papeete—the not very enviable gentlemen who pay them, and the Chinese underlings who do the dirty work.

CHAPTER IX—THE HOUSE OF TEMOANA

The history of the Marquesas is, of late years, much confused by the coming and going of the French. At least twice they have seized the archipelago, at least once deserted it; and in the meanwhile the natives pursued almost without interruption their desultory cannibal wars. Through these events and changing dynasties, a single considerable figure may be seen to move: that of the high chief, a king, Temoana. Odds and ends of his history came to my ears: how he was at first a convert to the Protestant mission; how he was kidnapped or exiled from his native land, served as cook aboard a whaler, and was shown, for small charge, in English seaports; how he returned at last to the Marquesas, fell under the strong and benign influence of the late bishop, extended his influence in the group, was for a while joint ruler with the prelate, and died at last the chief supporter of Catholicism and the French. His widow remains in receipt of two pounds a month from the French Government. Queen she is usually called, but in the official almanac she figures as 'Madame Vaekehu, Grande Chefesse.' His son (natural or adoptive, I know not which), Stanislao Moanatini, chief of Akaui, serves in Tai-o-hae as a kind of Minister of Public Works; and the daughter of Stanislao is High Chiefess of the southern island of Tauata. These, then, are the greatest folk of the archipelago; we thought them also the most estimable. This is the rule in Polynesia, with few exceptions; the higher the family, the better the man—better in sense, better in manners, and usually taller and stronger in body. A stranger advances blindfold. He scrapes acquaintance as he can. Save the tattoo in the Marquesas, nothing indicates the difference of rank; and yet almost invariably we found, after we had made them, that our friends were persons of station. I have said 'usually taller and stronger.' I might have been more absolute,—over all Polynesia, and a part of Micronesia, the rule holds good; the great ones of the isle, and even of the village, are greater of bone and muscle, and often heavier of flesh, than any commoner. The usual explanation—that the high-born child is more industriously shampooed, is probably the true one. In New Caledonia, at least, where the difference does not exist, has never been remarked, the practice of shampooing seems to be itself unknown. Doctors would be well employed in a study of the point.

Vaekehu lives at the other end of the town from the Residency, beyond the buildings of the mission. Her house is on the European plan: a table in the midst of the chief room; photographs and religious pictures on the wall. It commands to either hand a charming vista: through the front door, a peep of green lawn, scurrying pigs, the pendent fans of the coco-palm and splendour of the bursting surf: through the back, mounting forest glades and coronals of precipice. Here, in the strong thorough-draught, Her Majesty received us in a simple gown of print, and with no mark of royalty but the exquisite finish of her tattooed mittens, the elaboration of her manners, and the gentle falsetto in which all the highly refined among Marquesan ladies (and Vaekehu above all others) delight to sing their language. An adopted daughter interpreted, while we gave the news, and rehearsed by name our friends of Anaho. As we talked, we could see, through the landward door, another lady of the household at her toilet under the green trees; who presently, when her hair was arranged, and her hat wreathed with flowers, appeared upon the back verandah with gracious salutations.

Vaekehu is very deaf; 'merci' is her only word of French; and I do not know that she seemed clever. An exquisite, kind refinement, with a shade of quietism, gathered perhaps from the nuns, was what chiefly struck us. Or rather, upon that first occasion, we were conscious of a sense as of district-visiting on our part, and reduced evangelical gentility on the part of our hostess. The other impression followed after she was more at ease, and came with Stanislao and his little girl to dine on board the Casco. She had dressed for the occasion: wore white, which very well became her strong brown face; and sat among us, eating or smoking her cigarette, quite cut off from all society, or only now and then included through the intermediary of her son. It was a position that might have been ridiculous, and she made it ornamental; making believe to hear and to be entertained; her face, whenever she met our eyes, lighting with the smile of good society; her contributions to the talk, when she made any, and that was seldom, always complimentary and pleasing. No attention was paid to the child, for instance, but what she remarked and thanked us for. Her parting with each, when she came to leave, was gracious and pretty, as had been every step of her behaviour. When Mrs. Stevenson held out her hand to say good-bye, Vaekehu took it, held it, and a moment smiled upon her; dropped it, and then, as upon a kindly after-thought, and with a sort of warmth of condescension, held out both hands and kissed my wife upon both cheeks. Given the same relation of years and of rank, the thing would have been so done on the boards of the Comédie Française; just so might Madame Brohan have warmed and condescended to Madame Broisat in the Marquis de Villemer. It was my part to accompany our guests ashore: when I kissed the little girl good-bye at the pier steps, Vaekehu gave a cry of gratification, reached down her hand into the boat, took mine, and pressed it with that flattering softness which seems the coquetry of the old lady in every quarter of the earth. The next moment she had taken Stanislao's arm, and they moved off along the pier in the moonlight, leaving me bewildered. This was a queen of cannibals; she was tattooed from hand to foot, and perhaps the greatest masterpiece of that art now extant, so that a while ago, before she was grown prim, her leg was one of the sights of Tai-o-hae; she had been passed from chief to chief; she had been fought for and taken in war; perhaps, being so great a lady, she had sat on the high place, and throned it there, alone of her sex, while the drums were going twenty strong and the priests carried up the blood-stained baskets of long-pig. And now behold her, out of that past of violence and sickening feasts, step forth, in her age, a quiet, smooth, elaborate old lady, such as you might find at home (mittened also, but not often so well-mannered) in a score of country houses. Only Vaekehu's mittens were of dye, not of silk; and they had been paid for, not in money, but the cooked flesh of men. It came in my mind with a clap, what she could think of it herself, and whether at heart, perhaps, she might not regret and aspire after the barbarous and stirring past. But when I asked Stanislao—'Ah!' said he, 'she is content; she is religious, she passes all her days with the sisters.'

Stanislao (Stanislaos, with the final consonant evaded after the Polynesian habit) was sent by Bishop Dordillon to South America, and there educated by the fathers. His French is fluent, his talk sensible and spirited, and in his capacity of ganger-in-chief, he is of excellent service to the French. With the prestige of his name and family, and with the stick when needful, he keeps the natives working and the roads passable. Without Stanislao and the convicts, I am in doubt what would become of the present regimen in Nuka-hiva; whether the highways might not be suffered to close up, the pier to wash away, and the Residency to fall piecemeal about the ears of impotent officials. And yet though the hereditary favourer, and one of the chief props of French authority, he has always an eye upon the past. He showed me where the old public place had stood, still to be traced by random piles of stone; told me how great and fine it was, and surrounded on all sides by populous houses, whence, at the beating of the drums, the folk crowded to make holiday. The drum-beat of the Polynesian has a strange and gloomy stimulation for the nerves of all. White persons feel it—at these precipitate sounds their hearts beat faster; and, according to old residents, its effect on the natives was extreme. Bishop Dordillon might entreat; Temoana himself command and threaten; at the note of the drum wild instincts triumphed. And now it might beat upon these ruins, and who should assemble? The houses are down, the people dead, their lineage extinct; and the sweepings and fugitives of distant bays and islands encamp upon their graves. The decline of the dance Stanislao especially laments. 'Chaque pays a ses coutumes,' said he; but in the report of any gendarme, perhaps corruptly eager to increase the number of délits and the instruments of his own power, custom after custom is placed on the expurgatorial index. 'Tenez, une danse qui n'est pas permise,' said Stanislao: 'je ne sais pas pourquoi, elle est très jolie, elle va comme ça,' and sticking his umbrella upright in the road, he sketched the steps and gestures. All his criticisms of the present, all his regrets for the past, struck me as temperate and sensible. The short term of office of the Resident he thought the chief defect of the administration; that officer having scarce begun to be efficient ere he was recalled. I thought I gathered, too, that he regarded with some fear the coming change from a naval to a civil governor. I am sure at least that I regard it so myself; for the civil servants of France have never appeared to any foreigner as at all the flower of their country, while her naval officers may challenge competition with the world. In all his talk, Stanislao was particular to speak of his own country as a land of savages; and when he stated an opinion of his own, it was with some apologetic preface, alleging that he was 'a savage who had travelled.' There was a deal, in this elaborate modesty, of honest pride. Yet there was something in the precaution that saddened me; and I could not but fear he was only forestalling a taunt that he had heard too often.

I recall with interest two interviews with Stanislao. The first was a certain afternoon of tropic rain, which we passed together in the verandah of the club; talking at times with heightened voices as the showers redoubled overhead, passing at times into the billiard-room, to consult, in the dim, cloudy daylight, that map of the world which forms its chief adornment. He was naturally ignorant of English history, so that I had much of news to communicate. The story of Gordon I told him in full, and many episodes of the Indian Mutiny, Lucknow, the second battle of Cawn-pore, the relief of Arrah, the death of poor Spottis-woode, and Sir Hugh Rose's hotspur, midland campaign. He was intent to hear; his brown face, strongly marked with small-pox, kindled and changed with each vicissitude. His eyes glowed with the reflected light of battle; his questions were many and intelligent, and it was chiefly these that sent us so often to the map. But it is of our parting that I keep the strongest sense. We were to sail on the morrow, and the night had fallen, dark, gusty, and rainy, when we stumbled up the hill to bid farewell to Stanislao. He had already loaded us with gifts; but more were waiting. We sat about the table over cigars and green cocoa-nuts; claps of wind blew through the house and extinguished the lamp, which was always instantly relighted with a single match; and these recurrent intervals of darkness were felt as a relief. For there was something painful and embarrassing in the kindness of that separation. 'Ah, vous devriez rester ici, mon cher ami!' cried Stanislao. 'Vous êtes les gens qu'il faut pour les Kanaques; vous êtes doux, vous et votre famille; vous seriez obéis dans toutes les îles.' We had been civil; not always that, my conscience told me, and never anything beyond; and all this to-do is a measure, not of our considerateness, but of the want of it in others. The rest of the evening, on to Vaekehu's and back as far as to the pier, Stanislao walked with my arm and sheltered me with his umbrella; and after the boat had put off, we could still distinguish, in the murky darkness, his gestures of farewell. His words, if there were any, were drowned by the rain and the loud surf.

I have mentioned presents, a vexed question in the South Seas; and one which well illustrates the common, ignorant habit of regarding races in a lump. In many quarters the Polynesian gives only to receive. I have visited islands where the population mobbed me for all the world like dogs after the waggon of cat's-meat; and where the frequent proposition, 'You my pleni (friend),' or (with more of pathos) 'You all 'e same my father,' must be received with hearty laughter and a shout. And perhaps everywhere, among the greedy and rapacious, a gift is regarded as a sprat to catch a whale. It is the habit to give gifts and to receive returns, and such characters, complying with the custom, will look to it nearly that they do not lose. But for persons of a different stamp the statement must be reversed. The shabby Polynesian is anxious till he has received the return gift; the generous is uneasy until he has made it. The first is disappointed if you have not given more than he; the second is miserable if he thinks he has given less than you. This is my experience; if it clash with that of others, I pity their fortune, and praise mine: the circumstances cannot change what I have seen, nor lessen what I have received. And indeed I find that those who oppose me often argue from a ground of singular presumptions; comparing Polynesians with an ideal person, compact of generosity and gratitude, whom I never had the pleasure of encountering; and forgetting that what is almost poverty to us is wealth almost unthinkable to them. I will give one instance: I chanced to speak with consideration of these gifts of Stanislao's with a certain clever man, a great hater and contemner of Kanakas. 'Well! what were they?' he cried. 'A pack of old men's beards. Trash!' And the same gentleman, some half an hour later, being upon a different train of thought, dwelt at length on the esteem in which the Marquesans held that sort of property, how they preferred it to all others except land, and what fancy prices it would fetch. Using his own figures, I computed that, in this commodity alone, the gifts of Vaekehu and Stanislao represented between two and three hundred dollars; and the queen's official salary is of two hundred and forty in the year.

But generosity on the one hand, and conspicuous meanness on the other, are in the South Seas, as at home, the exception. It is neither with any hope of gain, nor with any lively wish to please, that the ordinary Polynesian chooses and presents his gifts. A plain social duty lies before him, which he performs correctly, but without the least enthusiasm. And we shall best understand his attitude of mind, if we examine our own to the cognate absurdity of marriage presents. There we give without any special thought of a return; yet if the circumstance arise, and the return be withheld, we shall judge ourselves insulted. We give them usually without affection, and almost never with a genuine desire to please; and our gift is rather a mark of our own status than a measure of our love to the recipients. So in a great measure and with the common run of the Polynesians; their gifts are formal; they imply no more than social recognition; and they are made and reciprocated, as we pay and return our morning visits. And the practice of marking and measuring events and sentiments by presents is universal in the island world. A gift plays with them the part of stamp and seal; and has entered profoundly into the mind of islanders. Peace and war, marriage, adoption and naturalisation, are celebrated or declared by the acceptance or the refusal of gifts; and it is as natural for the islander to bring a gift as for us to carry a card-case.

CHAPTER X—A PORTRAIT AND A STORY

I have had occasion several times to name the late bishop, Father Dordillon, 'Monseigneur,' as he is still almost universally called, Vicar-Apostolic of the Marquesas and Bishop of Cambysopolis in partibus. Everywhere in the islands, among all classes and races, this fine, old, kindly, cheerful fellow is remembered with affection and respect. His influence with the natives was paramount. They reckoned him the highest of men—higher than an admiral; brought him their money to keep; took his advice upon their purchases; nor would they plant trees upon their own land till they had the approval of the father of the islands. During the time of the French exodus he singly represented Europe, living in the Residency, and ruling by the hand of Temoana. The first roads were made under his auspices and by his persuasion. The old road between Hatiheu and Anaho was got under way from either side on the ground that it would be pleasant for an evening promenade, and brought to completion by working on the rivalry of the two villages. The priest would boast in Hatiheu of the progress made in Anaho, and he would tell the folk of Anaho, 'If you don't take care, your neighbours will be over the hill before you are at the top.' It could not be so done to-day; it could then; death, opium, and depopulation had not gone so far; and the people of Hatiheu, I was told, still vied with each other in fine attire, and used to go out by families, in the cool of the evening, boat-sailing and racing in the bay. There seems some truth at least in the common view, that this joint reign of Temoana and the bishop was the last and brief golden age of the Marquesas. But the civil power returned, the mission was packed out of the Residency at twenty-four hours' notice, new methods supervened, and the golden age (whatever it quite was) came to an end. It is the strongest proof of Father Dordillon's prestige that it survived, seemingly without loss, this hasty deposition.

His method with the natives was extremely mild. Among these barbarous children he still played the part of the smiling father; and he was careful to observe, in all indifferent matters, the Marquesan etiquette. Thus, in the singular system of artificial kinship, the bishop had been adopted by Vaekehu as a grandson; Miss Fisher, of Hatiheu, as a daughter. From that day, Monseigneur never addressed the young lady except as his mother, and closed his letters with the formalities of a dutiful son. With Europeans he could be strict, even to the extent of harshness. He made no distinction against heretics, with whom he was on friendly terms; but the rules of his own Church he would see observed; and once at least he had a white man clapped in jail for the desecration of a saint's day. But even this rigour, so intolerable to laymen, so irritating to Protestants, could not shake his popularity. We shall best conceive him by examples nearer home; we may all have known some divine of the old school in Scotland, a literal Sabbatarian, a stickler for the letter of the law, who was yet in private modest, innocent, genial and mirthful. Much such a man, it seems, was Father Dordillon. And his popularity bore a test yet stronger. He had the name, and probably deserved it, of a shrewd man in business and one that made the mission pay. Nothing so much stirs up resentment as the inmixture in commerce of religious bodies; but even rival traders spoke well of Monseigneur.

His character is best portrayed in the story of the days of his decline. A time came when, from the failure of sight, he must desist from his literary labours: his Marquesan hymns, grammars, and dictionaries; his scientific papers, lives of saints, and devotional poetry. He cast about for a new interest: pitched on gardening, and was to be seen all day, with spade and water-pot, in his childlike eagerness, actually running between the borders. Another step of decay, and he must leave his garden also. Instantly a new occupation was devised, and he sat in the mission cutting paper flowers and wreaths. His diocese was not great enough for his activity; the churches of the Marquesas were papered with his handiwork, and still he must be making more. 'Ah,' said he, smiling, 'when I am dead what a fine time you will have clearing out my trash!' He had been dead about six months; but I was pleased to see some of his trophies still exposed, and looked upon them with a smile: the tribute (if I have read his cheerful character aright) which he would have preferred to any useless tears. Disease continued progressively to disable him; he who had clambered so stalwartly over the rude rocks of the Marquesas, bringing peace to warfaring clans, was for some time carried in a chair between the mission and the church, and at last confined to bed, impotent with dropsy, and tormented with bed-sores and sciatica. Here he lay two months without complaint; and on the 11th January 1888, in the seventy-ninth year of his life, and the thirty-fourth of his labours in the Marquesas, passed away.

Those who have a taste for hearing missions, Protestant or Catholic, decried, must seek their pleasure elsewhere than in my pages. Whether Catholic or Protestant, with all their gross blots, with all their deficiency of candour, of humour, and of common sense, the missionaries are the best and the most useful whites in the Pacific. This is a subject which will follow us throughout; but there is one part of it that may conveniently be treated here. The married and the celibate missionary, each has his particular advantage and defect. The married missionary, taking him at the best, may offer to the native what he is much in want of—a higher picture of domestic life; but the woman at his elbow tends to keep him in touch with Europe and out of touch with Polynesia, and to perpetuate, and even to ingrain, parochial decencies far best forgotten. The mind of the female missionary tends, for instance, to be continually busied about dress. She can be taught with extreme difficulty to think any costume decent but that to which she grew accustomed on Clapham Common; and to gratify this prejudice, the native is put to useless expense, his mind is tainted with the morbidities of Europe, and his health is set in danger. The celibate missionary, on the other hand, and whether at best or worst, falls readily into native ways of life; to which he adds too commonly what is either a mark of celibate man at large, or an inheritance from mediæval saints—I mean slovenly habits and an unclean person. There are, of course, degrees in this; and the sister (of course, and all honour to her) is as fresh as a lady at a ball. For the diet there is nothing to be said—it must amaze and shock the Polynesian—but for the adoption of native habits there is much. 'Chaque pays a ses coutumes,' said Stanislao; these it is the missionary's delicate task to modify; and the more he can do so from within, and from a native standpoint, the better he will do his work; and here I think the Catholics have sometimes the advantage; in the Vicariate of Dordillon, I am sure they had it. I have heard the bishop blamed for his indulgence to the natives, and above all because he did not rage with sufficient energy against cannibalism. It was a part of his policy to live among the natives like an elder brother; to follow where he could; to lead where it was necessary; never to drive; and to encourage the growth of new habits, instead of violently rooting up the old. And it might be better, in the long-run, if this policy were always followed.

It might be supposed that native missionaries would prove more indulgent, but the reverse is found to be the case. The new broom sweeps clean; and the white missionary of to-day is often embarrassed by the bigotry of his native coadjutor. What else should we expect? On some islands, sorcery, polygamy, human sacrifice, and tobacco-smoking have been prohibited, the dress of the native has been modified, and himself warned in strong terms against rival sects of Christianity; all by the same man, at the same period of time, and with the like authority. By what criterion is the convert to distinguish the essential from the unessential? He swallows the nostrum whole; there has been no play of mind, no instruction, and, except for some brute utility in the prohibitions, no advance. To call things by their proper names, this is teaching superstition. It is unfortunate to use the word; so few people have read history, and so many have dipped into little atheistic manuals, that the majority will rush to a conclusion, and suppose the labour lost. And far from that: These semi-spontaneous superstitions, varying with the sect of the original evangelist and the customs of the island, are found in practice to be highly fructifying; and in particular those who have learned and who go forth again to teach them offer an example to the world. The best specimen of the Christian hero that I ever met was one of these native missionaries. He had saved two lives at the risk of his own; like Nathan, he had bearded a tyrant in his hour of blood; when a whole white population fled, he alone stood to his duty; and his behaviour under domestic sorrow with which the public has no concern filled the beholder with sympathy and admiration. A poor little smiling laborious man he looked; and you would have thought he had nothing in him but that of which indeed he had too much—facile good-nature. [86]

It chances that the only rivals of Monseigneur and his mission in the Marquesas were certain of these brown-skinned evangelists, natives from Hawaii. I know not what they thought of Father Dordillon: they are the only class I did not question; but I suspect the prelate to have regarded them askance, for he was eminently human. During my stay at Tai-o-hae, the time of the yearly holiday came round at the girls' school; and a whole fleet of whale-boats came from Ua-pu to take the daughters of that island home. On board of these was Kauwealoha, one of the pastors, a fine, rugged old gentleman, of that leonine type so common in Hawaii. He paid me a visit in the Casco, and there entertained me with a tale of one of his colleagues, Kekela, a missionary in the great cannibal isle of Hiva-oa. It appears that shortly after a kidnapping visit from a Peruvian slaver, the boats of an American whaler put into a bay upon that island, were attacked, and made their escape with difficulty, leaving their mate, a Mr. Whalon, in the hands of the natives. The captive, with his arms bound behind his back, was cast into a house; and the chief announced the capture to Kekela. And here I begin to follow the version of Kauwealoha; it is a good specimen of Kanaka English; and the reader is to conceive it delivered with violent emphasis and speaking pantomime.

"'I got 'Melican mate," the chief he say. "What you go do 'Melican mate?" Kekela he say. "I go make fire, I go kill, I go eat him," he say; "you come to-mollow eat piece." "I no want eat 'Melican mate!" Kekela he say; "why you want?" "This bad shippee, this slave shippee," the chief he say. "One time a shippee he come from Pelu, he take away plenty Kanaka, he take away my son. 'Melican mate he bad man. I go eat him; you eat piece." "I no want eat 'Melican mate!" Kekela he say; and he cly—all night he cly! To-mollow Kekela he get up, he put on blackee coat, he go see chief; he see Missa Whela, him hand tie' like this. (Pantomime.) Kekela he cly. He say chief:—"Chief, you like things of mine? you like whale-boat?" "Yes," he say. "You like file-a'm?" (fire-arms). "Yes," he say. "You like blackee coat?" "Yes," he say. Kekela he take Missa Whela by he shoul'a' (shoulder), he take him light out house; he give chief he whale-boat, he file-a'm, he blackee coat. He take Missa Whela he house, make him sit down with he wife and chil'en. Missa Whela all-the-same pelison (prison); he wife, he chil'en in Amelica; he cly—O, he cly. Kekela he solly. One day Kekela he see ship. (Pantomime.) He say Missa Whela, "Ma' Whala?" Missa Whela he say, "Yes." Kanaka they begin go down beach. Kekela he get eleven Kanaka, get oa' (oars), get evely thing. He say Missa Whela, "Now you go quick." They jump in whale-boat. "Now you low!" Kekela he say: "you low quick, quick!" (Violent pantomime, and a change indicating that the narrator has left the boat and returned to the beach.) All the Kanaka they say, "How! 'Melican mate he go away?"—jump in boat; low afta. (Violent pantomime, and change again to boat.) Kekela he say, "Low quick!"'

Here I think Kauwealoha's pantomime had confused me; I have no more of his ipsissima verba; and can but add, in my own less spirited manner, that the ship was reached, Mr. Whalon taken aboard, and Kekela returned to his charge among the cannibals. But how unjust it is to repeat the stumblings of a foreigner in a language only partly acquired! A thoughtless reader might conceive Kauwealoha and his colleague to be a species of amicable baboon; but I have here the anti-dote. In return for his act of gallant charity, Kekela was presented by the American Government with a sum of money, and by President Lincoln personally with a gold watch. From his letter of thanks, written in his own tongue, I give the following extract. I do not envy the man who can read it without emotion.

> 'When I saw one of your countrymen, a citizen of your great nation, ill-treated, and about to be baked and eaten, as a pig is eaten, I ran to save him, full of pity and grief at the evil deed of these benighted people. I gave my boat for the stranger's life. This boat came from James Hunnewell, a gift of friendship. It became the ransom of this countryman of yours, that he might not be eaten by the savages who knew not Jehovah. This was Mr. Whalon, and the date, Jan. 14, 1864.
>
> 'As to this friendly deed of mine in saving Mr. Whalon, its seed came from your great land, and was brought by certain of your countrymen, who had received the love of God. It was planted in Hawaii, and I

brought it to plant in this land and in these dark regions, that they might receive the root of all that is good and true, which is love.

'1. Love to Jehovah.

'2. Love to self.

'3. Love to our neighbour.

'If a man have a sufficiency of these three, he is good and holy, like his God, Jehovah, in his triune character (Father, Son, and Holy Ghost), one-three, three-one. If he have two and wants one, it is not well; and if he have one and wants two, indeed, is not well; but if he cherishes all three, then is he holy, indeed, after the manner of the Bible.

'This is a great thing for your great nation to boast of, before all the nations of the earth. From your great land a most precious seed was brought to the land of darkness. It was planted here, not by means of guns and men-of-war and threatening. It was planted by means of the ignorant, the neglected, the despised. Such was the introduction of the word of the Almighty God into this group of Nuuhiwa. Great is my debt to Americans, who have taught me all things pertaining to this life and to that which is to come.

'How shall I repay your great kindness to me? Thus David asked of Jehovah, and thus I ask of you, the President of the United States. This is my only payment—that which I have received of the Lord, love—(aloha).'

CHAPTER XI—LONG-PIG—A CANNIBAL HIGH PLACE

Nothing more strongly arouses our disgust than cannibalism, nothing so surely unmortars a society; nothing, we might plausibly argue, will so harden and degrade the minds of those that practise it. And yet we ourselves make much the same appearance in the eyes of the Buddhist and the vegetarian. We consume the carcasses of creatures of like appetites, passions, and organs with ourselves; we feed on babes, though not our own; and the slaughter-house resounds daily with screams of pain and fear. We distinguish, indeed; but the unwillingness of many nations to eat the dog, an animal with whom we live on terms of the next intimacy, shows how precariously the distinction is grounded. The pig is the main element of animal food among the islands; and I had many occasions, my mind being quickened by my cannibal surroundings, to observe his character and the manner of his death. Many islanders live with their pigs as we do with our dogs; both crowd around the hearth with equal freedom; and the island pig is a fellow of activity, enterprise, and sense. He husks his own cocoa-nuts, and (I am told) rolls them into the sun to burst; he is the terror of the shepherd. Mrs. Stevenson, senior, has seen one fleeing to the woods with a lamb in his mouth; and I saw another come rapidly (and erroneously) to the conclusion that the Casco was going down, and swim through the flush water to the rail in search of an escape. It was told us in childhood that pigs cannot swim; I have known one to leap overboard, swim five hundred yards to shore, and return to the house of his original owner. I was once, at Tautira, a pig-master on a considerable scale; at first, in my pen, the utmost good feeling prevailed; a little sow with a belly-ache came and appealed to us for help in the manner of a child; and there was one shapely black boar, whom we called Catholicus, for he was a particular present from the Catholics of the village, and who early displayed the marks of courage and friendliness; no other animal, whether dog or pig, was suffered to approach him at his food, and for human beings he showed a full measure of that toadying fondness so common in the lower animals, and possibly their chief title to the name. One day, on visiting my piggery, I was amazed to see Catholicus draw back from my approach with cries of terror; and if I was amazed at the change, I was truly embarrassed when I learnt its reason. One of the pigs had been that morning killed; Catholicus had seen the murder, he had discovered he was dwelling in the shambles, and from that time his confidence and his delight in life were ended. We still reserved him a long while, but he could not endure the sight of any two-legged creature, nor could we, under the circumstances, encounter his eye without confusion. I have assisted besides, by the ear, at the act of butchery itself; the victim's cries of pain I think I could have borne, but the execution was mismanaged, and his expression of terror was contagious: that small heart moved to the same tune with ours. Upon such 'dread foundations' the life of the European reposes, and yet the European is among the less cruel of races. The paraphernalia of murder, the preparatory brutalities of his existence, are all hid away; an extreme sensibility reigns upon the surface; and ladies will faint at the recital of one tithe of what they daily expect of their butchers. Some will be even crying out upon me in their hearts for the coarseness of this paragraph. And so with the island cannibals. They were not cruel; apart from this custom, they are a race of the most kindly; rightly speaking, to cut a man's flesh after he is dead is far less hateful than to oppress him whilst he lives; and even the victims of their appetite were gently used in life and suddenly and painlessly despatched at last. In island circles of refinement it was doubtless thought bad taste to expatiate on what was ugly in the practice.

Cannibalism is traced from end to end of the Pacific, from the Marquesas to New Guinea, from New Zealand to Hawaii, here in the lively haunt of its exercise, there by scanty but significant survivals. Hawaii is the most doubtful. We find cannibalism chronicled in Hawaii, only in the history of a single war, where it seems to have been thought exception, as in the case of mountain outlaws, such as fell by the hand of Theseus. In Tahiti, a single circumstance survived, but that appears conclusive. In historic times, when human oblation was made in the marae, the eyes of the victim were formally offered to the chief: a delicacy to the leading guest. All Melanesia appears tainted. In Micronesia, in the Marshalls, with which my acquaintance is no more than that of a tourist, I could find no trace at all; and even in the Gilbert zone I long looked and asked in vain. I was told tales indeed of men who had been eaten in a famine; but these were nothing to my purpose, for the same thing is done under the same stress by all kindreds and generations of men. At last, in some manuscript notes of Dr. Turner's, which I was allowed to consult at Malua, I came on one damning evidence: on the island of Onoatoa the punishment for theft was to be killed and eaten. How shall we account for the universality of the practice over so vast an area, among people of such varying civilisation, and, with whatever intermixture, of such different blood? What circumstance is common to them all, but that they lived on islands destitute, or very nearly so, of animal food? I can never find it in my appetite that man was meant to live on vegetables only. When our stores ran low among the islands, I grew to weary for the recurrent day when economy allowed us to open another tin of miserable mutton. And in at least one ocean language, a particular word denotes that a man is 'hungry for fish,' having reached that stage when vegetables can no longer satisfy, and his soul, like those of the Hebrews in the desert, begins to lust after flesh-pots. Add to this the evidences of over-population and imminent famine already adduced, and I think we see some ground of indulgence for the island cannibal.

It is right to look at both sides of any question; but I am far from making the apology of this worse than bestial vice. The higher Polynesian races, such as the Tahitians, Hawaiians, and Samoans, had one and all outgrown, and some of them had in part forgot, the practice, before Cook or Bougainville had shown a top-sail in their waters. It lingered only in some low islands where life was difficult to maintain, and among inveterate savages like the New-Zealanders or the Marquesans. The Marquesans intertwined man-eating with the whole texture of their lives; long-pig was in a sense their currency and sacrament; it formed the hire of the artist, illustrated public events, and was the occasion and attraction of a feast. To-day they are paying the penalty of this bloody commixture. The civil power, in its crusade against man-eating, has had to examine one after another all Marquesan arts and pleasures, has found them one after another tainted with a cannibal element, and one after another has placed them on the proscript list. Their art of tattooing stood by itself, the execution exquisite, the designs most beautiful and intricate; nothing more handsomely sets off a handsome man; it may cost some pain in the beginning, but I doubt if it be near so painful in the long-run, and I am sure it is far more becoming than the ignoble European practice of tight-lacing among women. And now it has been found needful to forbid the art. Their songs and dances were numerous (and the law has had to abolish them by the dozen). They now face empty-handed the tedium of their uneventful days; and who shall pity them? The least rigorous will say that they were justly served.

Death alone could not satisfy Marquesan vengeance: the flesh must be eaten. The chief who seized Mr. Whalon preferred to eat him; and he thought he had justified the wish when he explained it was a vengeance. Two or three years ago, the people of a valley seized and slew a wretch who had offended them. His offence, it is to be supposed, was dire; they could not bear to leave their vengeance incomplete, and, under the eyes of the French, they did not dare to hold a public festival. The body was accordingly divided; and every man retired to his own house to consummate the rite in secret, carrying his proportion of the dreadful meat in a Swedish match-box. The barbarous substance of the drama and the European properties employed offer a seizing contrast to the imagination. Yet more striking is another incident of the very year when I was there myself, 1888. In the spring, a man and woman skulked about the school-house in Hiva-oa till they found a particular child alone. Him they approached with honeyed words and carneying manners—'You are So-and-so, son of So-and-so?' they asked; and caressed and beguiled him deeper in the woods. Some instinct woke in the child's bosom, or some look betrayed the horrid purpose of his deceivers. He sought to break from them; he screamed; and they, casting off the mask, seized him the more strongly and began to run. His cries were heard; his schoolmates, playing not far off, came running to the rescue; and the sinister couple fled and vanished in the woods. They were never identified; no prosecution followed; but it was currently supposed they had some grudge against the boy's father, and designed to eat him in revenge. All over the islands, as at home among our own ancestors, it will be observed that the avenger takes no particular heed to strike an individual. A family, a class, a village, a whole valley or island, a whole race of mankind, share equally the guilt of any member. So, in the above story, the son was to pay the penalty for his father; so Mr. Whalon, the mate of an American whaler, was to bleed and be eaten for the misdeeds of a Peruvian slaver. I am reminded of an incident in Jaluit in the Marshall group, which was told me by an eye-witness, and which I tell here again for the strangeness of the scene. Two men had awakened the animosity of the Jaluit chiefs; and it was their wives who were selected to be punished. A single native served as executioner. Early in the morning, in the face of a large concourse of spectators, he waded out upon the reef between his victims. These neither complained nor resisted; accompanied their destroyer patiently; stooped down, when they had waded deep enough, at his command; and he (laying one hand upon the shoulders of each) held them under water till they drowned. Doubtless, although my informant did not tell me so, their families would be lamenting aloud upon the beach.

It was from Hatiheu that I paid my first visit to a cannibal high place.

The day was sultry and clouded. Drenching tropical showers succeeded bursts of sweltering sunshine. The green pathway of the road wound steeply upward. As we went, our little schoolboy guide a little ahead of us, Father Simeon had his portfolio in his hand, and named the trees for me, and read aloud from his notes the abstract of their virtues. Presently the road, mounting, showed us the vale of Hatiheu, on a larger scale; and the priest, with occasional reference to our guide, pointed out the boundaries and told me the names of the larger tribes that lived at perpetual war in the old days: one on the north-east, one along the beach, one behind upon the mountain. With a survivor of this latter clan Father Simeon had spoken; until the pacification he had never been to the sea's edge, nor, if I remember exactly, eaten of sea-fish. Each in its own district, the septs lived cantoned and beleaguered. One step without the boundaries was to affront death. If famine came, the men must out to the woods to gather chestnuts and small fruits; even as to this day, if the parents are backward in their weekly doles, school must be broken up and the scholars sent foraging. But in the old days, when there was trouble in one clan, there would be activity in all its neighbours; the woods would be laid full of ambushes; and he who went after vegetables for himself might remain to be a joint for his hereditary foes. Nor was the pointed occasion needful. A dozen different natural signs and social junctures called this people to the war-path and the cannibal hunt. Let one of chiefly rank have finished his tattooing, the wife of one be near upon her time, two of the debauching streams have deviated nearer on the beach of Hatiheu, a certain bird have been heard to sing, a certain ominous formation of cloud observed above the northern sea; and instantly the arms were oiled, and the man-hunters swarmed into the wood to lay their fratricidal ambuscades. It appears besides that occasionally, perhaps in famine, the priest would shut himself in his house, where he lay for a stated period like a person dead. When he came forth it was to run for three days through the territory of the clan, naked and starving, and to sleep at night alone in the high place. It was now the turn of the others to keep the house, for to encounter the priest upon his rounds was death. On the eve of the fourth day the time of the running was over; the priest returned to his roof, the laymen came forth, and in the morning the number of the victims was announced. I have this tale of the priest on one authority—I think a good one,—but I set it down with diffidence. The particulars are so striking that, had they been true, I almost think I must have heard them oftener referred to. Upon one point there seems to be no question: that the feast was sometimes furnished from within the clan. In times of scarcity, all who were not protected by their family connections—in the Highland expression, all the commons of the clan—had cause to tremble. It was vain to resist, it was useless to flee. They were begirt upon all hands by cannibals; and the oven was ready to smoke for them abroad in the country of their foes, or at home in the valley of their fathers.

At a certain corner of the road our scholar-guide struck off to his left into the twilight of the forest. We were now on one of the ancient native roads, plunged in a high vault of wood, and clambering, it seemed, at random over boulders and dead trees; but the lad wound in and out and up and down without a check, for these paths are to the natives as marked as the king's highway is to us; insomuch that, in the days of the man-hunt, it was their labour rather to block and deface than to improve them. In the crypt of the wood the air was clammy and hot and cold; overhead, upon the leaves, the tropical rain uproariously poured, but only here and there, as through holes in a leaky roof, a single drop would fall, and make a spot upon my mackintosh. Presently the huge trunk of a banyan hove in sight, standing upon what seemed the ruins of an ancient fort; and our guide, halting and holding forth his arm, announced that we had reached the paepae tapu.

Paepae signifies a floor or platform such as a native house is built on; and even such a paepae—a paepae hae—may be called a paepae tapu in a lesser sense when it is deserted and becomes the haunt of spirits; but the public high place, such as I was now treading, was a thing on a great scale. As far as my eyes could pierce through the dark undergrowth, the floor of the forest was all paved. Three tiers of terrace ran on the slope of the hill; in front, a crumbling parapet contained the main arena; and the pavement of that was pierced and parcelled out with several wells and small enclosures. No trace remained of any superstructure, and the scheme of the amphitheatre was difficult to seize. I visited another in Hiva-oa, smaller but more perfect, where it was easy to follow rows of benches, and to distinguish isolated seats of honour for eminent persons; and where, on the upper platform, a single joist of the temple or dead-house still remained, its uprights richly carved. In the old days the high place was sedulously tended. No tree except the sacred banyan was suffered to encroach upon its grades, no dead leaf to rot upon the pavement. The stones were smoothly set, and I am told they were kept bright with oil. On all sides the guardians lay encamped in their subsidiary huts to watch and cleanse it. No other foot of man was suffered to draw near; only the priest, in the days of his running, came there to sleep—perhaps to dream of his ungodly errand; but, in the time of the feast, the clan trooped to the high place in a body, and each had his appointed seat. There were places for the chiefs, the drummers, the dancers, the women, and the priests. The drums—perhaps twenty strong, and some of them twelve feet high—continuously throbbed in time. In time the singers kept up their long-drawn, lugubrious, ululating song; in time, too, the dancers, tricked out in singular finery, stepped, leaped, swayed, and gesticulated—their plumed fingers fluttering in the air like butterflies. The sense of time, in all these ocean races, is extremely perfect; and I conceive in such a festival that almost every sound and movement fell in one. So much the more unanimously must have grown the agitation of the feasters; so much the more wild must have been the scene to any European who could have beheld them there, in the strong sun and the strong shadow of the banyan, rubbed with saffron to throw in a more high relief the arabesque of the tattoo; the women bleached by days of confinement to a complexion almost European; the chiefs crowned with silver plumes of old men's beards and girt with kirtles of the hair of dead women. All manner of island food was meanwhile spread for the women and the commons; and, for those who were privileged to eat of it, there were carried up to the dead-house the baskets of long-pig. It is told that the feasts were long kept up; the people came from them brutishly exhausted with debauchery, and the chiefs heavy with their beastly food. There are certain sentiments which we call emphatically human—denying the honour of that name to those who lack them. In such feasts—particularly where the victim has been slain at home, and men banqueted on the poor clay of a comrade with whom they had played in infancy, or a woman whose favours they had shared—the whole body of these sentiments is outraged. To consider it too closely is to understand, if not to excuse, the fervours of self-righteous old ship-captains, who would man their guns, and open fire in passing, on a cannibal island.

And yet it was strange. There, upon the spot, as I stood under the high, dripping vault of the forest, with the young priest on the one hand, in his kilted gown, and the bright-eyed Marquesan schoolboy on the other, the whole business appeared infinitely distant, and fallen in the cold perspective and dry light of history. The bearing of the priest, perhaps, affected me. He smiled; he jested with the boy, the heir both of these feasters and their meat; he clapped his hands, and gave me a stave of one of the old, ill-omened choruses. Centuries might have come and gone since this slimy theatre was last in operation; and I beheld the place with no more emotion than I might have felt in visiting Stonehenge. In Hiva-oa, as I began to appreciate that the thing was still living and latent about my footsteps, and that it was still within the bounds of possibility that I might hear the cry of the trapped victim, my historic attitude entirely failed, and I was sensible of some repugnance for the natives. But here, too, the priests maintained their jocular attitude: rallying the cannibals as upon an eccentricity rather absurd than horrible; seeking, I should say, to shame them from the practice by good-natured ridicule, as we shame a child from stealing sugar. We may here recognise the temperate and sagacious mind of Bishop Dordillon.

CHAPTER XII—THE STORY OF A PLANTATION

Taahauku, on the south-westerly coast of the island of Hiva-oa—Tahuku, say the slovenly whites—may be called the port of Atuona. It is a narrow and small anchorage, set between low cliffy points, and opening above upon a woody valley: a little French fort, now disused and deserted, overhangs the valley and the inlet. Atuona itself, at the head of the next bay, is framed in a theatre of mountains, which dominate the more immediate settling of Taahauku and give the salient character of the scene. They are reckoned at no higher than four thousand feet; but Tahiti with eight thousand, and Hawaii with fifteen, can offer no such picture of abrupt, melancholy alps. In the morning, when the sun falls directly on their front, they stand like a vast wall:

green to the summit, if by any chance the summit should be clear—watercourses here and there delineated on their face, as narrow as cracks. Towards afternoon, the light falls more obliquely, and the sculpture of the range comes in relief, huge gorges sinking into shadow, huge, tortuous buttresses standing edged with sun. At all hours of the day they strike the eye with some new beauty, and the mind with the same menacing gloom.

The mountains, dividing and deflecting the endless airy deluge of the Trade, are doubtless answerable for the climate. A strong draught of wind blew day and night over the anchorage. Day and night the same fantastic and attenuated clouds fled across the heavens, the same dusky cap of rain and vapour fell and rose on the mountain. The land-breezes came very strong and chill, and the sea, like the air, was in perpetual bustle. The swell crowded into the narrow anchorage like sheep into a fold; broke all along both sides, high on the one, low on the other; kept a certain blowhole sounding and smoking like a cannon; and spent itself at last upon the beach.

On the side away from Atuona, the sheltering promontory was a nursery of coco-trees. Some were mere infants, none had attained to any size, none had yet begun to shoot skyward with that whip-like shaft of the mature palm. In the young trees the colour alters with the age and growth. Now all is of a grass-like hue, infinitely dainty; next the rib grows golden, the fronds remaining green as ferns; and then, as the trunk continues to mount and to assume its final hue of grey, the fans put on manlier and more decided depths of verdure, stand out dark upon the distance, glisten against the sun, and flash like silver fountains in the assault of the wind. In this young wood of Taahauku, all these hues and combinations were exampled and repeated by the score. The trees grew pleasantly spaced upon a hilly sward, here and there interspersed with a rack for drying copra, or a tumble-down hut for storing it. Every here and there the stroller had a glimpse of the Casco tossing in the narrow anchorage below; and beyond he had ever before him the dark amphitheatre of the Atuona mountains and the cliffy bluff that closes it to seaward. The trade-wind moving in the fans made a ceaseless noise of summer rain; and from time to time, with the sound of a sudden and distant drum-beat, the surf would burst in a sea-cave.

At the upper end of the inlet, its low, cliffy lining sinks, at both sides, into a beach. A copra warehouse stands in the shadow of the shoreside trees, flitted about for ever by a clan of dwarfish swallows; and a line of rails on a high wooden staging bends back into the mouth of the valley. Walking on this, the new-landed traveller becomes aware of a broad fresh-water lagoon (one arm of which he crosses), and beyond, of a grove of noble palms, sheltering the house of the trader, Mr. Keane. Overhead, the cocos join in a continuous and lofty roof; blackbirds are heard lustily singing; the island cock springs his jubilant rattle and airs his golden plumage; cow-bells sound far and near in the grove; and when you sit in the broad verandah, lulled by this symphony, you may say to yourself, if you are able: 'Better fifty years of Europe . . .' Farther on, the floor of the valley is flat and green, and dotted here and there with stripling coco-palms. Through the midst, with many changes of music, the river trots and brawls; and along its course, where we should look for willows, puraos grow in clusters, and make shadowy pools after an angler's heart. A vale more rich and peaceful, sweeter air, a sweeter voice of rural sounds, I have found nowhere. One circumstance alone might strike the experienced: here is a convenient beach, deep soil, good water, and yet nowhere any paepaes, nowhere any trace of island habitation.

It is but a few years since this valley was a place choked with jungle, the debatable land and battle-ground of cannibals. Two clans laid claim to it—neither could substantiate the claim, and the roads lay desert, or were only visited by men in arms. It is for this very reason that it wears now so smiling an appearance: cleared, planted, built upon, supplied with railways, boat-houses, and bath-houses. For, being no man's land, it was the more readily ceded to a stranger. The stranger was Captain John Hart: Ima Hati, 'Broken-arm,' the natives call him, because when he first visited the islands his arm was in a sling. Captain Hart, a man of English birth, but an American subject, had conceived the idea of cotton culture in the Marquesas during the American War, and was at first rewarded with success. His plantation at Anaho was highly productive; island cotton fetched a high price, and the natives used to debate which was the stronger power, Ima Hati or the French: deciding in favour of the captain, because, though the French had the most ships, he had the more money.

He marked Taahauku for a suitable site, acquired it, and offered the superintendence to Mr. Robert Stewart, a Fifeshire man, already some time in the islands, who had just been ruined by a war on Tauata. Mr. Stewart was somewhat averse to the adventure, having some acquaintance with Atuona and its notorious chieftain, Moipu. He had once landed there, he told me, about dusk, and found the remains of a man and woman partly eaten. On his starting and sickening at the sight, one of Moipu's young men picked up a human foot, and provocatively staring at the stranger, grinned and nibbled at the heel. None need be surprised if Mr. Stewart fled incontinently to the bush, lay there all night in a great horror of mind, and got off to sea again by daylight on the morrow. 'It was always a bad place, Atuona,' commented Mr. Stewart, in his homely Fifeshire voice. In spite of this dire introduction, he accepted the captain's offer, was landed at Taahauku with three Chinamen, and proceeded to clear the jungle.

War was pursued at that time, almost without interval, between the men of Atuona and the men of Haamau; and one day, from the opposite sides of the valley, battle—or I should rather say the noise of battle—raged all the afternoon: the shots and insults of the opposing clans passing from hill to hill over the heads of Mr. Stewart and his Chinamen. There was no genuine fighting; it was like a bicker of schoolboys, only some fool had given the children guns. One man died of his exertions in running, the only casualty. With night the shots and insults ceased; the men of Haamau withdrew; and victory, on some occult principle, was scored to Moipu. Perhaps, in consequence, there came a day when Moipu made a feast, and a party from Haamau came under safe-conduct to eat of it. These passed early by Taahauku, and some of Moipu's young men were there to be a guard of honour. They were not long gone before there came down from Haamau, a man, his wife, and a girl of twelve, their daughter, bringing fungus. Several Atuona lads were hanging round the store; but the day being one of truce none apprehended danger. The fungus was weighed and paid for; the man of Haamau proposed he should have his axe ground in the bargain; and Mr. Stewart demurring at the trouble, some of the Atuona lads offered to grind it for him, and set it on the wheel. While the axe was grinding, a friendly native whispered Mr. Stewart to have a care of himself, for there was trouble in hand; and, all at once, the man of Haamau was seized, and his head and arm stricken from his body, the head at one sweep of his own newly sharpened axe. In the first alert, the girl escaped among the cotton; and Mr. Stewart, having thrust the wife into the house and locked her in from the outside, supposed the affair was over. But the business had not passed without noise, and it reached the ears of an older girl who had loitered by the way, and who now came hastily down the valley, crying as she came for her father. Her, too, they seized and beheaded; I know not what they had done with the axe, it was a blunt knife that served their butcherly turn upon the girl; and the blood spurted in fountains and painted them from head to foot. Thus horrible from crime, the party returned to Atuona, carrying the heads to Moipu. It may be fancied how the feast broke up; but it is notable that the guests were honourably suffered to retire. These passed back through Taahauku in extreme disorder; a little after the valley began to be overrun with shouting and triumphing braves; and a letter of warning coming at the same time to Mr. Stewart, he and his Chinamen took refuge with the Protestant missionary in Atuona. That night the store was gutted, and the bodies cast in a pit and covered with leaves. Three days later the schooner had come in; and things appearing quieter, Mr. Stewart and the captain landed in Taahauku to compute the damage and to view the grave, which was already indicated by the stench. While they were so employed, a party of Moipu's young men, decked with red flannel to indicate martial sentiments, came over the hills from Atuona, dug up the bodies, washed them in the river, and carried them away on sticks. That night the feast began.

Those who knew Mr. Stewart before this experience declare the man to be quite altered. He stuck, however, to his post; and somewhat later, when the plantation was already well established, and gave employment to sixty Chinamen and seventy natives, he found himself once more in dangerous times. The men of Haamau, it was reported, had sworn to plunder and erase the settlement; letters came continually from the Hawaiian missionary, who acted as intelligence department; and for six weeks Mr. Stewart and three other whites slept in the cotton-house at night in a rampart of bales, and (what was their best defence) ostentatiously practised rifle-shooting by day upon the beach. Natives were often there to watch them; the practice was excellent; and the assault was never delivered—if it ever was intended, which I doubt, for the natives are more famous for false rumours than for deeds of energy. I was told the late French war was a case in point; the tribes on the beach accusing those in the mountains of designs which they had never the hardihood to entertain. And the same testimony to their backwardness in open battle reached me from all sides. Captain Hart once landed after an engagement in a certain bay; one man had his hand hurt, an old woman and two children had been slain; and the captain improved the occasion by poulticing the hand, and taunting both sides upon so wretched an affair. It is true these wars were often merely formal—comparable with duels to the first blood. Captain Hart visited a bay where such a war was being carried on between two brothers, one of whom had been thought wanting in civility to the guests of the other. About one-half of the population served day about on alternate sides, so as to be well with each when the inevitable peace should follow. The forts of the belligerents were over against each other, and close by. Pigs were cooking. Well-oiled braves, with well-oiled muskets, strutted on the paepae or sat down to feast. No business, however needful, could be done, and all thoughts were supposed to be centred in this mockery of war. A few days later, by a regrettable accident, a man was killed; it was felt at once the thing had gone too far, and the quarrel was instantly patched up. But the more serious wars were prosecuted in a similar spirit; a gift of pigs and a feast made their inevitable end; the killing of a single man was a great victory, and the murder of defenceless solitaries counted a heroic deed.

The foot of the cliffs, about all these islands, is the place of fishing. Between Taahauku and Atuona we saw men, but chiefly women, some nearly naked, some in thin white or crimson dresses, perched in little surf-beat promontories—the brown precipice overhanging them, and the convolvulus overhanging that, as if to cut them off the more completely from assistance. There they would angle much of the morning; and as fast as they caught any fish, eat them, raw and living, where they stood. It was such helpless ones that the warriors from the opposite island of Tauata slew, and carried home and ate, and were thereupon accounted mighty men of valour. Of one such exploit I can give the account of an eye-witness. 'Portuguese Joe,' Mr. Keane's cook, was once pulling an oar in an Atuona boat, when they spied a stranger in a canoe with some fish and a piece of tapu. The Atuona men cried upon him to draw near and have a smoke. He complied, because, I suppose, he had no choice; but he knew, poor devil, what he was coming to, and (as Joe said) 'he didn't seem to care about the smoke.' A few questions followed, as to where he came from, and what was his business. These he must needs answer, as he must needs draw at the unwelcome pipe, his heart the while drying in his bosom. And then, of a sudden, a big fellow in Joe's boat leaned over, plucked the stranger from his canoe, struck him with a knife in the neck—inward and downward, as Joe showed in pantomime more expressive than his words—and held him under water, like a fowl, until his struggles ceased. Whereupon the long-pig was hauled on board, the boat's head turned about for Atuona, and these Marquesan braves pulled home rejoicing. Moipu was on the beach and rejoiced with them on their arrival. Poor Joe toiled at his oar that day with a white face, yet he had no fear for himself. 'They were very good to me—gave me plenty grub: never wished to eat white man,' said he.

If the most horrible experience was Mr. Stewart's, it was Captain Hart himself who ran the nearest danger. He had bought a piece of land from Timau, chief of a neighbouring bay, and put some Chinese there to work. Visiting the station with one of the Godeffroys, he found his Chinamen trooping to the beach in terror: Timau had driven them out, seized their effects, and was in war attire with his young men. A boat was despatched to Taahauku for reinforcement; as they awaited her return, they could see, from the deck of the schooner, Timau and his young men dancing the war-dance on the hill-top till past twelve at night; and so soon as the boat came (bringing three gendarmes, armed with chassepots, two white men from Taahauku station, and some native warriors) the party set out to seize the chief before he should awake. Day was not come, and it was a very bright moonlight morning, when they reached the hill-top where (in a house of palm-leaves) Timau was sleeping off his debauch. The assailants were fully exposed, the interior of the hut quite dark; the position far from sound. The gendarmes knelt with their pieces ready, and Captain Hart advanced alone. As he drew near the door he heard the snap of a gun cocking from within, and in sheer self-defence—there being no other escape—sprang into the house and grappled Timau. 'Timau, come with me!' he cried. But Timau—a great fellow, his eyes blood-red with the abuse of kava, six foot three in stature—cast him on one side; and the captain, instantly expecting to be either shot or brained, discharged his pistol in the dark. When they carried Timau out at the door into the moonlight, he was already dead, and, upon this unlooked-for termination of their sally, the whites appeared to have lost all conduct, and retreated to the boats, fired upon by the natives as they went. Captain Hart, who almost rivals Bishop Dordillon in popularity, shared with him the policy of extreme indulgence to the natives, regarding them as children, making light of their defects, and constantly in favour of mild measures. The death of Timau has thus somewhat weighed upon his mind; the more so, as the chieftain's musket was found in the house unloaded. To a less delicate conscience the matter will seem light. If a drunken savage elects to cock a fire-arm, a gentleman advancing towards him in the open cannot wait to make sure if it be charged.

I have touched on the captain's popularity. It is one of the things that most strikes a stranger in the Marquesas. He comes instantly on two names, both new to him, both locally famous, both mentioned by all with affection and respect—the bishop's and the captain's. It gave me a strong desire to meet with the survivor, which was subsequently gratified—to the enrichment of these pages. Long after that again, in the Place Dolorous—Molokai—I came once more on the traces of that affectionate popularity. There was a blind white leper there, an old sailor—'an old tough,' he called himself—who had long sailed among the eastern islands. Him I used to visit, and, being fresh from the scenes of his activity, gave him the news. This (in the true island style) was largely a chronicle of wrecks; and it chanced I mentioned the case of one not very successful captain, and how he had lost a vessel for Mr. Hart; thereupon the blind leper broke forth in lamentation. 'Did he lose a ship of John Hart's?' he cried; 'poor John Hart! Well, I'm sorry it was Hart's,' with needless force of epithet, which I neglect to reproduce.

Perhaps, if Captain Hart's affairs had continued to prosper, his popularity might have been different. Success wins glory, but it kills affection, which misfortune fosters. And the misfortune which overtook the captain's enterprise was truly singular. He was at the top of his career. Ile Masse belonged to him, given by the French as an indemnity for the robberies at Taahauku. But the Ile Masse was only suitable for cattle; and his two chief stations were Anaho, in Nuka-hiva, facing the north-east, and Taahauku in Hiva-oa, some hundred miles to the southward, and facing the south-west. Both these were on the same day swept by a tidal wave, which was not felt in any other bay or island of the group. The south coast of Hiva-oa was bestrewn with building timber and camphor-wood chests, containing goods; which, on the promise of a reasonable salvage, the natives very honestly brought back, the chests apparently not opened, and some of the wood after it had been built into their houses. But the recovery of such jetsam could not affect the result. It was impossible the captain should withstand this partiality of fortune; and with his fall the prosperity of the Marquesas ended. Anaho is truly extinct, Taahauku but a shadow of itself; nor has any new plantation arisen in their stead.

CHAPTER XIII—CHARACTERS

There was a certain traffic in our anchorage at Atuona; different indeed from the dead inertia and quiescence of the sister island, Nuka-hiva. Sails were seen steering from its mouth; now it would be a whale-boat manned with native rowdies, and heavy with copra for sale; now perhaps a single canoe come after commodities to buy. The anchorage was besides frequented by fishers; not only the lone females perched in niches of the cliff, but whole parties, who would sometimes camp and build a fire upon the beach, and sometimes lie in their canoes in the midst of the haven and jump by turns in the water; which they would cast eight or nine feet high, to drive, as we supposed, the fish into their nets. The goods the purchasers came to buy were sometimes quaint. I remarked one outrigger returning with a single ham swung from a pole in the stern. And one day there came into Mr. Keane's store a charming lad, excellently mannered, speaking French correctly though with a babyish accent; very handsome too, and much of a dandy, as was shown not only in his shining raiment, but by the nature of his purchases. These were five ship-biscuits, a bottle of scent, and two balls of washing blue. He was from Tauata, whither he returned the same night in an outrigger, daring the deep with these young-ladyish treasures. The gross of the native passengers were more ill-favoured: tall, powerful fellows, well tattooed, and with disquieting manners. Something coarse and jeering distinguished them, and I was often reminded of the slums of some great city. One night, as dusk was falling, a whale-boat put in on that part of the beach where I chanced to be alone. Six or seven ruffianly fellows scrambled out; all had enough English to give me 'good-bye,' which was the ordinary salutation; or 'good-morning,' which they seemed to regard as an intensitive; jests followed, they surrounded me with harsh laughter and rude looks, and I was glad to move away. I had not yet encountered Mr. Stewart, or I should have been reminded of his first landing at Atuona and the humorist who nibbled at the heel. But their neighbourhood depressed me; and I felt, if I had been there a castaway and out of reach of help, my heart would have been sick.

Nor was the traffic altogether native. While we lay in the anchorage there befell a strange coincidence. A schooner was observed at sea and aiming to enter. We knew all the schooners in the group, but this appeared larger than any; she was rigged, besides, after the English manner; and, coming to an anchor some way outside the Casco, showed at last the blue ensign. There were at that time, according to rumour, no fewer than four yachts in the Pacific; but it was strange that any two of them should thus lie side by side in that outlandish inlet: stranger still that in the owner of the Nyanza, Captain Dewar, I should find a man of the same country and the same county with myself, and one whom I had seen walking as a boy on the shores of the Alpes Maritimes.

We had besides a white visitor from shore, who came and departed in a crowded whale-boat manned by natives; having read of yachts in the Sunday papers, and being fired with the desire to see one. Captain Chase, they called him, an old whaler-man, thickset and white-bearded, with a strong Indiana drawl; years old in the country, a good backer in battle, and one of those dead shots whose practice at the target struck terror in the braves of Haamau. Captain Chase dwelt farther east in a bay called Hanamate, with a Mr. M'Callum; or rather they had dwelt together once, and were now amicably separated. The captain is to be found near one end of the bay, in a wreck of a house, and waited on by a Chinese. At the point of the opposing corner another habitation stands on a tall paepae. The surf runs there exceeding heavy, seas of seven and eight feet high bursting under the walls of the house, which is thus continually filled with their clamour, and rendered fit only for solitary, or at least for silent, inmates. Here it is that Mr. M'Callum, with a Shakespeare and a Burns, enjoys the society of the breakers. His name and his Burns testify to Scottish blood; but he is an American born, somewhere far east; followed the trade of a ship-carpenter; and was long employed, the captain of a hundred Indians, breaking up wrecks about Cape Flattery. Many of the whites who are to be found scattered in the South Seas represent the more artistic portion of their class; and not only enjoy the poetry of that new life, but came there on purpose to enjoy it. I have been shipmates with a man, no longer young, who sailed upon that voyage, his first time to sea, for the mere love of Samoa; and it was a few letters in a newspaper that sent him on that pilgrimage. Mr. M'Callum was another instance of the same. He had read of the South Seas; loved to read of them; and let their image fasten in his heart: till at length he could refrain no longer—must set forth, a new Rudel, for that unseen homeland—and has now dwelt for years in Hiva-oa, and will lay his bones there in the end with full content; having no desire to behold again the places of his boyhood, only, perhaps—once, before he dies—the rude and wintry landscape of Cape Flattery. Yet he is an active man, full of schemes; has bought land of the natives; has planted five thousand coco-palms; has a desert island in his eye, which he desires to lease, and a schooner in the stocks, which he has laid and built himself, and even hopes to finish. Mr. M'Callum and I did not meet, but, like gallant troubadours, corresponded in verse. I hope he will not consider it a breach of copyright if I give here a specimen of his muse. He and Bishop Dordillon are the two European bards of the Marquesas.

'Sail, ho! Ahoy! *Casco,*
  First among the pleasure fleet
  That came around to greet
These isles from San Francisco,

And first, too; only one

Among the literary men

That this way has ever been—

Welcome, then, to Stevenson.

Please not offended be

At this little notice

Of the *Casco,* Captain Otis,

With the novelist's family.

Avoir une voyage magnifical

Is our wish sincere,

That you'll have from here

Allant sur la Grande Pacifical.'

But our chief visitor was one Mapiao, a great Tahuku—which seems to mean priest, wizard, tattooer, practiser of any art, or, in a word, esoteric person—and a man famed for his eloquence on public occasions and witty talk in private. His first appearance was typical of the man. He came down clamorous to the eastern landing, where the surf was running very high; scorned all our signals to go round the bay; carried his point, was brought aboard at some hazard to our skiff, and set down in one corner of the cockpit to his appointed task. He had been hired, as one cunning in the art, to make my old men's beards into a wreath: what a wreath for Celia's arbour! His own beard (which he carried, for greater safety, in a sailor's knot) was not merely the adornment of his age, but a substantial piece of property. One hundred dollars was the estimated value; and as Brother Michel never knew a native to deposit a greater sum with Bishop Dordillon, our friend was a rich man in virtue of his chin. He had something of an East Indian cast, but taller and stronger: his nose hooked, his face narrow, his forehead very high, the whole elaborately tattooed. I may say I have never entertained a guest so trying. In the least particular he must be waited on; he would not go to the scuttle-butt for water; he would not even reach to get the glass, it must be given him in his hand; if aid were denied him, he would fold his arms, bow his head, and go without: only the work would suffer. Early the first forenoon he called aloud for biscuit and salmon; biscuit and ham were brought; he looked on them inscrutably, and signed they should be set aside. A number of considerations crowded on my mind; how the sort of work on which he was engaged was probably tapu in a high degree; should by rights, perhaps, be transacted on a tapu platform which no female might approach; and it was possible that fish might be the essential diet. Some salted fish I therefore brought him, and along with that a glass of rum: at sight of which Mapiao displayed extraordinary animation, pointed to the zenith, made a long speech in which I picked up umati—the word for the sun—and signed to me once more to place these dainties out of reach. At last I had understood, and every day the programme was the same. At an early period of the morning his dinner must be set forth on the roof of the house and at a proper distance, full in view but just out of reach; and not until the fit hour, which was the point of noon, would the artificer partake. This solemnity was the cause of an absurd misadventure. He was seated plaiting, as usual, at the beards, his dinner arrayed on the roof, and not far off a glass of water standing. It appears he desired to drink; was of course far too great a gentleman to rise and get the water for himself; and spying Mrs. Stevenson, imperiously signed to her to hand it. The signal was misunderstood; Mrs. Stevenson was, by this time, prepared for any eccentricity on the part of our guest; and instead of passing him the water, flung his dinner overboard. I must do Mapiao justice: all laughed, but his laughter rang the loudest.

These troubles of service were at worst occasional; the embarrassment of the man's talk incessant. He was plainly a practised conversationalist; the nicety of his inflections, the elegance of his gestures, and the fine play of his expression, told us that. We, meanwhile, sat like aliens in a playhouse; we could see the actors were upon some material business and performing well, but the plot of the drama remained undiscoverable. Names of places, the name of Captain Hart, occasional disconnected words, tantalised without enlightening us; and the less we understood, the more gallantly, the more copiously, and with still the more explanatory gestures, Mapiao returned to the assault. We could see his vanity was on the rack; being come to a place where that fine jewel of his conversational talent could earn him no respect; and he had times of despair when he desisted from the endeavour, and instants of irritation when he regarded us with unconcealed contempt. Yet for me, as the practitioner of some kindred mystery to his own, he manifested to the last a measure of respect. As we sat under the awning in opposite corners of the cockpit, he braiding hairs from dead men's chins, I forming runes upon a sheet of folio paper, he would nod across to me as one Tahuku to another, or, crossing the cockpit, study for a while my shapeless scrawl and encourage me with a heartfelt 'mitai!—good!' So might a deaf painter sympathise far off with a musician, as the slave and master of some uncomprehended and yet kindred art. A silly trade, he doubtless considered it; but a man must make allowance for barbarians—chaque pays a ses coutumes—and he felt the principle was there.

The time came at last when his labours, which resembled those rather of Penelope than Hercules, could be no more spun out, and nothing remained but to pay him and say farewell. After a long, learned argument in Marquesan, I gathered that his mind was set on fish-hooks; with three of which, and a brace of dollars, I thought he was not ill rewarded for passing his forenoons in our cockpit, eating, drinking, delivering his opinions, and pressing the ship's company into his menial service. For all that, he was a man of so high a bearing, and so like an uncle of my own who should have gone mad and got tattooed, that I applied to him, when we were both on shore, to know if he were satisfied. 'Mitai ehipe?' I asked. And he, with rich unction, offering at the same time his hand—'Mitai ehipe, mitai kaehae; kaoha nui!'—or, to translate freely: 'The ship is good, the victuals are up to the mark, and we part in friendship.' Which testimonial uttered, he set off along the beach with his head bowed and the air of one deeply injured.

I saw him go, on my side, with relief. It would be more interesting to learn how our relation seemed to Mapiao. His exigence, we may suppose, was merely loyal. He had been hired by the ignorant to do a piece of work; and he was bound that he would do it the right way. Countless obstacles, continual ignorant ridicule, availed not to dissuade him. He had his dinner laid out; watched it, as was fit, the while he worked; ate it at the fit hour; was in all things served and waited on; and could take his hire in the end with a clear conscience, telling himself the mystery was performed duly, the beards rightfully braided, and we (in spite of ourselves) correctly served. His view of our stupidity, even he, the mighty talker, must have lacked language to express. He never interfered with my Tahuku work; civilly praised it, idle as it seemed; civilly supposed that I was competent in my own mystery: such being the attitude of the intelligent and the polite. And we, on the other hand—who had yet the most to gain or lose, since the product was to be ours—who had professed our disability by the very act of hiring him to do it—were never weary of impeding his own more important labours, and sometimes lacked the sense and the civility to refrain from laughter.

CHAPTER XIV—IN A CANNIBAL VALLEY

The road from Taahauku to Atuona skirted the north-westerly side of the anchorage, somewhat high up, edged, and sometimes shaded, by the splendid flowers of the flamboyant—its English name I do not know. At the turn of the hand, Atuona came in view: a long beach, a heavy and loud breach of surf, a shore-side village scattered among trees, and the guttered mountains drawing near on both sides above a narrow and rich ravine. Its infamous repute perhaps affected me; but I thought it the loveliest, and by far the most ominous and gloomy, spot on earth. Beautiful it surely was; and even more salubrious. The healthfulness of the whole group is amazing; that of Atuona almost in the nature of a miracle. In Atuona, a village planted in a shore-side marsh, the houses standing everywhere intermingled with the pools of a taro-garden, we find every condition of tropical danger and discomfort; and yet there are not even mosquitoes—not even the hateful day-fly of Nuka-hiva—and fever, and its concomitant, the island fe'efe'e, [122] are unknown.

This is the chief station of the French on the man-eating isle of Hiva-oa. The sergeant of gendarmerie enjoys the style of the vice-resident, and hoists the French colours over a quite extensive compound. A Chinaman, a waif from the plantation, keeps a restaurant in the rear quarters of the village; and the mission is well represented by the sister's school and Brother Michel's church. Father Orens, a wonderful octogenarian, his frame scarce bowed, the fire of his eye undimmed, has lived, and trembled, and suffered in this place since 1843. Again and again, when Moipu had made coco-brandy, he has been driven from his house into the woods. 'A mouse that dwelt in a cat's ear' had a more easy resting-place; and yet I have never seen a man that bore less mark of years. He must show us the church, still decorated with the bishop's artless ornaments of paper—the last work of industrious old hands, and the last earthly amusement of a man that was much of a hero. In the sacristy we must see his sacred vessels, and, in particular, a vestment which was a 'vraie curiosité,' because it had been given by a gendarme. To the Protestant there is always something embarrassing in the eagerness with which grown and holy men regard these trifles; but it was touching and pretty to see Orens, his aged eyes shining in his head, display his sacred treasures.

August 26.—The vale behind the village, narrowing swiftly to a mere ravine, was choked with profitable trees. A river gushed in the midst. Overhead, the tall coco-palms made a primary covering; above that, from one wall of the mountain to another, the ravine was roofed with cloud; so that we moved below, amid teeming vegetation, in a covered house of heat. On either hand, at every hundred yards, instead of the houseless, disembowelling paepaes of Nuka-hiva, populous houses turned out their inhabitants to cry 'Kaoha!' to the passers-by. The road, too, was busy: strings of girls, fair and foul, as in less favoured countries; men bearing breadfruit; the sisters, with a little guard of pupils; a fellow bestriding a horse—passed and greeted us continually; and now it was a Chinaman who came to the gate of his flower-yard, and gave us 'Good-day' in excellent English; and a little farther on it would be some natives who set us down by the wayside, made us a feast of mummy-apple, and entertained us as we ate with drumming on a tin case. With all this fine plenty of men and fruit, death is at work here also. The population, according to the highest estimate, does not exceed six hundred in the whole vale of Atuona; and yet, when I once chanced to put the question, Brother Michel counted up ten whom he knew to be sick beyond recovery. It was here, too, that I could at last gratify my curiosity with the sight of a native house in the very article of dissolution. It had fallen flat along the paepae, its poles sprawling ungainly; the rains and the mites contended against it; what remained seemed sound enough, but much was gone already; and it was easy to see how the insects consumed the walls as if they had been bread, and the air and the rain ate into them like vitriol.

A little ahead of us, a young gentleman, very well tattooed, and dressed in a pair of white trousers and a flannel shirt, had been marching unconcernedly. Of a sudden, without apparent cause, he turned back, took us in possession, and led us undissuadably along a by-path to the river's edge. There, in a nook of the most attractive amenity, he bade us to sit down: the stream splashing at our elbow, a shock of nondescript greenery enshrining us from above; and thither, after a brief absence, he brought us a cocoa-nut, a lump of sandal-wood, and a stick he had begun to carve: the nut for present refreshment, the sandal-wood for a precious gift, and the stick—in the simplicity of his vanity—to harvest premature praise. Only one section was yet carved, although the whole was pencil-marked in lengths; and when I proposed to buy it, Poni (for that was the artist's name) recoiled in horror. But I was not to be moved, and simply refused restitution, for I had long wondered why a people who displayed, in their tattooing, so great a gift of arabesque invention, should display it nowhere else. Here, at last, I had found something of the same talent in another medium; and I held the incompleteness, in these days of world-wide brummagem, for a happy mark of authenticity. Neither my reasons nor my purpose had I the means of making clear to Poni; I could only hold on to the stick, and bid the artist follow me to the gendarmerie, where I should find interpreters and money; but we gave him, in the meanwhile, a boat-call in return for his sandal-wood. As he came behind us down the vale he sounded upon this continually. And continually, from the wayside houses, there poured forth little groups of girls in crimson, or of men in white. And to these must Poni pass the news of who the strangers were, of what they had been doing, of why it was that Poni had a boat-whistle; and of why he was now being haled to the vice-residency, uncertain whether to be punished or rewarded, uncertain whether he had lost a stick or made a bargain, but hopeful on the whole, and in the meanwhile highly consoled by the boat-whistle. Whereupon he would tear himself away from this particular group of inquirers, and once more we would hear the shrill call in our wake.

August 27.—I made a more extended circuit in the vale with Brother

Michel. We were mounted on a pair of sober nags, suitable to these rude paths; the weather was exquisite, and the company in which I found myself no less agreeable than the scenes through which I passed. We mounted at first by a steep grade along the summit of one of those twisted spurs that, from a distance, mark out provinces of sun and shade upon the mountain-side. The ground fell away on either hand with an extreme declivity. From either hand, out of profound ravines, mounted the song of falling water and the smoke of household fires. Here and there the hills of foliage would divide, and our eye would plunge down upon one of these deep-nested habitations. And still, high in front, arose the precipitous barrier of the mountain, greened over where it seemed that scarce a harebell could find root, barred with the zigzags of a human road where it seemed that not a goat could scramble. And in truth, for all the labour that it cost, the road is regarded even by the Marquesans as impassable; they will not risk a horse on that ascent; and those who lie to the westward come and go in their canoes. I never knew a hill to lose so little on a near approach: a consequence, I must suppose, of its surprising steepness. When we turned about, I was amazed to behold so deep a view behind, and so high a shoulder of blue sea, crowned by the whale-like island of Motane. And yet the wall of mountain had not visibly dwindled, and I could even have fancied, as I raised my eyes to measure it, that it loomed higher than before.

We struck now into covert paths, crossed and heard more near at hand the bickering of the streams, and tasted the coolness of those recesses where the houses stood. The birds sang about us as we descended. All along our path my guide was being hailed by voices: 'Mikaël—Kaoha, Mikaël!' From the doorstep, from the cotton-patch, or out of the deep grove of island-chestnuts, these friendly cries arose, and were cheerily answered as we passed. In a sharp angle of a glen, on a rushing brook and under fathoms of cool foliage, we struck a house upon a well-built paepae, the fire brightly burning under the popoi-shed against the evening meal; and here the cries became a chorus, and the house folk, running out, obliged us to dismount and breathe. It seemed a numerous family: we saw eight at least; and one of these honoured me with a particular attention. This was the mother, a woman naked to the waist, of an aged countenance, but with hair still copious and black, and breasts still erect and youthful. On our arrival I could see she remarked me, but instead of offering any greeting, disappeared at once into the bush. Thence she returned with two crimson flowers. 'Good-bye!' was her salutation, uttered not without coquetry; and as she said it she pressed the flowers into my hand—'Good-bye! I speak Inglis.' It was from a whaler-man, who (she informed me) was 'a plenty good chap,' that she had learned my language; and I could not but think how handsome she must have been in these times of her youth, and could not but guess that some memories of the dandy whaler-man prompted her attentions to myself. Nor could I refrain from wondering what had befallen her lover; in the rain and mire of what sea-ports he had tramped since then; in what close and garish drinking-dens had found his pleasure; and in the ward of what infirmary dreamed his last of the Marquesas. But she, the more fortunate, lived on in her green island. The talk, in this lost house upon the mountains, ran chiefly upon Mapiao and his visits to the Casco: the news of which had probably gone abroad by then to all the island, so that there was no paepae in Hiva-oa where they did not make the subject of excited comment.

Not much beyond we came upon a high place in the foot of the ravine. Two roads divided it, and met in the midst. Save for this intersection the amphitheatre was strangely perfect, and had a certain ruder air of things Roman. Depths of foliage and the bulk of the mountain kept it in a grateful shadow. On the benches several young folk sat clustered or apart. One of these, a girl perhaps fourteen years of age, buxom and comely, caught the eye of Brother Michel. Why was she not at school?—she was done with school now. What was she doing here?—she lived here now. Why so?—no answer but a deepening blush. There was no severity in Brother Michel's manner; the girl's own confusion told her story. 'Elle a honte,' was the missionary's comment, as we rode away. Near by in the stream, a grown girl was bathing naked in a goyle between two stepping-stones; and it amused me to see with what alacrity and real alarm she bounded on her many-coloured under-clothes. Even in these daughters of cannibals shame was eloquent.

It is in Hiva-oa, owing to the inveterate cannibalism of the natives, that local beliefs have been most rudely trodden underfoot. It was here that three religious chiefs were set under a bridge, and the women of the valley made to defile over their heads upon the road-way: the poor, dishonoured fellows sitting there (all observers agree) with streaming tears. Not only was one road driven across the high place, but two roads intersected in its midst. There is no reason to suppose that the last was done of purpose, and perhaps it was impossible entirely to avoid the numerous sacred places of the islands. But these things are not done without result. I have spoken already of the regard of Marquesans for the dead, making (as it does) so strange a contrast with their unconcern for death. Early on this day's ride, for instance, we encountered a petty chief, who inquired (of course) where we were going, and suggested by way of amendment. 'Why do you not rather show him the cemetery?' I saw it; it was but newly opened, the third within eight years. They are great builders here in Hiva-oa; I saw in my ride paepaes that no European dry-stone mason could have equalled, the black volcanic stones were laid so justly, the corners were so precise, the levels so true; but the retaining-wall of the new graveyard stood apart, and seemed to be a work of love. The sentiment of honour for the dead is therefore not extinct. And yet observe the consequence of violently countering men's opinions. Of the four prisoners in Atuona gaol, three were of course thieves; the fourth was there for sacrilege. He had levelled up a piece of the graveyard—to give a feast upon, as he informed the court—and declared he had no thought of doing wrong. Why should he? He had been forced at the point of the bayonet to destroy the sacred places of his own piety; when he had recoiled from the task, he had been jeered at for a superstitious fool. And now it is supposed he will respect our European superstitions as by second nature.

CHAPTER XV—THE TWO CHIEFS OF ATUONA

It had chanced (as the Casco beat through the Bordelais Straits for Taahauku) she approached on one board very near the land in the opposite isle of Tauata, where houses were to be seen in a grove of tall coco-palms. Brother Michel pointed out the spot. 'I am at home now,' said he. 'I believe I have a large share in these cocoa-nuts; and in that house madame my mother lives with her two husbands!' 'With two husbands?' somebody inquired. 'C'est ma honte,' replied the brother drily.

A word in passing on the two husbands. I conceive the brother to have expressed himself loosely. It seems common enough to find a native lady with two consorts; but these are not two husbands. The first is still the husband; the wife continues to be referred to by his name; and the position of the coadjutor, or pikio, although quite regular, appears undoubtedly subordinate. We had opportunities to observe one household of the sort. The pikio was recognised; appeared openly along with the husband when the lady was thought to be insulted, and the pair made common cause like brothers. At home the inequality was more apparent. The husband sat to receive and entertain visitors; the pikio was running the while to fetch cocoa-nuts like a hired servant, and I remarked he was sent on these errands in preference even to the son. Plainly we have here no second husband; plainly we have the tolerated lover. Only, in the Marquesas, instead of carrying his lady's fan and mantle, he must turn his hand to do the husband's housework.

The sight of Brother Michel's family estate led the conversation for some while upon the method and consequence of artificial kinship. Our curiosity became extremely whetted; the brother offered to have the whole of us adopted, and some two days later we became accordingly the children of Paaaeua, appointed chief of Atuona. I was unable to be present at the ceremony, which was primitively simple. The two Mrs. Stevensons and Mr. Osbourne, along with Paaaeua, his wife, and an adopted child of theirs, son of a shipwrecked Austrian, sat down to an excellent island meal, of which the principal and the only necessary dish was pig. A concourse watched them through the apertures of the house; but none, not even Brother Michel, might partake; for the meal was sacramental, and either creative or declaratory of the new relationship. In Tahiti things are not so strictly ordered; when Ori and I 'made brothers,' both our families sat with us at table, yet only he and I, who had eaten with intention were supposed to be affected by the ceremony. For the adoption of an infant I believe no formality to be required; the child is handed over by the natural parents, and grows up to inherit the estates of the adoptive. Presents are doubtless exchanged, as at all junctures of island life, social or international; but I never heard of any banquet—the child's presence at the daily board perhaps sufficing. We may find the rationale in the ancient Arabian idea that a common diet makes a common blood, with its derivative axiom that 'he is the father who gives the child its morning draught.' In the

Marquesan practice, the sense would thus be evanescent; from the Tahitian, a mere survival, it will have entirely fled. An interesting parallel will probably occur to many of my readers.

What is the nature of the obligation assumed at such a festival? It will vary with the characters of those engaged, and with the circumstances of the case. Thus it would be absurd to take too seriously our adoption at Atuona. On the part of Paaaeua it was an affair of social ambition; when he agreed to receive us in his family the man had not so much as seen us, and knew only that we were inestimably rich and travelled in a floating palace. We, upon our side, ate of his baked meats with no true animus affiliandi, but moved by the single sentiment of curiosity. The affair was formal, and a matter of parade, as when in Europe sovereigns call each other cousin. Yet, had we stayed at Atuona, Paaaeua would have held himself bound to establish us upon his land, and to set apart young men for our service, and trees for our support. I have mentioned the Austrian. He sailed in one of two sister ships, which left the Clyde in coal; both rounded the Horn, and both, at several hundred miles of distance, though close on the same point of time, took fire at sea on the Pacific. One was destroyed; the derelict iron frame of the second, after long, aimless cruising, was at length recovered, refitted, and hails to-day from San Francisco. A boat's crew from one of these disasters reached, after great hardships, the isle of Hiva-oa. Some of these men vowed they would never again confront the chances of the sea; but alone of them all the Austrian has been exactly true to his engagement, remains where he landed, and designs to die where he has lived. Now, with such a man, falling and taking root among islanders, the processes described may be compared to a gardener's graft. He passes bodily into the native stock; ceases wholly to be alien; has entered the commune of the blood, shares the prosperity and consideration of his new family, and is expected to impart with the same generosity the fruits of his European skill and knowledge. It is this implied engagement that so frequently offends the ingrafted white. To snatch an immediate advantage—to get (let us say) a station for his store—he will play upon the native custom and become a son or a brother for the day, promising himself to cast down the ladder by which he shall have ascended, and repudiate the kinship so soon as it shall grow burdensome. And he finds there are two parties to the bargain.

Perhaps his Polynesian relative is simple, and conceived the blood-bond literally; perhaps he is shrewd, and himself entered the covenant with a view to gain. And either way the store is ravaged, the house littered with lazy natives; and the richer the man grows, the more numerous, the more idle, and the more affectionate he finds his native relatives. Most men thus circumstanced contrive to buy or brutally manage to enforce their independence; but many vegetate without hope, strangled by parasites.

We had no cause to blush with Brother Michel. Our new parents were kind, gentle, well-mannered, and generous in gifts; the wife was a most motherly woman, the husband a man who stood justly high with his employers. Enough has been said to show why Moipu should be deposed; and in Paaaeua the French had found a reputable substitute. He went always scrupulously dressed, and looked the picture of propriety, like a dark, handsome, stupid, and probably religious young man hot from a European funeral. In character he seemed the ideal of what is known as the good citizen. He wore gravity like an ornament. None could more nicely represent the desired character as an appointed chief, the outpost of civilisation and reform. And yet, were the French to go and native manners to revive, fancy beholds him crowned with old men's beards and crowding with the first to a man-eating festival. But I must not seem to be unjust to Paaaeua. His respectability went deeper than the skin; his sense of the becoming sometimes nerved him for unexpected rigours.

One evening Captain Otis and Mr. Osbourne were on shore in the village. All was agog; dancing had begun; it was plain it was to be a night of festival, and our adventurers were overjoyed at their good fortune. A strong fall of rain drove them for shelter to the house of Paaaeua, where they were made welcome, wiled into a chamber, and shut in. Presently the rain took off, the fun was to begin in earnest, and the young bloods of Atuona came round the house and called to my fellow-travellers through the interstices of the wall. Late into the night the calls were continued and resumed, and sometimes mingled with taunts; late into the night the prisoners, tantalised by the noises of the festival, renewed their efforts to escape. But all was vain; right across the door lay that god-fearing householder, Paaaeua, feigning sleep;

and my friends had to forego their junketing. In this incident, so delightfully European, we thought we could detect three strands of sentiment. In the first place, Paaaeua had a charge of souls: these were young men, and he judged it right to withhold them from the primrose path. Secondly, he was a public character, and it was not fitting that his guests should countenance a festival of which he disapproved. So might some strict clergyman at home address a worldly visitor: 'Go to the theatre if you like, but, by your leave, not from my house!' Thirdly, Paaaeua was a man jealous, and with some cause (as shall be shown) for jealousy; and the feasters were the satellites of his immediate rival, Moipu.

For the adoption had caused much excitement in the village; it made the strangers popular. Paaaeua, in his difficult posture of appointed chief, drew strength and dignity from their alliance, and only Moipu and his followers were malcontent. For some reason nobody (except myself) appears to dislike Moipu. Captain Hart, who has been robbed and threatened by him; Father Orens, whom he has fired at, and repeatedly driven to the woods; my own family, and even the French officials—all seemed smitten with an irrepressible affection for the man. His fall had been made soft; his son, upon his death, was to succeed Paaaeua in the chieftaincy; and he lived, at the time of our visit, in the shoreward part of the village in a good house, and with a strong following of young men, his late braves and pot-hunters. In this society, the coming of the Casco, the adoption, the return feast on board, and the presents exchanged between the whites and their new parents, were doubtless eagerly and bitterly canvassed. It was felt that a few years ago the honours would have gone elsewhere. In this unwonted business, in this reception of some hitherto undreamed-of and outlandish potentate—some Prester John or old Assaracus—a few years back it would have been the part of Moipu to play the hero and the host, and his young men would have accompanied and adorned the various celebrations as the acknowledged leaders of society. And now, by a malign vicissitude of fortune, Moipu must sit in his house quite unobserved; and his young men could but look in at the door while their rivals feasted. Perhaps M. Grévy felt a touch of bitterness towards his successor when he beheld him figure on the broad stage of the centenary of eighty-nine; the visit of the Casco which Moipu had missed by so few years was a more unusual occasion in Atuona than a centenary in France; and the dethroned chief determined to reassert himself in the public eye.

Mr. Osbourne had gone into Atuona photographing; the population of the village had gathered together for the occasion on the place before the church, and Paaaeua, highly delighted with this new appearance of his family, played the master of ceremonies. The church had been taken, with its jolly architect before the door; the nuns with their pupils; sundry damsels in the ancient and singularly unbecoming robes of tapa; and Father Orens in the midst of a group of his parishioners. I know not what else was in hand, when the photographer became aware of a sensation in the crowd, and, looking around, beheld a very noble figure of a man appear upon the margin of a thicket and stroll nonchalantly near. The nonchalance was visibly affected; it was plain he came there to arouse attention, and his success was instant. He was introduced; he was civil, he was obliging, he was always ineffably superior and certain of himself; a well-graced actor. It was presently suggested that he should appear in his war costume; he gracefully consented; and returned in that strange, inappropriate and ill-omened array (which very well became his handsome person) to strut in a circle of admirers, and be thenceforth the centre of photography. Thus had Moipu effected his introduction, as by accident, to the white strangers, made it a favour to display his finery, and reduced his rival to a secondary rôle on the theatre of the disputed village. Paaaeua felt the blow; and, with a spirit which we never dreamed he could possess, asserted his priority. It was found impossible that day to get a photograph of Moipu alone; for whenever he stood up before the camera his successor placed himself unbidden by his side, and gently but firmly held to his position. The portraits of the pair, Jacob and Esau, standing shoulder to shoulder, one in his careful European dress, one in his barbaric trappings, figure the past and present of their island. A graveyard with its humble crosses would be the aptest symbol of the future.

We are all impressed with the belief that Moipu had planned his campaign from the beginning to the end. It is certain that he lost no time in pushing his advantage. Mr. Osbourne was inveigled to his house; various gifts were fished out of an old sea-chest; Father Orens was called into service as interpreter, and Moipu formally proposed to 'make brothers' with Mata-Galahi—Glass-Eyes,—the not very euphonious name under which Mr. Osbourne passed in the Marquesas. The feast of brotherhood took place on board the Casco. Paaaeua had arrived with his family, like a plain man; and his presents, which had been numerous, had followed one another, at intervals through several days. Moipu, as if to mark at every point the opposition, came with a certain feudal pomp, attended by retainers bearing gifts of all descriptions, from plumes of old men's beard to little, pious, Catholic engravings.

I had met the man before this in the village, and detested him on sight; there was something indescribably raffish in his looks and ways that raised my gorge; and when man-eating was referred to, and he laughed a low, cruel laugh, part boastful, part bashful, like one reminded of some dashing peccadillo, my repugnance was mingled with nausea. This is no very human attitude, nor one at all becoming in a traveller. And, seen more privately, the man improved. Something negroid in character and face was still displeasing; but his ugly mouth became attractive when he smiled, his figure and bearing were certainly noble, and his eyes superb. In his appreciation of jams and pickles, in is delight in the reverberating mirrors of the dining cabin, and consequent endless repetition of Moipus and Mata-Galahis, he showed himself engagingly a child. And yet I am not sure; and what seemed childishness may have been rather courtly art. His manners struck me as beyond the mark; they were refined and caressing to the point of grossness, and when I think of the serene absent-mindedness with which he first strolled in upon our party, and then recall him running on hands and knees along the cabin sofas, pawing the velvet, dipping into the beds, and bleating commendatory 'mitais' with exaggerated emphasis, like some enormous over-mannered ape, I feel the more sure that both must have been calculated. And I sometimes wonder next, if Moipu were quite alone in this polite duplicity, and ask myself whether the Casco were quite so much admired in the Marquesas as our visitors desired us to suppose.

I will complete this sketch of an incurable cannibal grandee with two incongruous traits. His favourite morsel was the human hand, of which he speaks to-day with an ill-favoured lustfulness. And when he said good-bye to

Mrs. Stevenson, holding her hand, viewing her with tearful eyes, and chanting his farewell improvisation in the falsetto of Marquesan high society, he wrote upon her mind a sentimental impression which I try in vain to share.\

PART II: THE PAUMOTUS

CHAPTER I—THE DANGEROUS ARCHIPELAGO—ATOLLS AT A DISTANCE

In the early morning of 4th September a whale-boat manned by natives dragged us down the green lane of the anchorage and round the spouting promontory. On the shore level it was a hot, breathless, and yet crystal morning; but high overhead the hills of Atuona were all cowled in cloud, and the ocean-river of the trades streamed without pause. As we crawled from under the immediate shelter of the land, we reached at last the limit of their influence. The wind fell upon our sails in puffs, which strengthened and grew more continuous; presently the Casco heeled down to her day's work; the whale-boat, quite outstripped, clung for a noisy moment to her quarter; the stipulated bread, rum, and tobacco were passed in; a moment more and the boat was in our wake, and our late pilots were cheering our departure.

This was the more inspiriting as we were bound for scenes so different, and though on a brief voyage, yet for a new province of creation. That wide field of ocean, called loosely the South Seas, extends from tropic to tropic, and from perhaps 123 degrees W. to 150 degrees E., a parallelogram of one hundred degrees by forty-seven, where degrees are the most spacious. Much of it lies vacant, much is closely sown with isles, and the isles are of two sorts. No distinction is so continually dwelt upon in South Sea talk as that between the 'low' and the 'high' island, and there is none more broadly marked in nature. The Himalayas are not more different from the Sahara. On the one hand, and chiefly in groups of from eight to a dozen, volcanic islands rise above the sea; few reach an altitude of less than 4000 feet; one exceeds 13,000; their tops are often obscured in cloud, they are all clothed with various forests, all abound in food, and are all remarkable for picturesque and solemn scenery. On the other hand, we have the atoll; a thing of problematic origin and history, the reputed creature of an insect apparently unidentified; rudely annular in shape; enclosing a lagoon; rarely extending beyond a quarter of a mile at its chief width; often rising at its highest point to less than the stature of a man—man himself, the rat and the land crab, its chief inhabitants; not more variously supplied with plants; and offering to the eye, even when perfect, only a ring of glittering beach and verdant foliage, enclosing and enclosed by the blue sea.

In no quarter are the atolls so thickly congregated, in none are they so varied in size from the greatest to the least, and in none is navigation so beset with perils, as in that archipelago that we were now to thread. The huge system of the trades is, for some reason, quite confounded by this multiplicity of reefs, the wind intermits, squalls are frequent from the west and south-west, hurricanes are known. The currents are, besides, inextricably intermixed; dead reckoning becomes a farce; the charts are not to be trusted; and such is the number and similarity of these islands that, even when you have picked one up, you may be none the wiser. The reputation of the place is consequently infamous; insurance offices exclude it from their field, and it was not without misgiving that my captain risked the Casco in such waters. I believe, indeed, it is almost understood that yachts are to avoid this baffling archipelago; and it required all my instances—and all Mr. Otis's private taste for adventure—to deflect our course across its midst.

For a few days we sailed with a steady trade, and a steady westerly current setting us to leeward; and toward sundown of the seventh it was supposed we should have sighted Takaroa, one of Cook's so-called King George Islands. The sun set; yet a while longer the old moon—semi-brilliant herself, and with a silver belly, which was her successor—sailed among gathering clouds; she, too, deserted us; stars of every degree of sheen, and clouds of every variety of form disputed the sub-lustrous night; and still we gazed in vain for Takaroa. The mate stood on the bowsprit, his tall grey figure slashing up and down against the stars, and still

'nihil astra praeter

Vidit et undas.

The rest of us were grouped at the port anchor davit, staring with no less assiduity, but with far less hope on the obscure horizon. Islands we beheld in plenty, but they were of 'such stuff as dreams are made on,' and vanished at a wink, only to appear in other places; and by and by not only islands, but refulgent and revolving lights began to stud the darkness; lighthouses of the mind or of the wearied optic nerve, solemnly shining and winking as we passed. At length the mate himself despaired, scrambled on board again from his unrestful perch, and announced that we had missed our destination. He was the only man of practice in these waters, our sole pilot, shipped for that end at Tai-o-hae. If he declared we had missed Takaroa, it was not for us to quarrel with the fact, but, if we could, to explain it. We had certainly run down our southing. Our canted wake upon the sea and our somewhat drunken-looking course upon the chart both testified with no less certainty to an impetuous westward current. We had no choice but to conclude we were again set down to leeward; and the best we could do was to bring the Casco to the wind, keep a good watch, and expect morning.

I slept that night, as was then my somewhat dangerous practice, on deck upon the cockpit bench. A stir at last awoke me, to see all the eastern heaven dyed with faint orange, the binnacle lamp already dulled against the brightness of the day, and the steersman leaning eagerly across the wheel. 'There it is, sir!' he cried, and pointed in the very eyeball of the dawn. For awhile I could see nothing but the bluish ruins of the morning bank, which lay far along the horizon, like melting icebergs. Then the sun rose, pierced a gap in these débris of vapours, and displayed an inconsiderable islet, flat as a plate upon the sea, and spiked with palms of disproportioned altitude.

So far, so good. Here was certainly an atoll; and we were certainly got among the archipelago. But which? And where? The isle was too small for either Takaroa: in all our neighbourhood, indeed, there was none so inconsiderable, save only Tikei; and Tikei, one of Roggewein's so-called Pernicious Islands, seemed beside the question. At that rate, instead of drifting to the west, we must have fetched up thirty miles to windward. And how about the current? It had been setting us down, by observation, all these days: by the deflection of our wake, it should be setting us down that moment. When had it stopped? When had it begun again? and what kind of torrent was that which had swept us eastward in the interval? To these questions, so typical of navigation in that range of isles, I have no answer. Such were at least the facts; Tikei our island turned out to be; and it was our first experience of the dangerous archipelago, to make our landfall thirty miles out.

The sight of Tikei, thrown direct against the splendour of the morning, robbed of all its colour, and deformed with disproportioned trees like bristles on a broom, had scarce prepared us to be much in love with atolls. Later the same day we saw under more fit conditions the island of Taiaro. Lost in the Sea is possibly the meaning of the name. And it was so we saw it; lost in blue sea and sky: a ring of white beach, green underwood, and tossing palms, gem-like in colour; of a fairy, of a heavenly prettiness. The surf ran all around it, white as snow, and broke at one point, far to seaward, on what seems an uncharted reef. There was no smoke, no sign of man; indeed, the isle is not inhabited, only visited at intervals. And yet a trader (Mr. Narii Salmon) was watching from the shore and wondering at the unexpected ship. I have spent since then long months upon low islands; I know the tedium of their undistinguished days; I know the burden of their diet. With whatever envy we may have looked from the deck on these green coverts, it was with a tenfold greater that Mr. Salmon and his comrades saw us steer, in our trim ship, to seaward.

The night fell lovely in the extreme. After the moon went down, the heaven was a thing to wonder at for stars. And as I lay in the cockpit and looked upon the steersman I was haunted by Emerson's verses:

'And the lone seaman all the night

Sails astonished among stars.'

By this glittering and imperfect brightness, about four bells in the first watch we made our third atoll, Raraka. The low line of the isle lay straight along the sky; so that I was at first reminded of a towpath, and we seemed to be mounting some engineered and navigable stream. Presently a red star appeared, about the height and brightness of a danger signal, and with that my simile was changed; we seemed rather to skirt the embankment of a railway, and the eye began to look instinctively for the telegraph-posts, and the ear to expect the coming of a train. Here and there, but rarely, faint tree-tops broke the level. And the sound of the surf accompanied us, now in a drowsy monotone, now with a menacing swing.

The isle lay nearly east and west, barring our advance on Fakarava. We must, therefore, hug the coast until we gained the western end, where, through a passage eight miles wide, we might sail southward between Raraka and the next isle, Kauehi. We had the wind free, a lightish air; but clouds of an inky blackness were beginning to arise, and at times it lightened—without thunder. Something, I know not what, continually set us up upon the island. We lay more and more to the nor'ard; and you would have thought the shore copied our manœuvre and outsailed us. Once and twice Raraka headed us again—again, in the sea fashion, the quite innocent steersman was abused—and again the Casco kept away. Had I been called on, with no more light than that of our experience, to draw the configuration of that island, I should have shown a series of bow-window promontories, each overlapping the other to the nor'ard, and the trend of the land from the south-east to the north-west, and behold, on the chart it lay near east and west in a straight line.

We had but just repeated our manœuvre and kept away—for not more than five minutes the railway embankment had been lost to view and the surf to hearing—when I was aware of land again, not only on the weather bow, but dead ahead. I played the part of the judicious landsman, holding my peace till the last moment; and presently my mariners perceived it for themselves.

'Land ahead!' said the steersman.

'By God, it's Kauehi!' cried the mate.

And so it was. And with that I began to be sorry for cartographers. We were scarce doing three and a half; and they asked me to believe that (in five minutes) we had dropped an island, passed eight miles of open water, and run almost high and dry upon the next. But my captain was more sorry for himself to be afloat in such a labyrinth; laid the Casco to, with the log line up and down, and sat on the stern rail and watched it till the morning. He had enough of night in the Paumotus.

By daylight on the 9th we began to skirt Kauehi, and had now an opportunity to see near at hand the geography of atolls. Here and there, where it was high, the farther side loomed up; here and there the near side dipped entirely and showed a broad path of water into the lagoon; here and there both sides were equally abased, and we could look right through the discontinuous ring to the sea horizon on the south. Conceive, on a vast scale, the submerged hoop of the duck-hunter, trimmed with green rushes to conceal his head—water within, water without—you have the image of the perfect atoll. Conceive one that has been partly plucked of its rush fringe; you have the atoll of Kauehi. And for either shore of it at closer quarters, conceive the line of some old Roman highway traversing a wet morass, and here sunk out of view and there re-arising, crowned with a green tuft of thicket; only instead of the stagnant waters of a marsh, the live ocean now boiled against, now buried the frail barrier. Last night's impression in the dark was thus confirmed by day, and not corrected. We sailed indeed by a mere causeway in the sea, of nature's handiwork, yet of no greater magnitude than many of the works of man.

The isle was uninhabited; it was all green brush and white sand, set in transcendently blue water; even the coco-palms were rare, though some of these completed the bright harmony of colour by hanging out a fan of golden yellow. For long there was no sign of life beyond the vegetable, and no sound but the continuous grumble of the surf. In silence and desertion these fair shores slipped past, and were submerged and rose again with clumps of thicket from the sea. And then a bird or two appeared, hovering and crying; swiftly these became more numerous, and presently, looking ahead, we were aware of a vast effervescence of winged life. In this place the annular isle was mostly under water, carrying here and there on its submerged line a wooded islet. Over one of these the birds hung and flew with an incredible density like that of gnats or hiving bees; the mass flashed white and black, and heaved and quivered, and the screaming of the creatures rose over the voice of the surf in a shrill clattering whirr. As you descend some inland valley a not dissimilar sound announces the nearness of a mill and pouring river. Some stragglers, as I said, came to meet our approach; a few still hung about the ship as we departed. The crying died away, the last pair of wings was left behind, and once more the low shores of Kauehi streamed past our eyes in silence like a picture. I supposed at the time that the birds lived, like ants or citizens, concentred where we saw them. I have been told since (I know not if correctly) that the whole isle, or much of it, is similarly peopled; and that the effervescence at a single spot would be the mark of a boat's crew of egg-hunters from one of the neighbouring inhabited atolls. So that here at Kauehi, as the day before at Taiaro, the Casco sailed by under the fire of unsuspected eyes. And one thing is surely true, that even on these ribbons of land an army might lie hid and no passing mariner divine its presence.

CHAPTER II—FAKARAVA: AN ATOLL AT HAND

By a little before noon we were running down the coast of our destination, Fakarava: the air very light, the sea near smooth; though still we were accompanied by a continuous murmur from the beach, like the sound of a distant train. The isle is of a huge longitude, the enclosed lagoon thirty miles by ten or twelve, and the coral tow-path, which they call the land, some eighty or ninety miles by (possibly) one furlong. That part by which we sailed was all raised; the underwood excellently green, the topping wood of coco-palms continuous—a mark, if I had known it, of man's intervention. For once more, and once more unconsciously, we were within hail of fellow-creatures, and that vacant beach was but a pistol-shot from the capital city of the archipelago. But the life of an atoll, unless it be enclosed, passes wholly on the shores of the lagoon; it is there the villages are seated, there the canoes ply and are drawn up; and the beach of the ocean is a place accursed and deserted, the fit scene only for wizardry and shipwreck, and in the native belief a haunting ground of murderous spectres.

By and by we might perceive a breach in the low barrier; the woods ceased; a glittering point ran into the sea, tipped with an emerald shoal the mark of entrance. As we drew near we met a little run of sea—the private sea of the lagoon having there its origin and end, and here, in the jaws of the gateway, trying vain conclusions with the more majestic heave of the Pacific. The Casco scarce avowed a shock; but there are times and circumstances when these harbour mouths of inland basins vomit floods, deflecting, burying, and dismasting ships. For, conceive a lagoon perfectly sealed but in the one point, and that of merely navigable width; conceive the tide and wind to have heaped for hours together in that coral fold a superfluity of waters, and the tide to change and the wind fall—the open sluice of some great reservoirs at home will give an image of the unstemmable effluxion.

We were scarce well headed for the pass before all heads were craned over the rail. For the water, shoaling under our board, became changed in a moment to surprising hues of blue and grey; and in its transparency the coral branched and blossomed, and the fish of the inland sea cruised visibly below us, stained and striped, and even beaked like parrots. I have paid in my time to view many curiosities; never one so curious as that first sight over the ship's rail in the lagoon of Fakarava. But let not the reader be deceived with hope. I have since entered, I suppose, some dozen atolls in different parts of the Pacific, and the experience has never been repeated. That exquisite hue and transparency of submarine day, and these shoals of rainbow fish, have not enraptured me again.

Before we could raise our eyes from that engaging spectacle the schooner had slipped betwixt the pierheads of the reef, and was already quite committed to the sea within. The containing shores are so little erected, and the lagoon itself is so great, that, for the more part, it seemed to extend without a check to the horizon. Here and there, indeed, where the reef carried an inlet, like a signet-ring upon a finger, there would be a pencilling of palms; here and there, the green wall of wood ran solid for a length of miles; and on the port hand, under the highest grove of trees, a few houses sparkled white—Rotoava, the metropolitan settlement of the Paumotus. Hither we beat in three tacks, and came to an anchor close in shore, in the first smooth water since we had left San Francisco, five fathoms deep, where a man might look overboard all day at the vanishing cable, the coral patches, and the many-coloured fish.

Fakarava was chosen to be the seat of Government from nautical considerations only. It is eccentrically situate; the productions, even for a low island, poor; the population neither many nor—for Low Islanders—industrious. But the lagoon has two good passages, one to leeward, one to windward, so that in all states of the wind it can be left and entered, and this advantage, for a government of scattered islands, was decisive. A pier of coral, landing-stairs, a harbour light upon a staff and pillar, and two spacious Government bungalows in a handsome fence, give to the northern end of Rotoava a great air of consequence. This is confirmed on the one hand by an empty prison, on the other by a gendarmerie pasted over with hand-bills in Tahitian, land-law notices from Papeete, and republican sentiments from Paris, signed (a little after date) 'Jules Grévy, Perihidente.' Quite at the far end a belfried Catholic chapel concludes the town; and between, on a smooth floor of white coral sand and under the breezy canopy of coco-palms, the houses of the natives stand irregularly scattered, now close on the lagoon for the sake of the breeze, now back under the palms for love of shadow.

Not a soul was to be seen. But for the thunder of the surf on the far side, it seemed you might have heard a pin drop anywhere about that capital city. There was something thrilling in the unexpected silence, something yet more so in the unexpected sound. Here before us a sea reached to the horizon, rippling like an inland mere; and behold! close at our back another sea assaulted with assiduous fury the reverse of the position. At night the lantern was run up and lit a vacant pier. In one house lights were seen and voices heard, where the population (I was told) sat playing cards. A little beyond, from deep in the darkness of the palm-grove, we saw the glow and smelt the aromatic odour of a coal of cocoa-nut husk, a relic of the evening kitchen. Crickets sang; some shrill thing whistled in a tuft of weeds; and the mosquito hummed and stung. There was no other trace that night of man, bird, or insect in the isle. The moon, now three days old, and as yet but a silver crescent on a still visible sphere, shone through the palm canopy with vigorous and scattered lights. The alleys where we walked were smoothed and weeded like a boulevard; here and there were plants set out; here and there dusky cottages clustered in the shadow, some with verandahs. A public garden by night, a rich and fashionable watering-place in a by-season, offer sights and vistas not dissimilar. And still, on the one side, stretched the lapping mere, and from the other the deep sea still growled in the night. But it was most of all on board, in the dead hours, when I had been better sleeping, that the spell of Fakarava seized and held me. The moon was down. The harbour lantern and two of the greater planets drew vari-coloured wakes on the lagoon. From shore the cheerful watch-cry of cocks rang out at intervals above the organ-point of surf. And the thought of this depopulated capital, this protracted thread of annular island with its crest of coco-palms and fringe of breakers, and that tranquil inland sea that stretched before me till it touched the stars, ran in my head for hours with delight.

So long as I stayed upon that isle these thoughts were constant. I lay down to sleep, and woke again with an unblunted sense of my surroundings. I was never weary of calling up the image of that narrow causeway, on which I had my dwelling, lying coiled like a serpent, tail to mouth, in the outrageous ocean, and I was never weary of passing—a mere quarter-deck parade—from the one side to the other, from the shady, habitable shores of the lagoon to the blinding desert and uproarious breakers of the opposite beach. The sense of insecurity in such a thread of residence is more than fanciful. Hurricanes and tidal waves over-leap these humble obstacles; Oceanus remembers his strength, and, where houses stood and palms flourished, shakes his white beard again over the barren coral. Fakarava itself has suffered; the trees immediately beyond my house were all of recent replantation; and Anaa is only now recovered from a heavier stroke. I knew one who was then dwelling in the isle. He told me that he and two ship captains walked to the sea beach. There for a while they viewed the oncoming breakers, till one of the captains clapped suddenly his hand before his eyes and cried aloud that he could endure no longer to behold them. This was in the afternoon; in the dark hours of the night the sea burst upon the island like a flood; the settlement was razed all but the church and presbytery; and, when day returned, the survivors saw themselves clinging in an abattis of uprooted coco-palms and ruined houses.

Danger is but a small consideration. But men are more nicely sensible of a discomfort; and the atoll is a discomfortable home. There are some, and these probably ancient, where a deep soil has formed and the most valuable fruit-trees prosper. I have walked in one, with equal admiration and surprise, through a forest of huge breadfruits, eating bananas and stumbling among taro as I went. This was in the atoll of Namorik in the Marshall group, and stands alone in my experience. To give the opposite extreme, which is yet far more near the average, I will describe the soil and productions of Fakarava. The surface of that narrow strip is for the more part of broken coral lime-stone, like volcanic clinkers, and excruciating to the naked foot; in some atolls, I believe, not in Fakarava, it gives a fine metallic ring when struck. Here and there you come upon a bank of sand, exceeding fine and white, and these parts are the least productive. The plants (such as they are) spring from and love the broken coral, whence they grow with that wonderful verdancy that makes the beauty of the atoll from the sea. The coco-palm in particular luxuriates in that stern solum, striking down his roots to the brackish, percolated water, and bearing his green head in the wind with every evidence of health and pleasure. And yet even the coco-palm must be helped in infancy with some extraneous nutriment, and through much of the low archipelago there is planted with each nut a piece of ship's biscuit and a rusty nail. The pandanus comes next in importance, being also a food tree; and he, too, does bravely. A green bush called miki runs everywhere; occasionally a purao is seen; and there are several useless weeds. According to M. Cuzent, the whole number of plants on an atoll such as Fakarava will scarce exceed, even if it reaches to, one score. Not a blade of grass appears; not a grain of humus, save when a sack or two has been imported to make the semblance of a garden; such gardens as bloom in cities on the window-sill. Insect life is sometimes dense; a cloud o' mosquitoes, and, what is far worse, a plague of flies blackening our food, has sometimes driven us from a meal on Apemama; and even in Fakarava the mosquitoes were a pest. The land crab may be seen scuttling to his hole, and at night the rats besiege the houses and the artificial gardens. The crab is good eating; possibly so is the rat; I have not tried. Pandanus fruit is made, in the Gilberts, into an agreeable sweetmeat, such as a man may trifle with at the end of a long dinner; for a substantial meal I have no use for it. The rest of the food-supply, in a destitute atoll such as Fakarava, can be summed up in the favourite jest of the archipelago—cocoa-nut beefsteak. Cocoa-nut green, cocoa-nut ripe, cocoa-nut germinated; cocoa-nut to eat and cocoa-nut to drink; cocoa-nut raw and cooked, cocoa-nut hot and cold—such is the bill of fare. And some of the entrées are no doubt delicious. The germinated nut, cooked in the shell and eaten with a spoon, forms a good pudding; cocoa-nut milk—the expressed juice of a ripe nut, not the water of a green one—goes well in coffee, and is a valuable adjunct in cookery through the South Seas; and cocoa-nut salad, if you be a millionaire, and can afford to eat the value of a field of corn for your dessert, is a dish to be remembered with affection. But when all is done there is a sameness, and the Israelites of the low islands murmur at their manna.

The reader may think I have forgot the sea. The two beaches do certainly abound in life, and they are strangely different. In the lagoon the water shallows slowly on a bottom of the fine slimy sand, dotted with clumps of growing coral. Then comes a strip of tidal beach on which the ripples lap. In the coral clumps the great holy-water clam (Tridacna) grows plentifully; a little deeper lie the beds of the pearl-oyster and sail the resplendent fish that charmed us at our entrance; and these are all more or less vigorously coloured. But the other shells are white like lime, or faintly tinted with a little pink, the palest possible display; many of them dead besides, and badly rolled. On the ocean side, on the mounds of the steep beach, over all the width of the reef right out to where the surf is bursting, in every cranny, under every scattered fragment of the coral, an incredible plenty of marine life displays the most wonderful variety and brilliancy of hues. The reef itself has no passage of colour but is imitated by some shell. Purple and red and white, and green and yellow, pied and striped and clouded, the living shells wear in every combination the livery of the dead reef—if the reef be dead—so that the eye is continually baffled and the collector continually deceived. I have taken shells for stones and stones for shells, the one as often as the other. A prevailing character of the coral is to be dotted with small spots of red, and it is wonderful how many varieties of shell have adopted the same fashion and donned the disguise of the red spot. A shell I had found in plenty in the Marquesas I found here also unchanged in all things else, but there were the red spots. A lively little crab wore the same markings. The case of the hermit or soldier crab was more conclusive, being the result of conscious choice. This nasty little wrecker, scavenger, and squatter has learned the value of a spotted house; so it be of the right colour he will choose the smallest shard, tuck himself in a mere corner of a broken whorl, and go about the world half naked; but I never found him in this imperfect armour unless it was marked with the red spot.

Some two hundred yards distant is the beach of the lagoon. Collect the shells from each, set them side by side, and you would suppose they came from different hemispheres; the one so pale, the other so brilliant; the one prevalently white, the other of a score of hues, and infected with the scarlet spot like a disease. This seems the more strange, since the hermit crabs pass and repass the island, and I have met them by the Residency well, which is about central, journeying either way. Without doubt many of the shells in the lagoon are dead. But why are they dead? Without doubt the living shells have a very different background set for imitation. But why are these so different? We are only on the threshold of the mysteries.

Either beach, I have said, abounds with life. On the sea-side and in certain atolls this profusion of vitality is even shocking: the rock under foot is mined with it. I have broken off—notably in Funafuti and Arorai [156]—great lumps of ancient weathered rock that rang under my blows like iron, and the fracture has been full of pendent worms as long as my hand, as thick as a child's finger, of a slightly pinkish white, and set as close as three or even four to the square inch. Even in the lagoon, where certain shell-fish seem to sicken, others (it is notorious) prosper exceedingly and make the riches of these islands. Fish, too, abound; the lagoon is a closed fish-pond, such as might rejoice the fancy of an abbot; sharks swarm there, and chiefly round the passages, to feast upon this plenty, and you would suppose that man had only to prepare his angle. Alas! it is not so. Of these painted fish that came in hordes about the entering Casco, some bore poisonous spines, and others were poisonous if eaten. The stranger must refrain, or take his chance of painful and dangerous sickness. The native, on his own isle, is a safe guide; transplant him to the next, and he is helpless as yourself. For it is a question both of time and place. A fish caught in a lagoon may be deadly; the same fish caught the same day at sea, and only a few hundred yards without the passage, will be wholesome eating: in a neighbouring isle perhaps the case will be reversed; and perhaps a fortnight later you shall be able to eat of them indifferently from within and from without. According to the natives, these bewildering vicissitudes are ruled by the movement of the heavenly bodies. The beautiful planet Venus plays a great part in all island tales and customs; and among other functions, some of them more awful, she regulates the season of good fish. With Venus in one phase, as we had her, certain fish were poisonous in the lagoon: with Venus in another, the same fish was harmless and a valued article of diet. White men explain these changes by the phases of the coral.

It adds a last touch of horror to the thought of this precarious annular gangway in the sea, that even what there is of it is not of honest rock, but organic, part alive, part putrescent; even the clean sea and the bright fish about it poisoned, the most stubborn boulder burrowed in by worms, the lightest dust venomous as an apothecary's drugs.

CHAPTER III—A HOUSE TO LET IN A LOW ISLAND

Never populous, it was yet by a chapter of accidents that I found the island so deserted that no sound of human life diversified the hours; that we walked in that trim public garden of a town, among closed houses, without even a lodging-bill in a window to prove some tenancy in the back quarters; and, when we visited the Government bungalow, that Mr. Donat, acting Vice-Resident, greeted us alone, and entertained us with cocoa-nut punches in the Sessions Hall and seat of judgment of that widespread archipelago, our glasses standing arrayed with summonses and census returns. The unpopularity of a late Vice-Resident had begun the movement of exodus, his native employés resigning court appointments and retiring each to his own coco-patch in the remoter districts of the isle. Upon the back of that, the Governor in Papeete issued a decree: All land in the Paumotus must be defined and registered by a certain date. Now, the folk of the archipelago are half nomadic; a man can scarce be said to belong to a particular atoll; he belongs to several, perhaps holds a stake and counts cousinship in half a score; and the inhabitants of Rotoava in particular, man, woman, and child, and from the gendarme to the Mormon prophet and the schoolmaster, owned—I was going to say land—owned at least coral blocks and growing coco-palms in some adjacent isle. Thither—from the gendarme to the babe in arms, the pastor followed by his flock, the schoolmaster carrying along with him his scholars, and the scholars with their books and slates—they had taken ship some two days previous to our arrival, and were all now engaged disputing boundaries. Fancy overhears the shrillness of their disputation mingle with the surf and scatter sea-fowl. It was admirable to observe the completeness of their flight, like that of hibernating birds; nothing left but empty houses, like old nests to be reoccupied in spring; and even the harmless necessary dominie borne with them in their transmigration. Fifty odd set out, and only seven, I was informed, remained. But when I made a feast on board the Casco, more than seven, and nearer seven times seven, appeared to be my guests. Whence they appeared, how they were summoned, whither they vanished when the feast was eaten, I have no guess. In view of Low Island tales, and that awful frequentation which makes men avoid the seaward beaches of an atoll, some two score of those that ate with us may have returned, for the occasion, from the kingdom of the dead.

It was this solitude that put it in our minds to hire a house, and become, for the time being, indwellers of the isle—a practice I have ever since, when it was possible, adhered to. Mr. Donat placed us, with that intent, under the convoy of one Taniera Mahinui, who combined the incongruous characters of catechist and convict. The reader may smile, but I affirm he was well qualified for either part. For that of convict, first of all, by a good substantial felony, such as in all lands casts the perpetrator in chains and dungeons. Taniera was a man of birth—the chief a while ago, as he loved to tell, of a district in Anaa of 800 souls. In an evil hour it occurred to the authorities in Papeete to charge the chiefs with the collection of the taxes. It is a question if much were collected; it is certain that nothing was handed on; and Taniera, who had distinguished himself by a visit to Papeete and some high living in restaurants, was chosen for the scapegoat. The reader must understand that not Taniera but the authorities in Papeete were first in fault. The charge imposed was disproportioned. I have not yet heard of any Polynesian capable of such a burden; honest and upright Hawaiians—one in particular, who was admired even by the whites as an inflexible magistrate—have stumbled in the narrow path of the trustee. And Taniera, when the pinch came, scorned to denounce accomplices; others had shared the spoil, he bore the penalty alone. He was condemned in five years. The period, when I had the pleasure of his friendship, was not yet expired; he still drew prison rations, the sole and not unwelcome reminder of his chains, and, I believe, looked forward to the date of his enfranchisement with mere alarm. For he had no sense of shame in the position; complained of nothing but the defective table of his place of exile; regretted nothing but the fowls and eggs and fish of his own more favoured island. And as for his parishioners, they did not think one hair the less of him. A schoolboy, mulcted in ten thousand lines of Greek and dwelling sequestered in the dormitories, enjoys unabated consideration from his fellows. So with Taniera: a marked man, not a dishonoured; having fallen under the lash of the unthinkable gods; a Job, perhaps, or say a Taniera in the den of lions. Songs are likely made and sung about this saintly Robin Hood. On the other hand, he was even highly qualified for his office in the Church; being by nature a grave, considerate, and kindly man; his face rugged and serious, his smile bright; the master of several trades, a builder both of boats and houses; endowed with a fine pulpit voice; endowed besides with such a gift of eloquence that at the grave of the late chief of Fakarava he set all the assistants weeping. I never met a man of a mind more ecclesiastical; he loved to dispute and to inform himself of doctrine and the history of sects; and when I showed him the cuts in a volume of Chambers's Encyclopædia—except for one of an ape—reserved his whole enthusiasm for cardinals' hats, censers, candlesticks, and cathedrals. Methought when he looked upon the cardinal's hat a voice said low in his ear: 'Your foot is on the ladder.'

Under the guidance of Taniera we were soon installed in what I believe to have been the best-appointed private house in Fakarava. It stood just beyond the church in an oblong patch of cultivation. More than three hundred sacks of soil were imported from Tahiti for the Residency garden; and this must shortly be renewed, for the earth blows away, sinks in crevices of the coral, and is sought for at last in vain. I know not how much earth had gone to the garden of my villa; some at least, for an alley of prosperous bananas ran to the gate, and over the rest of the enclosure, which was covered with the usual clinker-like fragments of smashed coral, not only coco-palms and mikis but also fig-trees flourished, all of a delicious greenness. Of course there was no blade of grass. In front a picket fence divided us from the white road, the palm-fringed margin of the lagoon, and the lagoon itself, reflecting clouds by day and stars by night. At the back, a bulwark of uncemented coral enclosed us from the narrow belt of bush and the nigh ocean beach where the seas thundered, the roar and wash of them still humming in the chambers of the house.

This itself was of one story, verandahed front and back. It contained three rooms, three sewing-machines, three sea-chests, chairs, tables, a pair of beds, a cradle, a double-barrelled gun, a pair of enlarged coloured photographs, a pair of coloured prints after Wilkie and Mulready, and a French lithograph with the legend: 'Le brigade du Général Lepasset brûlant son drapeau devant Metz.' Under the stilts of the house a stove was rusting, till we drew it forth and put it in commission. Not far off was the burrow in the coral whence we supplied ourselves with brackish water. There was live stock, besides, on the estate—cocks and hens and a brace of ill-regulated cats, whom Taniera came every morning with the sun to feed on grated cocoa-nut. His voice was our regular réveille, ringing pleasantly about the garden: 'Pooty—pooty—poo—poo—poo!'

Far as we were from the public offices, the nearness of the chapel made our situation what is called eligible in advertisements, and gave us a side look on some native life. Every morning, as soon as he had fed the fowls, Taniera set the bell agoing in the small belfry; and the faithful, who were not very numerous, gathered to prayers. I was once present: it was the Lord's day, and seven females and eight males composed the congregation. A woman played precentor, starting with a longish note; the catechist joined in upon the second bar; and then the faithful in a body. Some had printed hymn-books which they followed; some of the rest filled up with 'eh—eh—eh,' the Paumotuan tol-de-rol. After the hymn, we had an antiphonal prayer or two; and then Taniera rose from the front bench, where he had been sitting in his catechist's robes, passed within the altar-rails, opened his Tahitian Bible, and began to preach from notes. I understood one word—the name of God; but the preacher managed his voice with taste, used rare and expressive gestures, and made a strong impression of sincerity. The plain service, the vernacular Bible, the hymn-tunes mostly on an English pattern—'God save the Queen,' I was informed, a special favourite,—all, save some paper flowers upon the altar, seemed not merely but austerely Protestant. It is thus the Catholics have met their low island proselytes half-way.

Taniera had the keys of our house; it was with him I made my bargain, if that could be called a bargain in which all was remitted to my generosity; it was he who fed the cats and poultry, he who came to call and pick a meal with us like an acknowledged friend; and we long fondly supposed he was our landlord. This belief was not to bear the test of experience; and, as my chapter has to relate, no certainty succeeded it.

We passed some days of airless quiet and great heat; shell-gatherers were warned from the ocean beach, where sunstroke waited them from ten till four; the highest palm hung motionless, there was no voice audible but that of the sea on the far side. At last, about four of a certain afternoon, long cat's-paws flawed the face of the lagoon; and presently in the tree-tops there awoke the grateful bustle of the trades, and all the houses and alleys of the island were fanned out. To more than one enchanted ship, that had lain long becalmed in view of the green shore, the wind brought deliverance; and by daylight on the morrow a schooner and two cutters lay moored in the port of Rotoava. Not only in the outer sea, but in the lagoon itself, a certain traffic woke with the reviving breeze; and among the rest one François, a half-blood, set sail with the first light in his own half-decked cutter. He had held before a court appointment; being, I believe, the Residency sweeper-out. Trouble arising with the unpopular Vice-Resident, he had thrown his honours down, and fled to the far parts of the atoll to plant cabbages—or at least coco-palms. Thence he was now driven by such need as even a Cincinnatus must acknowledge, and fared for the capital city, the seat of his late functions, to exchange half a ton of copra for necessary flour. And here, for a while, the story leaves to tell of his voyaging.

It must tell, instead, of our house, where, toward seven at night, the catechist came suddenly in with his pleased air of being welcome; armed besides with a considerable bunch of keys. These he proceeded to try on the sea-chests, drawing each in turn from its place against the wall. Heads of strangers appeared in the doorway and volunteered suggestions. All in vain. Either they were the wrong keys or the wrong boxes, or the wrong man was trying them. For a little Taniera fumed and fretted; then had recourse to the more summary method of the hatchet; one of the chests was broken open, and an armful of clothing, male and female, baled out and handed to the strangers on the verandah.

These were François, his wife, and their child. About eight a.m., in the midst of the lagoon, their cutter had capsized in jibbing. They got her righted, and though she was still full of water put the child on board. The mainsail had been carried away, but the jib still drew her sluggishly along, and François and the woman swam astern and worked the rudder with their hands. The cold was cruel; the fatigue, as time went on, became excessive; and in that preserve of sharks, fear hunted them. Again and again, François, the half-breed, would have desisted and gone down; but the woman, whole blood of an amphibious race, still supported him with cheerful words. I am reminded of a woman of Hawaii who swam with her husband, I dare not say how many miles, in a high sea, and came ashore at last with his dead body in her arms. It was about five in the evening, after nine hours' swimming, that François and his wife reached land at Rotoava. The gallant fight was won, and instantly the more childish side of native character appears. They had supped, and told and retold their story, dripping as they came; the flesh of the woman, whom Mrs. Stevenson helped to shift, was cold as stone; and François, having changed to a dry cotton shirt and trousers, passed the remainder of the evening on my floor and between open doorways, in a thorough draught. Yet François, the son of a French father, speaks excellent French himself and seems intelligent.

It was our first idea that the catechist, true to his evangelical vocation, was clothing the naked from his superfluity. Then it came out that François was but dealing with his own. The clothes were his, so was the chest, so was the house. François was in fact the landlord. Yet you observe he had hung back on the verandah while Taniera tried his 'prentice hand upon the locks: and even now, when his true character appeared, the only use he made of the estate was to leave the clothes of his family drying on the fence. Taniera was still the friend of the house, still fed the poultry, still came about us on his daily visits, François, during the remainder of his stay, holding bashfully aloof. And there was stranger matter. Since François had lost the whole load of his cutter, the half ton of copra, an axe, bowls, knives, and clothes—since he had in a manner to begin the world again, and his necessary flour was not yet bought or paid for—I proposed to advance him what he needed on the rent. To my enduring amazement he refused, and the reason he gave—if that can be called a reason which but darkens counsel—was that Taniera was his friend. His friend, you observe; not his creditor. I inquired into that, and was assured that Taniera, an exile in a strange isle, might possibly be in debt himself, but certainly was no man's creditor.

Very early one morning we were awakened by a bustling presence in the yard, and found our camp had been surprised by a tall, lean old native lady, dressed in what were obviously widow's weeds. You could see at a glance she was a notable woman, a housewife, sternly practical, alive with energy, and with fine possibilities of temper. Indeed, there was nothing native about her but the skin; and the type abounds, and is everywhere respected, nearer home. It did us good to see her scour the grounds, examining the plants and chickens; watering, feeding, trimming them; taking angry, purpose-like possession. When she neared the house our sympathy abated; when she came to the broken chest I wished I were elsewhere. We had scarce a word in common; but her whole lean body spoke for her with indignant eloquence. 'My chest!' it cried, with a stress on the possessive. 'My chest—broken open! This is a fine state of things!' I hastened to lay the blame where it belonged—on François and his wife—and found I had made things worse instead of better. She repeated the names at first with incredulity, then with despair. A while she seemed stunned, next fell to disembowelling the box, piling the goods on the floor, and visibly computing the extent of François's ravages; and presently after she was observed in high speech with Taniera, who seemed to hang an ear like one reproved.

Here, then, by all known marks, should be my land-lady at last; here was every character of the proprietor fully developed. Should I not approach her on the still depending question of my rent? I carried the point to an adviser. 'Nonsense!' he cried. 'That's the old woman, the mother. It doesn't belong to her. I believe that's the man the house belongs to,' and he pointed to one of the coloured photographs on the wall. On this I gave up all desire of understanding; and when the time came for me to leave, in the judgment-hall of the archipelago, and with the awful countenance of the acting Governor, I duly paid my rent to Taniera. He was satisfied, and so was I. But what had he to do with it? Mr. Donat, acting magistrate and a man of kindred blood, could throw no light upon the mystery; a plain private person, with a taste for letters, cannot be expected to do more.

CHAPTER IV—TRAITS AND SECTS IN THE PAUMOTUS

The most careless reader must have remarked a change of air since the Marquesas. The house, crowded with effects, the bustling housewife counting her possessions, the serious, indoctrinated island pastor, the long fight for life in the lagoon: here are traits of a new world. I read in a pamphlet (I will not give the author's name) that the Marquesan especially resembles the Paumotuan. I should take the two races, though so near in neighbourhood, to be extremes of Polynesian diversity. The Marquesan is certainly the most beautiful of human races, and one of the tallest—the Paumotuan averaging a good inch shorter, and not even handsome; the Marquesan open-handed, inert, insensible to religion, childishly self-indulgent—the Paumotuan greedy, hardy, enterprising, a religious disputant, and with a trace of the ascetic character.

Yet a few years ago, and the people of the archipelago were crafty savages. Their isles might be called sirens' isles, not merely from the attraction they exerted on the passing mariner, but from the perils that awaited him on shore. Even to this day, in certain outlying islands, danger lingers; and the civilized Paumotuan dreads to land and hesitates to accost his backward brother. But, except in these, to-day the peril is a memory. When our generation were yet in the cradle and playroom it was still a living fact. Between 1830 and 1840, Hao, for instance, was a place of the most dangerous approach, where ships were seized and crews kidnapped. As late as 1856, the schooner Sarah Ann sailed from Papeete and was seen no more. She had women on board, and children, the captain's wife, a nursemaid, a baby, and the two young sons of a Captain Steven on their way to the mainland for schooling. All were supposed to have perished in a squall. A year later, the captain of the Julia, coasting along the island variously called Bligh, Lagoon, and Tematangi saw armed natives follow the course of his schooner, clad in many-coloured stuffs. Suspicion was at once aroused; the mother of the lost children was profuse of money; and one expedition having found the place deserted, and returned content with firing a few shots, she raised and herself accompanied another. None appeared to greet or to oppose them; they roamed a while among abandoned huts and empty thickets; then formed two parties and set forth to beat, from end to end, the pandanus jungle of the island. One man remained alone by the landing-place—Teina, a chief of Anaa, leader of the armed natives who made the strength of the expedition. Now that his comrades were departed this way and that, on their laborious exploration, the silence fell profound; and this silence was the ruin of the islanders. A sound of stones rattling caught the ear of Teina. He looked, thinking to perceive a crab, and saw instead the brown hand of a human being issue from a fissure in the ground. A shout recalled the search parties and announced their doom to the buried caitiffs. In the cave below, sixteen were found crouching among human bones and singular and horrid curiosities. One was a head of golden hair, supposed to be a relic of the captain's wife; another was half of the body of a European child, sun-dried and stuck upon a stick, doubtless with some design of wizardry.

The Paumotuan is eager to be rich. He saves, grudges, buries money, fears not work. For a dollar each, two natives passed the hours of daylight cleaning our ship's copper. It was strange to see them so indefatigable and so much at ease in the water—working at times with their pipes lighted, the smoker at times submerged and only the glowing bowl above the surface; it was stranger still to think they were next congeners to the incapable Marquesan. But the Paumotuan not only saves, grudges, and works, he steals besides; or, to be more precise, he swindles. He will never deny a debt, he only flees his creditor. He is always keen for an advance; so soon as he has fingered it he disappears. He knows your ship; so soon as it nears one island, he is off to another. You may think you know his name; he has already changed it. Pursuit in that infinity of isles were fruitless. The result can be given in a nutshell. It has been actually proposed in a Government report to secure debts by taking a photograph of the debtor; and the other day in Papeete credits on the Paumotus to the amount of sixteen thousand pounds were sold for less than forty—quatre cent mille francs pour moins de mille francs. Even so, the purchase was thought hazardous; and only the man who made it and who had special opportunities could have dared to give so much.

The Paumotuan is sincerely attached to those of his own blood and household. A touching affection sometimes unites wife and husband. Their children, while they are alive, completely rule them; after they are dead, their bones or their mummies are often jealously preserved and carried from atoll to atoll in the wanderings of the family. I was told there were many houses in Fakarava with the mummy of a child locked in a sea-chest; after I heard it, I would glance a little jealously at those by my own bed; in that cupboard, also, it was possible there was a tiny skeleton.

The race seems in a fair way to survive. From fifteen islands, whose rolls I had occasion to consult, I found a proportion of 59 births to 47 deaths for 1887. Dropping three out of the fifteen, there remained for the other twelve the comfortable ratio of 50 births to 32 deaths. Long habits of hardship and activity doubtless explain the contrast with Marquesan figures. But the Paumotuan displays, besides, a certain concern for health and the rudiments of a sanitary discipline. Public talk with these free-spoken people plays the part of the Contagious Diseases Act; in-comers to fresh islands anxiously inquire if all be well; and syphilis, when contracted, is successfully treated with indigenous herbs. Like their neighbours of Tahiti, from whom they have perhaps imbibed the error, they regard leprosy with comparative indifference, elephantiasis with disproportionate fear. But, unlike indeed to the Tahitian, their alarm puts on the guise of self-defence. Any one stricken with this painful and ugly malady is confined to the ends of villages, denied the use of paths and highways, and condemned to transport himself between his house and coco-patch by water only, his very footprint being held infectious. Fe'efe'e, being a creature of marshes and the sequel of malarial fever, is not original in atolls. On the single isle of Makatea, where the lagoon is now a marsh, the disease has made a home. Many suffer; they are excluded (if Mr. Wilmot be right) from much of the comfort of society; and it is believed they take a secret vengeance. The defections of the sick are considered highly poisonous. Early in the morning, it is narrated, aged and malicious persons creep into the sleeping village, and stealthily make water at the doors of the houses of young men. Thus they propagate disease; thus they breathe on and obliterate comeliness and health, the objects of their envy. Whether horrid fact or more abominable legend, it equally depicts that something bitter and energetic which distinguishes Paumotuan man.

The archipelago is divided between two main religions, Catholic and Mormon. They front each other proudly with a false air of permanence; yet are but shapes, their membership in a perpetual flux. The Mormon attends mass with devotion: the Catholic sits attentive at a Mormon sermon, and to-morrow each may have transferred allegiance. One man had been a pillar of the Church of Rome for fifteen years; his wife dying, he decided that must be a poor religion that could not save a man his wife, and turned Mormon. According to one informant, Catholicism was the more fashionable in health, but on the approach of sickness it was judged prudent to secede. As a Mormon, there were five chances out of six you might recover; as a Catholic, your hopes were small; and this opinion is perhaps founded on the comfortable rite of unction.

We all know what Catholics are, whether in the Paumotus or at home. But the Paumotuan Mormon seemed a phenomenon apart. He marries but the one wife, uses the Protestant Bible, observes Protestant forms of worship, forbids the use of liquor and tobacco, practises adult baptism by immersion, and after every public sin, rechristens the backslider. I advised with Mahinui, whom I found well informed in the history of the American Mormons, and he declared against the least connection. 'Pour moi,' said he, with a fine charity, 'les Mormons ici un petit Catholiques.' Some months later I had an opportunity to consult an orthodox fellow-countryman, an old dissenting Highlander, long settled in Tahiti, but still breathing of the heather of Tiree. 'Why do they call themselves Mormons?' I asked. 'My dear, and that is my question!' he exclaimed. 'For by all that I can hear of their doctrine, I have nothing to say against it, and their life, it is above reproach.' And for all that, Mormons they are, but of the earlier sowing: the so-called Josephites, the followers of Joseph Smith, the opponents of Brigham Young.

Grant, then, the Mormons to be Mormons. Fresh points at once arise: What are the Israelites? and what the Kanitus? For a long while back the sect had been divided into Mormons proper and so-called Israelites, I never could hear why. A few years since there came a visiting missionary of the name of Williams, who made an excellent collection, and retired, leaving fresh disruption imminent. Something irregular (as I was told) in his way of 'opening the service' had raised partisans and enemies; the church was once more rent asunder; and a new sect, the Kanitu, issued from the division. Since then Kanitus and Israelites, like the Cameronians and the United Presbyterians, have made common cause; and the ecclesiastical history of the Paumotus is, for the moment, uneventful. There will be more doing before long, and these isles bid fair to be the Scotland of the South. Two things I could never learn. The nature of the innovations of the Rev. Mr. Williams none would tell me, and of the meaning of the name Kanitu none had a guess. It was not Tahitian, it was not Marquesan; it formed no part of that ancient speech of the Paumotus, now passing swiftly into obsolescence. One man, a priest, God bless him! said it was the Latin for a little dog. I have found it since as the name of a god in New Guinea; it must be a bolder man than I who should hint at a connection. Here, then, is a singular thing: a brand-new sect, arising by popular acclamation, and a nonsense word invented for its name.

The design of mystery seems obvious, and according to a very intelligent observer, Mr. Magee of Mangareva, this element of the mysterious is a chief attraction of the Mormon Church. It enjoys some of the status of Freemasonry at home, and there is for the convert some of the exhilaration of adventure. Other attractions are certainly conjoined. Perpetual rebaptism, leading to a succession of baptismal feasts, is found, both from the social and the spiritual side, a pleasing feature. More important is the fact that all the faithful enjoy office; perhaps more important still, the strictness of the discipline. 'The veto on liquor,' said Mr. Magee, 'brings them plenty members.' There is no doubt these islanders are fond of drink, and no doubt they refrain from the indulgence; a bout on a feast-day, for instance, may be followed by a week or a month of rigorous sobriety. Mr. Wilmot attributes this to Paumotuan frugality and the love of hoarding; it goes far deeper. I have mentioned that I made a feast on board the Casco. To wash down ship's bread and jam, each guest was given the choice of rum or syrup, and out of the whole number only one man voted—in a defiant tone, and amid shouts of mirth—for 'Trum'! This was in public. I had the meanness to repeat the experiment, whenever I had a chance, within the four walls of my house; and three at least, who had refused at the festival, greedily drank rum behind a door. But there were others thoroughly consistent. I said the virtues of the race were bourgeois and puritan; and how bourgeois is this! how puritanic! how Scottish! and how Yankee!—the temptation, the resistance, the public hypocritical conformity, the Pharisees, the Holy Willies, and the true disciples. With such a people the popularity of an ascetic Church appears legitimate; in these strict rules, in this perpetual supervision, the weak find their advantage, the strong a certain pleasure; and the doctrine of rebaptism, a clean bill and a fresh start, will comfort many staggering professors.

There is yet another sect, or what is called a sect—no doubt improperly—that of the Whistlers. Duncan Cameron, so clear in favour of the Mormons, was no less loud in condemnation of the Whistlers. Yet I do not know; I still fancy there is some connection, perhaps fortuitous, probably disavowed. Here at least are some doings in the house of an Israelite clergyman (or prophet) in the island of Anaa, of which I am equally sure that Duncan would disclaim and the Whistlers hail them for an imitation of their own. My informant, a Tahitian and a Catholic, occupied one part of the house; the prophet and his family lived in the other. Night after night the Mormons, in the one end, held their evening sacrifice of song; night after night, in the other, the wife of the Tahitian lay awake and listened to their singing with amazement. At length she could contain herself no longer, woke her husband, and asked him what he heard. 'I hear several persons singing hymns,' said he. 'Yes,' she returned, 'but listen again! Do you not hear something supernatural?' His attention thus directed, he was aware of a strange buzzing voice—and yet he declared it was beautiful—which justly accompanied the singers. The next day he made inquiries. 'It is a spirit,' said the prophet, with entire simplicity, 'which has lately made a practice of joining us at family worship.' It did not appear the thing was visible, and like other spirits raised nearer home in these degenerate days, it was rudely ignorant, at first could only buzz, and had only learned of late to bear a part correctly in the music.

The performances of the Whistlers are more business-like. Their meetings are held publicly with open doors, all being 'cordially invited to attend.' The faithful sit about the room—according to one informant, singing hymns; according to another, now singing and now whistling; the leader, the wizard—let me rather say, the medium—sits in the midst, enveloped in a sheet and silent; and presently, from just above his head, or sometimes from the midst of the roof, an aerial whistling proceeds, appalling to the inexperienced. This, it appears, is the language of the dead; its purport is taken down progressively by one of the experts, writing, I was told, 'as fast as a telegraph operator'; and the communications are at last made public. They are of the baldest triviality; a schooner is, perhaps, announced, some idle gossip reported of a neighbour, or if the spirit shall have been called to consultation on a case of sickness, a remedy may be suggested. One of these, immersion in scalding water, not long ago proved fatal to the patient. The whole business is very dreary, very silly, and very European; it has none of the picturesque qualities of similar conjurations in New Zealand; it seems to possess no kernel of possible sense, like some that I shall describe among the Gilbert islanders. Yet I was told that many hardy, intelligent natives were inveterate Whistlers. 'Like Mahinui?' I asked, willing to have a standard; and I was told 'Yes.' Why should I wonder? Men more enlightened than my convict-catechist sit down at home to follies equally sterile and dull.

The medium is sometimes female. It was a woman, for instance, who introduced these practices on the north coast of Taiarapu, to the scandal of her own connections, her brother-in-law in particular declaring she was drunk. But what shocked Tahiti might seem fit enough in the Paumotus, the more so as certain women there possess, by the gift of nature, singular and useful powers. They say they are honest, well-intentioned ladies, some of them embarrassed by their weird inheritance. And indeed the trouble caused by this endowment is so great, and the protection afforded so infinitesimally small, that I hesitate whether to call it a gift or a hereditary curse. You may rob this lady's coco-patch, steal her canoes, burn down her house, and slay her family scatheless; but one thing you must not do: you must not lay a hand upon her sleeping-mat, or your belly will swell, and you can only be cured by the lady or her husband. Here is the report of an eye-witness, Tasmanian born, educated, a man who has made money—certainly no fool. In 1886 he was present in a house on Makatea, where two lads began to skylark on the mats, and were (I think) ejected. Instantly after, their bellies began to swell; pains took hold on them; all manner of island remedies were exhibited in vain, and rubbing only magnified their sufferings. The man of the house was called, explained the nature of the visitation, and prepared the cure. A cocoa-nut was husked, filled with herbs, and with all the ceremonies of a launch, and the utterance of spells in the Paumotuan language, committed to the sea. From that moment the pains began to grow more easy and the swelling to subside. The reader may stare. I can assure him, if he moved much among old residents of the archipelago, he would be driven to admit one thing of two—either that there is something in the swollen bellies or nothing in the evidence of man.

I have not met these gifted ladies; but I had an experience of my own, for I have played, for one night only, the part of the whistling spirit. It had been blowing wearily all day, but with the fall of night the wind abated, and the moon, which was then full, rolled in a clear sky. We went southward down the island on the side of the lagoon, walking through long-drawn forest aisles of palm, and on a floor of snowy sand. No life was abroad, nor sound of life; till in a clear part of the isle we spied the embers of a fire, and not far off, in a dark house, heard natives talking softly. To sit without a light, even in company, and under cover, is for a Paumotuan a somewhat hazardous extreme. The whole scene—the strong moonlight and crude shadows on the sand, the scattered coals, the sound of the low voices from the house, and the lap of the lagoon along the beach—put me (I know not how) on thoughts of superstition. I was barefoot, I observed my steps were noiseless, and drawing near to the dark house, but keeping well in shadow, began to whistle. 'The Heaving of the Lead' was my air—no very tragic piece. With the first note the conversation and all movement ceased; silence accompanied me while I continued; and when I passed that way on my return I found the lamp was lighted in the house, but the tongues were still mute. All night, as I now think, the wretches shivered and were silent. For indeed, I had no guess at the time at the nature and magnitude of the terrors I inflicted, or with what grisly images the notes of that old song had peopled the dark house.

CHAPTER V—A PAUMOTUAN FUNERAL

No, I had no guess of these men's terrors. Yet I had received ere that a hint, if I had understood; and the occasion was a funeral.

A little apart in the main avenue of Rotoava, in a low hut of leaves that opened on a small enclosure, like a pigsty on a pen, an old man dwelt solitary with his aged wife. Perhaps they were too old to migrate with the others; perhaps they were too poor, and had no possessions to dispute. At least they had remained behind; and it thus befell that they were invited to my feast. I dare say it was quite a piece of politics in the pigsty whether to come or not to come, and the husband long swithered between curiosity and age, till curiosity conquered, and they came, and in the midst of that last merrymaking death tapped him on the shoulder. For some days, when the sky was bright and the wind cool, his mat would be spread in the main highway of the village, and he was to be seen lying there inert, a mere handful of a man, his wife inertly seated by his head. They seemed to have outgrown alike our needs and faculties; they neither spoke nor listened; they suffered us to pass without a glance; the wife did not fan, she seemed not to attend upon her husband, and the two poor antiques sat juxtaposed under the high canopy of palms, the human tragedy reduced to its bare elements, a sight beyond pathos, stirring a thrill of curiosity. And yet there was one touch of the pathetic haunted me: that so much youth and expectation should have run in these starved veins, and the man should have squandered all his lees of life on a pleasure party.

On the morning of 17th September the sufferer died, and, time pressing, he was buried the same day at four. The cemetery lies to seaward behind Government House; broken coral, like so much road-metal, forms the surface; a few wooden crosses, a few inconsiderable upright stones, designate graves; a mortared wall, high enough to lean on, rings it about; a clustering shrub surrounds it with pale leaves. Here was the grave dug that morning, doubtless by uneasy diggers, to the sound of the nigh sea and the cries of sea-birds; meanwhile the dead man waited in his house, and the widow and another aged woman leaned on the fence before the door, no speech upon their lips, no speculation in their eyes.

Sharp at the hour the procession was in march, the coffin wrapped in white and carried by four bearers; mourners behind—not many, for not many remained in Rotoava, and not many in black, for these were poor; the men in straw hats, white coats, and blue trousers or the gorgeous parti-coloured pariu, the Tahitian kilt; the women, with a few exceptions, brightly habited. Far in the rear came the widow, painfully carrying the dead man's mat; a creature aged beyond humanity, to the likeness of some missing link.

The dead man had been a Mormon; but the Mormon clergyman was gone with the rest to wrangle over boundaries in the adjacent isle, and a layman took his office. Standing at the head of the open grave, in a white coat and blue pariu, his Tahitian Bible in his hand and one eye bound with a red handkerchief, he read solemnly that chapter in Job which has been read and heard over the bones of so many of our fathers, and with a good voice offered up two prayers. The wind and the surf bore a burthen. By the cemetery gate a mother in crimson suckled an infant rolled in blue. In the midst the widow sat upon the ground and polished one of the coffin-stretchers with a piece of coral; a little later she had turned her back to the grave and was playing with a leaf. Did she understand? God knows. The officiant paused a moment, stooped, and gathered and threw reverently on the coffin a handful of rattling coral. Dust to dust: but the grains of this dust were gross like cherries, and the true dust that was to follow sat near by, still cohering (as by a miracle) in the tragic semblance of a female ape.

So far, Mormon or not, it was a Christian funeral. The well-known passage had been read from Job, the prayers had been rehearsed, the grave was filled, the mourners straggled homeward. With a little coarser grain of covering earth, a little nearer outcry of the sea, a stronger glare of sunlight on the rude enclosure, and some incongruous colours of attire, the well-remembered form had been observed.

By rights it should have been otherwise. The mat should have been buried with its owner; but, the family being poor, it was thriftily reserved for a fresh service. The widow should have flung herself upon the grave and raised the voice of official grief, the neighbours have chimed in, and the narrow isle rung for a space with lamentation. But the widow was old; perhaps she had forgotten, perhaps never understood, and she played like a child with leaves and coffin-stretchers. In all ways my guest was buried with maimed rites. Strange to think that his last conscious pleasure was the Casco and my feast; strange to think that he had limped there, an old child, looking for some new good. And the good thing, rest, had been allotted him.

But though the widow had neglected much, there was one part she must not utterly neglect. She came away with the dispersing funeral; but the dead man's mat was left behind upon the grave, and I learned that by set of sun she must return to sleep there. This vigil is imperative. From sundown till the rising of the morning star the Paumotuan must hold his watch above the ashes of his kindred. Many friends, if the dead have been a man of mark, will keep the watchers company; they will be well supplied with coverings against the weather; I believe they bring food, and the rite is persevered in for two weeks. Our poor survivor, if, indeed, she properly survived, had little to cover, and few to sit with her; on the night of the funeral a strong squall chased her from her place of watch; for days the weather held uncertain and outrageous; and ere seven nights were up she had desisted, and returned to sleep in her low roof. That she should be at the pains of returning for so short a visit to a solitary house, that this borderer of the grave should fear a little wind and a wet blanket, filled me at the time with musings. I could not say she was indifferent; she was so far beyond me in experience that the court of my criticism waived jurisdiction; but I forged excuses, telling myself she had perhaps little to lament, perhaps suffered much, perhaps understood nothing. And lo! in the whole affair there was no question whether of tenderness or piety, and the sturdy return of this old remnant was a mark either of uncommon sense or of uncommon fortitude.

Yet one thing had occurred that partly set me on the trail. I have said the funeral passed much as at home. But when all was over, when we were trooping in decent silence from the graveyard gate and down the path to the settlement, a sudden inbreak of a different spirit startled and perhaps dismayed us. Two people walked not far apart in our procession: my friend Mr. Donat—Donat-Rimarau: 'Donat the much-handed'—acting Vice-Resident, present ruler of the archipelago, by far the man of chief importance on the scene, but known besides for one of an unshakable good temper; and a certain comely, strapping young Paumotuan woman, the comeliest on the isle, not (let us hope) the bravest or the most polite. Of a sudden, ere yet the grave silence of the funeral was broken, she made a leap at the Resident, with pointed finger, shrieked a few words, and fell back again with a laughter, not a natural mirth. 'What did she say to you?' I asked. 'She did not speak to me,' said Donat, a shade perturbed; 'she spoke to the ghost of the dead man.' And the purport of her speech was this: 'See there! Donat will be a fine feast for you to-night.'

'M. Donat called it a jest,' I wrote at the time in my diary. 'It seemed to me more in the nature of a terrified conjuration, as though she would divert the ghost's attention from herself. A cannibal race may well have cannibal phantoms.' The guesses of the traveller appear foredoomed to be erroneous; yet in these I was precisely right. The woman had stood by in terror at the funeral, being then in a dread spot, the graveyard. She looked on in terror to the coming night, with that ogre, a new spirit, loosed upon the isle. And the words she had cried in Donat's face were indeed a terrified conjuration, basely to shield herself, basely to dedicate another in her stead. One thing is to be said in her excuse. Doubtless she partly chose Donat because he was a man of great good-nature, but partly, too, because he was a man of the half-caste. For I believe all natives regard white blood as a kind of talisman against the powers of hell. In no other way can they explain the unpunished recklessness of Europeans.

CHAPTER VI—GRAVEYARD STORIES

With my superstitious friend, the islander, I fear I am not wholly frank, often leading the way with stories of my own, and being always a grave and sometimes an excited hearer. But the deceit is scarce mortal, since I am as pleased to hear as he to tell, as pleased with the story as he with the belief; and, besides, it is entirely needful. For it is scarce possible to exaggerate the extent and empire of his superstitions; they mould his life, they colour his thinking; and when he does not speak to me of ghosts, and gods, and devils, he is playing the dissembler and talking only with his lips. With thoughts so different, one must indulge the other; and I would rather that I should indulge his superstition than he my incredulity. Of one thing, besides, I may be sure: Let me indulge it as I please, I shall not hear the whole; for he is already on his guard with me, and the amount of the lore is boundless.

I will give but a few instances at random, chiefly from my own doorstep in Upolu, during the past month (October 1890). One of my workmen was sent the other day to the banana patch, there to dig; this is a hollow of the mountain, buried in woods, out of all sight and cry of mankind; and long before dusk Lafaele was back again beside the cook-house with embarrassed looks; he dared not longer stay alone, he was afraid of 'spirits in the bush.' It seems these are the souls of the unburied dead, haunting where they fell, and wearing woodland shapes of pig, or bird, or insect; the bush is full of them, they seem to eat nothing, slay solitary wanderers apparently in spite, and at times, in human form, go down to villages and consort with the inhabitants undetected. So much I learned a day or so after, walking in the bush with a very intelligent youth, a native. It was a little before noon; a grey day and squally; and perhaps I had spoken lightly. A dark squall burst on the side of the mountain; the woods shook and cried; the dead leaves rose from the ground in clouds, like butterflies; and my companion came suddenly to a full stop. He was afraid, he said, of the trees falling; but as soon as I had changed the subject of our talk he proceeded with alacrity. A day or two before a messenger came up the mountain from Apia with a letter; I was in the bush, he must await my return, then wait till I had answered: and before I was done his voice sounded shrill with terror of the coming night and the long forest road. These are the commons. Take the chiefs. There has been a great coming and going of signs and omens in our group. One river ran down blood; red eels were captured in another; an unknown fish was thrown upon the coast, an ominous word found written on its scales. So far we might be reading in a monkish chronicle; now we come on a fresh note, at once modern and Polynesian. The gods of Upolu and Savaii, our two chief islands, contended recently at cricket. Since then they are at war. Sounds of battle are heard to roll along the coast. A woman saw a man swim from the high seas and plunge direct into the bush; he was no man of that neighbourhood; and it was known he was one of the gods, speeding to a council. Most perspicuous of all, a missionary on Savaii, who is also a medical man, was disturbed late in the night by knocking; it was no hour for the dispensary, but at length he woke his servant and sent him to inquire; the servant, looking from a window, beheld crowds of persons, all with grievous wounds, lopped limbs, broken heads, and bleeding bullet-holes; but when the door was opened all had disappeared. They were gods from the field of battle. Now these reports have certainly significance; it is not hard to trace them to political grumblers or to read in them a threat of coming trouble; from that merely human side I found them ominous myself. But it was the spiritual side of their significance that was discussed in secret council by my rulers. I shall best depict this mingled habit of the Polynesian mind by two connected instances. I once lived in a village, the name of which I do not mean to tell. The chief and his sister were persons perfectly intelligent: gentlefolk, apt of speech. The sister was very religious, a great church-goer, one that used to reprove me if I stayed away; I found afterwards that she privately worshipped a shark. The chief himself was somewhat of a freethinker; at the least, a latitudinarian: he was a man, besides, filled with European knowledge and accomplishments; of an impassive, ironical habit; and I should as soon have expected superstition in Mr. Herbert Spencer. Hear the sequel. I had discovered by unmistakable signs that they buried too shallow in the village graveyard, and I took my friend, as the responsible authority, to task. 'There is something wrong about your graveyard,' said I, 'which you must attend to, or it may have very bad results.' 'Something wrong? What is it?' he asked, with an emotion that surprised me. 'If you care to go along there any evening about nine o'clock you can see for yourself,' said I. He stepped backward. 'A ghost!' he cried.

In short, in the whole field of the South Seas, there is not one to blame another. Half blood and whole, pious and debauched, intelligent and dull, all men believe in ghosts, all men combine with their recent Christianity fear of and a lingering faith in the old island deities. So, in Europe, the gods of Olympus slowly dwindled into village bogies; so to-day, the theological Highlander sneaks from under the eye of the Free Church divine to lay an offering by a sacred well.

I try to deal with the whole matter here because of a particular quality in Paumotuan superstitions. It is true I heard them told by a man with a genius for such narrations. Close about our evening lamp, within sound of the island surf, we hung on his words, thrilling. The reader, in far other scenes, must listen close for the faint echo.

This bundle of weird stories sprang from the burial and the woman's selfish conjuration. I was dissatisfied with what I heard, harped upon questions, and struck at last this vein of metal. It is from sundown to about four in the morning that the kinsfolk camp upon the grave; and these are the hours of the spirits' wanderings. At any time of the night—it may be earlier, it may be later—a sound is to be heard below, which is the noise of his liberation; at four sharp, another and a louder marks the instant of the re-imprisonment; between-whiles, he goes his malignant rounds. 'Did you ever see an evil spirit?' was once asked of a Paumotuan. 'Once.' 'Under what form?' 'It was in the form of a crane.' 'And how did you know that crane to be a spirit?' was asked. 'I will tell you,' he answered; and this was the purport of his inconclusive narrative. His father had been dead nearly a fortnight; others had wearied of the watch; and as the sun was setting, he found himself by the grave alone. It was not yet dark, rather the hour of the afterglow, when he was aware of a snow-white crane upon the coral mound; presently more cranes came, some white, some black; then the cranes vanished, and he saw in their place a white cat, to which there was silently joined a great company of cats of every hue conceivable; then these also disappeared, and he was left astonished.

This was an anodyne appearance. Take instead the experience of Rua-a-mariterangi on the isle of Katiu. He had a need for some pandanus, and crossed the isle to the sea-beach, where it chiefly flourishes. The day was still, and Rua was surprised to hear a crashing sound among the thickets, and then the fall of a considerable tree. Here must be some one building a canoe; and he entered the margin of the wood to find and pass the time of day with this chance neighbour. The crashing sounded more at hand; and then he was aware of something drawing swiftly near among the tree-tops. It swung by its heels downward, like an ape, so that its hands were free for murder; it depended safely by the slightest twigs; the speed of its coming was incredible; and soon Rua recognised it for a corpse, horrible with age, its bowels hanging as it came. Prayer was the weapon of Christian in the Valley of the Shadow, and it is to prayer that Rua-a-mariterangi attributes his escape. No merely human expedition had availed.

This demon was plainly from the grave; yet you will observe he was abroad by day. And inconsistent as it may seem with the hours of the night watch and the many references to the rising of the morning star, it is no singular exception. I could never find a case of another who had seen this ghost, diurnal and arboreal in its habits; but others have heard the fall of the tree, which seems the signal of its coming. Mr. Donat was once pearling on the uninhabited isle of Haraiki. It was a day without a breath of wind, such as alternate in the archipelago with days of contumelious breezes. The divers were in the midst of the lagoon upon their employment; the cook, a boy of ten, was over his pots in the camp. Thus were all souls accounted for except a single native who accompanied Donat into the wood in quest of sea-fowls' eggs. In a moment, out of the stillness, came the sound of the fall of a great tree. Donat would have passed on to find the cause. 'No,' cried his companion, 'that was no tree. It was something not right. Let us go back to camp.' Next Sunday the divers were turned on, all that part of the isle was thoroughly examined, and sure enough no tree had fallen. A little later Mr. Donat saw one of his divers flee from a similar sound, in similar unaffected panic, on the same isle. But neither would explain, and it was not till afterwards, when he met with Rua, that he learned the occasion of their terrors.

But whether by day or night, the purpose of the dead in these abhorred activities is still the same. In Samoa, my informant had no idea of the food of the bush spirits; no such ambiguity would exist in the mind of a Paumotuan. In that hungry archipelago, living and dead must alike toil for nutriment; and the race having been cannibal in the past, the spirits are so still. When the living ate the dead, horrified nocturnal imagination drew the shocking inference that the dead might eat the living. Doubtless they slay men, doubtless even mutilate them, in mere malice. Marquesan spirits sometimes tear out the eyes of travellers; but even that may be more practical than appears, for the eye is a cannibal dainty. And certainly the root-idea of the dead, at least in the far eastern islands, is to prowl for food. It was as a dainty morsel for a meal that the woman denounced Donat at the funeral. There are spirits besides who prey in particular not on the bodies but on the souls of the dead. The point is clearly made in a Tahitian story. A child fell sick, grew swiftly worse, and at last showed signs of death. The mother hastened to the house of a sorcerer, who lived hard by. 'You are yet in time,' said he; 'a spirit has just run past my door carrying the soul of your child wrapped in the leaf of a purao; but I have a spirit stronger and swifter who will run him down ere he has time to eat it.' Wrapped in a leaf: like other things edible and corruptible.

Or take an experience of Mr. Donat's on the island of Anaa. It was a night of a high wind, with violent squalls; his child was very sick, and the father, though he had gone to bed, lay wakeful, hearkening to the gale. All at once a fowl was violently dashed on the house wall. Supposing he had forgot to put it in shelter with the rest, Donat arose, found the bird (a cock) lying on the verandah, and put it in the hen-house, the door of which he securely fastened. Fifteen minutes later the business was repeated, only this time, as it was being dashed against the wall, the bird crew. Again Donat replaced it, examining the hen-house thoroughly and finding it quite perfect; as he was so engaged the wind puffed out his light, and he must grope back to the door a good deal shaken. Yet a third time the bird was dashed upon the wall; a third time Donat set it, now near dead, beside its mates; and he was scarce returned before there came a rush, like that of a furious strong man, against the door, and a whistle as loud as that of a railway engine rang about the house. The sceptical reader may here detect the finger of the tempest; but the women gave up all for lost and clustered on the beds lamenting. Nothing followed, and I must suppose the gale somewhat abated, for presently after a chief came visiting. He was a bold man to be abroad so late, but doubtless carried a bright lantern. And he was certainly a man of counsel, for as soon as he heard the details of these disturbances he was in a position to explain their nature. 'Your child,' said he, 'must certainly die. This is the evil spirit of our island who lies in wait to eat the spirits of the newly dead.' And then he went on to expatiate on the strangeness of the spirit's conduct. He was not usually, he explained, so open of assault, but sat silent on the house-top waiting, in the guise of a bird, while within the people tended the dying and bewailed the dead, and had no thought of peril. But when the day came and the doors were opened, and men began to go abroad, blood-stains on the wall betrayed the tragedy.

This is the quality I admire in Paumotuan legend. In Tahiti the spirit-eater is said to assume a vesture which has much more of pomp, but how much less of horror. It has been seen by all sorts and conditions, native and foreign; only the last insist it is a meteor. My authority was not so sure. He was riding with his wife about two in the morning; both were near asleep, and the horses not much better. It was a brilliant and still night, and the road wound over a mountain, near by a deserted marae (old Tahitian temple). All at once the appearance passed above them: a form of light; the head round and greenish; the body long, red, and with a focus of yet redder brilliancy about the midst. A buzzing hoot accompanied its passage; it flew direct out of one marae, and direct for another down the mountain side. And this, as my informant argued, is suggestive. For why should a mere meteor frequent the altars of abominable gods? The horses, I should say, were equally dismayed with their riders. Now I am not dismayed at all—not even agreeably. Give me rather the bird upon the house-top and the morning blood-gouts on the wall.

But the dead are not exclusive in their diet. They carry with them to the grave, in particular, the Polynesian taste for fish, and enter at times with the living into a partnership in fishery. Rua-a-mariterangi is again my authority; I feel it diminishes the credit of the fact, but how it builds up the image of this inveterate ghost-seer! He belongs to the miserably poor island of Taenga, yet his father's house was always well supplied. As Rua grew up he was called at last to go a-fishing with this fortunate parent. They rowed the lagoon at dusk, to an unlikely place, and the lay down in the stern, and the father began vainly to cast his line over the bows. It is to be supposed that Rua slept; and when he awoke there was the figure of another beside his father, and his father was pulling in the fish hand over hand. 'Who is that man, father?' Rua asked. 'It is none of your business,' said the father; and Rua supposed the stranger had swum off to them from shore. Night after night they fared into the lagoon, often to the most unlikely places; night after night the stranger would suddenly be seen on board, and as suddenly be missed; and morning after morning the canoe returned laden with fish. 'My father is a very lucky man,' thought Rua. At last, one fine day, there came first one boat party and then another, who must be entertained; father and son put off later than usual into the lagoon; and before the canoe was landed it was four o'clock, and the morning star was close on the horizon. Then the stranger appeared seized with some distress; turned about, showing for the first time his face, which was that of one long dead, with shining eyes; stared into the east, set the tips of his fingers to his mouth like one a-cold, uttered a strange, shuddering sound between a whistle and a moan—a thing to freeze the blood; and, the day-star just rising from the sea, he suddenly was not. Then Rua understood why his father prospered, why his fishes rotted early in the day, and why some were always carried to the cemetery and laid upon the graves. My informant is a man not certainly averse to superstition, but he keeps his head, and takes a certain superior interest, which I may be allowed to call scientific. The last point reminding him of some parallel practice in Tahiti, he asked Rua if the fish were left, or carried home again after a formal dedication. It appears old Mariterangi practised both methods; sometimes treating his shadowy partner to a mere oblation, sometimes honestly leaving his fish to rot upon the grave.

It is plain we have in Europe stories of a similar complexion; and the Polynesian varua ino or aitu o le vao is clearly the near kinsman of the Transylvanian vampire. Here is a tale in which the kinship appears broadly marked. On the atoll of Penrhyn, then still partly savage, a certain chief was long the salutary terror of the natives. He died, he was buried; and his late neighbours had scarce tasted the delights of licence ere his ghost appeared about the village. Fear seized upon all; a council was held of the chief men and sorcerers; and with the approval of the Rarotongan missionary, who was as frightened as the rest, and in the presence of several whites—my friend Mr. Ben Hird being one—the grave was opened, deepened until water came, and the body re-interred face down. The still recent staking of suicides in England and the decapitation of vampires in the east of Europe form close parallels.

So in Samoa only the spirits of the unburied awake fear. During the late war many fell in the bush; their bodies, sometimes headless, were brought back by native pastors and interred; but this (I know not why) was insufficient, and the spirit still lingered on the theatre of death. When peace returned a singular scene was enacted in many places, and chiefly round the high gorges of Lotoanuu, where the struggle was long centred and the loss had been severe. Kinswomen of the dead came carrying a mat or sheet and guided by survivors of the fight. The place of death was earnestly sought out; the sheet was spread upon the ground; and the women, moved with pious anxiety, sat about and watched it. If any living thing alighted it was twice brushed away; upon the third coming it was known to be the spirit of the dead, was folded in, carried home and buried beside the body; and the aitu rested. The rite was practised beyond doubt in simple piety; the repose of the soul was its object: its motive, reverent affection. The present king disowns indeed all knowledge of a dangerous aitu; he declares the souls of the unburied were only wanderers in limbo, lacking an entrance to the proper country of the dead, unhappy, nowise hurtful. And this severely classic opinion doubtless represents the views of the enlightened. But the flight of my Lafaele marks the grosser terrors of the ignorant.

This belief in the exorcising efficacy of funeral rites perhaps explains a fact, otherwise amazing, that no Polynesian seems at all to share our European horror of human bones and mummies. Of the first they made their cherished ornaments; they preserved them in houses or in mortuary caves; and the watchers of royal sepulchres dwelt with their children among the bones of generations. The mummy, even in the making, was as little feared. In the Marquesas, on the extreme coast, it was made by the household with continual unction and exposure to the sun; in the Carolines, upon the farthest west, it is still cured in the smoke of the family hearth. Head-hunting, besides, still lives around my doorstep in Samoa. And not ten years ago, in the Gilberts, the widow must disinter, cleanse, polish, and thenceforth carry about her, by day and night, the head of her dead husband. In all these cases we may suppose the process, whether of cleansing or drying, to have fully exorcised the aitu.

But the Paumotuan belief is more obscure. Here the man is duly buried, and he has to be watched. He is duly watched, and the spirit goes abroad in spite of watches. Indeed, it is not the purpose of the vigils to prevent these wanderings; only to mollify by polite attention the inveterate malignity of the dead. Neglect (it is supposed) may irritate and thus invite his visits, and the aged and weakly sometimes balance risks and stay at home. Observe, it is the dead man's kindred and next friends who thus deprecate his fury with nocturnal watchings. Even the placatory vigil is held perilous, except in company, and a boy was pointed out to me in Rotoava, because he had watched alone by his own father. Not the ties of the dead, nor yet their proved character, affect the issue. A late Resident, who died in Fakarava of sunstroke, was beloved in life and is still remembered with affection; none the less his spirit went about the island clothed with terrors, and the neighbourhood of Government House was still avoided after dark. We may sum up the cheerful doctrine thus: All men become vampires, and the vampire spares none. And here we come face to face with a tempting inconsistency. For the whistling spirits are notoriously clannish; I understood them to wait upon and to enlighten kinsfolk only, and that the medium was always of the race of the communicating spirit. Here, then, we have the bonds of the family, on the one hand, severed at the hour of death; on the other, helpfully persisting.

The child's soul in the Tahitian tale was wrapped in leaves. It is the spirits of the newly dead that are the dainty. When they are slain, the house is stained with blood. Rua's dead fisherman was decomposed; so—and horribly—was his arboreal demon. The spirit, then, is a thing material; and it is by the material ensigns of corruption that he is distinguished from the living man. This opinion is widespread, adds a gross terror to the more ugly Polynesian tales, and sometimes defaces the more engaging with a painful and incongruous touch. I will give two examples sufficiently wide apart, one from Tahiti, one from Samoa.

And first from Tahiti. A man went to visit the husband of his sister, then some time dead. In her life the sister had been dainty in the island fashion, and went always adorned with a coronet of flowers. In the midst of the night the brother awoke and was aware of a heavenly fragrance going to and fro in the dark house. The lamp I must suppose to have burned out; no Tahitian would have lain down without one lighted. A while he lay wondering and delighted; then called upon the rest. 'Do none of you smell flowers?' he asked. 'O,' said his brother-in-law, 'we are used to that here.' The next morning these two men went walking, and the widower confessed that his dead wife came about the house continually, and that he had even seen her. She was shaped and dressed and crowned with flowers as in her lifetime; only she moved a few inches above the earth with a very easy progress, and flitted dryshod above the surface of the river. And now comes my point: It was always in a back view that she appeared; and these brothers-in-law, debating the affair, agreed that this was to conceal the inroads of corruption.

Now for the Samoan story. I owe it to the kindness of Dr. F. Otto Sierich, whose collection of folk-tales I expect with a high degree of interest. A man in Manu'a was married to two wives and had no issue. He went to Savaii, married there a third, and was more fortunate. When his wife was near her time he remembered he was in a strange island, like a poor man; and when his child was born he must be shamed for lack of gifts. It was in vain his wife dissuaded him. He returned to his father in Manu'a seeking help; and with what he could get he set off in the night to re-embark. Now his wives heard of his coming; they were incensed that he did not stay to visit them; and on the beach, by his canoe, intercepted and slew him. Now the third wife lay asleep in Savaii;—her babe was born and slept by her side; and she was awakened by the spirit of her husband. 'Get up,' he said, 'my father is sick in Manu'a and we must go to visit him.' 'It is well,' said she; 'take you the child, while I carry its mats.' 'I cannot carry the child,' said the spirit; 'I am too cold from the sea.' When they were got on board the canoe the wife smelt carrion. 'How is this?' she said. 'What have you in the canoe that I should smell carrion?' 'It is nothing in the canoe,' said the spirit. 'It is the land-wind blowing down the mountains, where some beast lies dead.' It appears it was still night when they reached Manu'a—the swiftest passage on record—and as they entered the reef the bale-fires burned in the village. Again she asked him to carry the child; but now he need no more dissemble. 'I cannot carry your child,' said he, 'for I am dead, and the fires you see are burning for my funeral.'

The curious may learn in Dr. Sierich's book the unexpected sequel of the tale. Here is enough for my purpose. Though the man was but new dead, the ghost was already putrefied, as though putrefaction were the mark and of the essence of a spirit. The vigil on the Paumotuan grave does not extend beyond two weeks, and they told me this period was thought to coincide with that of the resolution of the body. The ghost always marked with decay—the danger seemingly ending with the process of dissolution—here is tempting matter for the theorist. But it will not do. The lady of the flowers had been long dead, and her spirit was still supposed to bear the brand of perishability. The Resident had been more than a fortnight buried, and his vampire was still supposed to go the rounds.

Of the lost state of the dead, from the lurid Mangaian legend, in which infernal deities hocus and destroy the souls of all, to the various submarine and aerial limbos where the dead feast, float idle, or resume the occupations of their life on earth, it would be wearisome to tell. One story I give, for it is singular in itself, is well-known in Tahiti, and has this of interest, that it is post-Christian, dating indeed from but a few years back. A princess of the reigning house died; was transported to the neighbouring isle of Raiatea; fell there under the empire of a spirit who condemned her to climb coco-palms all day and bring him the nuts; was found after some time in this miserable servitude by a second spirit, one of her own house; and by him, upon her lamentations, reconveyed to Tahiti, where she found her body still waked, but already swollen with the approaches of corruption. It is a lively point in the tale that, on the sight of this dishonoured tabernacle, the princess prayed she might continue to be numbered with the dead. But it seems it was too late, her spirit was replaced by the least dignified of entrances, and her startled family beheld the body move. The seemingly purgatorial labours, the helpful kindred spirit, and the horror of the princess at the sight of her tainted body, are all points to be remarked.

The truth is, the tales are not necessarily consistent in themselves; and they are further darkened for the stranger by an ambiguity of language. Ghosts, vampires, spirits, and gods are all confounded. And yet I seem to perceive that (with exceptions) those whom we would count gods were less maleficent. Permanent spirits haunt and do murder in corners of Samoa; but those legitimate gods of Upolu and Savaii, whose wars and cricketings of late convulsed society, I did not gather to be dreaded, or not with a like fear. The spirit of Aana that ate souls is certainly a fearsome inmate; but the high gods, even of the archipelago, seem helpful. Mahinui—from whom our convict-catechist had been named—the spirit of the sea, like a Proteus endowed with endless avatars, came to the assistance of the shipwrecked and carried them ashore in the guise of a ray fish. The same divinity bore priests from isle to isle about the archipelago, and by his aid, within the century, persons have been seen to fly. The tutelar deity of each isle is likewise helpful, and by a particular form of wedge-shaped cloud on the horizon announces the coming of a ship.

To one who conceives of these atolls, so narrow, so barren, so beset with sea, here would seem a superfluity of ghostly denizens. And yet there are more. In the various brackish pools and ponds, beautiful women with long red hair are seen to rise and bathe; only (timid as mice) on the first sound of feet upon the coral they dive again for ever. They are known to be healthy and harmless living people, dwellers of an underworld; and the same fancy is current in Tahiti, where also they have the hair red. Tetea is the Tahitian name; the Paumotuan, Mokurea.

PART III: THE GILBERTS

CHAPTER I—BUTARITARI

At Honolulu we had said farewell to the Casco and to Captain Otis, and our next adventure was made in changed conditions. Passage was taken for myself, my wife, Mr. Osbourne, and my China boy, Ah Fu, on a pigmy trading schooner, the Equator, Captain Dennis Reid; and on a certain bright June day in 1889, adorned in the Hawaiian fashion with the garlands of departure, we drew out of port and bore with a fair wind for Micronesia.

The whole extent of the South Seas is a desert of ships; more especially that part where we were now to sail. No post runs in these islands; communication is by accident; where you may have designed to go is one thing, where you shall be able to arrive another. It was my hope, for instance, to have reached the Carolines, and returned to the light of day by way of Manila and the China ports; and it was in Samoa that we were destined to re-appear and be once more refreshed with the sight of mountains. Since the sunset faded from the peaks of Oahu six months had intervened, and we had seen no spot of earth so high as an ordinary cottage. Our path had been still on the flat sea, our dwellings upon unerected coral, our diet from the pickle-tub or out of tins; I had learned to welcome shark's flesh for a variety; and a mountain, an onion, an Irish potato or a beef-steak, had been long lost to sense and dear to aspiration.

The two chief places of our stay, Butaritari and Apemama, lie near the line; the latter within thirty miles. Both enjoy a superb ocean climate, days of blinding sun and bracing wind, nights of a heavenly brightness. Both are somewhat wider than Fakarava, measuring perhaps (at the widest) a quarter of a mile from beach to beach. In both, a coarse kind of taro thrives; its culture is a chief business of the natives, and the consequent mounds and ditches make miniature scenery and amuse the eye. In all else they show the customary features of an atoll: the low horizon, the expanse of the lagoon, the sedge-like rim of palm-tops, the sameness and smallness of the land, the hugely superior size and interest of sea and sky. Life on such islands is in many points like life on shipboard. The atoll, like the ship, is soon taken for granted; and the islanders, like the ship's crew, become soon the centre of attention. The isles are populous, independent, seats of kinglets, recently civilised, little visited. In the last decade many changes have crept in; women no longer go unclothed till marriage; the widow no longer sleeps at night and goes abroad by day with the skull of her dead husband; and, fire-arms being introduced, the spear and the shark-tooth sword are sold for curiosities. Ten years ago all these things and practices were to be seen in use; yet ten years more, and the old society will have entirely vanished. We came in a happy moment to see its institutions still erect and (in Apemama) scarce decayed.

Populous and independent—warrens of men, ruled over with some rustic pomp—such was the first and still the recurring impression of these tiny lands. As we stood across the lagoon for the town of Butaritari, a stretch of the low shore was seen to be crowded with the brown roofs of houses; those of the palace and king's summer parlour (which are of corrugated iron) glittered near one end conspicuously bright; the royal colours flew hard by on a tall flagstaff; in front, on an artificial islet, the gaol played the part of a martello. Even upon this first and distant view, the place had scarce the air of what it truly was, a village; rather of that which it was also, a petty metropolis, a city rustic and yet royal.

The lagoon is shoal. The tide being out, we waded for some quarter of a mile in tepid shallows, and stepped ashore at last into a flagrant stagnancy of sun and heat. The lee side of a line island after noon is indeed a breathless place; on the ocean beach the trade will be still blowing, boisterous and cool; out in the lagoon it will be blowing also, speeding the canoes; but the screen of bush completely intercepts it from the shore, and sleep and silence and companies of mosquitoes brood upon the towns.

We may thus be said to have taken Butaritari by surprise. A few inhabitants were still abroad in the north end, at which we landed. As we advanced, we were soon done with encounter, and seemed to explore a city of the dead. Only, between the posts of open houses, we could see the townsfolk stretched in the siesta, sometimes a family together veiled in a mosquito-net, sometimes a single sleeper on a platform like a corpse on a bier.

The houses were of all dimensions, from those of toys to those of churches. Some might hold a battalion, some were so minute they could scarce receive a pair of lovers; only in the playroom, when the toys are mingled, do we meet such incongruities of scale. Many were open sheds; some took the form of roofed stages; others were walled and the walls pierced with little windows. A few were perched on piles in the lagoon; the rest stood at random on a green, through which the roadway made a ribbon of sand, or along the embankments of a sheet of water like a shallow dock. One and all were the creatures of a single tree; palm-tree wood and palm-tree leaf their materials; no nail had been driven, no hammer sounded, in their building, and they were held together by lashings of palm-tree sinnet.

In the midst of the thoroughfare, the church stands like an island, a lofty and dim house with rows of windows; a rich tracery of framing sustains the roof; and through the door at either end the street shows in a vista. The proportions of the place, in such surroundings, and built of such materials, appeared august; and we threaded the nave with a sentiment befitting visitors in a cathedral. Benches run along either side. In the midst, on a crazy dais, two chairs stand ready for the king and queen when they shall choose to worship; over their heads a hoop, apparently from a hogshead, depends by a strip of red cotton; and the hoop (which hangs askew) is dressed with streamers of the same material, red and white.

This was our first advertisement of the royal dignity, and presently we stood before its seat and centre. The palace is built of imported wood upon a European plan; the roof of corrugated iron, the yard enclosed with walls, the gate surmounted by a sort of lych-house. It cannot be called spacious; a labourer in the States is sometimes more commodiously lodged; but when we had the chance to see it within, we found it was enriched (beyond all island expectation) with coloured advertisements and cuts from the illustrated papers. Even before the gate some of the treasures of the crown stand public: a bell of a good magnitude, two pieces of cannon, and a single shell. The bell cannot be rung nor the guns fired; they are curiosities, proofs of wealth, a part of the parade of the royalty, and stand to be admired like statues in a square. A straight gut of water like a canal runs almost to the palace door; the containing quay-walls excellently built of coral; over against the mouth, by what seems an effect of landscape art, the martello-like islet of the gaol breaks the lagoon. Vassal chiefs with tribute, neighbour monarchs come a-roving, might here sail in, view with surprise these extensive public works, and be awed by these mouths of silent cannon. It was impossible to see the place and not to fancy it designed for pageantry. But the elaborate theatre then stood empty; the royal house deserted, its doors and windows gaping; the whole quarter of the town immersed in silence. On the opposite bank of the canal, on a roofed stage, an ancient gentleman slept publicly, sole visible inhabitant; and beyond on the lagoon a canoe spread a striped lateen, the sole thing moving.

The canal is formed on the south by a pier or causeway with a parapet. At the far end the parapet stops, and the quay expands into an oblong peninsula in the lagoon, the breathing-place and summer parlour of the king. The midst is occupied by an open house or permanent marquee—called here a maniapa, or, as the word is now pronounced, a maniap'—at the lowest estimation forty feet by sixty. The iron roof, lofty but exceedingly low-browed, so that a woman must stoop to enter, is supported externally on pillars of coral, within by a frame of wood. The floor is of broken coral, divided in aisles by the uprights of the frame; the house far enough from shore to catch the breeze, which enters freely and disperses the mosquitoes; and under the low eaves the sun is seen to glitter and the waves to dance on the lagoon.

It was now some while since we had met any but slumberers; and when we had wandered down the pier and stumbled at last into this bright shed, we were surprised to find it occupied by a society of wakeful people, some twenty souls in all, the court and guardsmen of Butaritari. The court ladies were busy making mats; the guardsmen yawned and sprawled. Half a dozen rifles lay on a rock and a cutlass was leaned against a pillar: the armoury of these drowsy musketeers. At the far end, a little closed house of wood displayed some tinsel curtains, and proved, upon examination, to be a privy on the

European model. In front of this, upon some mats, lolled Tebureimoa, the king; behind him, on the panels of the house, two crossed rifles represented fasces. He wore pyjamas which sorrowfully misbecame his bulk; his nose was hooked and cruel, his body overcome with sodden corpulence, his eye timorous and dull: he seemed at once oppressed with drowsiness and held awake by apprehension: a pepper rajah muddled with opium, and listening for the march of a Dutch army, looks perhaps not otherwise. We were to grow better acquainted, and first and last I had the same impression; he seemed always drowsy, yet always to hearken and start; and, whether from remorse or fear, there is no doubt he seeks a refuge in the abuse of drugs.

The rajah displayed no sign of interest in our coming. But the queen, who sat beside him in a purple sacque, was more accessible; and there was present an interpreter so willing that his volubility became at last the cause of our departure. He had greeted us upon our entrance:—'That is the honourable King, and I am his interpreter,' he had said, with more stateliness than truth. For he held no appointment in the court, seemed extremely ill-acquainted with the island language, and was present, like ourselves, upon a visit of civility. Mr. Williams was his name: an American darkey, runaway ship's cook, and bar-keeper at The Land we Live in tavern, Butaritari. I never knew a man who had more words in his command or less truth to communicate; neither the gloom of the monarch, nor my own efforts to be distant, could in the least abash him; and when the scene closed, the darkey was left talking.

The town still slumbered, or had but just begun to turn and stretch itself; it was still plunged in heat and silence. So much the more vivid was the impression that we carried away of the house upon the islet, the Micronesian Saul wakeful amid his guards, and his unmelodious David, Mr. Williams, chattering through the drowsy hours.

CHAPTER II—THE FOUR BROTHERS

The kingdom of Tebureimoa includes two islands, Great and Little Makin; some two thousand subjects pay him tribute, and two semi-independent chieftains do him qualified homage. The importance of the office is measured by the man; he may be a nobody, he may be absolute; and both extremes have been exemplified within the memory of residents.

On the death of king Tetimararoa, Tebureimoa's father, Nakaeia, the eldest son, succeeded. He was a fellow of huge physical strength, masterful, violent, with a certain barbaric thrift and some intelligence of men and business. Alone in his islands, it was he who dealt and profited; he was the planter and the merchant; and his subjects toiled for his behoof in servitude. When they wrought long and well their taskmaster declared a holiday, and supplied and shared a general debauch. The scale of his providing was at times magnificent; six hundred dollars' worth of gin and brandy was set forth at once; the narrow land resounded with the noise of revelry: and it was a common thing to see the subjects (staggering themselves) parade their drunken sovereign on the fore-hatch of a wrecked vessel, king and commons howling and singing as they went. At a word from Nakaeia's mouth the revel ended; Makin became once more an isle of slaves and of teetotalers; and on the morrow all the population must be on the roads or in the taro-patches toiling under his bloodshot eye.

The fear of Nakaeia filled the land. No regularity of justice was affected; there was no trial, there were no officers of the law; it seems there was but one penalty, the capital; and daylight assault and midnight murder were the forms of process. The king himself would play the executioner: and his blows were dealt by stealth, and with the help and countenance of none but his own wives. These were his oarswomen; one that caught a crab, he slew incontinently with the tiller; thus disciplined, they pulled him by night to the scene of his vengeance, which he would then execute alone and return well-pleased with his connubial crew. The inmates of the harem held a station hard for us to conceive. Beasts of draught, and driven by the fear of death, they were yet implicitly trusted with their sovereign's life; they were still wives and queens, and it was supposed that no man should behold their faces. They killed by the sight like basilisks; a chance view of one of those boatwomen was a crime to be wiped out with blood. In the days of Nakaeia the palace was beset with some tall coco-palms which commanded the enclosure. It chanced one evening, while Nakaeia sat below at supper with his wives, that the owner of the grove was in a tree-top drawing palm-tree wine; it chanced that he looked down, and the king at the same moment looking up, their eyes encountered. Instant flight preserved the involuntary criminal. But during the remainder of that reign he must lurk and be hid by friends in remote parts of the isle; Nakaeia hunted him without remission, although still in vain; and the palms, accessories to the fact, were ruthlessly cut down. Such was the ideal of wifely purity in an isle where nubile virgins went naked as in paradise. And yet scandal found its way into Nakaeia's well-guarded harem. He was at that time the owner of a schooner, which he used for a pleasure-house, lodging on board as she lay anchored; and thither one day he summoned a new wife. She was one that had been sealed to him; that is to say (I presume), that he was married to her sister, for the husband of an elder sister has the call of the cadets. She would be arrayed for the occasion; she would come scented, garlanded, decked with fine mats and family jewels, for marriage, as her friends supposed; for death, as she well knew. 'Tell me the man's name, and I will spare you,' said Nakaeia. But the girl was staunch; she held her peace, saved her lover and the queens strangled her between the mats.

Nakaeia was feared; it does not appear that he was hated. Deeds that smell to us of murder wore to his subjects the reverend face of justice; his orgies made him popular; natives to this day recall with respect the firmness of his government; and even the whites, whom he long opposed and kept at arm's-length, give him the name (in the canonical South Sea phrase) of 'a perfect gentleman when sober.'

When he came to lie, without issue, on the bed of death, he summoned his next brother, Nanteitei, made him a discourse on royal policy, and warned him he was too weak to reign. The warning was taken to heart, and for some while the government moved on the model of Nakaeia's. Nanteitei dispensed with guards, and walked abroad alone with a revolver in a leather mail-bag. To conceal his weakness he affected a rude silence; you might talk to him all day; advice, reproof, appeal, and menace alike remained unanswered.

The number of his wives was seventeen, many of them heiresses; for the royal house is poor, and marriage was in these days a chief means of buttressing the throne. Nakaeia kept his harem busy for himself; Nanteitei hired it out to others. In his days, for instance, Messrs. Wightman built a pier with a verandah at the north end of the town. The masonry was the work of the seventeen queens, who toiled and waded there like fisher lasses; but the man who was to do the roofing durst not begin till they had finished, lest by chance he should look down and see them.

It was perhaps the last appearance of the harem gang. For some time already Hawaiian missionaries had been seated at Butaritari—Maka and Kanoa, two brave childlike men. Nakaeia would none of their doctrine; he was perhaps jealous of their presence; being human, he had some affection for their persons. In the house, before the eyes of Kanoa, he slew with his own hand three sailors of Oahu, crouching on their backs to knife them, and menacing the missionary if he interfered; yet he not only spared him at the moment, but recalled him afterwards (when he had fled) with some expressions of respect. Nanteitei, the weaker man, fell more completely under the spell. Maka, a light-hearted, lovable, yet in his own trade very rigorous man, gained and improved an influence on the king which soon grew paramount. Nanteitei, with the royal house, was publicly converted; and, with a severity which liberal missionaries disavow, the harem was at once reduced. It was a compendious act. The throne was thus impoverished, its influence shaken, the queen's relatives mortified, and sixteen chief women (some of great possessions) cast in a body on the market. I have been shipmates with a Hawaiian sailor who was successively married to two of these impromptu widows, and successively divorced by both for misconduct. That two great and rich ladies (for both of these were rich) should have married 'a man from another island' marks the dissolution of society. The laws besides were wholly remodelled, not always for the better. I love Maka as a man; as a legislator he has two defects: weak in the punishment of crime, stern to repress innocent pleasures.

War and revolution are the common successors of reform; yet Nanteitei died (of an overdose of chloroform), in quiet possession of the throne, and it was in the reign of the third brother, Nabakatokia, a man brave in body and feeble of character, that the storm burst. The rule of the high chiefs and notables seems to have always underlain and perhaps alternated with monarchy. The Old Men (as they were called) have a right to sit with the king in the Speak House and debate: and the king's chief superiority is a form of closure—'The Speaking is over.' After the long monocracy of Nakaeia and the changes of Nanteitei, the Old Men were doubtless grown impatient of obscurity, and they were beyond question jealous of the influence of Maka. Calumny, or rather caricature, was called in use; a spoken cartoon ran round society; Maka was reported to have said in church that the king was the first man in the island and himself the second; and, stung by the supposed affront, the chiefs broke into rebellion and armed gatherings. In the space of one forenoon the throne of Nakaeia was humbled in the dust. The king sat in the maniap' before the palace gate expecting his recruits; Maka by his side, both anxious men; and meanwhile, in the door of a house at the north entry of the town, a chief had taken post and diverted the succours as they came. They came singly or in groups, each with his gun or pistol slung about his neck. 'Where are you going?' asked the chief. 'The king called us,' they would reply. 'Here is your place. Sit down,' returned the chief. With incredible disloyalty, all obeyed; and sufficient force being thus got together from both sides, Nabakatokia was summoned and surrendered. About this period, in almost every part of the group, the kings were murdered; and on Tapituea, the skeleton of the last hangs to this day in the chief Speak House of the isle, a menace to ambition. Nabakatokia was more fortunate; his life and the royal style were spared to him, but he was stripped of power. The Old Men enjoyed a festival of public speaking; the laws were continually changed, never enforced; the commons had an opportunity to regret the merits of Nakaeia; and the king, denied the resource of rich marriages and the service of a troop of wives, fell not only in disconsideration but in debt.

He died some months before my arrival on the islands, and no one regretted him; rather all looked hopefully to his successor. This was by repute the hero of the family. Alone of the four brothers, he had issue, a grown son, Natiata, and a daughter three years old; it was to him, in the hour of the revolution, that Nabakatokia turned too late for help; and in earlier days he had been the right hand of the vigorous Nakaeia. Nontemat', Mr. Corpse, was his appalling nickname, and he had earned it well. Again and again, at the command of Nakaeia, he had surrounded houses in the dead of night, cut down the mosquito bars and butchered families. Here was the hand of iron; here was Nakaeia redux. He came, summoned from the tributary rule of Little Makin: he was installed, he proved a puppet and a trembler, the unwieldy shuttlecock of orators; and the reader has seen the remains of him in his summer parlour under the name of Tebureimoa.

The change in the man's character was much commented on in the island, and variously explained by opium and Christianity. To my eyes, there seemed no change at all, rather an extreme consistency. Mr. Corpse was afraid of his brother: King Tebureimoa is afraid of the Old Men. Terror of the first nerved him for deeds of desperation; fear of the second disables him for the least act of government. He played his part of bravo in the past, following the line of least resistance, butchering others in his own defence: to-day, grown elderly and heavy, a convert, a reader of the Bible, perhaps a penitent, conscious at least of accumulated hatreds, and his memory charged with images of violence and blood, he capitulates to the Old Men, fuddles himself with opium, and sits among his guards in dreadful expectation. The same cowardice that put into his hand the knife of the assassin deprives him of the sceptre of a king.

A tale that I was told, a trifling incident that fell in my observation, depicts him in his two capacities. A chief in Little Makin asked, in an hour of lightness, 'Who is Kaeia?' A bird carried the saying; and Nakaeia placed the matter in the hands of a committee of three. Mr. Corpse was chairman; the second commissioner died before my arrival; the third was yet alive and green, and presented so venerable an appearance that we gave him the name of Abou ben Adhem. Mr. Corpse was troubled with a scruple; the man from Little Makin was his adopted brother; in such a case it was not very delicate to appear at all, to strike the blow (which it seems was otherwise expected of him) would be worse than awkward. 'I will strike the blow,' said the venerable Abou; and Mr. Corpse (surely with a sigh) accepted the compromise. The quarry was decoyed into the bush; he was set to carrying a log; and while his arms were raised Abou ripped up his belly at a blow. Justice being thus done, the commission, in a childish horror, turned to flee. But their victim recalled them to his side. 'You need not run away now,' he said. 'You have done this thing to me. Stay.' He was some twenty minutes dying, and his murderers sat with him the while: a scene for Shakespeare. All the stages of a violent death, the blood, the failing voice, the decomposing features, the changed hue, are thus present in the memory of Mr. Corpse; and since he studied them in the brother he betrayed, he has some reason to reflect on the possibilities of treachery. I was never more sure of anything than the tragic quality of the king's thoughts; and yet I had but the one sight of him at unawares. I had once an errand for his ear. It was once more the hour of the siesta; but there were loiterers abroad, and these directed us to a closed house on the bank of the canal where Tebureimoa lay unguarded. We entered without ceremony, being in some haste. He lay on the floor upon a bed of mats, reading in his Gilbert Island Bible with compunction. On our sudden entrance the unwieldy man reared himself half-sitting so that the Bible rolled on the floor, stared on us a moment with blank eyes, and, having recognised his visitors, sank again upon the mats. So Eglon looked on Ehud.

The justice of facts is strange, and strangely just; Nakaeia, the author of these deeds, died at peace discoursing on the craft of kings; his tool suffers daily death for his enforced complicity. Not the nature, but the congruity of men's deeds and circumstances damn and save them; and Tebureimoa from the first has been incongruously placed. At home, in a quiet bystreet of a village, the man had been a worthy carpenter, and, even bedevilled as he is, he shows some private virtues. He has no lands, only the use of such as are impignorate for fines; he cannot enrich himself in the old way by marriages; thrift is the chief pillar of his future, and he knows and uses it. Eleven foreign traders pay him a patent of a hundred dollars, some two thousand subjects pay capitation at the rate of a dollar for a man, half a dollar for a woman, and a shilling for a child: allowing for the exchange, perhaps a total of three hundred pounds a year. He had been some nine months on the throne: had bought his wife a silk dress and hat, figure unknown, and himself a uniform at three hundred dollars; had sent his brother's photograph to be enlarged in San Francisco at two hundred and fifty dollars; had greatly reduced that brother's legacy of debt and had still sovereigns in his pocket. An affectionate brother, a good economist; he was besides a handy carpenter, and cobbled occasionally on the woodwork of the palace. It is not wonderful that Mr. Corpse has virtues; that Tebureimoa should have a diversion filled me with surprise.

CHAPTER III—AROUND OUR HOUSE

When we left the palace we were still but seafarers ashore; and within the hour we had installed our goods in one of the six foreign houses of Butaritari, namely, that usually occupied by Maka, the Hawaiian missionary. Two San Francisco firms are here established, Messrs. Crawford and Messrs. Wightman Brothers; the first hard by the palace of the mid town, the second at the north entry; each with a store and bar-room. Our house was in the Wightman compound, betwixt the store and bar, within a fenced enclosure. Across the road a few native houses nestled in the margin of the bush, and the green wall of palms rose solid, shutting out the breeze. A little sandy cove of the lagoon ran in behind, sheltered by a verandah pier, the labour of queens' hands. Here, when the tide was high, sailed boats lay to be loaded; when the tide was low, the boats took ground some half a mile away, and an endless series of natives descended the pier stair, tailed across the sand in strings and clusters, waded to the waist with the bags of copra, and loitered backward to renew their charge. The mystery of the copra trade tormented me, as I sat and watched the profits drip on the stair and the sands.

In front, from shortly after four in the morning until nine at night, the folk of the town streamed by us intermittingly along the road: families going up the island to make copra on their lands; women bound for the bush to gather flowers against the evening toilet; and, twice a day, the toddy-cutters, each with his knife and shell. In the first grey of the morning, and again late in the afternoon, these would straggle past about their tree-top business, strike off here and there into the bush, and vanish from the face of the earth. At about the same hour, if the tide be low in the lagoon, you are likely to be bound yourself across the island for a bath, and may enter close at their heels alleys of the palm wood. Right in front, although the sun is not yet risen, the east is already lighted with preparatory fires, and the huge accumulations of the trade-wind cloud glow with and heliograph the coming day. The breeze is in your face; overhead in the tops of the palms, its playthings, it maintains a lively bustle; look where you will, above or below, there is no human presence, only the earth and shaken forest. And right overhead the song of an invisible singer breaks from the thick leaves; from farther on a second tree-top answers;

and beyond again, in the bosom of the woods, a still more distant minstrel perches and sways and sings. So, all round the isle, the toddy-cutters sit on high, and are rocked by the trade, and have a view far to seaward, where they keep watch for sails, and like huge birds utter their songs in the morning. They sing with a certain lustiness and Bacchic glee; the volume of sound and the articulate melody fall unexpected from the tree-top, whence we anticipate the chattering of fowls. And yet in a sense these songs also are but chatter; the words are ancient, obsolete, and sacred; few comprehend them, perhaps no one perfectly; but it was understood the cutters 'prayed to have good toddy, and sang of their old wars.' The prayer is at least answered; and when the foaming shell is brought to your door, you have a beverage well 'worthy of a grace.' All forenoon you may return and taste; it only sparkles, and sharpens, and grows to be a new drink, not less delicious; but with the progress of the day the fermentation quickens and grows acid; in twelve hours it will be yeast for bread, in two days more a devilish intoxicant, the counsellor of crime.

The men are of a marked Arabian cast of features, often bearded and mustached, often gaily dressed, some with bracelets and anklets, all stalking hidalgo-like, and accepting salutations with a haughty lip. The hair (with the dandies of either sex) is worn turban-wise in a frizzled bush; and like the daggers of the Japanese a pointed stick (used for a comb) is thrust gallantly among the curls. The women from this bush of hair look forth enticingly: the race cannot be compared with the Tahitian for female beauty; I doubt even if the average be high; but some of the prettiest girls, and one of the handsomest women I ever saw, were Gilbertines. Butaritari, being the commercial centre of the group, is Europeanised; the coloured sacque or the white shift are common wear, the latter for the evening; the trade hat, loaded with flowers, fruit, and ribbons, is unfortunately not unknown; and the characteristic female dress of the Gilberts no longer universal. The ridi is its name: a cutty petticoat or fringe of the smoked fibre of cocoa-nut leaf, not unlike tarry string: the lower edge not reaching the mid-thigh, the upper adjusted so low upon the haunches that it seems to cling by accident. A sneeze, you think, and the lady must surely be left destitute. 'The perilous, hairbreadth ridi' was our word for it; and in the conflict that rages over women's dress it has the misfortune to please neither side, the prudish condemning it as insufficient, the more frivolous finding it unlovely in itself. Yet if a pretty Gilbertine would look her best, that must be her costume. In that and naked otherwise, she moves with an incomparable liberty and grace and life, that marks the poetry of Micronesia. Bundle her in a gown, the charm is fled, and she wriggles like an Englishwoman.

Towards dusk the passers-by became more gorgeous. The men broke out in all the colours of the rainbow—or at least of the trade-room,—and both men and women began to be adorned and scented with new flowers. A small white blossom is the favourite, sometimes sown singly in a woman's hair like little stars, now composed in a thick wreath. With the night, the crowd sometimes thickened in the road, and the padding and brushing of bare feet became continuous; the promenades mostly grave, the silence only interrupted by some giggling and scampering of girls; even the children quiet. At nine, bed-time struck on a bell from the cathedral, and the life of the town ceased. At four the next morning the signal is repeated in the darkness, and the innocent prisoners set free; but for seven hours all must lie—I was about to say within doors, of a place where doors, and even walls, are an exception—housed, at least, under their airy roofs and clustered in the tents of the mosquito-nets. Suppose a necessary errand to occur, suppose it imperative to send abroad, the messenger must then go openly, advertising himself to the police with a huge brand of cocoa-nut, which flares from house to house like a moving bonfire. Only the police themselves go darkling, and grope in the night for misdemeanants. I used to hate their treacherous presence; their captain in particular, a crafty old man in white, lurked nightly about my premises till I could have found it in my heart to beat him. But the rogue was privileged.

Not one of the eleven resident traders came to town, no captain cast anchor in the lagoon, but we saw him ere the hour was out. This was owing to our position between the store and the bar—the Sans Souci, as the last was called. Mr. Rick was not only Messrs. Wightman's manager, but consular agent for the States; Mrs. Rick was the only white woman on the island, and one of the only two in the archipelago; their house besides, with its cool verandahs, its bookshelves, its comfortable furniture, could not be rivalled nearer than Jaluit or Honolulu. Every one called in consequence, save such as might be prosecuting a South Sea quarrel, hingeing on the price of copra and the odd cent, or perhaps a difference about poultry. Even these, if they did not appear upon the north, would be presently visible to the southward, the Sans Souci drawing them as with cords. In an island with a total population of twelve white persons, one of the two drinking-shops might seem superfluous: but every bullet has its billet, and the double accommodation of Butaritari is found in practice highly convenient by the captains and the crews of ships: The Land we Live in being tacitly resigned to the forecastle, the Sans Souci tacitly reserved for the afterguard. So aristocratic were my habits, so commanding was my fear of Mr. Williams, that I have never visited the first; but in the other, which was the club or rather the casino of the island, I regularly passed my evenings. It was small, but neatly fitted, and at night (when the lamp was lit) sparkled with glass and glowed with coloured pictures like a theatre at Christmas. The pictures were advertisements, the glass coarse enough, the carpentry amateur; but the effect, in that incongruous isle, was of unbridled luxury and inestimable expense. Here songs were sung, tales told, tricks performed, games played. The Ricks, ourselves, Norwegian Tom the bar-keeper, a captain or two from the ships, and perhaps three or four traders come down the island in their boats or by the road on foot, made up the usual company. The traders, all bred to the sea, take a humorous pride in their new business; 'South Sea Merchants' is the title they prefer. 'We are all sailors here'—'Merchants, if you please'—'South Sea Merchants,'—was a piece of conversation endlessly repeated, that never seemed to lose in savour. We found them at all times simple, genial, gay, gallant, and obliging; and, across some interval of time, recall with pleasure the traders of Butaritari. There was one black sheep indeed. I tell of him here where he lived, against my rule; for in this case I have no measure to preserve, and the man is typical of a class of ruffians that once disgraced the whole field of the South Seas, and still linger in the rarely visited isles of Micronesia. He had the name on the beach of 'a perfect gentleman when sober,' but I never saw him otherwise than drunk. The few shocking and savage traits of the Micronesian he has singled out with the skill of a collector, and planted in the soil of his original baseness. He has been accused and acquitted of a treacherous murder; and has since boastfully owned it, which inclines me to suppose him innocent. His daughter is defaced by his erroneous cruelty, for it was his wife he had intended to disfigure, and in the darkness of the night and the frenzy of coco-brandy, fastened on the wrong victim. The wife has since fled and harbours in the bush with natives; and the husband still demands from deaf ears her forcible restoration. The best of his business is to make natives drink, and then advance the money for the fine upon a lucrative mortgage. 'Respect for whites' is the man's word: 'What is the matter with this island is the want of respect for whites.' On his way to Butaritari, while I was there, he spied his wife in the bush with certain natives and made a dash to capture her; whereupon one of her companions drew a knife and the husband retreated: 'Do you call that proper respect for whites?' he cried. At an early stage of the acquaintance we proved our respect for his kind of white by forbidding him our enclosure under pain of death. Thenceforth he lingered often in the neighbourhood with I knew not what sense of envy or design of mischief; his white, handsome face (which I beheld with loathing) looked in upon us at all hours across the fence; and once, from a safe distance, he avenged himself by shouting a recondite island insult, to us quite inoffensive, on his English lips incredibly incongruous.

Our enclosure, round which this composite of degradations wandered, was of some extent. In one corner was a trellis with a long table of rough boards. Here the Fourth of July feast had been held not long before with memorable consequences, yet to be set forth; here we took our meals; here entertained to a dinner the king and notables of Makin. In the midst was the house, with a verandah front and back, and three is rooms within. In the verandah we slung our man-of-war hammocks, worked there by day, and slept at night. Within were beds, chairs, a round table, a fine hanging lamp, and portraits of the royal family of Hawaii. Queen Victoria proves nothing; Kalakaua and Mrs. Bishop are diagnostic; and the truth is we were the stealthy tenants of the parsonage. On the day of our arrival Maka was away; faithless trustees unlocked his doors; and the dear rigorous man, the sworn foe of liquor and tobacco, returned to find his verandah littered with cigarettes and his parlour horrible with bottles. He made but one condition—on the round table, which he used in the celebration of the sacraments, he begged us to refrain from setting liquor; in all else he bowed to the accomplished fact, refused rent, retired across the way into a native house, and, plying in his boat, beat the remotest quarters of the isle for provender. He found us pigs—I could not fancy where—no other pigs were visible; he brought us fowls and taro; when we gave our feast to the monarch and gentry, it was he who supplied the wherewithal, he who superintended the cooking, he who asked grace at table, and when the king's health was proposed, he also started the cheering with an English hip-hip-hip. There was never a more fortunate conception; the heart of the fatted king exulted in his bosom at the sound.

Take him for all in all, I have never known a more engaging creature than this parson of Butaritari: his mirth, his kindness, his noble, friendly feelings, brimmed from the man in speech and gesture. He loved to exaggerate, to act and overact the momentary part, to exercise his lungs and muscles, and to speak and laugh with his whole body. He had the morning cheerfulness of birds and healthy children; and his humour was infectious. We were next neighbours and met daily, yet our salutations lasted minutes at a stretch—shaking hands, slapping shoulders, capering like a pair of Merry-Andrews, laughing to split our sides upon some pleasantry that would scarce raise a titter in an infant-school. It might be five in the morning, the toddy-cutters just gone by, the road empty, the shade of the island lying far on the lagoon: and the ebullition cheered me for the day.

Yet I always suspected Maka of a secret melancholy—these jubilant extremes could scarce be constantly maintained. He was besides long, and lean, and lined, and corded, and a trifle grizzled; and his Sabbath countenance was even saturnine. On that day we made a procession to the church, or (as I must always call it) the cathedral: Maka (a blot on the hot landscape) in tall hat, black frock-coat, black trousers; under his arm the hymn-book and the Bible; in his face, a reverent gravity:—beside him Mary his wife, a quiet, wise, and handsome elderly lady, seriously attired:—myself following with singular and moving thoughts. Long before, to the sound of bells and streams and birds, through a green Lothian glen, I had accompanied Sunday by Sunday a minister in whose house I lodged; and the likeness, and the difference, and the series of years and deaths, profoundly touched me. In the great, dusky, palm-tree cathedral the congregation rarely numbered thirty: the men on one side, the women on the other, myself posted (for a privilege) amongst the women, and the small missionary contingent gathered close around the platform, we were lost in that round vault. The lessons were read antiphonally, the flock was catechised, a blind youth repeated weekly a long string of psalms, hymns were sung—I never heard worse singing,—and the sermon followed. To say I understood nothing were untrue; there were points that I learned to expect with certainty; the name of Honolulu, that of Kalakaua, the word Cap'n-man-o'-wa', the word ship, and a description of a storm at sea, infallibly occurred; and I was not seldom rewarded with the name of my own Sovereign in the bargain. The rest was but sound to the ears, silence for the mind: a plain expanse of tedium, rendered unbearable by heat, a hard chair, and the sight through the wide doors of the more happy heathen on the green. Sleep breathed on my joints and eyelids, sleep hummed in my ears; it reigned in the dim cathedral. The congregation stirred and stretched; they moaned, they groaned aloud; they yawned upon a singing note, as you may sometimes hear a dog when he has reached the tragic bitterest of boredom. In vain the preacher thumped the table; in vain he singled and addressed by name particular hearers. I was myself perhaps a more effective excitant; and at least to one old gentleman the spectacle of my successful struggles against sleep—and I hope they were successful—cheered the flight of time. He, when he was not catching flies or playing tricks upon his neighbours, gloated with a fixed, truculent eye upon the stages of my agony; and once, when the service was drawing towards a close, he winked at me across the church.

I write of the service with a smile; yet I was always there—always with respect for Maka, always with admiration for his deep seriousness, his burning energy, the fire of his roused eye, the sincere and various accents of his voice. To see him weekly flogging a dead horse and blowing a cold fire was a lesson in fortitude and constancy. It may be a question whether if the mission were fully supported, and he was set free from business avocations, more might not result; I think otherwise myself; I think not neglect but rigour has reduced his flock, that rigour which has once provoked a revolution, and which to-day, in a man so lively and engaging, amazes the beholder. No song, no dance, no tobacco, no liquor, no alleviative of life—only toil and church-going; so says a voice from his face; and the face is the face of the Polynesian Esau, but the voice is the voice of a Jacob from a different world. And a Polynesian at the best makes a singular missionary in the Gilberts, coming from a country recklessly unchaste to one conspicuously strict; from a race hag-ridden with bogies to one comparatively bold against the terrors of the dark. The thought was stamped one morning in my mind, when I chanced to be abroad by moonlight, and saw all the town lightless, but the lamp faithfully burning by the missionary's bed. It requires no law, no fire, and no scouting police, to withhold Maka and his countrymen from wandering in the night unlighted.

CHAPTER IV—A TALE OF A TAPU

On the morrow of our arrival (Sunday, 14th July 1889) our photographers were early stirring. Once more we traversed a silent town; many were yet abed and asleep; some sat drowsily in their open houses; there was no sound of intercourse or business. In that hour before the shadows, the quarter of the palace and canal seemed like a landing-place in the Arabian Nights or from the classic poets; here were the fit destination of some 'faery frigot,' here some adventurous prince might step ashore among new characters and incidents; and the island prison, where it floated on the luminous face of the lagoon, might have passed for the repository of the Grail. In such a scene, and at such an hour, the impression received was not so much of foreign travel—rather of past ages; it seemed not so much degrees of latitude that we had crossed, as centuries of time that we had re-ascended; leaving, by the same steps, home and to-day. A few children followed us, mostly nude, all silent; in the clear, weedy waters of the canal some silent damsels waded, baring their brown thighs; and to one of the maniap's before the palace gate we were attracted by a low but stirring hum of speech.

The oval shed was full of men sitting cross-legged. The king was there in striped pyjamas, his rear protected by four guards with Winchesters, his air and bearing marked by unwonted spirit and decision; tumblers and black bottles went the round; and the talk, throughout loud, was general and animated. I was inclined at first to view this scene with suspicion. But the hour appeared unsuitable for a carouse; drink was besides forbidden equally by the law of the land and the canons of the church; and while I was yet hesitating, the king's rigorous attitude disposed of my last doubt. We had come, thinking to photograph him surrounded by his guards, and at the first word of the design his piety revolted. We were reminded of the day—the Sabbath, in which thou shalt take no photographs—and returned with a flea in our ear, bearing the rejected camera.

At church, a little later, I was struck to find the throne unoccupied. So nice a Sabbatarian might have found the means to be present; perhaps my doubts revived; and before I got home they were transformed to certainties. Tom, the bar-keeper of the Sans Souci, was in conversation with two emissaries from the court. The 'keen,' they said, wanted 'din,' failing which 'perandi.' [231] No din, was Tom's reply, and no perandi; but 'pira' if they pleased. It seems they had no use for beer, and departed sorrowing.

'Why, what is the meaning of all this?' I asked. 'Is the island on the spree?'

Such was the fact. On the 4th of July a feast had been made, and the king, at the suggestion of the whites, had raised the tapu against liquor. There is a proverb about horses; it scarce applies to the superior animal, of whom it may be rather said, that any one can start him drinking, not any twenty can prevail on him to stop. The tapu, raised ten days before, was not yet re-imposed; for ten days the town had been passing the bottle or lying (as we had seen it the afternoon before) in hoggish sleep; and the king, moved by the Old Men and his own appetites, continued to maintain the liberty, to squander his savings on liquor, and to join in and lead the debauch. The whites were the authors of this crisis; it was upon their own proposal that the freedom had been granted at the first; and for a while, in the interests of trade, they were doubtless pleased it should continue. That pleasure had now sometime ceased; the bout had been prolonged (it was conceded) unduly; and it now began to be a question how it might conclude. Hence Tom's refusal. Yet that refusal was avowedly only for the moment, and it was avowedly unavailing; the king's foragers, denied by Tom at the Sans Souci, would be supplied at The Land we Live in by the gobbling Mr. Williams.

The degree of the peril was not easy to measure at the time, and I am inclined to think now it was easy to exaggerate. Yet the conduct of drunkards even at home is always matter for anxiety; and at home our populations are not armed from the highest to the lowest with revolvers and repeating rifles, neither do we go on a debauch by the whole townful—and I might rather say, by the whole polity—king, magistrates, police, and army joining in one common scene of drunkenness. It must be thought besides that we were here in barbarous islands, rarely visited, lately and partly civilised. First and last, a really considerable number of whites have perished in the Gilberts, chiefly through their own misconduct; and the natives have displayed in at least one instance a disposition to conceal an accident under a butchery, and leave nothing but dumb bones. This last was the chief consideration against a sudden closing of the bars; the bar-keepers stood in the immediate breach and dealt direct with madmen; too surly a refusal might at any moment precipitate a blow, and the blow might prove the signal for a massacre.

Monday, 15th.—At the same hour we returned to the same muniap'. Kümmel (of all drinks) was served in tumblers; in the midst sat the crown prince, a fatted youth, surrounded by fresh bottles and busily plying the corkscrew; and king, chief, and commons showed the loose mouth, the uncertain joints, and the blurred and animated eye of the early drinker. It was plain we were impatiently expected; the king retired with alacrity to dress, the guards were despatched after their uniforms; and we were left to await the issue of these preparations with a shedful of tipsy natives. The orgie had proceeded further than on Sunday. The day promised to be of great heat; it was already sultry, the courtiers were already fuddled; and still the kümmel continued to go round, and the crown prince to play butler. Flemish freedom followed upon Flemish excess; and a funny dog, a handsome fellow, gaily dressed, and with a full turban of frizzed hair, delighted the company with a humorous courtship of a lady in a manner not to be described. It was our diversion, in this time of waiting, to observe the gathering of the guards. They have European arms, European uniforms, and (to their sorrow) European shoes. We saw one warrior (like Mars) in the article of being armed; two men and a stalwart woman were scarce strong enough to boot him; and after a single appearance on parade the army is crippled for a week.

At last, the gates under the king's house opened; the army issued, one behind another, with guns and epaulettes; the colours stooped under the gateway; majesty followed in his uniform bedizened with gold lace; majesty's wife came next in a hat and feathers, and an ample trained silk gown; the royal imps succeeded; there stood the pageantry of Makin marshalled on its chosen theatre. Dickens might have told how serious they were; how tipsy; how the king melted and streamed under his cocked hat; how he took station by the larger of his two cannons—austere, majestic, but not truly vertical; how the troops huddled, and were straightened out, and clubbed again; how they and their firelocks raked at various inclinations like the masts of ships; and how an amateur photographer reviewed, arrayed, and adjusted them, to see his dispositions change before he reached the camera.

The business was funny to see; I do not know that it is graceful to laugh at; and our report of these transactions was received on our return with the shaking of grave heads.

The day had begun ill; eleven hours divided us from sunset; and at any moment, on the most trifling chance, the trouble might begin. The Wightman compound was in a military sense untenable, commanded on three sides by houses and thick bush; the town was computed to contain over a thousand stand of excellent new arms; and retreat to the ships, in the case of an alert, was a recourse not to be thought of. Our talk that morning must have closely reproduced the talk in English garrisons before the Sepoy mutiny; the sturdy doubt that any mischief was in prospect, the sure belief that (should any come) there was nothing left but to go down fighting, the half-amused, half-anxious attitude of mind in which we were awaiting fresh developments.

The kümmel soon ran out; we were scarce returned before the king had followed us in quest of more. Mr. Corpse was now divested of his more awful attitude, the lawless bulk of him again encased in striped pyjamas; a guardsman brought up the rear with his rifle at the trail: and his majesty was further accompanied by a Rarotongan whalerman and the playful courtier with the turban of frizzed hair. There was never a more lively deputation. The whalerman was gapingly, tearfully tipsy: the courtier walked on air; the king himself was even sportive. Seated in a chair in the Ricks' sitting-room, he bore the brunt of our prayers and menaces unmoved. He was even rated, plied with historic instances, threatened with the men-of-war, ordered to restore the tapu on the spot—and nothing in the least affected him. It should be done to-morrow, he said; to-day it was beyond his power, to-day he durst not. 'Is that royal?' cried indignant Mr. Rick. No, it was not royal; had the king been of a royal character we should ourselves have held a different language; and royal or not, he had the best of the dispute. The terms indeed were hardly equal; for the king was the only man who could restore the tapu, but the Ricks were not the only people who sold drink. He had but to hold his ground on the first question, and they were sure to weaken on the second. A little struggle they still made for the fashion's sake; and then one exceedingly tipsy deputation departed, greatly rejoicing, a case of brandy wheeling beside them in a barrow. The Rarotongan (whom I had never seen before) wrung me by the hand like a man bound on a far voyage. 'My dear frien'!' he cried, 'good-bye, my dear frien'!'—tears of kümmel standing in his eyes; the king lurched as he went, the courtier ambled,—a strange party of intoxicated children to be entrusted with that barrowful of madness.

You could never say the town was quiet; all morning there was a ferment in the air, an aimless movement and congregation of natives in the street. But it was not before half-past one that a sudden hubbub of voices called us from the house, to find the whole white colony already gathered on the spot as by concerted signal. The Sans Souci was overrun with rabble, the stair and verandah thronged. From all these throats an inarticulate babbling cry went up incessantly; it sounded like the bleating of young lambs, but angrier. In the road his royal highness (whom I had seen so lately in the part of butler) stood crying upon Tom; on the top step, tossed in the hurly-burly, Tom was shouting to the prince. Yet a while the pack swayed about the bar, vociferous. Then came a brutal impulse; the mob reeled, and returned, and was rejected; the stair showed a stream of heads; and there shot into view, through the disbanding ranks, three men violently dragging in their midst a fourth. By his hair and his hands, his head forced as low as his knees, his face concealed, he was wrenched from the verandah and whisked along the road into the village, howling as he disappeared. Had his face been raised, we should have seen it bloodied, and the blood was not his own. The courtier with the turban of frizzed hair had paid the costs of this disturbance with the lower part of one ear.

So the brawl passed with no other casualty than might seem comic to the inhumane. Yet we looked round on serious faces and—a fact that spoke volumes—Tom was putting up the shutters on the bar. Custom might go elsewhere, Mr. Williams might profit as he pleased, but Tom had had enough of bar-keeping for that day. Indeed the event had hung on a hair. A man had sought to draw a revolver—on what quarrel I could never learn, and perhaps he himself could not have told; one shot, when the room was so crowded, could scarce have failed to take effect; where many were armed and all tipsy, it could scarce have failed to draw others; and the woman who spied the weapon and the man who seized it may very well have saved the white community.

The mob insensibly melted from the scene; and for the rest of the day our neighbourhood was left in peace and a good deal in solitude. But the tranquillity was only local; din and perandi still flowed in other quarters: and we had one more sight of Gilbert Island violence. In the church, where we had wandered photographing, we were startled by a sudden piercing outcry. The scene, looking forth from the doors of that great hall of shadow, was unforgettable. The palms, the quaint and scattered houses, the flag of the island streaming from its tall staff, glowed with intolerable sunshine. In the midst two women rolled fighting on the grass. The combatants were the more easy to be distinguished, because the one was stripped to the ridi and the other wore a holoku (sacque) of some lively colour. The first was uppermost, her teeth locked in her adversary's face, shaking her like a dog; the other impotently fought and scratched. So for a moment we saw them wallow and grapple there like vermin; then the mob closed and shut them in.

It was a serious question that night if we should sleep ashore. But we were travellers, folk that had come far in quest of the adventurous; on the first sign of an adventure it would have been a singular inconsistency to have withdrawn; and we sent on board instead for our revolvers. Mindful of Taahauku, Mr. Rick, Mr. Osbourne, and Mrs. Stevenson held an assault of arms on the public highway, and fired at bottles to the admiration of the natives. Captain Reid of the Equator stayed on shore with us to be at hand in case of trouble, and we retired to bed at the accustomed hour, agreeably excited by the day's events. The night was exquisite, the silence enchanting; yet as I lay in my hammock looking on the strong moonshine and the quiescent palms, one ugly picture haunted me of the two women, the naked and the clad, locked in that hostile embrace. The harm done was probably not much, yet I could have looked on death and massacre with less revolt. The return to these primeval weapons, the vision of man's beastliness, of his ferality, shocked in me a deeper sense than that with which we count the cost of battles. There are elements in our state and history which it is a pleasure to forget, which it is perhaps the better wisdom not to dwell on. Crime, pestilence, and death are in the day's work; the imagination readily accepts them. It instinctively rejects, on the contrary, whatever shall call up the image of our race upon its lowest terms, as the partner of beasts, beastly itself, dwelling pell-mell and hugger-mugger, hairy man with hairy woman, in the caves of old. And yet to be just to barbarous islanders we must not forget the slums and dens of our cities; I must not forget that I have passed dinnerward through Soho, and seen that which cured me of my dinner.

CHAPTER V—A TALE OF A TAPU—continued

Tuesday, July 16.—It rained in the night, sudden and loud, in Gilbert Island fashion. Before the day, the crowing of a cock aroused me and I wandered in the compound and along the street. The squall was blown by, the moon shone with incomparable lustre, the air lay dead as in a room, and yet all the isle sounded as under a strong shower, the eaves thickly pattering, the lofty palms dripping at larger intervals and with a louder note. In this bold nocturnal light the interior of the houses lay inscrutable, one lump of blackness, save when the moon glinted under the roof, and made a belt of silver, and drew the slanting shadows of the pillars on the floor. Nowhere in all the town was any lamp or ember; not a creature stirred; I thought I was alone to be awake; but the police were faithful to their duty; secretly vigilant, keeping account of time; and a little later, the watchman struck slowly and repeatedly on the cathedral bell; four o'clock, the warning signal. It seemed strange that, in a town resigned to drunkenness and tumult, curfew and réveille should still be sounded and still obeyed.

The day came, and brought little change. The place still lay silent; the people slept, the town slept. Even the few who were awake, mostly women and children, held their peace and kept within under the strong shadow of the thatch, where you must stop and peer to see them. Through the deserted streets, and past the sleeping houses, a deputation took its way at an early hour to the palace; the king was suddenly awakened, and must listen (probably with a headache) to unpalatable truths. Mrs. Rick, being a sufficient mistress of that difficult tongue, was spokeswoman; she explained to the sick monarch that I was an intimate personal friend of Queen Victoria's; that immediately on my return I should make her a report upon Butaritari; and that if my house should have been again invaded by natives, a man-of-war would be despatched to make reprisals. It was scarce the fact—rather a just and necessary parable of the fact, corrected for latitude; and it certainly told upon the king. He was much affected; he had conceived the notion (he said) that I was a man of some importance, but not dreamed it was as bad as this; and the missionary house was tapu'd under a fine of fifty dollars.

So much was announced on the return of the deputation; not any more; and I gathered subsequently that much more had passed. The protection gained was welcome. It had been the most annoying and not the least alarming feature of the day before, that our house was periodically filled with tipsy natives, twenty or thirty at a time, begging drink, fingering our goods, hard to be dislodged, awkward to quarrel with. Queen Victoria's friend (who was soon promoted to be her son) was free from these intrusions. Not only my house, but my neighbourhood as well, was left in peace; even on our walks abroad we were guarded and prepared for; and, like great persons visiting a hospital, saw only the fair side. For the matter of a week we were thus suffered to go out and in and live in a fool's paradise, supposing the king to have kept his word, the tapu to be revived and the island once more sober.

Tuesday, July 23.—We dined under a bare trellis erected for the Fourth of July; and here we used to linger by lamplight over coffee and tobacco. In that climate evening approaches without sensible chill; the wind dies out before sunset; heaven glows a while and fades, and darkens into the blueness of the tropical night; swiftly and insensibly the shadows thicken, the stars multiply their number; you look around you and the day is gone. It was then that we would see our Chinaman draw near across the compound in a lurching sphere of light, divided by his shadows; and with the coming of the lamp the night closed about the table. The faces of the company, the spars of the trellis, stood out suddenly bright on a ground of blue and silver, faintly designed with palm-tops and the peaked roofs of houses. Here and there the gloss upon a leaf, or the fracture of a stone, returned an isolated sparkle. All else had vanished. We hung there, illuminated like a galaxy of stars in vacuo; we sat, manifest and blind, amid the general ambush of the darkness; and the islanders, passing with light footfalls and low voices in the sand of the road, lingered to observe us, unseen.

On Tuesday the dusk had fallen, the lamp had just been brought, when a missile struck the table with a rattling smack and rebounded past my ear. Three inches to one side and this page had never been written; for the thing travelled like a cannon ball. It was supposed at the time to be a nut, though even at the time I thought it seemed a small one and fell strangely.

Wednesday, July 24.—The dusk had fallen once more, and the lamp been just brought out, when the same business was repeated. And again the missile whistled past my ear. One nut I had been willing to accept; a second, I rejected utterly. A cocoa-nut does not come slinging along on a windless evening, making an angle of about fifteen degrees with the horizon; cocoa-nuts do not fall on successive nights at the same hour and spot; in both cases, besides, a specific moment seemed to have been chosen, that when the lamp was just carried out, a specific person threatened, and that the head of the family. I may have been right or wrong, but I believed I was the mark of some intimidation; believed the missile was a stone, aimed not to hit, but to frighten.

No idea makes a man more angry. I ran into the road, where the natives were as usual promenading in the dark; Maka joined me with a lantern; and I ran from one to another, glared in quite innocent faces, put useless questions, and proffered idle threats. Thence I carried my wrath (which was worthy the son of any queen in history) to the Ricks. They heard me with depression, assured me this trick of throwing a stone into a family dinner was not new;

that it meant mischief, and was of a piece with the alarming disposition of the natives. And then the truth, so long concealed from us, came out. The king had broken his promise, he had defied the deputation; the tapu was still dormant, The Land we Live in still selling drink, and that quarter of the town disturbed and menaced by perpetual broils. But there was worse ahead: a feast was now preparing for the birthday of the little princess; and the tributary chiefs of Kuma and Little Makin were expected daily. Strong in a following of numerous and somewhat savage clansmen, each of these was believed, like a Douglas of old, to be of doubtful loyalty. Kuma (a little pot-bellied fellow) never visited the palace, never entered the town, but sat on the beach on a mat, his gun across his knees, parading his mistrust and scorn; Karaiti of Makin, although he was more bold, was not supposed to be more friendly; and not only were these vassals jealous of the throne, but the followers on either side shared in the animosity. Brawls had already taken place; blows had passed which might at any moment be repaid in blood. Some of the strangers were already here and already drinking; if the debauch continued after the bulk of them had come, a collision, perhaps a revolution, was to be expected.

The sale of drink is in this group a measure of the jealousy of traders; one begins, the others are constrained to follow; and to him who has the most gin, and sells it the most recklessly, the lion's share of copra is assured. It is felt by all to be an extreme expedient, neither safe, decent, nor dignified. A trader on Tarawa, heated by an eager rivalry, brought many cases of gin. He told me he sat afterwards day and night in his house till it was finished, not daring to arrest the sale, not venturing to go forth, the bush all round him filled with howling drunkards. At night, above all, when he was afraid to sleep, and heard shots and voices about him in the darkness, his remorse was black.

'My God!' he reflected, 'if I was to lose my life on such a wretched business!' Often and often, in the story of the Gilberts, this scene has been repeated; and the remorseful trader sat beside his lamp, longing for the day, listening with agony for the sound of murder, registering resolutions for the future. For the business is easy to begin, but hazardous to stop. The natives are in their way a just and law-abiding people, mindful of their debts, docile to the voice of their own institutions; when the tapu is re-enforced they will cease drinking; but the white who seeks to antedate the movement by refusing liquor does so at his peril.

Hence, in some degree, the anxiety and helplessness of Mr. Rick. He and Tom, alarmed by the rabblement of the Sans Souci, had stopped the sale; they had done so without danger, because The Land we Live in still continued selling; it was claimed, besides, that they had been the first to begin. What step could be taken? Could Mr. Rick visit Mr. Muller (with whom he was not on terms) and address him thus: 'I was getting ahead of you, now you are getting ahead of me, and I ask you to forego your profit. I got my place closed in safety, thanks to your continuing; but now I think you have continued long enough. I begin to be alarmed; and because I am afraid I ask you to confront a certain danger'? It was not to be thought of. Something else had to be found; and there was one person at one end of the town who was at least not interested in copra. There was little else to be said in favour of myself as an ambassador. I had arrived in the Wightman schooner, I was living in the Wightman compound, I was the daily associate of the Wightman coterie. It was egregious enough that I should now intrude unasked in the private affairs of Crawford's agent, and press upon him the sacrifice of his interests and the venture of his life. But bad as I might be, there was none better; since the affair of the stone I was, besides, sharp-set to be doing, the idea of a delicate interview attracted me, and I thought it policy to show myself abroad.

The night was very dark. There was service in the church, and the building glimmered through all its crevices like a dim Kirk Allowa'. I saw few other lights, but was indistinctly aware of many people stirring in the darkness, and a hum and sputter of low talk that sounded stealthy. I believe (in the old phrase) my beard was sometimes on my shoulder as I went. Muller's was but partly lighted, and quite silent, and the gate was fastened. I could by no means manage to undo the latch. No wonder, since I found it afterwards to be four or five feet long—a fortification in itself. As I still fumbled, a dog came on the inside and sniffed suspiciously at my hands, so that I was reduced to calling 'House ahoy!' Mr. Muller came down and put his chin across the paling in the dark. 'Who is that?' said he, like one who has no mind to welcome strangers.

'My name is Stevenson,' said I.

'O, Mr. Stevens! I didn't know you. Come inside.' We stepped into the dark store, when I leaned upon the counter and he against the wall. All the light came from the sleeping-room, where I saw his family being put to bed; it struck full in my face, but Mr. Muller stood in shadow. No doubt he expected what was Coming, and sought the advantage of position; but for a man who wished to persuade and had nothing to conceal, mine was the preferable.

'Look here,' I began, 'I hear you are selling to the natives.'

'Others have done that before me,' he returned pointedly.

'No doubt,' said I, 'and I have nothing to do with the past, but the future. I want you to promise you will handle these spirits carefully.'

'Now what is your motive in this?' he asked, and then, with a sneer, 'Are you afraid of your life?'

'That is nothing to the purpose,' I replied. 'I know, and you know, these spirits ought not to be used at all.'

'Tom and Mr. Rick have sold them before.'

'I have nothing to do with Tom and Mr. Rick. All I know is I have heard them both refuse.'

'No, I suppose you have nothing to do with them. Then you are just afraid of your life.'

'Come now,' I cried, being perhaps a little stung, 'you know in your heart I am asking a reasonable thing. I don't ask you to lose your profit—though I would prefer to see no spirits brought here, as you would—'

'I don't say I wouldn't. I didn't begin this,' he interjected.

'No, I don't suppose you did,' said I. 'And I don't ask you to lose; I ask you to give me your word, man to man, that you will make no native drunk.'

Up to now Mr. Muller had maintained an attitude very trying to my temper; but he had maintained it with difficulty, his sentiment being all upon my side; and here he changed ground for the worse. 'It isn't me that sells,' said he.

'No, it's that nigger,' I agreed. 'But he's yours to buy and sell; you have your hand on the nape of his neck; and I ask you—I have my wife here—to use the authority you have.'

He hastily returned to his old ward. 'I don't deny I could if I wanted,' said he. 'But there's no danger, the natives are all quiet. You're just afraid of your life.'

I do not like to be called a coward, even by implication; and here I lost my temper and propounded an untimely ultimatum. 'You had better put it plain,' I cried. 'Do you mean to refuse me what I ask?'

'I don't want either to refuse it or grant it,' he replied.

'You'll find you have to do the one thing or the other, and right now!' I cried, and then, striking into a happier vein, 'Come,' said I, 'you're a better sort than that. I see what's wrong with you—you think I came from the opposite camp. I see the sort of man you are, and you know that what I ask is right.'

Again he changed ground. 'If the natives get any drink, it isn't safe to stop them,' he objected.

'I'll be answerable for the bar,' I said. 'We are three men and four revolvers; we'll come at a word, and hold the place against the village.'

'You don't know what you're talking about; it's too dangerous!' he cried.

'Look here,' said I, 'I don't mind much about losing that life you talk so much of; but I mean to lose it the way I want to, and that is, putting a stop to all this beastliness.'

He talked a while about his duty to the firm; I minded not at all, I was secure of victory. He was but waiting to capitulate, and looked about for any potent to relieve the strain. In the gush of light from the bedroom door I spied a cigar-holder on the desk. 'That is well coloured,' said I.

'Will you take a cigar?' said he.

I took it and held it up unlighted. 'Now,' said I, 'you promise me.'

'I promise you-you won't have any trouble from natives that have drunk at my place,' he replied.

'That is all I ask,' said I, and showed it was not by immediately offering to try his stock.

So far as it was anyway critical our interview here ended. Mr. Muller had thenceforth ceased to regard me as an emissary from his rivals, dropped his defensive attitude, and spoke as he believed. I could make out that he would already, had he dared, have stopped the sale himself. Not quite daring, it may be imagined how he resented the idea of interference from those who had (by his own statement) first led him on, then deserted him in the breach, and now (sitting themselves in safety) egged him on to a new peril, which was all gain to them, all loss to him! I asked him what he thought of the danger from the feast.

'I think worse of it than any of you,' he answered. 'They were shooting around here last night, and I heard the balls too. I said to myself, "That's bad." What gets me is why you should be making this row up at your end. I should be the first to go.'

It was a thoughtless wonder. The consolation of being second is not great; the fact, not the order of going—there was our concern.

Scott talks moderately of looking forward to a time of fighting 'with a feeling that resembled pleasure.' The resemblance seems rather an identity. In modern life, contact is ended; man grows impatient of endless manœuvres; and to approach the fact, to find ourselves where we can push an advantage home, and stand a fair risk, and see at last what we are made of, stirs the blood. It was so at least with all my family, who bubbled with delight at the approach of trouble; and we sat deep into the night like a pack of schoolboys, preparing the revolvers and arranging plans against the morrow. It promised certainly to be a busy and eventful day. The Old Men were to be summoned to confront me on the question of the tapu; Muller might call us at any moment to garrison his bar; and suppose Muller to fail, we decided in a family council to take that matter into our own hands, The Land we Live in at the pistol's mouth, and with the polysyllabic Williams, dance to a new tune. As I recall our humour I think it would have gone hard with the mulatto.

Wednesday, July 24.—It was as well, and yet it was disappointing that these thunder-clouds rolled off in silence. Whether the Old Men recoiled from an interview with Queen Victoria's son, whether Muller had secretly intervened, or whether the step flowed naturally from the fears of the king and the nearness of the feast, the tapu was early that morning re-enforced; not a day too soon, from the manner the boats began to arrive thickly, and the town was filled with the big rowdy vassals of Karaiti.

The effect lingered for some time on the minds of the traders; it was with the approval of all present that I helped to draw up a petition to the United States, praying for a law against the liquor trade in the Gilberts; and it was at this request that I added, under my own name, a brief testimony of what had passed;—useless pains; since the whole reposes, probably unread and possibly unopened, in a pigeon-hole at Washington.

Sunday, July 28.—This day we had the afterpiece of the debauch. The king and queen, in European clothes, and followed by armed guards, attended church for the first time, and sat perched aloft in a precarious dignity under the barrel-hoops. Before sermon his majesty clambered from the dais, stood lopsidedly upon the gravel floor, and in a few words abjured drinking. The queen followed suit with a yet briefer allocution. All the men in church were next addressed in turn; each held up his right hand, and the affair was over—throne and church were reconciled.

CHAPTER VI—THE FIVE DAYS' FESTIVAL

Thursday, July 25.—The street was this day much enlivened by the presence of the men from Little Makin; they average taller than Butaritarians, and being on a holiday, went wreathed with yellow leaves and gorgeous in vivid colours. They are said to be more savage, and to be proud of the distinction. Indeed, it seemed to us they swaggered in the town, like plaided Highlanders upon the streets of Inverness, conscious of barbaric virtues.

In the afternoon the summer parlour was observed to be packed with people; others standing outside and stooping to peer under the eaves, like children at home about a circus. It was the Makin company, rehearsing for the day of competition. Karaiti sat in the front row close to the singers, where we were summoned (I suppose in honour of Queen Victoria) to join him. A strong breathless heat reigned under the iron roof, and the air was heavy with the scent of wreaths. The singers, with fine mats about their loins, cocoa-nut feathers set in rings upon their fingers, and their heads crowned with yellow leaves, sat on the floor by companies. A varying number of soloists stood up for different songs; and these bore the chief part in the music. But the full force of the companies, even when not singing, contributed continuously to the effect, and marked the ictus of the measure, mimicking, grimacing, casting up their heads and eyes, fluttering the feathers on their fingers, clapping hands, or beating (loud as a kettledrum) on the left breast; the time was exquisite, the music barbarous, but full of conscious art. I noted some devices constantly employed. A sudden change would be introduced (I think of key) with no break of the measure, but emphasised by a sudden dramatic heightening of the voice and a swinging, general gesticulation. The voices of the soloists would begin far apart in a rude discord, and gradually draw together to a unison; which, when, they had reached, they were joined and drowned by the full chorus. The ordinary, hurried, barking unmelodious movement of the voices would at times be broken and glorified by a psalm-like strain of melody, often well constructed, or seeming so by contrast. There was much variety of measure, and towards the end of each piece, when the fun became fast and furious, a recourse to this figure—

It is difficult to conceive what fire and devilry they get into these hammering finales; all go together, voices, hands, eyes, leaves, and fluttering finger-rings; the chorus swings to the eye, the song throbs on the ear; the faces are convulsed with enthusiasm and effort.

Presently the troop stood up in a body, the drums forming a half-circle for the soloists, who were sometimes five or even more in number. The songs that followed were highly dramatic; though I had none to give me any explanation, I would at times make out some shadowy but decisive outline of a plot; and I was continually reminded of certain quarrelsome concerted scenes in grand operas at home; just so the single voices issue from and fall again into the general volume; just so do the performers separate and crowd together, brandish the raised hand, and roll the eye to heaven—or the gallery. Already this is beyond the Thespian model; the art of this people is already past the embryo: song, dance, drums, quartette and solo—it is the drama full developed although still in miniature. Of all so-called dancing in the South Seas, that which I saw in Butaritari stands easily the first. The hula, as it may be viewed by the speedy globe-trotter in Honolulu, is surely the most dull of man's inventions, and the spectator yawns under its length as at a college lecture or a parliamentary debate. But the Gilbert Island dance leads on the mind; it thrills, rouses, subjugates; it has the essence of all art, an unexplored imminent significance. Where so many are engaged, and where all must make (at a given moment) the same swift, elaborate, and often arbitrary movement, the toil of rehearsal is of course extreme. But they begin as children. A child and a man may often be seen together in a maniap': the man sings and gesticulates, the child stands before him with streaming tears and tremulously copies him in act and sound; it is the Gilbert Island artist learning (as all artists must) his art in sorrow.

I may seem to praise too much; here is a passage from my wife's diary, which proves that I was not alone in being moved, and completes the picture:—'The conductor gave the cue, and all the dancers, waving their arms, swaying their bodies, and clapping their breasts in perfect time, opened with an introductory. The performers remained seated, except two, and once three, and twice a single soloist. These stood in the group, making a slight movement with the feet and rhythmical quiver of the body as they sang. There was a pause after the introductory, and then the real business of the opera—for it was no less—began; an opera where every singer was an accomplished actor. The leading man, in an impassioned ecstasy which possessed him from head to foot, seemed transfigured; once it was as though a strong wind had swept over the stage—their arms, their feathered fingers thrilling with an emotion that shook my nerves as well: heads and bodies followed like a field of grain before a gust. My blood came hot and cold, tears pricked my eyes, my head whirled, I felt an almost irresistible impulse to join the dancers. One drama, I think, I very nearly understood. A fierce and savage old man took the solo part. He sang of the birth of a prince, and how he was tenderly rocked in his mother's arms; of his boyhood, when he excelled his fellows in swimming, climbing, and all athletic sports; of his youth, when he went out to sea with his boat and fished; of his manhood, when he married a wife who cradled a son of his own in her arms. Then came the alarm of war, and a great battle, of which for a time the issue was doubtful; but the hero conquered, as he always does, and with a tremendous burst of the victors the piece closed. There were also comic pieces, which caused great amusement. During one, an old man behind me clutched me by the arm, shook his finger in my face with a roguish smile, and said something with a chuckle, which I took to be the equivalent of "O, you women, you women; it is true of you all!" I fear it was not complimentary. At no time was there the least sign of the ugly indecency of the eastern islands. All was poetry pure and simple. The music itself was as complex as our own, though constructed on an entirely different basis; once or twice I was startled by a bit of something very like the best English sacred music, but it was only for an instant. At last there was a longer pause, and this time the dancers were all on their feet. As the drama went on, the interest grew. The performers appealed to each other, to the audience, to the heaven above; they took counsel with each other, the conspirators drew together in a knot; it was just an opera, the drums coming in at proper intervals, the tenor, baritone, and bass all where they should be—except that the voices were all of the same calibre. A woman once sang from the back row with a very fine contralto voice spoilt by being made artificially nasal; I notice all the women affect that unpleasantness. At one time a boy of angelic beauty was the soloist; and at another, a child of six or eight, doubtless an infant phenomenon being trained, was placed in the centre. The little fellow was desperately frightened and embarrassed at first, but towards the close warmed up to his work and showed much dramatic talent. The changing expressions on the faces of the dancers were so speaking, that it seemed a great stupidity not to understand them.'

Our neighbour at this performance, Karaiti, somewhat favours his Butaritarian majesty in shape and feature, being, like him, portly, bearded, and Oriental. In character he seems the reverse: alert, smiling, jovial, jocular, industrious. At home in his own island, he labours himself like a slave, and makes his people labour like a slave-driver. He takes an interest in ideas. George the trader told him about flying-machines. 'Is that true, George?' he asked. 'It is in the papers,' replied George. 'Well,' said Karaiti, 'if that man can do it with machinery, I can do it without'; and he designed and made a pair of wings, strapped them on his shoulders, went to the end of a pier, launched himself into space, and fell bulkily into the sea. His wives fished him out, for his wings hindered him in swimming. 'George,' said he, pausing as he went up to change, 'George, you lie.' He had eight wives, for his small realm still follows ancient customs; but he showed embarrassment when this was mentioned to my wife. 'Tell her I have only brought one here,' he said anxiously. Altogether the Black Douglas pleased us much; and as we heard fresh details of the king's uneasiness, and saw for ourselves that all the weapons in the summer parlour had been hid, we watched with the more admiration the cause of all this anxiety rolling on his big legs, with his big smiling face, apparently unarmed, and certainly unattended, through the hostile town. The Red Douglas, pot-bellied Kuma, having perhaps heard word of the debauch, remained upon his fief; his vassals thus came uncommanded to the feast, and swelled the following of Karaiti.

Friday, July 26.—At night in the dark, the singers of Makin paraded in the road before our house and sang the song of the princess. 'This is the day; she was born to-day; Nei Kamaunave was born to-day—a beautiful princess, Queen of Butaritari.' So I was told it went in endless iteration. The song was of course out of season, and the performance only a rehearsal. But it was a serenade besides; a delicate attention to ourselves from our new friend, Karaiti.

Saturday, July 27.—We had announced a performance of the magic lantern to-night in church; and this brought the king to visit us. In honour of the Black Douglas (I suppose) his usual two guardsmen were now increased to four; and the squad made an outlandish figure as they straggled after him, in straw hats, kilts and jackets. Three carried their arms reversed, the butts over their shoulders, the muzzles menacing the king's plump back; the fourth had passed his weapon behind his neck, and held it there with arms extended like a backboard. The visit was extraordinarily long. The king, no longer galvanised with gin, said and did nothing. He sat collapsed in a chair and let a cigar go out. It was hot, it was sleepy, it was cruel dull; there was no resource but to spy in the countenance of Tebureimoa for some remaining trait of Mr. Corpse the butcher. His hawk nose, crudely depressed and flattened at the point, did truly seem to us to smell of midnight murder. When he took his leave, Maka bade me observe him going down the stair (or rather ladder) from the verandah. 'Old man,' said Maka. 'Yes,' said I, 'and yet I suppose not old man.' 'Young man,' returned Maka, 'perhaps fo'ty.' And I have heard since he is most likely younger.

While the magic lantern was showing, I skulked without in the dark. The voice of Maka, excitedly explaining the Scripture slides, seemed to fill not the church only, but the neighbourhood. All else was silent. Presently a distant sound of singing arose and approached; and a procession drew near along the road, the hot clean smell of the men and women striking in my face delightfully. At the corner, arrested by the voice of Maka and the lightening and darkening of the church, they paused. They had no mind to go nearer, that was plain. They were Makin people, I believe, probably staunch heathens, contemners of the missionary and his works. Of a sudden, however, a man broke from their company, took to his heels, and fled into the church; next moment three had followed him; the next it was a covey of near upon a score, all pelting for their lives. So the little band of the heathen paused irresolute at the corner, and melted before the attractions of a magic lantern, like a glacier in spring. The more staunch vainly taunted the deserters; three fled in a guilty silence, but still fled; and when at length the leader found the wit or the authority to get his troop in motion and revive the singing, it was with much diminished forces that they passed musically on up the dark road.

Meanwhile inside the luminous pictures brightened and faded. I stood for some while unobserved in the rear of the spectators, when I could hear just in front of me a pair of lovers following the show with interest, the male playing the part of interpreter and (like Adam) mingling caresses with his lecture. The wild animals, a tiger in particular, and that old school-treat favourite, the sleeper and the mouse, were hailed with joy; but the chief marvel and delight was in the gospel series. Maka, in the opinion of his aggrieved wife, did not properly rise to the occasion. 'What is the matter with the man? Why can't he talk?' she cried. The matter with the man, I think, was the greatness of the opportunity; he reeled under his good fortune; and whether he did ill or well, the exposure of these pious 'phantoms' did as a matter of fact silence in all that part of the island the voice of the scoffer. 'Why then,' the word went round, 'why then, the Bible is true!' And on our return afterwards we were told the impression was yet lively, and those who had seen might be heard telling those who had not, 'O yes, it is all true; these things all happened, we have seen the pictures.' The argument is not so childish as it seems; for I doubt if these islanders are acquainted with any other mode of representation but photography; so that the picture of an event (on the old melodrama principle that 'the camera cannot lie, Joseph,') would appear strong proof of its occurrence. The fact amused us the more because our slides were some of them ludicrously silly, and one (Christ before Pilate) was received with shouts of merriment, in which even Maka was constrained to join.

Sunday, July 28.—Karaiti came to ask for a repetition of the 'phantoms'—this was the accepted word—and, having received a promise, turned and left my humble roof without the shadow of a salutation. I felt it impolite to have the least appearance of pocketing a slight; the times had been too difficult, and were still too doubtful; and Queen Victoria's son was bound to maintain the honour of his house. Karaiti was accordingly summoned that evening to the Ricks, where Mrs. Rick fell foul of him in words, and Queen Victoria's son assailed him with indignant looks. I was the ass with the lion's skin; I could not roar in the language of the Gilbert Islands; but I could stare. Karaiti declared he had meant no offence; apologised in a sound, hearty, gentlemanly manner; and became at once at his ease. He had in a dagger to examine, and announced he would come to price it on the morrow, to-day being Sunday; this nicety in a heathen with eight wives surprised me. The dagger was 'good for killing fish,' he said roguishly; and was supposed to have his eye upon fish upon two legs. It is at least odd that in Eastern Polynesia fish was the accepted euphemism for the human sacrifice. Asked as to the population of his island, Karaiti called out to his vassals who sat waiting him outside the door, and they put it at four hundred and fifty; but (added Karaiti jovially) there will soon be plenty more, for all the women are in the family way. Long before we separated I had quite forgotten his offence. He, however, still bore it in mind; and with a very courteous inspiration returned early on the next day, paid us a long visit, and punctiliously said farewell when he departed.

Monday, July 29.—The great day came round at last. In the first hours the night was startled by the sound of clapping hands and the chant of Nei Kamaunava; its melancholy, slow, and somewhat menacing measures broken at intervals by a formidable shout. The little morsel of humanity thus celebrated in the dark hours was observed at midday playing on the green entirely naked, and equally unobserved and unconcerned.

The summer parlour on its artificial islet, relieved against the shimmering lagoon, and shimmering itself with sun and tinned iron, was all day crowded about by eager men and women. Within, it was boxed full of islanders, of any age and size, and in every degree of nudity and finery. So close we squatted, that at one time I had a mighty handsome woman on my knees, two little naked urchins having their feet against my back. There might be a dame in full attire of holoku and hat and flowers; and her next neighbour might the next moment strip some little rag of a shift from her fat shoulders and come out a monument of flesh, painted rather than covered by the hairbreadth ridi. Little ladies who thought themselves too great to appear undraped upon so high a festival were seen to pause outside in the bright sunshine, their miniature ridis in their hand; a moment more and they were full-dressed and entered the concert-room.

At either end stood up to sing, or sat down to rest, the alternate companies of singers; Kuma and Little Makin on the north, Butaritari and its conjunct hamlets on the south; both groups conspicuous in barbaric bravery.

In the midst, between these rival camps of troubadours, a bench was placed; and here the king and queen throned it, some two or three feet above the crowded audience on the floor—Tebureimoa as usual in his striped pyjamas with a satchel strapped across one shoulder, doubtless (in the island fashion) to contain his pistols; the queen in a purple holoku, her abundant hair let down, a fan in her hand. The bench was turned facing to the strangers, a piece of well-considered civility; and when it was the turn of Butaritari to sing, the pair must twist round on the bench, lean their elbows on the rail, and turn to us the spectacle of their broad backs. The royal couple occasionally solaced themselves with a clay pipe; and the pomp of state was further heightened by the rifles of a picket of the guard.

With this kingly countenance, and ourselves squatted on the ground, we heard several songs from one side or the other. Then royalty and its guards withdrew, and Queen Victoria's son and daughter-in-law were summoned by acclamation to the vacant throne. Our pride was perhaps a little modified when we were joined on our high places by a certain thriftless loafer of a white; and yet I was glad too, for the man had a smattering of native, and could give me some idea of the subject of the songs. One was patriotic, and dared Tembinok' of Apemama, the terror of the group, to an invasion. One mixed the planting of taro and the harvest-home. Some were historical, and commemorated kings and the illustrious chances of their time, such as a bout of drinking or a war. One, at least, was a drama of domestic interest, excellently played by the troop from Makin. It told the story of a man who has lost his wife, at first bewails her loss, then seeks another: the earlier strains (or acts) are played exclusively by men; but towards the end a woman appears, who has just lost her husband; and I suppose the pair console each other, for the finale seemed of happy omen. Of some of the songs my informant told me briefly they were 'like about the weemen'; this I could have guessed myself. Each side (I should have said) was strengthened by one or two women. They were all soloists, did not very often join in the performance, but stood disengaged at the back part of the stage, and looked (in ridi, necklace, and dressed hair) for all the world like European ballet-dancers. When the song was anyway broad these ladies came particularly to the front; and it was singular to see that, after each entry, the première danseuse pretended to be overcome by shame, as though led on beyond what she had meant, and her male assistants made a feint of driving her away like one who had disgraced herself. Similar affectations accompany certain truly obscene dances of Samoa, where they are very well in place. Here it was different. The words, perhaps, in this free-spoken world, were gross enough to make a carter blush; and the most suggestive feature was this feint of shame. For such parts the women showed some disposition; they were pert, they were neat, they were acrobatic, they were at times really amusing, and some of them were pretty. But this is not the artist's field; there is the whole width of heaven between such capering and ogling, and the strange rhythmic gestures, and strange, rapturous, frenzied faces with which the best of the male dancers held us spellbound through a Gilbert Island ballet.

Almost from the first it was apparent that the people of the city were defeated. I might have thought them even good, only I had the other troop before my eyes to correct my standard, and remind me continually of 'the little more, and how much it is.' Perceiving themselves worsted, the choir of Butaritari grew confused, blundered, and broke down; amid this hubbub of unfamiliar intervals I should not myself have recognised the slip, but the audience were quick to catch it, and to jeer. To crown all, the Makin company began a dance of truly superlative merit. I know not what it was about, I was too much absorbed to ask. In one act a part of the chorus, squealing in some strange falsetto, produced very much the effect of our orchestra; in another, the dancers, leaping like jumping-jacks, with arms extended, passed through and through each other's ranks with extraordinary speed, neatness, and humour. A more laughable effect I never saw; in any European theatre it would have brought the house down, and the island audience roared with laughter and applause. This filled up the measure for the rival company, and they forgot themselves and decency. After each act or figure of the ballet, the performers pause a moment standing, and the next is introduced by the clapping of hands in triplets. Not until the end of the whole ballet do they sit down, which is the signal for the rivals to stand up. But now all rules were to be broken. During the interval following on this great applause, the company of Butaritari leaped suddenly to their feet and most unhandsomely began a performance of their own. It was strange to see the men of Makin staring; I have seen a tenor in Europe stare with the same blank dignity into a hissing theatre; but presently, to my surprise, they sobered down, gave up the unsung remainder of their ballet, resumed their seats, and suffered their ungallant adversaries to go on and finish. Nothing would suffice. Again, at the first interval, Butaritari unhandsomely cut in; Makin, irritated in turn, followed the example; and the two companies of dancers remained permanently standing, continuously clapping hands, and regularly cutting across each other at each pause. I expected blows to begin with any moment; and our position in the midst was highly unstrategical. But the Makin people had a better thought; and upon a fresh interruption turned and trooped out of the house. We followed them, first because these were the artists, second because they were guests and had been scurvily ill-used. A large population of our neighbours did the same, so that the causeway was filled from end to end by the procession of deserters; and the Butaritari choir was left to sing for its own pleasure in an empty house, having gained the point and lost the audience. It was surely fortunate that there was no one drunk; but, drunk or sober, where else would a scene so irritating have concluded without blows?

The last stage and glory of this auspicious day was of our own providing—the second and positively the last appearance of the phantoms. All round the church, groups sat outside, in the night, where they could see nothing; perhaps ashamed to enter, certainly finding some shadowy pleasure in the mere proximity. Within, about one-half of the great shed was densely packed with people. In the midst, on the royal dais, the lantern luminously smoked; chance rays of light struck out the earnest countenance of our Chinaman grinding the hand-organ; a fainter glimmer showed off the rafters and their shadows in the hollow of the roof; the pictures shone and vanished on the screen; and as each appeared, there would run a hush, a whisper, a strong shuddering rustle, and a chorus of small cries among the crowd. There sat by me the mate of a wrecked schooner. 'They would think this a strange sight in Europe or the States,' said he, 'going on in a building like this, all tied with bits of string.'

CHAPTER VII—HUSBAND AND WIFE

The trader accustomed to the manners of Eastern Polynesia has a lesson to learn among the Gilberts. The ridi is but a spare attire; as late as thirty years back the women went naked until marriage; within ten years the custom lingered; and these facts, above all when heard in description, conveyed a very false idea of the manners of the group. A very intelligent missionary described it (in its former state) as a 'Paradise of naked women' for the resident whites. It was at least a platonic Paradise, where Lothario ventured at his peril. Since 1860, fourteen whites have perished on a single island, all for the same cause, all found where they had no business, and speared by some indignant father of a family; the figure was given me by one of their contemporaries who had been more prudent and survived. The strange persistence of these fourteen martyrs might seem to point to monomania or a series of romantic passions; gin is the more likely key. The poor buzzards sat alone in their houses by an open case; they drank; their brain was fired; they stumbled towards the nearest houses on chance; and the dart went through their liver. In place of a Paradise the trader found an archipelago of fierce husbands and of virtuous women. 'Of course if you wish to make love to them, it's the same as anywhere else,' observed a trader innocently; but he and his companions rarely so choose.

The trader must be credited with a virtue: he often makes a kind and loyal husband. Some of the worst beachcombers in the Pacific, some of the last of the old school, have fallen in my path, and some of them were admirable to their native wives, and one made a despairing widower. The position of a trader's wife in the Gilberts is, besides, unusually enviable. She shares the immunities of her husband. Curfew in Butaritari sounds for her in vain. Long after the bell is rung and the great island ladies are confined for the night to their own roof, this chartered libertine may scamper and giggle through the deserted streets or go down to bathe in the dark. The resources of the store are at her hand; she goes arrayed like a queen, and feasts delicately everyday upon tinned meats. And she who was perhaps of no regard or station among natives sits with captains, and is entertained on board of schooners. Five of these privileged dames were some time our neighbours. Four were handsome skittish lasses, gamesome like children, and like children liable to fits of pouting. They wore dresses by day, but there was a tendency after dark to strip these lendings and to career and squall about the compound in the aboriginal ridi. Games of cards were continually played, with shells for counters; their course was much marred by cheating; and the end of a round (above all if a man was of the party) resolved itself into a scrimmage for the counters. The fifth was a matron. It was a picture to see her sail to church on a Sunday, a parasol in hand, a nursemaid following, and the baby buried in a trade hat and armed with a patent feeding-bottle. The service was enlivened by her continual supervision and correction of the maid. It was impossible not to fancy the baby was a doll, and the church some European playroom. All these women were legitimately married. It is true that the certificate of one, when she proudly showed it, proved to run thus, that she was 'married for one night,' and her gracious partner was at liberty to 'send her to hell' the next morning; but she was none the wiser or the worse for the dastardly trick. Another, I heard, was married on a work of mine in a pirated edition; it answered the purpose as well as a Hall Bible. Notwithstanding all these allurements of social distinction, rare food and raiment, a comparative vacation from toil, and legitimate marriage contracted on a pirated edition, the trader must sometimes seek long before he can be mated. While I was in the group one had been eight months on the quest, and he was still a bachelor.

Within strictly native society the old laws and practices were harsh, but not without a certain stamp of high-mindedness. Stealthy adultery was punished with death; open elopement was properly considered virtue in comparison, and compounded for a fine in land. The male adulterer alone seems to have been punished. It is correct manners for a jealous man to hang himself; a jealous woman has a different remedy—she bites her rival. Ten or twenty years ago it was a capital offence to raise a woman's ridi; to this day it is still punished with a heavy fine; and the garment itself is still symbolically sacred. Suppose a piece of land to be disputed in Butaritari, the claimant who shall first hang a ridi on the tapu-post has gained his cause, since no one can remove or touch it but himself.

The ridi was the badge not of the woman but the wife, the mark not of her sex but of her station. It was the collar on the slave's neck, the brand on merchandise. The adulterous woman seems to have been spared; were the husband offended, it would be a poor consolation to send his draught cattle to the shambles. Karaiti, to this day, calls his eight wives 'his horses,' some trader having explained to him the employment of these animals on farms; and Nanteitei hired out his wives to do mason-work. Husbands, at least when of high rank, had the power of life and death; even whites seem to have possessed it; and their wives, when they had transgressed beyond forgiveness, made haste to pronounce the formula of deprecation—I Kana Kim. This form of words had so much virtue that a condemned criminal repeating it on a particular day to the king who had condemned him, must be instantly released. It is an offer of abasement, and, strangely enough, the reverse—the imitation—is a common vulgar insult in Great Britain to this day. I give a scene between a trader and his Gilbert Island wife, as it was told me by the husband, now one of the oldest residents, but then a freshman in the group.

'Go and light a fire,' said the trader, 'and when I have brought this oil I will cook some fish.' The woman grunted at him, island fashion. 'I am not a pig that you should grunt at me,' said he.

'I know you are not a pig,' said the woman, 'neither am I your slave.'

'To be sure you are not my slave, and if you do not care to stop with me, you had better go home to your people,' said he. 'But in the mean time go and light the fire; and when I have brought this oil I will cook some fish.'

She went as if to obey; and presently when the trader looked she had built a fire so big that the cook-house was catching in flames.

'I Kana Kim!' she cried, as she saw him coming; but he recked not, and hit her with a cooking-pot. The leg pierced her skull, blood spouted, it was thought she was a dead woman, and the natives surrounded the house in a menacing expectation. Another white was present, a man of older experience. 'You will have us both killed if you go on like this,' he cried. 'She had said I Kana Kim!' If she had not said I Kana Kim he might have struck her with a caldron. It was not the blow that made the crime, but the disregard of an accepted formula.

Polygamy, the particular sacredness of wives, their semi-servile state, their seclusion in kings' harems, even their privilege of biting, all would seem to indicate a Mohammedan society and the opinion of the soullessness of woman. And not so in the least. It is a mere appearance. After you have studied these extremes in one house, you may go to the next and find all reversed, the woman the mistress, the man only the first of her thralls. The authority is not with the husband as such, nor the wife as such. It resides in the chief or the chief-woman; in him or her who has inherited the lands of the clan, and stands to the clansman in the place of parent, exacting their service, answerable for their fines. There is but the one source of power and the one ground of dignity—rank. The king married a chief-woman; she became his menial, and must work with her hands on Messrs. Wightman's pier. The king divorced her; she regained at once her former state and power. She married the Hawaiian sailor, and behold the man is her flunkey and can be shown the door at pleasure. Nay, and such low-born lords are even corrected physically, and, like grown but dutiful children, must endure the discipline.

We were intimate in one such household, that of Nei Takauti and Nan Tok'; I put the lady first of necessity. During one week of fool's paradise, Mrs. Stevenson had gone alone to the sea-side of the island after shells. I am very sure the proceeding was unsafe; and she soon perceived a man and woman watching her. Do what she would, her guardians held her steadily in view; and when the afternoon began to fall, and they thought she had stayed long enough, took her in charge, and by signs and broken English ordered her home. On the way the lady drew from her earring-hole a clay pipe, the husband lighted it, and it was handed to my unfortunate wife, who knew not how to refuse the incommodious favour; and when they were all come to our house, the pair sat down beside her on the floor, and improved the occasion with prayer. From that day they were our family friends; bringing thrice a day the beautiful island garlands of white flowers, visiting us any evening, and frequently carrying us down to their own maniap' in return, the woman leading Mrs. Stevenson by the hand like one child with another.

Nan Tok', the husband, was young, extremely handsome, of the most approved good humour, and suffering in his precarious station from suppressed high spirits. Nei Takauti, the wife, was getting old; her grown son by a former marriage had just hanged himself before his mother's eyes in despair at a well-merited rebuke. Perhaps she had never been beautiful, but her face was full of character, her eye of sombre fire. She was a high chief-woman, but by a strange exception for a person of her rank, was small, spare, and sinewy, with lean small hands and corded neck. Her full dress of an evening was invariably a white chemise—and for adornment, green leaves (or sometimes white blossoms) stuck in her hair and thrust through her huge earring-holes. The husband on the contrary changed to view like a kaleidoscope. Whatever pretty thing my wife might have given to Nei Takauti—a string of beads, a ribbon, a piece of bright fabric—appeared the next evening on the person of Nan Tok'. It was plain he was a clothes-horse; that he wore livery; that, in a word, he was his wife's wife. They reversed the parts indeed, down to the least particular; it was the husband who showed himself the ministering angel in the hour of pain, while the wife displayed the apathy and heartlessness of the proverbial man.

When Nei Takauti had a headache Nan Tok' was full of attention and concern. When the husband had a cold and a racking toothache the wife heeded not, except to jeer. It is always the woman's part to fill and light the pipe; Nei Takauti handed hers in silence to the wedded page; but she carried it herself, as though the page were not entirely trusted. Thus she kept the money, but it was he who ran the errands, anxiously sedulous. A cloud on her face dimmed instantly his beaming looks; on an early visit to their maniap' my wife saw he had cause to be wary. Nan Tok' had a friend with him, a giddy young thing, of his own age and sex; and they had worked themselves into that stage of jocularity when consequences are too often disregarded. Nei Takauti mentioned her own name. Instantly Nan Tok' held up two fingers, his friend did likewise, both in an ecstasy of slyness. It was plain the lady had two names; and from the nature of their merriment, and the wrath that gathered on her brow, there must be something ticklish in the second. The husband pronounced it; a well-directed cocoa-nut from the hand of his wife caught him on the side of the head, and the voices and the mirth of these indiscreet young gentlemen ceased for the day.

The people of Eastern Polynesia are never at a loss; their etiquette is absolute and plenary; in every circumstance it tells them what to do and how to do it. The Gilbertines are seemingly more free, and pay for their freedom (like ourselves) in frequent perplexity. This was often the case with the topsy-turvy couple. We had once supplied them during a visit with a pipe and tobacco; and when they had smoked and were about to leave, they found themselves confronted with a problem: should they take or leave what remained of the tobacco? The piece of plug was taken up, it was laid down again, it was handed back and forth, and argued over, till the wife began to look haggard and the husband elderly. They ended by taking it, and I wager were not yet clear of the compound before they were sure they had decided wrong. Another time they had been given each a liberal cup of coffee, and Nan Tok' with difficulty and disaffection made an end of his. Nei Takauti had taken some, she had no mind for more, plainly conceived it would be a breach of manners to set down the cup unfinished, and ordered her wedded retainer to dispose of what was left. 'I have swallowed all I can, I cannot swallow more, it is a physical impossibility,' he seemed to say; and his stern officer reiterated her commands with secret imperative signals. Luckless dog! but in mere humanity we came to the rescue and removed the cup.

I cannot but smile over this funny household; yet I remember the good souls with affection and respect. Their attention to ourselves was surprising. The garlands are much esteemed, the blossoms must be sought far and wide; and though they had many retainers to call to their aid, we often saw themselves passing afield after the blossoms, and the wife engaged with her own in putting them together. It was no want of only that disregard so incident to husbands, that made Nei Takauti despise the sufferings of Nan Tok'. When my wife was unwell she proved a diligent and kindly nurse; and the pair, to the extreme embarrassment of the sufferer, became fixtures in the sick-room. This rugged, capable, imperious old dame, with the wild eyes, had deep and tender qualities: her pride in her young husband it seemed that she dissembled, fearing possibly to spoil him; and when she spoke of her dead son there came something tragic in her face. But I seemed to trace in the Gilbertines a virility of sense and sentiment which distinguishes them (like their harsh and uncouth language) from their brother islanders in the east.

PART IV: THE GILBERTS—APEMAMA

CHAPTER I—THE KING OF APEMAMA: THE ROYAL TRADER

There is one great personage in the Gilberts: Tembinok' of Apemama: solely conspicuous, the hero of song, the butt of gossip. Through the rest of the group the kings are slain or fallen in tutelage: Tembinok' alone remains, the last tyrant, the last erect vestige of a dead society. The white man is everywhere else, building his houses, drinking his gin, getting in and out of trouble with the weak native governments. There is only one white on Apemama, and he on sufferance, living far from court, and hearkening and watching his conduct like a mouse in a cat's ear. Through all the other islands a stream of native visitors comes and goes, travelling by families, spending years on the grand tour. Apemama alone is left upon one side, the tourist dreading to risk himself within the clutch of Tembinok'. And fear of the same Gorgon follows and troubles them at home. Maiana once paid him tribute; he once fell upon and seized Nonuti: first steps to the empire of the archipelago. A British warship coming on the scene, the conqueror was driven to disgorge, his career checked in the outset, his dear-bought armoury sunk in his own lagoon. But the impression had been made; periodical fear of him still shakes the islands; rumour depicts him mustering his canoes for a fresh onfall; rumour can name his destination; and Tembinok' figures in the patriotic war-songs of the Gilberts like Napoleon in those of our grandfathers.

We were at sea, bound from Mariki to Nonuti and Tapituea, when the wind came suddenly fair for Apemama. The course was at once changed; all hands were turned-to to clean ship, the decks holy-stoned, all the cabin washed, the trade-room overhauled. In all our cruising we never saw the Equator so smart as she was made for Tembinok'. Nor was Captain Reid alone in these coquetries; for, another schooner chancing to arrive during my stay in Apemama, I found that she also was dandified for the occasion. And the two cases stand alone in my experience of South Sea traders.

We had on board a family of native tourists, from the grandsire to the babe in arms, trying (against an extraordinary series of ill-luck) to regain their native island of Peru. [275] Five times already they had paid their fare and taken ship; five times they had been disappointed, dropped penniless upon strange islands, or carried back to Butaritari, whence they sailed. This last attempt had been no better-starred; their provisions were exhausted. Peru was beyond hope, and they had cheerfully made up their minds to a fresh stage of exile in Tapituea or Nonuti. With this slant of wind their random destination became once more changed; and like the Calendar's pilot, when the 'black mountains' hove in view, they changed colour and beat upon their breasts. Their camp, which was on deck in the ship's waist, resounded with complaint. They would be set to work, they must become slaves, escape was hopeless, they must live and toil and die in Apemama, in the tyrant's den. With this sort of talk they so greatly terrified their children, that one (a big hulking boy) must at last be torn screaming from the schooner's side. And their fears were wholly groundless. I have little doubt they were not suffered to be idle; but I can vouch for it that they were kindly and generously used. For, the matter of a year later, I was once more shipmate with these inconsistent wanderers on board the Janet Nicoll. Their fare was paid by Tembinok'; they who had gone ashore from the Equator destitute, reappeared upon the Janet with new clothes, laden with mats and presents, and bringing with them a magazine of food, on which they lived like fighting-cocks throughout the voyage; I saw them at length repatriated, and I must say they showed more concern on quitting Apemama than delight at reaching home.

We entered by the north passage (Sunday, September 1st), dodging among shoals. It was a day of fierce equatorial sunshine; but the breeze was strong and chill; and the mate, who conned the schooner from the cross-trees, returned shivering to the deck. The lagoon was thick with many-tinted wavelets; a continuous roaring of the outer sea overhung the anchorage; and the long, hollow crescent of palm ruffled and sparkled in the wind. Opposite our berth the beach was seen to be surmounted for some distance by a terrace of white coral seven or eight feet high and crowned in turn by the scattered and incongruous buildings of the palace. The village adjoins on the south, a cluster of high-roofed maniap's. And village and palace seemed deserted.

We were scarce yet moored, however, before distant and busy figures appeared upon the beach, a boat was launched, and a crew pulled out to us bringing the king's ladder. Tembinok' had once an accident; has feared ever since to entrust his person to the rotten chandlery of South Sea traders; and devised in consequence a frame of wood, which is brought on board a ship as soon as she appears, and remains lashed to her side until she leave. The boat's crew, having applied this engine, returned at once to shore. They might not come on board; neither might we land, or not without danger of offence; the king giving pratique in person. An interval followed, during which dinner was delayed for the great man—the prelude of the ladder, giving us some notion of his weighty body and sensible, ingenious character, had highly whetted our curiosity; and it was with something like excitement that we saw the beach and terrace suddenly blacken with attendant vassals, the king and party embark, the boat (a man-of-war gig) come flying towards us dead before the wind, and the royal coxswain lay us cleverly aboard, mount the ladder with a jealous diffidence, and descend heavily on deck.

Not long ago he was overgrown with fat, obscured to view, and a burthen to himself. Captains visiting the island advised him to walk; and though it broke the habits of a life and the traditions of his rank, he practised the remedy with benefit. His corpulence is now portable; you would call him lusty rather than fat; but his gait is still dull, stumbling, and elephantine. He neither stops nor hastens, but goes about his business with an implacable deliberation. We could never see him and not be struck with his extraordinary natural means for the theatre: a beaked profile like Dante's in the mask, a mane of long black hair, the eye brilliant, imperious, and inquiring: for certain parts, and to one who could have used it, the face was a fortune. His voice matched it well, being shrill, powerful, and uncanny, with a note like a sea-bird's. Where there are no fashions, none to set them, few to follow them if they were set, and none to criticise, he dresses—as Sir Charles Grandison lived—'to his own heart.' Now he wears a woman's frock, now a naval uniform; now (and more usually) figures in a masquerade costume of his own design: trousers and a singular jacket with shirt tails, the cut and fit wonderful for island workmanship, the material always handsome, sometimes green velvet, sometimes cardinal red silk. This masquerade becomes him admirably. In the woman's frock he looks ominous and weird beyond belief. I see him now come pacing towards me in the cruel sun, solitary, a figure out of Hoffmann.

A visit on board ship, such as that at which we now assisted, makes a chief part and by far the chief diversion of the life of Tembinok'. He is not only the sole ruler, he is the sole merchant of his triple kingdom, Apemama, Aranuka, and Kuria, well-planted islands. The taro goes to the chiefs, who divide as they please among their immediate adherents; but certain fish, turtles—which abound in Kuria,—and the whole produce of the coco-palm, belong exclusively to Tembinok'. 'A' cobra [279a] berong me,' observed his majesty with a wave of his hand; and he counts and sells it by the houseful. 'You got copra, king?' I have heard a trader ask. 'I got two, three outches,' [279b] his majesty replied: 'I think three.' Hence the commercial importance of Apemama, the trade of three islands being centred there in a single hand; hence it is that so many whites have tried in vain to gain or to preserve a footing; hence ships are adorned, cooks have special orders, and captains array themselves in smiles, to greet the king. If he be pleased with his welcome and the fare he may pass days on board, and, every day, and sometimes every hour, will be of profit to the ship. He oscillates between the cabin, where he is entertained with strange meats, and the trade-room, where he enjoys the pleasures of shopping on a scale to match his person. A few obsequious attendants squat by the house door, awaiting his least signal. In the boat, which has been suffered to drop astern, one or two of his wives lie covered from the sun under mats, tossed by the short sea of the lagoon, and enduring agonies of heat and tedium. This severity is now and then relaxed and the wives allowed on board. Three or four were thus favoured on the day of our arrival: substantial ladies airily attired in ridis. Each had a share of copra, her peculium, to dispose of for herself. The display in the trade-room—hats, ribbbons, dresses, scents, tins of salmon—the pride of the eye and the lust of the flesh—tempted them in vain. They had but the one idea—tobacco, the island currency, tantamount to minted gold; returned to shore with it, burthened but rejoicing; and late into the night, on the royal terrace, were to be seen counting the sticks by lamplight in the open air.

The king is no such economist. He is greedy of things new and foreign. House after house, chest after chest, in the palace precinct, is already crammed with clocks, musical boxes, blue spectacles, umbrellas, knitted waistcoats, bolts of stuff, tools, rifles, fowling-pieces, medicines, European foods, sewing-machines, and, what is more extraordinary, stoves: all that ever caught his eye, tickled his appetite, pleased him for its use, or puzzled him with its apparent inutility. And still his lust is unabated. He is possessed by the seven devils of the collector. He hears a thing spoken of, and a shadow comes on his face. 'I think I no got him,' he will say; and the treasures he has seem worthless in comparison. If a ship be bound for Apemama, the merchant racks his brain to hit upon some novelty. This he leaves carelessly in the main cabin or partly conceals in his own berth, so that the king shall spy it for himself. 'How much you want?' inquires Tembinok', passing and pointing. 'No, king; that too dear,' returns the trader. 'I think I like him,' says the king. This was a bowl of gold-fish. On another occasion it was scented soap. 'No, king; that cost too much,' said the trader; 'too good for a Kanaka.' 'How much you got? I take him all,' replied his majesty, and became the lord of seventeen boxes at two dollars a cake. Or again, the merchant feigns the article is not for sale, is private property, an heirloom or a gift; and the trick infallibly succeeds. Thwart the king and you hold him. His autocratic nature rears at the affront of opposition. He accepts it for a challenge; sets his teeth like a hunter going at a fence; and with no mark of emotion, scarce even of interest, stolidly piles up the price. Thus, for our sins, he took a fancy to my wife's dressing-bag, a thing entirely useless to the man, and sadly battered by years of service. Early one forenoon he came to our house, sat down, and abruptly offered to purchase it. I told him I sold nothing, and the bag at any rate was a present from a friend; but he was acquainted with these pretexts from of old, and knew what they were worth and how to meet them. Adopting what I believe is called 'the object method,' he drew out a bag of English gold, sovereigns and half-sovereigns, and began to lay them one by one in silence on the table; at each fresh piece reading our faces with a look. In vain I continued to protest I was no trader; he deigned not to reply. There must have been twenty pounds on the table, he was still going on, and irritation had begun to mingle with our embarrassment, when a happy idea came to our delivery. Since his majesty thought so much of the bag, we said, we must beg him to accept it as a present. It was the most surprising turn in Tembinok's experience.

He perceived too late that his persistence was unmannerly; hung his head a while in silence; then, lifting up a sheepish countenance, 'I 'shamed,' said the tyrant. It was the first and the last time we heard him own to a flaw in his behaviour. Half an hour after he sent us a camphor-wood chest worth only a few dollars—but then heaven knows what Tembinok' had paid for it.

Cunning by nature, and versed for forty years in the government of men, it must not be supposed that he is cheated blindly, or has resigned himself without resistance to be the milch-cow of the passing trader. His efforts have been even heroic. Like Nakaeia of Makin, he has owned schooners. More fortunate than Nakaeia, he has found captains. Ships of his have sailed as far as to the colonies. He has trafficked direct, in his own bottoms, with New Zealand. And even so, even there, the world-enveloping dishonesty of the white man prevented him; his profit melted, his ship returned in debt, the money for the insurance was embezzled, and when the Coronet came to be lost, he was astonished to find he had lost all. At this he dropped his weapons; owned he might as hopefully wrestle with the winds of heaven; and like an experienced sheep, submitted his fleece thenceforward to the shearers. He is the last man in the world to waste anger on the incurable; accepts it with cynical composure; asks no more in those he deals with than a certain decency of moderation; drives as good a bargain as he can; and when he considers he is more than usually swindled, writes it in his memory against the merchant's name. He once ran over to me a list of captains and supercargoes with whom he had done business, classing them under three heads: 'He cheat a litty'—'He cheat plenty'—and 'I think he cheat too much.' For the first two classes he expressed perfect toleration; sometimes, but not always, for the third. I was present when a certain merchant was turned about his business, and was the means (having a considerable influence ever since the bag) of patching up the dispute. Even on the day of our arrival there was like to have been a hitch with Captain Reid: the ground of which is perhaps worth recital. Among goods exported specially for Tembinok' there is a beverage known (and labelled) as Hennessy's brandy. It is neither Hennessy, nor even brandy; is about the colour of sherry, but is not sherry; tastes of kirsch, and yet neither is it kirsch. The king, at least, has grown used to this amazing brand, and rather prides himself upon the taste; and any substitution is a double offence, being at once to cheat him and to cast a doubt upon his palate. A similar weakness is to be observed in all connoisseurs. Now the last case sold by the Equator was found to contain a different and I would fondly fancy a superior distillation; and the conversation opened very black for Captain Reid. But Tembinok' is a moderate man. He was reminded and admitted that all men were liable to error, even himself; accepted the principle that a fault handsomely acknowledged should be condoned; and wound the matter up with this proposal: 'Tuppoti [283] I mi'take, you 'peakee me. Tuppoti you mi'take, I 'peakee you. Mo' betta.'

After dinner and supper in the cabin, a glass or two of 'Hennetti'—the genuine article this time, with the kirsch bouquet,—and five hours' lounging on the trade-room counter, royalty embarked for home. Three tacks grounded the boat before the palace; the wives were carried ashore on the backs of vassals; Tembinok' stepped on a railed platform like a steamer's gangway, and was borne shoulder high through the shallows, up the beach, and by an inclined plane, paved with pebbles, to the glaring terrace where he dwells.

CHAPTER II—THE KING OF APEMAMA: FOUNDATION OF EQUATOR TOWN

Our first sight of Tembinok' was a matter of concern, almost alarm, to my whole party. We had a favour to seek; we must approach in the proper courtly attitude of a suitor; and must either please him or fail in the main purpose of our voyage. It was our wish to land and live in Apemama, and see more near at hand the odd character of the man and the odd (or rather ancient) condition of his island. In all other isles of the South Seas a white man may land with his chest, and set up house for a lifetime, if he choose, and if he have the money or the trade; no hindrance is conceivable. But Apemama is a close island, lying there in the sea with closed doors; the king himself, like a vigilant officer, ready at the wicket to scrutinise and reject intrenching visitors. Hence the attraction of our enterprise; not merely because it was a little difficult, but because this social quarantine, a curiosity in itself, has been the preservative of others.

Tembinok', like most tyrants, is a conservative; like many conservatives, he eagerly welcomes new ideas, and, except in the field of politics, leans to practical reform. When the missionaries came, professing a knowledge of the truth, he readily received them; attended their worship, acquired the accomplishment of public prayer, and made himself a student at their feet. It is thus—it is by the cultivation of similar passing chances—that he has learned to read, to write, to cipher, and to speak his queer, personal English, so different from ordinary 'Beach de Mar,' so much more obscure, expressive, and condensed. His education attended to, he found time to become critical of the new inmates. Like Nakaeia of Makin, he is an admirer of silence in the island; broods over it like a great ear; has spies who report daily; and had rather his subjects sang than talked. The service, and in particular the sermon, were thus sure to become offences: 'Here, in my island, I 'peak,' he once observed to me. 'My chieps no 'peak—do what I talk.' He looked at the missionary, and what did he see? 'See Kanaka 'peak in a big outch!' he cried, with a strong ring of sarcasm. Yet he endured the subversive spectacle, and might even have continued to endure it, had not a fresh point arisen. He looked again, to employ his own figure; and the Kanaka was no longer speaking, he was doing worse—he was building a copra-house. The king was touched in his chief interests; revenue and prerogative were threatened. He considered besides (and some think with him) that trade is incompatible with the missionary claims. 'Tuppoti mitonary think "good man": very good. Tuppoti he think "cobra": no good. I send him away ship.' Such was his abrupt history of the evangelist in Apemama.

Similar deportations are common: 'I send him away ship' is the epitaph of not a few, his majesty paying the exile's fare to the next place of call. For instance, being passionately fond of European food, he has several times added to his household a white cook, and one after another these have been deported. They, on their side, swear they were not paid their wages; he, on his, that they robbed and swindled him beyond endurance: both perhaps justly. A more important case was that of an agent, despatched (as I heard the story) by a firm of merchants to worm his way into the king's good graces, become, if possible, premier, and handle the copra in the interest of his employers. He obtained authority to land, practised his fascinations, was patiently listened to by Tembinok', supposed himself on the highway to success; and behold!

when the next ship touched at Apemama, the would-be premier was flung into a boat—had on board—his fare paid, and so good-bye. But it is needless to multiply examples; the proof of the pudding is in the eating. When we came to Apemama, of so many white men who have scrambled for a place in that rich market, one remained—a silent, sober, solitary, niggardly recluse, of whom the king remarks, 'I think he good; he no 'peak.'

I was warned at the outset we might very well fail in our design: yet never dreamed of what proved to be the fact, that we should be left four-and-twenty hours in suspense and come within an ace of ultimate rejection. Captain Reid had primed himself; no sooner was the king on board, and the Hennetti question amicably settled, than he proceeded to express my request and give an abstract of my claims and virtues. The gammon about Queen Victoria's son might do for Butaritari; it was out of the question here; and I now figured as 'one of the Old Men of England,' a person of deep knowledge, come expressly to visit Tembinok's dominion, and eager to report upon it to the no less eager Queen Victoria. The king made no shadow of an answer, and presently began upon a different subject. We might have thought that he had not heard, or not understood; only that we found ourselves the subject of a constant study. As we sat at meals, he took us in series and fixed upon each, for near a minute at a time, the same hard and thoughtful stare. As he thus looked he seemed to forget himself, the subject and the company, and to become absorbed in the process of his thought; the look was wholly impersonal; I have seen the same in the eyes of portrait-painters. The counts upon which whites have been deported are mainly four: cheating Tembinok', meddling overmuch with copra, which is the source of his wealth, and one of the sinews of his power, 'peaking, and political intrigue. I felt guiltless upon all; but how to show it? I would not have taken copra in a gift: how to express that quality by my dinner-table bearing? The rest of the party shared my innocence and my embarrassment. They shared also in my mortification when after two whole meal-times and the odd moments of an afternoon devoted to this reconnoitring, Tembinok' took his leave in silence. Next morning, the same undisguised study, the same silence, was resumed; and the second day had come to its maturity before I was informed abruptly that I had stood the ordeal. 'I look your eye. You good man. You no lie,' said the king: a doubtful compliment to a writer of romance. Later he explained he did not quite judge by the eye only, but the mouth as well. 'Tuppoti I see man,' he explained. 'I no tavvy good man, bad man. I look eye, look mouth. Then I tavvy. Look eye, look mouth,' he repeated. And indeed in our case the mouth had the most to do with it, and it was by our talk that we gained admission to the island; the king promising himself (and I believe really amassing) a vast amount of useful knowledge ere we left.

The terms of our admission were as follows: We were to choose a site, and the king should there build us a town. His people should work for us, but the king only was to give them orders. One of his cooks should come daily to help mine, and to learn of him. In case our stores ran out, he would supply us, and be repaid on the return of the Equator. On the other hand, he was to come to meals with us when so inclined; when he stayed at home, a dish was to be sent him from our table; and I solemnly engaged to give his subjects no liquor or money (both of which they are forbidden to possess) and no tobacco, which they were to receive only from the royal hand. I think I remember to have protested against the stringency of this last article; at least, it was relaxed, and when a man worked for me I was allowed to give him a pipe of tobacco on the premises, but none to take away.

The site of Equator City—we named our city for the schooner—was soon chosen. The immediate shores of the lagoon are windy and blinding; Tembinok' himself is glad to grope blue-spectacled on his terrace; and we fled the neighbourhood of the red conjunctiva, the suppurating eyeball, and the beggar who pursues and beseeches the passing foreigner for eye wash. Behind the town the country is diversified; here open, sandy, uneven, and dotted with dwarfish palms; here cut up with taro trenches, deep and shallow, and, according to the growth of the plants, presenting now the appearance of a sandy tannery, now of an alleyed and green garden. A path leads towards the sea, mounting abruptly to the main level of the island—twenty or even thirty feet, although Findlay gives five; and just hard by the top of the rise, where the coco-palms begin to be well grown, we found a grove of pandanus, and a piece of soil pleasantly covered with green underbush. A well was not far off under a rustic well-house; nearer still, in a sandy cup of the land, a pond where we might wash our clothes. The place was out of the wind, out of the sun, and out of sight of the village. It was shown to the king, and the town promised for the morrow.

The morrow came, Mr. Osbourne landed, found nothing done, and carried his complaint to Tembinok'. He heard it, rose, called for a Winchester, stepped without the royal palisade, and fired two shots in the air. A shot in the air is the first Apemama warning; it has the force of a proclamation in more loquacious countries; and his majesty remarked agreeably that it would make his labourers 'mo' bright.' In less than thirty minutes, accordingly, the men had mustered, the work was begun, and we were told that we might bring our baggage when we pleased.

It was two in the afternoon ere the first boat was beached, and the long procession of chests and crates and sacks began to straggle through the sandy desert towards Equator Town. The grove of pandanus was practically a thing of the past. Fire surrounded and smoke rose in the green underbush. In a wide circuit the axes were still crashing. Those very advantages for which the place was chosen, it had been the king's first idea to abolish; and in the midst of this devastation there stood already a good-sized maniap' and a small closed house. A mat was spread near by for Tembinok'; here he sat superintending, in cardinal red, a pith helmet on his head, a meerschaum pipe in his mouth, a wife stretched at his back with custody of the matches and tobacco. Twenty or thirty feet in front of him the bulk of the workers squatted on the ground; some of the bush here survived and in this the commons sat nearly to their shoulders, and presented only an arc of brown faces, black heads, and attentive eyes fixed on his majesty. Long pauses reigned, during which the subjects stared and the king smoked. Then Tembinok' would raise his voice and speak shrilly and briefly. There was never a response in words; but if the speech were jesting, there came by way of answer discreet, obsequious laughter—such laughter as we hear in schoolrooms; and if it were practical, the sudden uprising and departure of the squad. Twice they so disappeared, and returned with further elements of the city: a second house and a second maniap'. It was singular to spy, far off through the coco stems, the silent oncoming of the maniap', at first (it seemed) swimming spontaneously in the air—but on a nearer view betraying under the eaves many score of moving naked legs. In all the affair servile obedience was no less remarkable than servile deliberation. The gang had here mustered by the note of a deadly weapon; the man who looked on was the unquestioned master of their lives; and except for civility, they bestirred themselves like so many American hotel clerks. The spectator was aware of an unobtrusive yet invincible inertia, at which the skipper of a trading dandy might have torn his hair.

Yet the work was accomplished. By dusk, when his majesty withdrew, the town was founded and complete, a new and ruder Amphion having called it from nothing with three cracks of a rifle. And the next morning the same conjurer obliged us with a further miracle: a mystic rampart fencing us, so that the path which ran by our doors became suddenly impassable, the inhabitants who had business across the isle must fetch a wide circuit, and we sat in the midst in a transparent privacy, seeing, seen, but unapproachable, like bees in a glass hive. The outward and visible sign of this glamour was no more than a few ragged coco-leaf garlands round the stems of the outlying palms; but its significance reposed on the tremendous sanction of the tapu and the guns of Tembinok'.

We made our first meal that night in the improvised city, where we were to stay two months, and which—so soon as we had done with it—was to vanish in a day as it appeared, its elements returning whence they came, the tapu raised, the traffic on the path resumed, the sun and the moon peering in vain between the palm-trees for the bygone work, the wind blowing over an empty site. Yet the place, which is now only an episode in some memories, seemed to have been built, and to be destined to endure, for years. It was a busy hamlet. One of the maniap's we made our dining-room, one the kitchen. The houses we reserved for sleeping. They were on the admirable Apemama plan: out and away the best house in the South Seas; standing some three feet above the ground on posts; the sides of woven flaps, which can be raised to admit light and air, or lowered to shut out the wind and the rain: airy, healthy, clean, and watertight. We had a hen of a remarkable kind: almost unique in my experience, being a hen that occasionally laid eggs. Not far off, Mrs. Stevenson tended a garden of salad and shalots. The salad was devoured by the hen—which was her bane. The shalots were served out a leaf at a time, and welcomed and relished like peaches. Toddy and green cocoa-nuts were brought us daily. We once had a present of fish from the king, and once of a turtle. Sometimes we shot so-called plover along on the shore, sometimes wild chicken in the bush. The rest of our diet was from tins.

Our occupations were very various. While some of the party would be away sketching, Mr. Osbourne and I hammered away at a novel. We read Gibbon and Carlyle aloud; we blew on flageolets, we strummed on guitars; we took photographs by the light of the sun, the moon, and flash-powder; sometimes we played cards. Pot-hunting engaged a part of our leisure. I have myself passed afternoons in the exciting but innocuous pursuit of winged animals with a revolver; and it was fortunate there were better shots of the party, and fortunate the king could lend us a more suitable weapon, in the form of an excellent fowling-piece, or our spare diet had been sparer still.

Night was the time to see our city, after the moon was up, after the lamps were lighted, and so long as the fire sparkled in the cook-house. We suffered from a plague of flies and mosquitoes, comparable to that of Egypt; our dinner-table (lent, like all our furniture, by the king) must be enclosed in a tent of netting, our citadel and refuge; and this became all luminous, and bulged and beaconed under the eaves, like the globe of some monstrous lamp under the margin of its shade. Our cabins, the sides being propped at a variety of inclinations, spelled out strange, angular patterns of brightness. In his roofed and open kitchen, Ah Fu was to be seen by lamp and firelight, dabbling among pots. Over all, there fell in the season an extraordinary splendour of mellow moonshine. The sand sparkled as with the dust of diamonds; the stars had vanished. At intervals, a dusky night-bird, slow and low flying, passed in the colonnade of the tree stems and uttered a hoarse croaking cry.

CHAPTER III—THE KING OF APEMAMA: THE PALACE OF MANY WOMEN

The palace, or rather the ground which it includes, is several acres in extent. A terrace encloses it toward the lagoon; on the side of the land, a palisade with several gates. These are scarce intended for defence; a man, if he were strong, might easily pluck down the palisade; he need not be specially active to leap from the beach upon the terrace. There is no parade of guards, soldiers, or weapons; the armoury is under lock and key; and the only sentinels are certain inconspicuous old women lurking day and night before the gates. By day, these crones were often engaged in boiling syrup or the like household occupation; by night, they lay ambushed in the shadow or crouched along the palisade, filling the office of eunuchs to this harem, sole guards upon a tyrant life.

Female wardens made a fit outpost for this palace of many women. Of the number of the king's wives I have no guess; and but a loose idea of their function. He himself displayed embarrassment when they were referred to as his wives, called them himself 'my pamily,' and explained they were his 'cutcheons'—cousins. We distinguished four of the crowd: the king's mother; his sister, a grave, trenchant woman, with much of her brother's intelligence; the queen proper, to whom (and to whom alone) my wife was formally presented; and the favourite of the hour, a pretty, graceful girl, who sat with the king daily, and once (when he shed tears) consoled him with caresses. I am assured that even with her his relations are platonic. In the background figured a multitude of ladies, the lean, the plump, and the elephantine, some in sacque frocks, some in the hairbreadth ridi; high-born and low, slave and mistress; from the queen to the scullion, from the favourite to the scraggy sentries at the palisade. Not all of these of course are of 'my pamily,'—many are mere attendants; yet a surprising number shared the responsibility of the king's trust. These were key-bearers, treasurers, wardens of the armoury, the napery, and the stores. Each knew and did her part to admiration. Should anything be required—a particular gun, perhaps, or a particular bolt of stuff,—the right queen was summoned; she came bringing the right chest, opened it in the king's presence, and displayed her charge in perfect preservation—the gun cleaned and oiled, the goods duly folded. Without delay or haste, and with the minimum of speech, the whole great establishment turned on wheels like a machine. Nowhere have I seen order more complete and pervasive. And yet I was always reminded of Norse tales of trolls and ogres who kept their hearts buried in the ground for the mere safety, and must confide the secret to their wives. For these weapons are the life of Tembinok'. He does not aim at popularity; but drives and braves his subjects, with a simplicity of domination which it is impossible not to admire, hard not to sympathise with. Should one out of so many prove faithless, should the armoury be secretly unlocked, should the crones have dozed by the palisade and the weapons find their way unseen into the village, revolution would be nearly certain, death the most probable result, and the spirit of the tyrant of Apemama flit to rejoin his predecessors of Mariki and Tapituea. Yet those whom he so trusts are all women, and all rivals.

There is indeed a ministry and staff of males: cook, steward, carpenter, and supercargoes: the hierarchy of a schooner. The spies, 'his majesty's daily papers,' as we called them, come every morning to report, and go again. The cook and steward are concerned with the table only. The supercargoes, whose business it is to keep tally of the copra at three pounds a month and a percentage, are rarely in the palace; and two at least are in the other islands. The carpenter, indeed, shrewd and jolly old Rubam—query, Reuben?—promoted on my last visit to the greater dignity of governor, is daily present, altering, extending, embellishing, pursuing the endless series of the king's inventions; and his majesty will sometimes pass an afternoon watching and talking with Rubam at his work. But the males are still outsiders; none seems to be armed, none is entrusted with a key; by dusk they are all usually departed from the palace; and the weight of the monarchy and of the monarch's life reposes unshared on the women.

Here is a household unlike, indeed, to one of ours; more unlike still to the Oriental harem: that of an elderly childless man, his days menaced, dwelling alone amid a bevy of women of all ages, ranks, and relationships,—the mother, the sister, the cousin, the legitimate wife, the concubine, the favourite, the eldest born, and she of yesterday; he, in their midst, the only master, the only male, the sole dispenser of honours, clothes, and luxuries, the sole mark of multitudinous ambitions and desires. I doubt if you could find a man in Europe so bold as to attempt this piece of tact and government. And seemingly Tembinok' himself had trouble in the beginning. I hear of him shooting at a wife for some levity on board a schooner. Another, on some more serious offence, he slew outright; he exposed her body in an open box, and (to make the warning more memorable) suffered it to putrefy before the palace gate. Doubtless his growing years have come to his assistance; for upon so large a scale it is more easy to play the father than the husband. And to-day, at least to the eye of a stranger, all seems to go smoothly, and the wives to be proud of their trust, proud of their rank, and proud of their cunning lord.

I conceived they made rather a hero of the man. A popular master in a girls' school might, perhaps, offer a figure of his preponderating station. But then the master does not eat, sleep, live, and wash his dirty linen in the midst of his admirers; he escapes, he has a room of his own, he leads a private life; if he had nothing else, he has the holidays, and the more unhappy Tembinok' is always on the stage and on the stretch.

In all my coming and going, I never heard him speak harshly or express the least displeasure. An extreme, rather heavy, benignity—the benignity of one sure to be obeyed—marked his demeanour; so that I was at times reminded of Samual Richardson in his circle of admiring women. The wives spoke up and seemed to volunteer opinions, like our wives at home—or, say, like doting but respectable aunts. Altogether, I conclude that he rules his seraglio much more by art than terror; and those who give a different account (and who have none of them enjoyed my opportunities of observation) perhaps failed to distinguish between degrees of rank, between 'my pamily' and the hangers-on, laundresses, and prostitutes.

A notable feature is the evening game of cards when lamps are set forth upon the terrace, and 'I and my pamily' play for tobacco by the hour. It is highly characteristic of Tembinok' that he must invent a game for himself; highly characteristic of his worshipping household that they should swear by the absurd invention. It is founded on poker, played with the honours out of many packs, and inconceivably dreary. But I have a passion for all games, studied it, and am supposed to be the only white who ever fairly grasped its principle: a fact for which the wives (with whom I was not otherwise popular) admired me with acclamation. It was impossible to be deceived; this was a genuine feeling: they were proud of their private game, had been cut to the quick by the want of interest shown in it by others, and expanded under the flattery of my attention. Tembinok' puts up a double stake, and receives in return two hands to choose from: a shallow artifice which the wives (in all these years) have not yet fathomed. He himself, when talking with me privately, made not the least secret that he was secure of winning; and it was thus he explained his recent liberality on board the Equator. He let the wives buy their own tobacco, which pleased them at the moment. He won it back at cards, which made him once more, and without fresh expense, that which he ought to be,—the sole fount of all indulgences. And he summed the matter up in that phrase with which he almost always concludes any account of his policy: 'Mo' betta.'

The palace compound is laid with broken coral, excruciating to the eyes and the bare feet, but exquisitely raked and weeded. A score or more of buildings lie in a sort of street along the palisade and scattered on the margin of the terrace; dwelling-houses for the wives and the attendants, storehouses for the king's curios and treasures, spacious maniap's for feast or council, some on pillars of wood, some on piers of masonry. One was still in hand, a new invention, the king's latest born: a European frame-house built for coolness inside a lofty maniap': its roof planked like a ship's deck to be a raised, shady, and yet private promenade. It was here the king spent hours with Rubam; here I would sometimes join them; the place had a most singular appearance; and I must say I was greatly taken with the fancy, and joined with relish in the counsels of the architects.

Suppose we had business with his majesty by day: we strolled over the sand and by the dwarfish palms, exchanged a 'Kõnamaori' with the crone on duty, and entered the compound. The wide sheet of coral glared before us deserted; all having stowed themselves in dark canvas from the excess of room. I have gone to and fro in that labyrinth of a place, seeking the king; and the only breathing creature I could find was when I peered under the eaves of a maniap', and saw the brawny body of one of the wives stretched on the floor, a naked Amazon plunged in noiseless slumber. If it were still the hour of the 'morning papers' the quest would be more easy, the half-dozen obsequious, sly dogs squatting on the ground outside a house, crammed as far as possible in its narrow shadow, and turning to the king a row of leering faces. Tembinok' would be within, the flaps of the cabin raised, the trade blowing through, hearing their report. Like journalists nearer home, when the day's news were scanty, these would make the more of it in words; and I have known one to fill up a barren morning with an imaginary conversation of two dogs. Sometimes the king deigns to laugh, sometimes to question or jest with them, his voice sounding shrilly from the cabin. By his side he may have the heir-apparent, Paul, his nephew and adopted son, six years old, stark naked, and a model of young human beauty. And there will always be the favourite and perhaps two other wives awake; four more lying supine under mats and whelmed in slumber. Or perhaps we came later, fell on a more private hour, and found Tembinok' retired in the house with the favourite, an earthenware spittoon, a leaden inkpot, and a commercial ledger. In the last, lying on his belly, he writes from day to day the uneventful history of his reign; and when thus employed he betrayed a touch of fretfulness on interruption with which I was well able to sympathise. The royal annalist once read me a page or so, translating as he went; but the passage being genealogical, and the author boggling extremely in his version, I own I have been sometimes better entertained. Nor does he confine himself to prose, but touches the lyre, too, in his leisure moments, and passes for the chief bard of his kingdom, as he is its sole public character, leading architect, and only merchant.

His competence, however, does not reach to music; and his verses, when they are ready, are taught to a professional musician, who sets them and instructs the chorus. Asked what his songs were about, Tembinok' replied, 'Sweethearts and trees and the sea. Not all the same true, all the same lie.' For a condensed view of lyrical poetry (except that he seems to have forgot the stars and flowers) this would be hard to mend. These multifarious occupations bespeak (in a native and an absolute prince) unusual activity of mind.

The palace court at noon is a spot to be remembered with awe, the visitor scrambling there, on the loose stones, through a splendid nightmare of light and heat; but the sweep of the wind delivers it from flies and mosquitoes; and with the set of sun it became heavenly. I remember it best on moonless nights. The air was like a bath of milk. Countless shining stars were overhead, the lagoon paved with them. Herds of wives squatted by companies on the gravel, softly chatting. Tembinok' would doff his jacket, and sit bare and silent, perhaps meditating songs; the favourite usually by him, silent also. Meanwhile in the midst of the court, the palace lanterns were being lit and marshalled in rank upon the ground—six or eight square yards of them; a sight that gave one strange ideas of the number of 'my pamily': such a sight as may be seen about dusk in a corner of some great terminus at home. Presently these fared off into all corners of the precinct, lighting the last labours of the day, lighting one after another to their rest that prodigious company of women. A few lingered in the middle of the court for the card-party, and saw the honours shuffled and dealt, and Tembinok' deliberating between his two; hands, and the queens losing their tobacco. Then these also were scattered and extinguished; and their place was taken by a great bonfire, the night-light of the palace. When this was no more, smaller fires burned likewise at the gates. These were tended by the crones, unseen, unsleeping—not always unheard. Should any approach in the dark hours, a guarded alert made the circuit of the palisade; each sentry signalled her neighbour with a stone; the rattle of falling pebbles passed and died away; and the wardens of Tembinok' crouched in their places silent as before.

CHAPTER IV—THE KING OF APEMAMA: EQUATOR TOWN AND THE PALACE

Five persons were detailed to wait upon us. Uncle Parker, who brought us toddy and green nuts, was an elderly, almost an old man, with the spirits, the industry, and the morals of a boy of ten. His face was ancient, droll, and diabolical, the skin stretched over taut sinews, like a sail on the guide-rope; and he smiled with every muscle of his head. His nuts must be counted every day, or he would deceive us in the tale; they must be daily examined, or some would prove to be unhusked; nothing but the king's name, and scarcely that, would hold him to his duty. After his toils were over he was given a pipe, matches, and tobacco, and sat on the floor in the maniap' to smoke. He would not seem to move from his position, and yet every day, when the things fell to be returned the plug had disappeared; he had found the means to conceal it in the roof, whence he could radiantly produce it on the morrow. Although this piece of legerdemain was performed regularly before three or four pairs of eyes, we could never catch him in the fact; although we searched after he was gone, we could never find the tobacco. Such were the diversions of Uncle Parker, a man nearing sixty. But he was punished according unto his deeds: Mrs. Stevenson took a fancy to paint him, and the sufferings of the sitter were beyond description.

Three lasses came from the palace to do our washing and racket with Ah Fu. They were of the lowest class, hangers-on kept for the convenience of merchant skippers, probably low-born, perhaps out-islanders, with little refinement whether of manner or appearance, but likely and jolly enough wenches in their way. We called one Guttersnipe, for you may find her image in the slums of any city; the same lean, dark-eyed, eager, vulgar face, the same sudden, hoarse guffaws, the same forward and yet anxious manner, as with a tail of an eye on the policeman: only the policeman here was a live king, and his truncheon a rifle. I doubt if you could find anywhere out of the islands, or often there, the parallel of Fatty, a mountain of a girl, who must have weighed near as many stones as she counted summers, could have given a good account of a life-guardsman, had the face of a baby, and applied her vast mechanical forces almost exclusively to play. But they were all three of the same merry spirit. Our washing was conducted in a game of romps; and they fled and pursued, and splashed, and pelted, and rolled each other in the sand, and kept up a continuous noise of cries and laughter like holiday children. Indeed, and however strange their own function in that austere establishment, were they not escaped for the day from the largest and strictest Ladies' School in the South Seas?

Our fifth attendant was no less a person than the royal cook. He was strikingly handsome both in face and body, lazy as a slave, and insolent as a butcher's boy. He slept and smoked on our premises in various graceful attitudes; but so far from helping Ah Fu, he was not at the pains to watch him. It may be said of him that he came to learn, and remained to teach; and his lessons were at times difficult to stomach. For example, he was sent to fill a bucket from the well. About half-way he found my wife watering her onions, changed buckets with her, and leaving her the empty, returned to the kitchen with the full. On another occasion he was given a dish of dumplings for the king, was told they must be eaten hot, and that he should carry them as fast as possible. The wretch set off at the rate of about a mile in the hour, head in air, toes turned out. My patience, after a month of trial, failed me at the sight. I pursued, caught him by his two big shoulders, and thrusting him before me, ran with him down the hill, over the sands, and through the applauding village, to the Speak House, where the king was then holding a pow-wow. He had the impudence to pretend he was internally injured by my violence, and to profess serious apprehensions for his life.

All this we endured; for the ways of Tembinok' are summary, and I was not yet ripe to take a hand in the man's death. But in the meanwhile, here was my unfortunate China boy slaving for the pair, and presently he fell sick. I was now in the position of Cimondain Lantenac, and indeed all the characters in Quatre-Vingt-Treize: to continue to spare the guilty, I must sacrifice the innocent. I took the usual course and tried to save both, with the usual consequence of failure. Well rehearsed, I went down to the palace, found the king alone, and obliged him with a vast amount of rigmarole. The cook was too old to learn: I feared he was not making progress; how if we had a boy instead?—boys were more teachable. It was all in vain; the king pierced through my disguises to the root of the fact; saw that the cook had desperately misbehaved; and sat a while glooming. 'I think he tavvy too much,' he said at last, with grim concision; and immediately turned the talk to other subjects. The same day another high officer, the steward, appeared in the cook's place, and, I am bound to say, proved civil and industrious.

As soon as I left, it seems the king called for a Winchester and strolled outside the palisade, awaiting the defaulter. That day Tembinok' wore the woman's frock; as like as not, his make-up was completed by a pith helmet and blue spectacles. Conceive the glaring stretch of sandhills, the dwarf palms with their noon-day shadows, the line of the palisade, the crone sentries (each by a small clear fire) cooking syrup on their posts—and this chimæra waiting with his deadly engine. To him, enter at last the cook, strolling down the sandhill from Equator Town, listless, vain and graceful; with no thought of alarm. As soon as he was well within range, the travestied monarch fired the six shots over his head, at his feet, and on either hand of him: the second Apemama warning, startling in itself, fatal in significance, for the next time his majesty will aim to hit. I am told the king is a crack shot; that when he aims to kill, the grave may be got ready; and when he aims to miss, misses by so near a margin that the culprit tastes six times the bitterness of death. The effect upon the cook I had an opportunity of seeing for myself. My wife and I were returning from the sea-side of the island, when we spied one coming to meet us at a very quick, disordered pace, between a walk and a run. As we drew nearer we saw it was the cook, beside himself with some emotion, his usual warm, mulatto colour declined into a bluish pallor. He passed us without word or gesture, staring on us with the face of a Satan, and plunged on across the wood for the unpeopled quarter of the island and the long, desert beach, where he might rage to and fro unseen, and froth out the vials of his wrath, fear, and humiliation. Doubtless in the curses that he there uttered to the bursting surf and the tropic birds, the name of the Kaupoi—the rich man—was frequently repeated. I had made him the laughing-stock of the village in the affair of the king's dumplings; I had brought him by my machinations into disgrace and the immediate jeopardy of his days; last, and perhaps bitterest, he had found me there by the way to spy upon him in the hour of his disorder.

Time passed, and we saw no more of him. The season of the full moon came round, when a man thinks shame to lie sleeping; and I continued until late—perhaps till twelve or one in the morning—to walk on the bright sand and in the tossing shadow of the palms. I played, as I wandered, on a flageolet, which occupied much of my attention; the fans overhead rattled in the wind with a metallic chatter; and a bare foot falls at any rate almost noiseless on that shifting soil. Yet when I got back to Equator Town, where all the lights were out, and my wife (who was still awake, and had been looking forth) asked me who it was that followed me, I thought she spoke in jest. 'Not at all,' she said. 'I saw him twice as you passed, walking close at your heels. He only left you at the corner of the maniap'; he must be still behind the cook-house.' Thither I ran—like a fool, without any weapon—and came face to face with the cook. He was within my tapu-line, which was death in itself; he could have no business there at such an hour but either to steal or to kill; guilt made him timorous; and he turned and fled before me in the night in silence. As he went I kicked him in that place where honour lies, and he gave tongue faintly like an injured mouse. At the moment I daresay he supposed it was a deadly instrument that touched him.

What had the man been after? I have found my music better qualified to scatter than to collect an audience. Amateur as I was, I could not suppose him interested in my reading of the Carnival of Venice, or that he would deny himself his natural rest to follow my variations on The Ploughboy. And whatever his design, it was impossible I should suffer him to prowl by night among the houses. A word to the king, and the man were not, his case being far beyond pardon. But it is one thing to kill a man yourself; quite another to bear tales behind his back and have him shot by a third party; and I determined to deal with the fellow in some method of my own. I told Ah Fu the story, and bade him fetch me the cook whenever he should find him. I had supposed this would be a matter of difficulty; and far from that, he came of his own accord: an act really of desperation, since his life hung by my silence, and the best he could hope was to be forgotten. Yet he came with an assured countenance, volunteered no apology or explanation, complained of injuries received, and pretended he was unable to sit down. I suppose I am the weakest man God made; I had kicked him in the least vulnerable part of his big carcase; my foot was bare, and I had not even hurt my foot. Ah Fu could not control his merriment. On my side, knowing what must be the nature of his apprehensions, I found in so much impudence a kind of gallantry, and secretly admired the man. I told him I should say nothing of his night's adventure to the king; that I should still allow him, when he had an errand, to come within my tapu-line by day; but if ever I found him there after the set of the sun I would shoot him on the spot; and to the proof showed him a revolver. He must have been incredibly relieved; but he showed no sign of it, took himself off with his usual dandy nonchalance, and was scarce seen by us again.

These five, then, with the substitution of the steward for the cook, came and went, and were our only visitors. The circle of the tapu held at arm's-length the inhabitants of the village. As for 'my pamily,' they dwelt like nuns in their enclosure; only once have I met one of them abroad, and she was the king's sister, and the place in which I found her (the island infirmary) was very likely privileged. There remains only the king to be accounted for. He would come strolling over, always alone, a little before a meal-time, take a chair, and talk and eat with us like an old family friend. Gilbertine etiquette appears defective on the point of leave-taking. It may be remembered we had trouble in the matter with Karaiti; and there was something childish and disconcerting in Tembinok's abrupt 'I want go home now,' accompanied by a kind of ducking rise, and followed by an unadorned retreat. It was the only blot upon his manners, which were otherwise plain, decent, sensible, and dignified. He never stayed long nor drank much, and copied our behaviour where he perceived it to differ from his own. Very early in the day, for instance, he ceased eating with his knife. It was plain he was determined in all things to wring profit from our visit, and chiefly upon etiquette. The quality of his white visitors puzzled and concerned him; he would bring up name after name, and ask if its bearer were a 'big chiep,' or even a 'chiep' at all—which, as some were my excellent good friends, and none were actually born in the purple, became at times embarrassing. He was struck to learn that our classes were distinguishable by their speech, and that certain words (for instance) were tapu on the quarter-deck of a man-of-war; and he begged in consequence that we should watch and correct him on the point. We were able to assure him that he was beyond correction. His vocabulary is apt and ample to an extraordinary degree. God knows where he collected it, but by some instinct or some accident he has avoided all profane or gross expressions. 'Obliged,' 'stabbed,' 'gnaw,' 'lodge,' 'power,' 'company,' 'slender,' 'smooth,' and 'wonderful,' are a few of the unexpected words that enrich his dialect. Perhaps what pleased him most was to hear about saluting the quarter-deck of a man-of-war. In his gratitude for this hint he became fulsome. 'Schooner cap'n no tell me,' he cried; 'I think no tavvy! You tavvy too much; tavvy 'teama', tavvy man-a-wa'. I think you tavvy everything.' Yet he gravelled me often enough with his perpetual questions; and the false Mr. Barlow stood frequently exposed before the royal Sandford. I remember once in particular. We were showing the magic-lantern; a slide of Windsor Castle was put in, and I told him there was the 'outch' of Victoreea. 'How many pathom he high?' he asked, and I was dumb before him. It was the builder, the indefatigable architect of palaces, that spoke; collector though he was, he did not collect useless information; and all his questions had a purpose. After etiquette, government, law, the police, money, and medicine were his chief interests—things vitally important to himself as a king and the father of his people. It was my part not only to supply new information, but to correct the old. 'My patha he tell me,' or 'White man he tell me,' would be his constant beginning; 'You think he lie?' Sometimes I thought he did. Tembinok' once brought me a difficulty of this kind, which I was long of comprehending. A schooner captain had told him of Captain Cook; the king was much interested in the story; and turned for more information—not to Mr. Stephen's Dictionary, not to the Britannica, but to the Bible in the Gilbert Island version (which consists chiefly of the New Testament and the Psalms). Here he sought long and earnestly; Paul he found, and Festus and Alexander the coppersmith: no word of Cook. The inference was obvious: the explorer was a myth. So hard it is, even for a man of great natural parts like Tembinok', to grasp the ideas of a new society and culture.

CHAPTER V—KING AND COMMONS

We saw but little of the commons of the isle. At first we met them at the well, where they washed their linen and we drew water for the table. The combination was distasteful; and, having a tyrant at command, we applied to the king and had the place enclosed in our tapu. It was one of the few favours which Tembinok' visibly boggled about granting, and it may be conceived how little popular it made the strangers. Many villagers passed us daily going afield; but they fetched a wide circuit round our tapu, and seemed to avert their looks. At times we went ourselves into the village—a strange place. Dutch by its canals, Oriental by the height and steepness of the roofs, which looked at dusk like temples; but we were rarely called into a house: no welcome, no friendship, was offered us; and of home life we had but the one view: the waking of a corpse, a frigid, painful scene: the widow holding on her lap the cold, bluish body of her husband, and now partaking of the refreshments which made the round of the company, now weeping and kissing the pale mouth. ('I fear you feel this affliction deeply,' said the Scottish minister. 'Eh, sir, and that I do!' replied the widow. 'I've been greetin' a' nicht; an' noo I'm just gaun to sup this bit parritch, and then I'll begin an' greet again.') In our walks abroad I have always supposed the islanders avoided us, perhaps from distaste, perhaps by order; and those whom we met we took generally by surprise. The surface of the isle is diversified with palm groves, thickets, and romantic dingles four feet deep, relics of old taro plantation; and it is thus possible to stumble unawares on folk resting or hiding from their work. About pistol-shot from our township there lay a pond in the bottom of a jungle; here the maids of the isle came to bathe, and were several times alarmed by our intrusion. Not for them are the bright cold rivers of Tahiti or Upolu, not for them to splash and laugh in the hour of the dusk with a villageful of gay companions; but to steal here solitary, to crouch in a place like a cow-wallow, and wash (if that can be called washing) in lukewarm mud, brown as their own skins. Other, but still rare, encounters occur to my memory. I was several times arrested by a tender sound in the bush of voices talking, soft as flutes and with quiet intonations. Hope told a flattering tale; I put aside the leaves; and behold! in place of the expected dryads, a pair of all too solid ladies squatting over a clay pipe in the ungraceful ridi. The beauty of the voice and the eye was all that remained to those vast dames; but that of the voice was indeed exquisite. It is strange I should have never heard a more winning sound of speech, yet the dialect should be one remarkable for violent, ugly, and outlandish vocables; so that Tembinok' himself declared it made him weary, and professed to find repose in talking English.

The state of this folk, of whom I saw so little, I can merely guess at. The king himself explains the situation with some art. 'No; I no pay them,' he once said. 'I give them tobacco. They work for me all the same brothers.' It is true there was a brother once in Arden! But we prefer the shorter word. They bear every servile mark,—levity like a child's, incurable idleness, incurious content. The insolence of the cook was a trait of his own; not so his levity, which he shared with the innocent Uncle Parker. With equal unconcern both gambolled under the shadow of the gallows, and took liberties with death that might have surprised a careless student of man's nature. I wrote of Parker that he behaved like a boy of ten: what was he else, being a slave of sixty? He had passed all his years in school, fed, clad, thought for, commanded; and had grown familiar and coquetted with the fear of punishment. By terror you may drive men long, but not far. Here, in Apemama, they work at the constant and the instant peril of their lives; and are plunged in a kind of lethargy of laziness. It is common to see one go afield in his stiff mat ungirt, so that he walks elbows-in like a trussed fowl; and whatsoever his right hand findeth to do, the other must be off duty holding on his clothes. It is common to see two men carrying between them on a pole a single bucket of water. To make two bites of a cherry is good enough: to make two burthens of a soldier's kit, for a distance of perhaps half a furlong, passes measure. Woman, being the less childish animal, is less relaxed by servile conditions. Even in the king's absence, even when they were alone, I have seen Apemama women work with constancy. But the outside to be hoped for in a man is that he may attack his task in little languid fits, and lounge between-whiles. So I have seen a painter, with his pipe going, and a friend by the studio fireside. You might suppose the race to lack civility, even vitality, until you saw them in the dance. Night after night, and sometimes day after day, they rolled out their choruses in the great Speak House—solemn andantes and adagios, led by the clapped hand, and delivered with an energy that shook the roof. The time was not so slow, though it was slow for the islands; but I have chosen rather to indicate the effect upon the hearer. Their music had a church-like character from near at hand, and seemed to European ears more regular than the run of island music. Twice I have heard a discord regularly solved. From farther off, heard at Equator Town for instance, the measures rose and fell and crepitated like the barking of hounds in a distant kennel.

The slaves are certainly not overworked—children of ten do more without fatigue—and the Apemama labourers have holidays, when the singing begins early in the afternoon. The diet is hard; copra and a sweetmeat of pounded pandanus are the only dishes I observed outside the palace; but there seems no defect in quantity, and the king shares with them his turtles. Three came in a boat from Kuria during our stay; one was kept for the palace, one sent to us, one presented to the village. It is the habit of the islanders to cook the turtle in its carapace; we had been promised the shells, and we asked a tapu on this foolish practice. The face of Tembinok' darkened and he answered nothing. Hesitation in the question of the well I could understand, for water is scarce on a low island; that he should refuse to interfere upon a point of cookery was more than I had dreamed of; and I gathered (rightly or wrongly) that he was scrupulous of touching in the least degree the private life and habits of his slaves. So that even here, in full despotism, public opinion has weight; even here, in the midst of slavery, freedom has a corner.

Orderly, sober, and innocent, life flows in the isle from day to day as in a model plantation under a model planter. It is impossible to doubt the beneficence of that stern rule. A curious politeness, a soft and gracious manner, something effeminate and courtly, distinguishes the islanders of Apemama; it is talked of by all the traders, it was felt even by residents so little beloved as ourselves, and noticeable even in the cook, and even in that scoundrel's hours of insolence. The king, with his manly and plain bearing, stood out alone; you might say he was the only Gilbert Islander in Apemama. Violence, so common in Butaritari, seems unknown. So are theft and drunkenness. I am assured the experiment has been made of leaving sovereigns on the beach before the village; they lay there untouched. In all our time on the island I was but once asked for drink. This was by a mighty plausible fellow, wearing European clothes and speaking excellent English—Tamaiti his name, or, as the whites have now corrupted it, 'Tom White': one of the king's supercargoes at three pounds a month and a percentage, a medical man besides, and in his private hours a wizard. He found me one day in the outskirts of the village, in a secluded place, hot and private, where the taro-pits are deep and the plants high. Here he buttonholed me, and, looking about him like a conspirator, inquired if I had gin.

I told him I had. He remarked that gin was forbidden, lauded the prohibition a while, and then went on to explain that he was a doctor, or 'dogstar' as he pronounced the word, that gin was necessary to him for his medical infusions, that he was quite out of it, and that he would be obliged to me for some in a bottle. I told him I had passed the king my word on landing; but since his case was so exceptional, I would go down to the palace at once, and had no doubt that Tembinok' would set me free. Tom White was immediately overwhelmed with embarrassment and terror, besought me in the most moving terms not to betray him, and fled my neighbourhood. He had none of the cook's valour; it was weeks before he dared to meet my eye; and then only by the order of the king and on particular business.

The more I viewed and admired this triumph of firm rule, the more I was haunted and troubled by a problem, the problem (perhaps) of to-morrow for ourselves. Here was a people protected from all serious misfortune, relieved of all serious anxieties, and deprived of what we call our liberty. Did they like it? and what was their sentiment toward the ruler? The first question I could not of course ask, nor perhaps the natives answer. Even the second was delicate; yet at last, and under charming and strange circumstances, I found my opportunity to put it and a man to reply. It was near the full of the moon, with a delicious breeze; the isle was bright as day—to sleep would have been sacrilege; and I walked in the bush, playing my pipe. It must have been the sound of what I am pleased to call my music that attracted in my direction another wanderer of the night. This was a young man attired in a fine mat, and with a garland on his hair, for he was new come from dancing and singing in the public hall; and his body, his face, and his eyes were all of an enchanting beauty. Every here and there in the Gilberts youths are to be found of this absurd perfection; I have seen five of us pass half an hour in admiration of a boy at Mariki; and Te Kop (my friend in the fine mat and garland) I had already several times remarked, and long ago set down as the loveliest animal in Apemama. The philtre of admiration must be very strong, or these natives specially susceptible to its effects, for I have scarce ever admired a person in the islands but what he has sought my particular acquaintance. So it was with Te Kop. He led me to the ocean side; and for an hour or two we sat smoking and talking on the resplendent sand and under the ineffable brightness of the moon. My friend showed himself very sensible of the beauty and amenity of the hour. 'Good night! Good wind!' he kept exclaiming, and as he said the words he seemed to hug myself. I had long before invented such reiterated expressions of delight for a character (Felipe, in the story of Olalla) intended to be partly bestial. But there was nothing bestial in Te Kop; only a childish pleasure in the moment. He was no less pleased with his companion, or was good enough to say so; honoured me, before he left, by calling me Te Kop; apostrophised me as 'My name!' with an intonation exquisitely tender, laying his hand at the same time swiftly on my knee; and after we had risen, and our paths began to separate in the bush, twice cried to me with a sort of gentle ecstasy, 'I like you too much!' From the beginning he had made no secret of his terror of the king; would not sit down nor speak above a whisper till he had put the whole breadth of the isle between himself and his monarch, then harmlessly asleep; and even there, even within a stone-cast of the outer sea, our talk covered by the sound of the surf and the rattle of the wind among the palms, continued to speak guardedly, softening his silver voice (which rang loud enough in the chorus) and looking about him like a man in fear of spies. The strange thing is that I should have beheld him no more. In any other island in the whole South Seas, if I had advanced half as far with any native, he would have been at my door next morning, bringing and expecting gifts. But Te Kop vanished in the bush for ever. My house, of course, was unapproachable; but he knew where to find me on the ocean beach, where I went daily. I was the Kaupoi, the rich man; my tobacco and trade were known to be endless: he was sure of a present. I am at a loss how to explain his behaviour, unless it be supposed that he recalled with terror and regret a passage in our interview. Here it is:

'The king, he good man?' I asked.

'Suppose he like you, he good man,' replied Te Kop: 'no like, no good.'

That is one way of putting it, of course. Te Kop himself was probably no favourite, for he scarce appealed to my judgment as a type of industry. And there must be many others whom the king (to adhere to the formula) does not like. Do these unfortunates like the king? Or is not rather the repulsion mutual? and the conscientious Tembinok', like the conscientious Braxfield before him, and many other conscientious rulers and judges before either, surrounded by a considerable body of 'grumbletonians'? Take the cook, for instance, when he passed us by, blue with rage and terror. He was very wroth with me; I think by all the old principles of human nature he was not very well pleased with his sovereign. It was the rich man he sought to waylay: I think it must have been by the turn of a hair that it was not the king he waylaid instead. And the king gives, or seems to give, plenty of opportunities; day and night he goes abroad alone, whether armed or not I can but guess; and the taro-patches, where his business must so often carry him, seem designed for assassination. The case of the cook was heavy indeed to my conscience. I did not like to kill my enemy at second-hand; but had I a right to conceal from the king, who had trusted me, the dangerous secret character of his attendant? And suppose the king should fall, what would be the fate of the king's friends? It was our opinion at the time that we should pay dear for the closing of the well; that our breath was in the king's nostrils; that if the king should by any chance be bludgeoned in a taro-patch, the philosophical and musical inhabitants of Equator Town might lay aside their pleasant instruments, and betake themselves to what defence they had, with a very dim prospect of success. These speculations were forced upon us by an incident which I am ashamed to betray. The schooner H. L. Haseltine (since capsized at sea, with the loss of eleven lives) put into Apemama in a good hour for us, who had near exhausted our supplies. The king, after his habit, spent day after day on board; the gin proved unhappily to his taste; he brought a store of it ashore with him; and for some time the sole tyrant of the isle was half-seas-over. He was not drunk—the man is not a drunkard, he has always stores of liquor at hand, which he uses with moderation,—but he was muzzy, dull, and confused. He came one day to lunch with us, and while the cloth was being laid fell asleep in his chair. His confusion, when he awoke and found he had been detected, was equalled by our uneasiness. When he was gone we sat and spoke of his peril, which we thought to be in some degree our own; of how easily the man might be surprised in such a state by grumbletonians; of the strange scenes that would follow—the royal treasures and stores at the mercy of the rabble, the palace overrun, the garrison of women turned adrift. And as we talked we were startled by a gun-shot and a sudden, barbaric outcry. I believe we all changed colour; but it was only the king firing at a dog and the chorus striking up in the Speak House. A day or two later I learned the king was very sick; went down, diagnosed the case; and took at once the highest medical degree by the exhibition of bicarbonate of soda. Within the hour Richard was himself again; and I found him at the unfinished house, enjoying the double pleasure of directing Rubam and making a dinner of cocoa-nut dumplings, and all eagerness to have the formula of this new sort of pain-killer—for pain-killer in the islands is the generic name of medicine. So ended the king's modest spree and our anxiety.

On the face of things, I ought to say, loyalty appeared unshaken. When the schooner at last returned for us, after much experience of baffling winds, she brought a rumour that Tebureimoa had declared war on Apemama.

Tembinok' became a new man; his face radiant; his attitude, as I saw him preside over a council of chiefs in one of the palace maniap's, eager as a boy's; his voice sounding abroad, shrill and jubilant, over half the compound. War is what he wants, and here was his chance. The English captain, when he flung his arms in the lagoon, had forbidden him (except in one case) all military adventures in the future: here was the case arrived. All morning the council sat; men were drilled, arms were bought, the sound of firing disturbed the afternoon; the king devised and communicated to me his plan of campaign, which was highly elaborate and ingenious, but perhaps a trifle fine-spun for the rough and random vicissitudes of war. And in all this bustle the temper of the people appeared excellent, an unwonted animation in every face, and even Uncle Parker burning with military zeal.

Of course it was a false alarm. Tebureimoa had other fish to fry. The ambassador who accompanied us on our return to Butaritari found him retired to a small island on the reef, in a huff with the Old Men, a tiff with the traders, and more fear of insurrection at home than appetite for wars abroad. The plenipotentiary had been placed under my protection; and we solemnly saluted when we met. He proved an excellent fisherman, and caught bonito over the ship's side. He pulled a good oar, and made himself useful for a whole fiery afternoon, towing the becalmed Equator off Mariki. He went to his post and did no good. He returned home again, having done no harm. O si sic omnes!

CHAPTER VI—THE KING OF APEMAMA: DEVIL-WORK

The ocean beach of Apemama was our daily resort. The coast is broken by shallow bays. The reef is detached, elevated, and includes a lagoon about knee-deep, the unrestful spending-basin of the surf. The beach is now of fine sand, now of broken coral. The trend of the coast being convex, scarce a quarter of a mile of it is to be seen at once; the land being so low, the horizon appears within a stone-cast; and the narrow prospect enhances the sense of privacy. Man avoids the place—even his footprints are uncommon; but a great number of birds hover and pipe there fishing, and leave crooked tracks upon the sand. Apart from these, the only sound (and I was going to say the only society), is that of the breakers on the reef.

On each projection of the coast, the bank of coral clinkers immediately above the beach has been levelled, and a pillar built, perhaps breast-high. These are not sepulchral; all the dead being buried on the inhabited side of the island, close to men's houses, and (what is worse) to their wells. I was told they were to protect the isle against inroads from the sea—divine or diabolical martellos, probably sacred to Taburik, God of Thunder.

The bay immediately opposite Equator Town, which we called Fu Bay, in honour of our cook, was thus fortified on either horn. It was well sheltered by the reef, the enclosed water clear and tranquil, the enclosing beach curved like a horseshoe, and both steep and broad. The path debouched about the midst of the re-entrant angle, the woods stopping some distance inland. In front, between the fringe of the wood and the crown of the beach, there had been designed a regular figure, like the court for some new variety of tennis, with borders of round stones imbedded, and pointed at the angles with low posts, likewise of stone. This was the king's Pray Place. When he prayed, what he prayed for, and to whom he addressed his supplications I could never learn. The ground was tapu.

In the angle, by the mouth of the path, stood a deserted maniap'. Near by there had been a house before our coming, which was now transported and figured for the moment in Equator Town. It had been, and it would be again when we departed, the residence of the guardian and wizard of the spot—Tamaiti. Here, in this lone place, within sound of the sea, he had his dwelling and uncanny duties. I cannot call to mind another case of a man living on the ocean side of any open atoll; and Tamaiti must have had strong nerves, the greater confidence in his own spells, or, what I believe to be the truth, an enviable scepticism. Whether Tamaiti had any guardianship of the Pray Place I never heard. But his own particular chapel stood farther back in the fringe of the wood. It was a tree of respectable growth. Around it there was drawn a circle of stones like those that enclosed the Pray Place; in front, facing towards the sea, a stone of a much greater size, and somewhat hollowed, like a piscina, stood close against the trunk; in front of that again a conical pile of gravel. In the hollow of what I have called the piscina (though it proved to be a magic seat) lay an offering of green cocoa-nuts; and when you looked up you found the boughs of the tree to be laden with strange fruit: palm-branches elaborately plaited, and beautiful models of canoes, finished and rigged to the least detail. The whole had the appearance of a mid-summer and sylvan Christmas-tree al fresco. Yet we were already well enough acquainted in the Gilberts to recognise it, at the first sight, for a piece of wizardry, or, as they say in the group, of Devil-work.

The plaited palms were what we recognised. We had seen them before on Apaiang, the most christianised of all these islands; where excellent Mr. Bingham lived and laboured and has left golden memories; whence all the education in the northern Gilberts traces its descent; and where we were boarded by little native Sunday-school misses in clean frocks, with demure faces, and singing hymns as to the manner born.

Our experience of Devil-work at Apaiang had been as follows:—It chanced we were benighted at the house of Captain Tierney. My wife and I lodged with a Chinaman some half a mile away; and thither Captain Reid and a native boy escorted us by torch-light. On the way the torch went out, and we took shelter in a small and lonely Christian chapel to rekindle it. Stuck in the rafters of the chapel was a branch of knotted palm. 'What is that?' I asked. 'O, that's Devil-work,' said the Captain. 'And what is Devil-work?' I inquired. 'If you like, I'll show you some when we get to Johnnie's,' he replied. 'Johnnie's' was a quaint little house upon the crest of the beach, raised some three feet on posts, approached by stairs; part walled, part trellised. Trophies of advertisement-photographs were hung up within for decoration. There was a table and a recess-bed, in which Mrs. Stevenson slept; while I camped on the matted floor with Johnnie, Mrs. Johnnie, her sister, and the devil's own regiment of cockroaches. Hither was summoned an old witch, who looked the part to horror. The lamp was set on the floor; the crone squatted on the threshold, a green palm-branch in her hand, the light striking full on her aged features and picking out behind her, from the black night, timorous faces of spectators. Our sorceress began with a chanted incantation; it was in the old tongue, for which I had no interpreter; but ever and again there ran among the crowd outside that laugh which every traveller in the islands learns so soon to recognise,—the laugh of terror. Doubtless these half-Christian folk were shocked, these half-heathen folk alarmed. Chench or Taburik thus invoked, we put our questions; the witch knotted the leaves, here a leaf and there a leaf, plainly on some arithmetical system; studied the result with great apparent contention of mind; and gave the answers. Sidney Colvin was in robust health and gone a journey; and we should have a fair wind upon the morrow: that was the result of our consultation, for which we paid a dollar. The next day dawned cloudless and breathless; but I think Captain Reid placed a secret reliance on the sibyl, for the schooner was got ready for sea. By eight the lagoon was flawed with long cat's-paws, and the palms tossed and rustled; before ten we were clear of the passage and skimming under all plain sail, with bubbling scuppers. So we had the breeze, which was well worth a dollar in itself; but the bulletin about my friend in England proved, some six months later, when I got my mail, to have been groundless. Perhaps London lies beyond the horizon of the island gods.

Tembinok', in his first dealings, showed himself sternly averse from superstition: and had not the Equator delayed, we might have left the island and still supposed him an agnostic. It chanced one day, however, that he came to our maniap', and found Mrs. Stevenson in the midst of a game of patience. She explained the game as well as she was able, and wound up jocularly by telling him this was her devil-work, and if she won, the Equator would arrive next day. Tembinok' must have drawn a long breath; we were not so high-and-dry after all; he need no longer dissemble, and he plunged at once into confessions. He made devil-work every day, he told us, to know if ships were coming in; and thereafter brought us regular reports of the results. It was surprising how regularly he was wrong; but he always had an explanation ready. There had been some schooner in the offing out of view; but either she was not bound for Apemama, or had changed her course, or lay becalmed. I used to regard the king with veneration as he thus publicly deceived himself. I saw behind him all the fathers of the Church, all the philosophers and men of science of the past; before him, all those that are to come; himself in the midst; the whole visionary series bowed over the same task of welding incongruities. To the end Tembinok' spoke reluctantly of the island gods and their worship, and I learned but little. Taburik is the god of thunder, and deals in wind and weather. A while since there were wizards who could call him down in the form of lightning. 'My patha he tell me he see: you think he lie?' Tienti—pronounced something like 'Chench,' and identified by his majesty with the devil—sends and removes bodily sickness. He is whistled for in the Paumotuan manner, and is said to appear; but the king has never seen him. The doctors treat disease by the aid of Chench: eclectic Tembinok' at the same time administering 'pain-killer' from his medicine-chest, so as to give the sufferer both chances. 'I think mo' betta,' observed his majesty, with more than his usual self-approval. Apparently the gods are not jealous, and placidly enjoy both shrine and priest in common. On Tamaiti's medicine-tree, for instance, the model canoes are hung up ex voto for a prosperous voyage, and must therefore be dedicated to Taburik, god of the weather; but the stone in front is the place of sick folk come to pacify Chench.

It chanced, by great good luck, that even as we spoke of these affairs, I found myself threatened with a cold. I do not suppose I was ever glad of a cold before, or shall ever be again; but the opportunity to see the sorcerers at work was priceless, and I called in the faculty of Apemama. They came in a body, all in their Sunday's best and hung with wreaths and shells, the insignia of the devil-worker. Tamaiti I knew already: Terutak' I saw for the first time—a tall, lank, raw-boned, serious North-Sea fisherman turned brown; and there was a third in their company whose name I never heard, and who played to Tamaiti the part of famulus. Tamaiti took me in hand first, and led me, conversing agreeably, to the shores of Fu Bay. The famulus climbed a tree for some green cocoa-nuts. Tamaiti himself disappeared a while in the bush and returned with coco tinder, dry leaves, and a spray of waxberry. I was placed on the stone, with my back to the tree and my face to windward; between me and the gravel-heap one of the green nuts was set; and then Tamaiti (having previously bared his feet, for he had come in canvas shoes, which tortured him) joined me within the magic circle, hollowed out the top of the gravel-heap, built his fire in the bottom, and applied a match: it was one of Bryant and May's. The flame was slow to catch, and the irreverent sorcerer filled in the time with talk of foreign places—of London, and 'companies,' and how much money they had; of San Francisco, and the nefarious fogs, 'all the same smoke,' which had been so nearly the occasion of his death. I tried vainly to lead him to the matter in hand. 'Everybody make medicine,' he said lightly.

And when I asked him if he were himself a good practitioner—'No savvy,' he replied, more lightly still. At length the leaves burst in a flame, which he continued to feed; a thick, light smoke blew in my face, and the flames streamed against and scorched my clothes. He in the meanwhile addressed, or affected to address, the evil spirit, his lips moving fast, but without sound; at the same time he waved in the air and twice struck me on the breast with his green spray. So soon as the leaves were consumed the ashes were buried, the green spray was imbedded in the gravel, and the ceremony was at an end.

A reader of the Arabian Nights felt quite at home. Here was the suffumigation; here was the muttering wizard; here was the desert place to which Aladdin was decoyed by the false uncle. But they manage these things better in fiction. The effect was marred by the levity of the magician, entertaining his patient with small talk like an affable dentist, and by the incongruous presence of Mr. Osbourne with a camera. As for my cold, it was neither better nor worse.

I was now handed over to Terutak', the leading practitioner or medical baronet of Apemama. His place is on the lagoon side of the island, hard by the palace. A rail of light wood, some two feet high, encloses an oblong piece of gravel like the king's Pray Place; in the midst is a green tree; below, a stone table bears a pair of boxes covered with a fine mat; and in front of these an offering of food, a cocoa-nut, a piece of taro or a fish, is placed daily. On two sides the enclosure is lined with maniap's; and one of our party, who had been there to sketch, had remarked a daily concourse of people and an extraordinary number of sick children; for this is in fact the infirmary of Apemama. The doctor and myself entered the sacred place alone; the boxes and the mat were displaced; and I was enthroned in their stead upon the stone, facing once more to the east. For a while the sorcerer remained unseen behind me, making passes in the air with a branch of palm. Then he struck lightly on the brim of my straw hat; and this blow he continued to repeat at intervals, sometimes brushing instead my arm and shoulder. I have had people try to mesmerise me a dozen times, and never with the least result. But at the first tap—on a quarter no more vital than my hat-brim, and from nothing more virtuous than a switch of palm wielded by a man I could not even see—sleep rushed upon me like an armed man. My sinews fainted, my eyes closed, my brain hummed, with drowsiness. I resisted, at first instinctively, then with a certain flurry of despair, in the end successfully; if that were indeed success which enabled me to scramble to my feet, to stumble home somnambulous, to cast myself at once upon my bed, and sink at once into a dreamless stupor. When I awoke my cold was gone. So I leave a matter that I do not understand.

Meanwhile my appetite for curiosities (not usually very keen) had been strangely whetted by the sacred boxes. They were of pandanus wood, oblong in shape, with an effect of pillaring along the sides like straw work, lightly fringed with hair or fibre and standing on four legs. The outside was neat as a toy; the inside a mystery I was resolved to penetrate. But there was a lion in the path. I might not approach Terutak', since I had promised to buy nothing in the island; I dared not have recourse to the king, for I had already received from him more gifts than I knew how to repay. In this dilemma (the schooner being at last returned) we hit on a device. Captain Reid came forward in my stead, professed an unbridled passion for the boxes, and asked and obtained leave to bargain for them with the wizard. That same afternoon the captain and I made haste to the infirmary, entered the enclosure, raised the mat, and had begun to examine the boxes at our leisure, when Terutak's wife bounced out of one of the nigh houses, fell upon us, swept up the treasures, and was gone. There was never a more absolute surprise. She came, she took, she vanished, we had not a guess whither; and we remained, with foolish looks and laughter on the empty field. Such was the fit prologue of our memorable bargaining.

Presently Terutak' came, bringing Tamaiti along with him, both smiling; and we four squatted without the rail. In the three maniap's of the infirmary a certain audience was gathered: the family of a sick child under treatment, the king's sister playing cards, a pretty girl, who swore I was the image of her father; in all perhaps a score. Terutak's wife had returned (even as she had vanished) unseen, and now sat, breathless and watchful, by her husband's side. Perhaps some rumour of our quest had gone abroad, or perhaps we had given the alert by our unseemly freedom: certain, at least, that in the faces of all present, expectation and alarm were mingled.

Captain Reid announced, without preface or disguise, that I was come to purchase; Terutak', with sudden gravity, refused to sell. He was pressed; he persisted. It was explained we only wanted one: no matter, two were necessary for the healing of the sick. He was rallied, he was reasoned with: in vain. He sat there, serious and still, and refused. All this was only a preliminary skirmish; hitherto no sum of money had been mentioned; but now the captain brought his great guns to bear. He named a pound, then two, then three. Out of the maniap's one person after another came to join the group, some with mere excitement, others with consternation in their faces. The pretty girl crept to my side; it was then that—surely with the most artless flattery—she informed me of my likeness to her father. Tamaiti the infidel sat with hanging head and every mark of dejection. Terutak' streamed with sweat, his eye was glazed, his face wore a painful rictus, his chest heaved like that of one spent with running. The man must have been by nature covetous; and I doubt if ever I saw moral agony more tragically displayed. His wife by his side passionately encouraged his resistance.

And now came the charge of the old guard. The captain, making a skip, named the surprising figure of five pounds. At the word the maniap's were emptied. The king's sister flung down her cards and came to the front to listen, a cloud on her brow. The pretty girl beat her breast and cried with wearisome iteration that if the box were hers I should have it. Terutak's wife was beside herself with pious fear, her face discomposed, her voice (which scarce ceased from warning and encouragement) shrill as a whistle. Even Terutak' lost that image-like immobility which he had hitherto maintained. He rocked on his mat, threw up his closed knees alternately, and struck himself on the breast after the manner of dancers. But he came gold out of the furnace; and with what voice was left him continued to reject the bribe.

And now came a timely interjection. 'Money will not heal the sick,' observed the king's sister sententiously; and as soon as I heard the remark translated my eyes were unsealed, and I began to blush for my employment. Here was a sick child, and I sought, in the view of its parents, to remove the medicine-box. Here was the priest of a religion, and I (a heathen millionaire) was corrupting him to sacrilege. Here was a greedy man, torn in twain betwixt greed and conscience; and I sat by and relished, and lustfully renewed his torments. Ave, Cæsar! Smothered in a corner, dormant but not dead, we have all the one touch of nature: an infant passion for the sand and blood of the arena. So I brought to an end my first and last experience of the joys of the millionaire, and departed amid silent awe. Nowhere else can I expect to stir the depths of human nature by an offer of five pounds; nowhere else, even at the expense of millions, could I hope to see the evil of riches stand so legibly exposed. Of all the bystanders, none but the king's sister retained any memory of the gravity and danger of the thing in hand. Their eyes glowed, the girl beat her breast, in senseless animal excitement. Nothing was offered them; they stood neither to gain nor to lose; at the mere name and wind of these great sums Satan possessed them.

From this singular interview I went straight to the palace; found the king; confessed what I had been doing; begged him, in my name, to compliment Terutak' on his virtue, and to have a similar box made for me against the return of the schooner. Tembinok', Rubam, and one of the Daily Papers—him we used to call 'the Facetiæ Column'—laboured for a while of some idea, which was at last intelligibly delivered. They feared I thought the box would cure me; whereas, without the wizard, it was useless; and when I was threatened with another cold I should do better to rely on pain-killer. I explained I merely wished to keep it in my 'outch' as a thing made in Apemama and these honest men were much relieved.

Late the same evening, my wife, crossing the isle to windward, was aware of singing in the bush. Nothing is more common in that hour and place than the jubilant carol of the toddy-cutter, swinging high overhead, beholding below him the narrow ribbon of the isle, the surrounding field of ocean, and the fires of the sunset. But this was of a graver character, and seemed to proceed from the ground-level. Advancing a little in the thicket, Mrs. Stevenson saw a clear space, a fine mat spread in the midst, and on the mat a wreath of white flowers and one of the devil-work boxes. A woman—whom we guess to have been Mrs. Terutak'—sat in front, now drooping over the box like a mother over a cradle, now lifting her face and directing her song to heaven. A passing toddy-cutter told my wife that she was praying. Probably she did not so much pray as deprecate; and perhaps even the ceremony was one of disenchantment. For the box was already doomed; it was to pass from its green medicine-tree, reverend precinct, and devout attendants; to be handled by the profane; to cross three seas; to come to land under the foolscap of St. Paul's; to be domesticated within the hail of Lillie Bridge; there to be dusted by the British housemaid, and to take perhaps the roar of London for the voice of the outer sea along the reef. Before even we had finished dinner Chench had begun his journey, and one of the newspapers had already placed the box upon my table as the gift of Tembinok'.

I made haste to the palace, thanked the king, but offered to restore the box, for I could not bear that the sick of the island should be made to suffer. I was amazed by his reply. Terutak', it appeared, had still three or four in reserve against an accident; and his reluctance, and the dread painted at first on every face, was not in the least occasioned by the prospect of medical destitution, but by the immediate divinity of Chench. How much more did I respect the king's command, which had been able to extort in a moment and for nothing a sacrilegious favour that I had in vain solicited with millions! But now I had a difficult task in front of me; it was not in my view that Terutak' should suffer by his virtue; and I must persuade the king to share my opinion, to let me enrich one of his subjects, and (what was yet more delicate) to pay for my present. Nothing shows the king in a more becoming light than the fact that I succeeded. He demurred at the principle; he exclaimed, when he heard it, at the sum. 'Plenty money!' cried he, with contemptuous displeasure. But his resistance was never serious; and when he had blown off his ill-humour—'A' right,' said he. 'You give him. Mo' betta.'

Armed with this permission, I made straight for the infirmary. The night was now come, cool, dark, and starry. On a mat hard by a clear fire of wood and coco shell, Terutak' lay beside his wife. Both were smiling; the agony was over, the king's command had reconciled (I must suppose) their agitating scruples; and I was bidden to sit by them and share the circulating pipe. I was a little moved myself when I placed five gold sovereigns in the wizard's hand; but there was no sign of emotion in Terutak' as he returned them, pointed to the palace, and named Tembinok'. It was a changed scene when I had managed to explain. Terutak', long, dour Scots fisherman as he was, expressed his satisfaction within bounds; but the wife beamed; and there was an old gentleman present—her father, I suppose—who seemed nigh translated. His eyes stood out of his head; 'Kaupoi, Kaupoi—rich, rich!' ran on his lips like a refrain; and he could not meet my eye but what he gurgled into foolish laughter.

I might now go home, leaving that fire-lit family party gloating over their new millions, and consider my strange day. I had tried and rewarded the virtue of Terutak'. I had played the millionaire, had behaved abominably, and then in some degree repaired my thoughtlessness. And now I had my box, and could open it and look within. It contained a miniature sleeping-mat and a white shell. Tamaiti, interrogated next day as to the shell, explained it was not exactly Chench, but a cell, or body, which he would at times inhabit. Asked why there was a sleeping-mat, he retorted indignantly, 'Why have you mats?' And this was the sceptical Tamaiti! But island scepticism is never deeper than the lips.

CHAPTER VII—THE KING OF APEMAMA

Thus all things on the island, even the priests of the gods, obey the word of Tembinok'. He can give and take, and slay, and allay the scruples of the conscientious, and do all things (apparently) but interfere in the cookery of a turtle. 'I got power' is his favourite word; it interlards his conversation; the thought haunts him and is ever fresh; and when be has asked and meditates of foreign countries, he looks up with a smile and reminds you, 'I got Power.' Nor is his delight only in the possession, but in the exercise. He rejoices in the crooked and violent paths of kingship like a strong man to run a race, or like an artist in his art. To feel, to use his power, to embellish his island and the picture of the island life after a private ideal, to milk the island vigorously, to extend his singular museum—these employ delightfully the sum of his abilities. I never saw a man more patently in the right trade.

It would be natural to suppose this monarchy inherited intact through generations. And so far from that, it is a thing of yesterday. I was already a boy at school while Apemama was yet republican, ruled by a noisy council of Old Men, and torn with incurable feuds. And Tembinok' is no Bourbon; rather the son of a Napoleon. Of course he is well-born. No man need aspire high in the isles of the Pacific unless his pedigree be long and in the upper regions mythical. And our king counts cousinship with most of the high families in the archipelago, and traces his descent to a shark and a heroic woman. Directed by an oracle, she swam beyond sight of land to meet her revolting paramour, and received at sea the seed of a predestined family. 'I think lie,' is the king's emphatic commentary; yet he is proud of the legend. From this illustrious beginning the fortunes of the race must have declined; and Teñkoruti, the grandfather of Tembinok', was the chief of a village at the north end of the island. Kuria and Aranuka were yet independent; Apemama itself the arena of devastating feuds. Through this perturbed period of history the figure of Teñkoruti stalks memorable. In war he was swift and bloody; several towns fell to his spear, and the inhabitants were butchered to a man. In civil life this arrogance was unheard of. When the council of Old Men was summoned, he went to the Speak House, delivered his mind, and left without waiting to be answered. Wisdom had spoken: let others opine according to their folly. He was feared and hated, and this was his pleasure. He was no poet; he cared not for arts or knowledge. 'My gran'patha one thing savvy, savvy pight,' observed the king. In some lull of their own disputes the Old Men of Apemama adventured on the conquest of Apemama; and this unlicked Caius Marcius was elected general of the united troops. Success attended him; the islands were reduced, and Teñkoruti returned to his own government, glorious and detested. He died about 1860, in the seventieth year of his age and the full odour of unpopularity. He was tall and lean, says his grandson, looked extremely old, and 'walked all the same young man.' The same observer gave me a significant detail. The survivors of that rough epoch were all defaced with spearmarks; there was none on the body of this skilful fighter. 'I see old man, no got a spear,' said the king.

Teñkoruti left two sons, Tembaitake and Tembinatake. Tembaitake, our king's father, was short, middling stout, a poet, a good genealogist, and something of a fighter; it seems he took himself seriously, and was perhaps scarce conscious that he was in all things the creature and nursling of his brother. There was no shadow of dispute between the pair: the greater man filled with alacrity and content the second place; held the breach in war, and all the portfolios in the time of peace; and, when his brother rated him, listened in silence, looking on the ground. Like Teñkoruti, he was tall and lean and a swift talker—a rare trait in the islands. He possessed every accomplishment. He knew sorcery, he was the best genealogist of his day, he was a poet, he could dance and make canoes and armour; and the famous mast of Apemama, which ran one joint higher than the mainmast of a full-rigged ship, was of his conception and design. But these were avocations, and the man's trade was war. 'When my uncle go make wa', he laugh,' said Tembinok'. He forbade the use of field fortification, that protractor of native hostilities; his men must fight in the open, and win or be beaten out of hand; his own activity inspired his followers; and the swiftness of his blows beat down, in one lifetime, the resistance of three islands. He made his brother sovereign, he left his nephew absolute. 'My uncle make all smooth,' said Tembinok'. 'I mo' king than my patha: I got power,' he said, with formidable relish.

Such is the portrait of the uncle drawn by the nephew. I can set beside it another by a different artist, who has often—I may say always—delighted me with his romantic taste in narrative, but not always—and I may say not often—persuaded me of his exactitude. I have already denied myself the use of so much excellent matter from the same source, that I begin to think it time to reward good resolution; and his account of Tembinatake agrees so well with the king's, that it may very well be (what I hope it is) the record of a fact, and not (what I suspect) the pleasing exercise of an imagination more than sailorly. A., for so I had perhaps better call him, was walking up the island after dusk, when he came on a lighted village of some size, was directed to the chief's house, and asked leave to rest and smoke a pipe. 'You will sit down, and smoke a pipe, and wash, and eat, and sleep,' replied the chief, 'and to-morrow you will go again.' Food was brought, prayers were held (for this was in the brief day of Christianity), and the chief himself prayed with eloquence and seeming sincerity. All evening A. sat and admired the man by the firelight. He was six feet high, lean, with the appearance of many years, and an extraordinary air of breeding and command. 'He looked like a man who would kill you laughing,' said A., in singular echo of one of the king's expressions. And again: 'I had been reading the Musketeer books, and he reminded me of Aramis.' Such is the portrait of Tembinatake, drawn by an expert romancer.

We had heard many tales of 'my patha'; never a word of my uncle till two days before we left. As the time approached for our departure Tembinok' became greatly changed; a softer, a more melancholy, and, in particular, a more confidential man appeared in his stead. To my wife he contrived laboriously to explain that though he knew he must lose his father in the course of nature, he had not minded nor realised it till the moment came; and that now he was to lose us he repeated the experience. We showed fireworks one evening on the terrace. It was a heavy business; the sense of separation was in all our minds, and the talk languished. The king was specially affected, sat disconsolate on his mat, and often sighed. Of a sudden one of the wives stepped forth from a cluster, came and kissed him in silence, and silently went again. It was just such a caress as we might give to a disconsolate child, and the king received it with a child's simplicity. Presently after we said good-night and withdrew; but Tembinok' detained Mr. Osbourne, patting the mat by his side and saying: 'Sit down. I feel bad, I like talk.' Osbourne sat down by him. 'You like some beer?' said he; and one of the wives produced a bottle. The king did not partake, but sat sighing and smoking a meerschaum pipe. 'I very sorry you go,' he said at last. 'Miss Stlevens he good man, woman he good man, boy he good man; all good man. Woman he smart all the same man. My woman' (glancing towards his wives) 'he good woman, no very smart. I think Miss Stlevens he is chiep all the same cap'n man-o-wa'. I think Miss Stlevens he rich man all the same me. All go schoona. I very sorry. My patha he go, my uncle he go, my cutcheons he go, Miss Stlevens he go: all go. You no see king cry before. King all the same man: feel bad, he cry. I very sorry.'

In the morning it was the common topic in the village that the king had wept. To me he said: 'Last night I no can 'peak: too much here,' laying his hand upon his bosom. 'Now you go away all the same my pamily. My brothers, my uncle go away. All the same.' This was said with a dejection almost passionate. And it was the first time I had heard him name his uncle, or indeed employ the word. The same day he sent me a present of two corselets, made in the island fashion of plaited fibre, heavy and strong. One had been worn by Teñkoruti, one by Tembaitake; and the gift being gratefully received, he sent me, on the return of his messengers, a third—that of Tembinatake. My curiosity was roused; I begged for information as to the three wearers; and the king entered with gusto into the details already given. Here was a strange thing, that he should have talked so much of his family, and not once mentioned that relative of whom he was plainly the most proud. Nay, more: he had hitherto boasted of his father; thenceforth he had little to say of him; and the qualities for which he had praised him in the past were now attributed where they were due,—to the uncle. A confusion might be natural enough among islanders, who call all the sons of their grandfather by the common name of father. But this was not the case with Tembinok'. Now the ice was broken the word uncle was perpetually in his mouth; he who had been so ready to confound was now careful to distinguish; and the father sank gradually into a self-complacent ordinary man, while the uncle rose to his true stature as the hero and founder of the race.

The more I heard and the more I considered, the more this mystery of Tembinok's behaviour puzzled and attracted me. And the explanation, when it came, was one to strike the imagination of a dramatist. Tembinok' had two brothers. One, detected in private trading, was banished, then forgiven, lives to this day in the island, and is the father of the heir-apparent, Paul. The other fell beyond forgiveness. I have heard it was a love-affair with one of the king's wives, and the thing is highly possible in that romantic archipelago. War was attempted to be levied; but Tembinok' was too swift for the rebels, and the guilty brother escaped in a canoe. He did not go alone. Tembinatake had a hand in the rebellion, and the man who had gained a kingdom for a weakling brother was banished by that brother's son. The fugitives came to shore in other islands, but Tembinok' remains to this day ignorant of their fate.

So far history. And now a moment for conjecture. Tembinok' confused habitually, not only the attributes and merits of his father and his uncle, but their diverse personal appearance. Before he had even spoken, or thought to speak, of Tembinatake, he had told me often of a tall, lean father, skilled in war, and his own schoolmaster in genealogy and island arts. How if both were fathers, one natural, one adoptive? How if the heir of Tembaitake, like the heir of Tembinok' himself, were not a son, but an adopted nephew? How if the founder of the monarchy, while he worked for his brother, worked at the same time for the child of his loins? How if on the death of Tembaitake, the two stronger natures, father and son, king and kingmaker, clashed, and Tembinok', when he drove out his uncle, drove out the author of his days? Here is at least a tragedy four-square.

The king took us on board in his own gig, dressed for the occasion in the naval uniform. He had little to say, he refused refreshments, shook us briefly by the hand, and went ashore again. That night the palm-tops of Apemama had dipped behind the sea, and the schooner sailed solitary under the stars.

THE END.

FOOTNOTES

[12] Where that word is used as a salutation I give that form.

[29] In English usually written 'taboo': 'tapu' is the correct Tahitian form.—[Ed.]

[86] The reference is to Maka, the Gawaiian missionary, at Butaritari in the Gilberts.

[122] Elephantiasis.

[156] Arorai is in the Gilberts, Funafuti in the Ellice Islands.—Ed.

[231] Gin and brandy.

[275] In the Gilbert group.

[279a] Copra: the dried kernel of the cocoa-nut, the chief article of commerce throughout the Pacific Islands.

[279b] Houses.

[283] Suppose.

SONGS OF TRAVEL AND OTHER VERSES

The following collection of verses, written at various times and places, principally after the author's final departure from England in 1887, was sent home by him for publication some months before his death. He had tried them in several different orders and under several different titles, as "Songs and Notes of Travel," "Posthumous Poems," etc., and in the end left their naming and arrangement to the present editor, with the suggestion that they should be added as Book III. to future editions of "Underwoods." This suggestion it is proposed to carry out; but in the meantime, for the benefit of those who possess "Underwoods" in its original form, it has been thought desirable to publish them separately in the present volume. They have already been included in the Edinburgh Edition of the author's works.

S. C.

I—THE VAGABOND

(To an air of Schubert)

Give to me the life I love,
  Let the lave go by me,
Give the jolly heaven above
  And the byway nigh me.
Bed in the bush with stars to see,
  Bread I dip in the river—
There's the life for a man like me,
  There's the life for ever.

Let the blow fall soon or late,
  Let what will be o'er me;
Give the face of earth around
  And the road before me.
Wealth I seek not, hope nor love,
  Nor a friend to know me;
All I seek, the heaven above
  And the road below me.

Or let autumn fall on me
  Where afield I linger,

Silencing the bird on tree,
  Biting the blue finger.
White as meal the frosty field—
  Warm the fireside haven—
Not to autumn will I yield,
  Not to winter even!

Let the blow fall soon or late,
  Let what will be o'er me;
Give the face of earth around,
  And the road before me.
Wealth I ask not, hope nor love,
  Nor a friend to know me;
All I ask, the heaven above
  And the road below me.

II—YOUTH AND LOVE—I

Once only by the garden gate
  Our lips we joined and parted.
I must fulfil an empty fate
  And travel the uncharted.

Hail and farewell! I must arise,
  Leave here the fatted cattle,

And paint on foreign lands and skies
  My Odyssey of battle.

The untented Kosmos my abode,
  I pass, a wilful stranger:
My mistress still the open road
  And the bright eyes of danger.

Come ill or well, the cross, the crown,
  The rainbow or the thunder,
I fling my soul and body down
  For God to plough them under.

III—YOUTH AND LOVE—II

To the heart of youth the world is a highwayside.
Passing for ever, he fares; and on either hand,
Deep in the gardens golden pavilions hide,
Nestle in orchard bloom, and far on the level land
Call him with lighted lamp in the eventide.

Thick as the stars at night when the moon is down,
Pleasures assail him. He to his nobler fate
Fares; and but waves a hand as he passes on,

Cries but a wayside word to her at the garden gate,

Sings but a boyish stave and his face is gone.

IV

In dreams, unhappy, I behold you stand
    As heretofore:
The unremembered tokens in your hand
    Avail no more.

No more the morning glow, no more the grace,
    Enshrines, endears.
Cold beats the light of time upon your face
    And shows your tears.

He came and went. Perchance you wept a while
    And then forgot.
Ah me! but he that left you with a smile
    Forgets you not.

V

She rested by the Broken Brook,
  She drank of Weary Well,
She moved beyond my lingering look,
  Ah, whither none can tell!

She came, she went. In other lands,
  Perchance in fairer skies,
Her hands shall cling with other hands,
  Her eyes to other eyes.

She vanished. In the sounding town,
  Will she remember too?
Will she recall the eyes of brown
  As I recall the blue?

VI

The infinite shining heavens
  Rose and I saw in the night
Uncountable angel stars
  Showering sorrow and light.

I saw them distant as heaven,
  Dumb and shining and dead,
And the idle stars of the night
  Were dearer to me than bread.

Night after night in my sorrow
  The stars stood over the sea,

Till lo! I looked in the dusk
  And a star had come down to me.

VII

Plain as the glistering planets shine
  When winds have cleaned the skies,
Her love appeared, appealed for mine,
  And wantoned in her eyes.

Clear as the shining tapers burned
  On Cytherea's shrine,
Those brimming, lustrous beauties turned,
  And called and conquered mine.

The beacon-lamp that Hero lit
  No fairer shone on sea,
No plainlier summoned will and wit,
  Than hers encouraged me.

I thrilled to feel her influence near,
  I struck my flag at sight.
Her starry silence smote my ear
  Like sudden drums at night.

I ran as, at the cannon's roar,
  The troops the ramparts man—
As in the holy house of yore
  The willing Eli ran.

Here, lady, lo! that servant stands
  You picked from passing men,
And should you need nor heart nor hands
  He bows and goes again.

VIII

To you, let snow and roses
  And golden locks belong.
These are the world's enslavers,
  Let these delight the throng.
For her of duskier lustre
  Whose favour still I wear,
The snow be in her kirtle,
  The rose be in her hair!

The hue of highland rivers
  Careering, full and cool,
From sable on to golden,

From rapid on to pool—
The hue of heather-honey,
The hue of honey-bees,
Shall tinge her golden shoulder,
Shall gild her tawny knees.

IX

Let Beauty awake in the morn from beautiful dreams,
Beauty awake from rest!
Let Beauty awake
For Beauty's sake
In the hour when the birds awake in the brake
And the stars are bright in the west!

Let Beauty awake in the eve from the slumber of day,
Awake in the crimson eve!
In the day's dusk end
When the shades ascend,
Let her wake to the kiss of a tender friend
To render again and receive!

X

I know not how it is with you—
I love the first and last,

The whole field of the present view,
  The whole flow of the past.

One tittle of the things that are,
  Nor you should change nor I—
One pebble in our path—one star
  In all our heaven of sky.

Our lives, and every day and hour,
  One symphony appear:
One road, one garden—every flower
  And every bramble dear.

XI

I will make you brooches and toys for your delight
Of bird-song at morning and star-shine at night.
I will make a palace fit for you and me
Of green days in forests and blue days at sea.

I will make my kitchen, and you shall keep your room,
Where white flows the river and bright blows the broom,
And you shall wash your linen and keep your body white
In rainfall at morning and dewfall at night.

And this shall be for music when no one else is near,
The fine song for singing, the rare song to hear!
That only I remember, that only you admire,
Of the broad road that stretches and the roadside fire.

XII—WE HAVE LOVED OF YORE

(To an air of Diabelli)

Berried brake and reedy island,
  Heaven below, and only heaven above,
Through the sky's inverted azure
  Softly swam the boat that bore our love.
    Bright were your eyes as the day;
    Bright ran the stream,
    Bright hung the sky above.
Days of April, airs of Eden,
  How the glory died through golden hours,
And the shining moon arising,
  How the boat drew homeward filled with flowers!
    Bright were your eyes in the night:
    We have lived, my love—
    O, we have loved, my love.

Frost has bound our flowing river,

Snow has whitened all our island brake,
And beside the winter fagot
Joan and Darby doze and dream and wake.
Still, in the river of dreams
Swims the boat of love—
Hark! chimes the falling oar!
And again in winter evens
When on firelight dreaming fancy feeds,
In those ears of agèd lovers
Love's own river warbles in the reeds.
Love still the past, O my love!
We have lived of yore,
O, we have loved of yore.

XIII—MATER TRIUMPHANS

Son of my woman's body, you go, to the drum and fife,
To taste the colour of love and the other side of life—
From out of the dainty the rude, the strong from out of the frail,
Eternally through the ages from the female comes the male.

The ten fingers and toes, and the shell-like nail on each,
The eyes blind as gems and the tongue attempting speech;
Impotent hands in my bosom, and yet they shall wield the sword!

Drugged with slumber and milk, you wait the day of the Lord.

Infant bridegroom, uncrowned king, unanointed priest,
Soldier, lover, explorer, I see you nuzzle the breast.
You that grope in my bosom shall load the ladies with rings,
You, that came forth through the doors, shall burst the doors of kings.

XIV

Bright is the ring of words
When the right man rings them,
Fair the fall of songs
When the singer sings them.
Still they are carolled and said—
On wings they are carried—
After the singer is dead
And the maker buried.

Low as the singer lies
In the field of heather,
Songs of his fashion bring
The swains together.
And when the west is red
With the sunset embers,

The lover lingers and sings
  And the maid remembers.

XV

In the highlands, in the country places,
Where the old plain men have rosy faces,
And the young fair maidens
Quiet eyes;
Where essential silence cheers and blesses,
And for ever in the hill-recesses
Her more lovely music
Broods and dies.

O to mount again where erst I haunted;
Where the old red hills are bird-enchanted,
And the low green meadows
Bright with sward;
And when even dies, the million-tinted,
And the night has come, and planets glinted,
Lo, the valley hollow
Lamp-bestarred!

O to dream, O to awake and wander

There, and with delight to take and render,

Through the trance of silence,

Quiet breath;

Lo! for there, among the flowers and grasses,

Only the mightier movement sounds and passes;

Only winds and rivers,

Life and death.

XVI

(To the tune of Wandering Willie)

Home no more home to me, whither must I wander?

  Hunger my driver, I go where I must.

Cold blows the winter wind over hill and heather;

  Thick drives the rain, and my roof is in the dust.

Loved of wise men was the shade of my roof-tree.

  The true word of welcome was spoken in the door—

Dear days of old, with the faces in the firelight,

  Kind folks of old, you come again no more.

Home was home then, my dear, full of kindly faces,

  Home was home then, my dear, happy for the child.

Fire and the windows bright glittered on the moorland;

  Song, tuneful song, built a palace in the wild.

Now, when day dawns on the brow of the moorland,
  Lone stands the house, and the chimney-stone is cold.
Lone let it stand, now the friends are all departed,
  The kind hearts, the true hearts, that loved the place of old.

Spring shall come, come again, calling up the moorfowl,
  Spring shall bring the sun and rain, bring the bees and flowers;
Red shall the heather bloom over hill and valley,
  Soft flow the stream through the even-flowing hours;
Fair the day shine as it shone on my childhood—
  Fair shine the day on the house with open door;
Birds come and cry there and twitter in the chimney—
  But I go for ever and come again no more.

XVII—WINTER

In rigorous hours, when down the iron lane
The redbreast looks in vain
For hips and haws,
Lo, shining flowers upon my window-pane
The silver pencil of the winter draws.

When all the snowy hill
And the bare woods are still;

When snipes are silent in the frozen bogs,
And all the garden garth is whelmed in mire,
Lo, by the hearth, the laughter of the logs—
More fair than roses, lo, the flowers of fire!

Saranac Lake.

XVIII

The stormy evening closes now in vain,
Loud wails the wind and beats the driving rain,
    While here in sheltered house
    With fire-ypainted walls,
    I hear the wind abroad,
    I hark the calling squalls—
'Blow, blow,' I cry, 'you burst your cheeks in vain!
Blow, blow,' I cry, 'my love is home again!'

Yon ship you chase perchance but yesternight
Bore still the precious freight of my delight,
    That here in sheltered house
    With fire-ypainted walls,
    Now hears the wind abroad,
    Now harks the calling squalls.
'Blow, blow,' I cry, 'in vain you rouse the sea,
My rescued sailor shares the fire with me!'

XIX—TO DR. HAKE

(On receiving a Copy of Verses)

In the belovèd hour that ushers day,
In the pure dew, under the breaking grey,
One bird, ere yet the woodland quires awake,
With brief réveillé summons all the brake:
Chirp, chirp, it goes; nor waits an answer long;
And that small signal fills the grove with song.

Thus on my pipe I breathed a strain or two;
It scarce was music, but 'twas all I knew.
It was not music, for I lacked the art,
Yet what but frozen music filled my heart?

Chirp, chirp, I went, nor hoped a nobler strain;
But Heaven decreed I should not pipe in vain,
For, lo! not far from there, in secret dale,
All silent, sat an ancient nightingale.
My sparrow notes he heard; thereat awoke;
And with a tide of song his silence broke.

XX—TO ---

I knew thee strong and quiet like the hills;

I knew thee apt to pity, brave to endure,
In peace or war a Roman full equipt;
And just I knew thee, like the fabled kings
Who by the loud sea-shore gave judgment forth,
From dawn to eve, bearded and few of words.
What, what, was I to honour thee? A child;
A youth in ardour but a child in strength,
Who after virtue's golden chariot-wheels
Runs ever panting, nor attains the goal.
So thought I, and was sorrowful at heart.

Since then my steps have visited that flood
Along whose shore the numerous footfalls cease,
The voices and the tears of life expire.
Thither the prints go down, the hero's way
Trod large upon the sand, the trembling maid's:
Nimrod that wound his trumpet in the wood,
And the poor, dreaming child, hunter of flowers,
That here his hunting closes with the great:
So one and all go down, nor aught returns.

For thee, for us, the sacred river waits,
For me, the unworthy, thee, the perfect friend;

There Blame desists, there his unfaltering dogs
He from the chase recalls, and homeward rides;
Yet Praise and Love pass over and go in.
So when, beside that margin, I discard
My more than mortal weakness, and with thee
Through that still land unfearing I advance:
If then at all we keep the touch of joy
Thou shalt rejoice to find me altered—I,
O Felix, to behold thee still unchanged.

XXI

The morning drum-call on my eager ear
Thrills unforgotten yet; the morning dew
Lies yet undried along my field of noon.

But now I pause at whiles in what I do,
And count the bell, and tremble lest I hear
(My work untrimmed) the sunset gun too soon.

XXII

I have trod the upward and the downward slope;
I have endured and done in days before;
I have longed for all, and bid farewell to hope;
And I have lived and loved, and closed the door.

XXIII

He hears with gladdened heart the thunder
  Peal, and loves the falling dew;
He knows the earth above and under—
  Sits and is content to view.

He sits beside the dying ember,
  God for hope and man for friend,
Content to see, glad to remember,
  Expectant of the certain end.

XXIV

Farewell, fair day and fading light!
The clay-born here, with westward sight,
Marks the huge sun now downward soar.
Farewell. We twain shall meet no more.

Farewell. I watch with bursting sigh
My late contemned occasion die.
I linger useless in my tent:
Farewell, fair day, so foully spent!

Farewell, fair day. If any God

At all consider this poor clod,
He who the fair occasion sent
Prepared and placed the impediment.

Let him diviner vengeance take—
Give me to sleep, give me to wake
Girded and shod, and bid me play
The hero in the coming day!

XXV—IF THIS WERE FAITH

God, if this were enough,
That I see things bare to the buff
And up to the buttocks in mire;
That I ask nor hope nor hire,
Nut in the husk,
Nor dawn beyond the dusk,
Nor life beyond death:
God, if this were faith?

Having felt thy wind in my face
Spit sorrow and disgrace,
Having seen thine evil doom
In Golgotha and Khartoum,
And the brutes, the work of thine hands,

Fill with injustice lands
And stain with blood the sea:
If still in my veins the glee
Of the black night and the sun
And the lost battle, run:
If, an adept,
The iniquitous lists I still accept
With joy, and joy to endure and be withstood,
And still to battle and perish for a dream of good:
God, if that were enough?

If to feel, in the ink of the slough,
And the sink of the mire,
Veins of glory and fire
Run through and transpierce and transpire,
And a secret purpose of glory in every part,
And the answering glory of battle fill my heart;
To thrill with the joy of girded men
To go on for ever and fail and go on again,
And be mauled to the earth and arise,
And contend for the shade of a word and a thing not seen with the eyes:
With the half of a broken hope for a pillow at night
That somehow the right is the right

And the smooth shall bloom from the rough:

Lord, if that were enough?

XXVI—MY WIFE

Trusty, dusky, vivid, true,

With eyes of gold and bramble-dew,

Steel-true and blade-straight,

The great artificer

Made my mate.

Honour, anger, valour, fire;

A love that life could never tire,

Death quench or evil stir,

The mighty master

Gave to her.

Teacher, tender, comrade, wife,

A fellow-farer true through life,

Heart-whole and soul-free

The august father

Gave to me.

XXVII—TO THE MUSE

Resign the rhapsody, the dream,

To men of larger reach;
Be ours the quest of a plain theme,
The piety of speech.

As monkish scribes from morning break
Toiled till the close of light,
Nor thought a day too long to make
One line or letter bright:

We also with an ardent mind,
Time, wealth, and fame forgot,
Our glory in our patience find
And skim, and skim the pot:

Till last, when round the house we hear
The evensong of birds,
One corner of blue heaven appear
In our clear well of words.

Leave, leave it then, muse of my heart!
Sans finish and sans frame,
Leave unadorned by needless art
The picture as it came.

XXVIII—TO AN ISLAND PRINCESS

Since long ago, a child at home,
I read and longed to rise and roam,
Where'er I went, whate'er I willed,
One promised land my fancy filled.
Hence the long roads my home I made;
Tossed much in ships; have often laid
Below the uncurtained sky my head,
Rain-deluged and wind-buffeted:
And many a thousand hills I crossed
And corners turned—Love's labour lost,
Till, Lady, to your isle of sun
I came, not hoping; and, like one
Snatched out of blindness, rubbed my eyes,
And hailed my promised land with cries.

Yes, Lady, here I was at last;
Here found I all I had forecast:
The long roll of the sapphire sea
That keeps the land's virginity;
The stalwart giants of the wood
Laden with toys and flowers and food;

The precious forest pouring out
To compass the whole town about;
The town itself with streets of lawn,
Loved of the moon, blessed by the dawn,
Where the brown children all the day
Keep up a ceaseless noise of play,
Play in the sun, play in the rain,
Nor ever quarrel or complain;—
And late at night, in the woods of fruit,
Hark! do you hear the passing flute?

I threw one look to either hand,
And knew I was in Fairyland.
And yet one point of being so
I lacked. For, Lady (as you know),
Whoever by his might of hand,
Won entrance into Fairyland,
Found always with admiring eyes
A Fairy princess kind and wise.
It was not long I waited; soon
Upon my threshold, in broad noon,
Gracious and helpful, wise and good,
The Fairy Princess Moë stood. [44]

Tantira, Tahiti, Nov. 5, 1888.

XXIX—TO KALAKAUA

(With a present of a Pearl)

The Silver Ship, my King—that was her name

In the bright islands whence your fathers came [45]—

The Silver Ship, at rest from winds and tides,

Below your palace in your harbour rides:

And the seafarers, sitting safe on shore,

Like eager merchants count their treasures o'er.

One gift they find, one strange and lovely thing,

Now doubly precious since it pleased a king.

The right, my liege, is ancient as the lyre

For bards to give to kings what kings admire.

'Tis mine to offer for Apollo's sake;

And since the gift is fitting, yours to take.

To golden hands the golden pearl I bring:

The ocean jewel to the island king.

Honolulu, Feb. 3, 1889.

XXX—TO PRINCESS KAIULANI

[Written in April to Kaiulani in the April of her age; and at Waikiki, within easy walk of Kaiulani's banyan! When she comes to my land and her father's, and the rain beats upon the window (as I fear it will), let her look at this page; it will be like a weed gathered and pressed at home; and she will remember her own islands, and the shadow of the mighty tree; and she will hear the peacocks screaming in the dusk and the wind blowing in the palms; and she will think of her father sitting there alone.—R. L. S.]

Forth from her land to mine she goes,

The island maid, the island rose,

Light of heart and bright of face:

The daughter of a double race.

Her islands here, in Southern sun,

Shall mourn their Kaiulani gone,

And I, in her dear banyan shade,

Look vainly for my little maid.

But our Scots islands far away

Shall glitter with unwonted day,

And cast for once their tempests by

To smile in Kaiulani's eye.

Honolulu.

XXXI—TO MOTHER MARYANNE

To see the infinite pity of this place,

The mangled limb, the devastated face,

The innocent sufferer smiling at the rod—

A fool were tempted to deny his God.

He sees, he shrinks. But if he gaze again,

Lo, beauty springing from the breast of pain!

He marks the sisters on the mournful shores;

And even a fool is silent and adores.

Guest House, Kalawao, Molokai.

XXXII—IN MEMORIAM E. H.

I knew a silver head was bright beyond compare,

I knew a queen of toil with a crown of silver hair.

Garland of valour and sorrow, of beauty and renown,

Life, that honours the brave, crowned her himself with the crown.

The beauties of youth are frail, but this was a jewel of age.

Life, that delights in the brave, gave it himself for a gage.

Fair was the crown to behold, and beauty its poorest part—

At once the scar of the wound and the order pinned on the heart.

The beauties of man are frail, and the silver lies in the dust,

And the queen that we call to mind sleeps with the brave and the just;

Sleeps with the weary at length; but, honoured and ever fair,

Shines in the eye of the mind the crown of the silver hair.

Honolulu.

XXXIII—TO MY WIFE

(A Fragment)

Long must elapse ere you behold again
Green forest frame the entry of the lane—
The wild lane with the bramble and the brier,
The year-old cart-tracks perfect in the mire,
The wayside smoke, perchance, the dwarfish huts,
And ramblers' donkey drinking from the ruts:—
Long ere you trace how deviously it leads,
Back from man's chimneys and the bleating meads
To the woodland shadow, to the sylvan hush,
When but the brooklet chuckles in the brush—
Back from the sun and bustle of the vale
To where the great voice of the nightingale
Fills all the forest like a single room,
And all the banks smell of the golden broom;
So wander on until the eve descends.
And back returning to your firelit friends,
You see the rosy sun, despoiled of light,
Hung, caught in thickets, like a schoolboy's kite.

Here from the sea the unfruitful sun shall rise,

Bathe the bare deck and blind the unshielded eyes;

The allotted hours aloft shall wheel in vain

And in the unpregnant ocean plunge again.

Assault of squalls that mock the watchful guard,

And pluck the bursting canvas from the yard,

And senseless clamour of the calm, at night

Must mar your slumbers. By the plunging light,

In beetle-haunted, most unwomanly bower

Of the wild-swerving cabin, hour by hour . . .

Schooner 'Equator.'

XXXIV—TO MY OLD FAMILIARS

Do you remember—can we e'er forget?—

How, in the coiled-perplexities of youth,

In our wild climate, in our scowling town,

We gloomed and shivered, sorrowed, sobbed and feared?

The belching winter wind, the missile rain,

The rare and welcome silence of the snows,

The laggard morn, the haggard day, the night,

The grimy spell of the nocturnal town,

Do you remember?—Ah, could one forget!

As when the fevered sick that all night long

Listed the wind intone, and hear at last
The ever-welcome voice of chanticleer
Sing in the bitter hour before the dawn,—
With sudden ardour, these desire the day:
So sang in the gloom of youth the bird of hope;
So we, exulting, hearkened and desired.
For lo! as in the palace porch of life
We huddled with chimeras, from within—
How sweet to hear!—the music swelled and fell,
And through the breach of the revolving doors
What dreams of splendour blinded us and fled!

I have since then contended and rejoiced;
Amid the glories of the house of life
Profoundly entered, and the shrine beheld:
Yet when the lamp from my expiring eyes
Shall dwindle and recede, the voice of love
Fall insignificant on my closing ears,
What sound shall come but the old cry of the wind
In our inclement city? what return
But the image of the emptiness of youth,
Filled with the sound of footsteps and that voice
Of discontent and rapture and despair?

So, as in darkness, from the magic lamp,
The momentary pictures gleam and fade
And perish, and the night resurges—these
Shall I remember, and then all forget.
Apemama.

XXXV

The tropics vanish, and meseems that I,
From Halkerside, from topmost Allermuir,
Or steep Caerketton, dreaming gaze again.
Far set in fields and woods, the town I see
Spring gallant from the shallows of her smoke,
Cragged, spired, and turreted, her virgin fort
Beflagged. About, on seaward-drooping hills,
New folds of city glitter. Last, the Forth
Wheels ample waters set with sacred isles,
And populous Fife smokes with a score of towns.

There, on the sunny frontage of a hill,
Hard by the house of kings, repose the dead,
My dead, the ready and the strong of word.
Their works, the salt-encrusted, still survive;
The sea bombards their founded towers; the night
Thrills pierced with their strong lamps. The artificers,

One after one, here in this grated cell,
Where the rain erases, and the rust consumes,
Fell upon lasting silence. Continents
And continental oceans intervene;
A sea uncharted, on a lampless isle,
Environs and confines their wandering child
In vain. The voice of generations dead
Summons me, sitting distant, to arise,
My numerous footsteps nimbly to retrace,
And, all mutation over, stretch me down
In that denoted city of the dead.
Apemama.

XXXVI—TO S. C.

I heard the pulse of the besieging sea
Throb far away all night. I heard the wind
Fly crying and convulse tumultuous palms.
I rose and strolled. The isle was all bright sand,
And flailing fans and shadows of the palm;
The heaven all moon and wind and the blind vault;
The keenest planet slain, for Venus slept.
  The king, my neighbour, with his host of wives,
Slept in the precinct of the palisade;
Where single, in the wind, under the moon,

Among the slumbering cabins, blazed a fire,
Sole street-lamp and the only sentinel.
  To other lands and nights my fancy turned—
To London first, and chiefly to your house,
The many-pillared and the well-beloved.
There yearning fancy lighted; there again
In the upper room I lay, and heard far off
The unsleeping city murmur like a shell;
The muffled tramp of the Museum guard
Once more went by me; I beheld again
Lamps vainly brighten the dispeopled street;
Again I longed for the returning morn,
The awaking traffic, the bestirring birds,
The consentaneous trill of tiny song
That weaves round monumental cornices
A passing charm of beauty. Most of all,
For your light foot I wearied, and your knock
That was the glad réveillé of my day.
  Lo, now, when to your task in the great house
At morning through the portico you pass,
One moment glance, where by the pillared wall
Far-voyaging island gods, begrimed with smoke,
Sit now unworshipped, the rude monument

Of faiths forgot and races undivined:

Sit now disconsolate, remembering well

The priest, the victim, and the songful crowd,

The blaze of the blue noon, and that huge voice,

Incessant, of the breakers on the shore.

As far as these from their ancestral shrine,

So far, so foreign, your divided friends

Wander, estranged in body, not in mind.

Apemama.

XXXVII—THE HOUSE OF TEMBINOKA

[At my departure from the island of Apemama, for which you will look in vain in most atlases, the King and I agreed, since we both set up to be in the poetical way, that we should celebrate our separation in verse. Whether or not his Majesty has been true to his bargain, the laggard posts of the Pacific may perhaps inform me in six months, perhaps not before a year. The following lines represent my part of the contract, and it is hoped, by their pictures of strange manners, they may entertain a civilised audience. Nothing throughout has been invented or exaggerated; the lady herein referred to as the author's muse has confined herself to stringing into rhyme facts or legends that I saw or heard during two months' residence upon the island.—R. L. S.]

ENVOI

Let us, who part like brothers, part like bards;

And you in your tongue and measure, I in mine,

Our now division duly solemnise.

Unlike the strains, and yet the theme is one:
The strains unlike, and how unlike their fate!
You to the blinding palace-yard shall call
The prefect of the singers, and to him,
Listening devout, your valedictory verse
Deliver; he, his attribute fulfilled,
To the island chorus hand your measures on,
Wed now with harmony: so them, at last,
Night after night, in the open hall of dance,
Shall thirty matted men, to the clapped hand,
Intone and bray and bark. Unfortunate!
Paper and print alone shall honour mine.

THE SONG

Let now the King his ear arouse
And toss the bosky ringlets from his brows,
The while, our bond to implement,
My muse relates and praises his descent.

I

Bride of the shark, her valour first I sing
Who on the lone seas quickened of a King.

She, from the shore and puny homes of men,
Beyond the climber's sea-discerning ken,
Swam, led by omens; and devoid of fear,
Beheld her monstrous paramour draw near.
She gazed; all round her to the heavenly pale,
The simple sea was void of isle or sail—
Sole overhead the unsparing sun was reared—
When the deep bubbled and the brute appeared.
But she, secure in the decrees of fate,
Made strong her bosom and received the mate,
And, men declare, from that marine embrace
Conceived the virtues of a stronger race.

II

Her stern descendant next I praise,
Survivor of a thousand frays:—
In the hall of tongues who ruled the throng;
Led and was trusted by the strong;
And when spears were in the wood,
Like a tower of vantage stood:—
Whom, not till seventy years had sped,
Unscarred of breast, erect of head,

Still light of step, still bright of look,

The hunter, Death, had overtook.

III

His sons, the brothers twain, I sing,

Of whom the elder reigned a King.

No Childeric he, yet much declined

From his rude sire's imperious mind,

Until his day came when he died,

He lived, he reigned, he versified.

But chiefly him I celebrate

That was the pillar of the state,

Ruled, wise of word and bold of mien,

The peaceful and the warlike scene;

And played alike the leader's part

In lawful and unlawful art.

His soldiers with emboldened ears

Heard him laugh among the spears.

He could deduce from age to age

The web of island parentage;

Best lay the rhyme, best lead the dance,

For any festal circumstance:

And fitly fashion oar and boat,
A palace or an armour coat.
None more availed than he to raise
The strong, suffumigating blaze,
Or knot the wizard leaf: none more,
Upon the untrodden windward shore
Of the isle, beside the beating main,
To cure the sickly and constrain,
With muttered words and waving rods,
The gibbering and the whistling gods.
But he, though thus with hand and head
He ruled, commanded, charmed, and led,
And thus in virtue and in might
Towered to contemporary sight—
Still in fraternal faith and love,
Remained below to reach above,
Gave and obeyed the apt command,
Pilot and vassal of the land.

IV

My Tembinok' from men like these
Inherited his palaces,
His right to rule, his powers of mind,

His cocoa-islands sea-enshrined.
Stern bearer of the sword and whip,
A master passed in mastership,
He learned, without the spur of need,
To write, to cipher, and to read;
From all that touch on his prone shore
Augments his treasury of lore,
Eager in age as erst in youth
To catch an art, to learn a truth,
To paint on the internal page
A clearer picture of the age.
His age, you say? But ah, not so!
In his lone isle of long ago,
A royal Lady of Shalott,
Sea-sundered, he beholds it not;
He only hears it far away.
The stress of equatorial day
He suffers; he records the while
The vapid annals of the isle;
Slaves bring him praise of his renown,
Or cackle of the palm-tree town;
The rarer ship and the rare boat
He marks; and only hears remote,

Where thrones and fortunes rise and reel,

The thunder of the turning wheel.

V

For the unexpected tears he shed

At my departing, may his lion head

Not whiten, his revolving years

No fresh occasion minister of tears;

At book or cards, at work or sport,

Him may the breeze across the palace court

For ever fan; and swelling near

For ever the loud song divert his ear.

Schooner 'Equator,' at Sea.

XXXVIII—THE WOODMAN

In all the grove, nor stream nor bird

Nor aught beside my blows was heard,

And the woods wore their noonday dress—

The glory of their silentness.

From the island summit to the seas,

Trees mounted, and trees drooped, and trees

Groped upward in the gaps. The green

Inarboured talus and ravine

By fathoms. By the multitude
The rugged columns of the wood
And bunches of the branches stood;
Thick as a mob, deep as a sea,
And silent as eternity.
With lowered axe, with backward head,
Late from this scene my labourer fled,
And with a ravelled tale to tell,
Returned. Some denizen of hell,
Dead man or disinvested god,
Had close behind him peered and trod,
And triumphed when he turned to flee.
How different fell the lines with me!
Whose eye explored the dim arcade
Impatient of the uncoming shade—
Shy elf, or dryad pale and cold,
Or mystic lingerer from of old:
Vainly. The fair and stately things,
Impassive as departed kings,
All still in the wood's stillness stood,
And dumb. The rooted multitude
Nodded and brooded, bloomed and dreamed,
Unmeaning, undivined. It seemed

No other art, no hope, they knew,
Than clutch the earth and seek the blue.
'Mid vegetable king and priest
And stripling, I (the only beast)
Was at the beast's work, killing; hewed
The stubborn roots across, bestrewed
The glebe with the dislustred leaves,
And bade the saplings fall in sheaves;
Bursting across the tangled math
A ruin that I called a path,
A Golgotha that, later on,
When rains had watered, and suns shone,
And seeds enriched the place, should bear
And be called garden. Here and there,
I spied and plucked by the green hair
A foe more resolute to live,
The toothed and killing sensitive.
He, semi-conscious, fled the attack;
He shrank and tucked his branches back;
And straining by his anchor-strand,
Captured and scratched the rooting hand.
I saw him crouch, I felt him bite;
And straight my eyes were touched with sight.

I saw the wood for what it was:
The lost and the victorious cause,
The deadly battle pitched in line,
Saw silent weapons cross and shine:
Silent defeat, silent assault,
A battle and a burial vault.

Thick round me in the teeming mud
Brier and fern strove to the blood:
The hooked liana in his gin
Noosed his reluctant neighbours in:
There the green murderer throve and spread,
Upon his smothering victims fed,
And wantoned on his climbing coil.
Contending roots fought for the soil
Like frightened demons: with despair
Competing branches pushed for air.
Green conquerors from overhead
Bestrode the bodies of their dead:
The Caesars of the sylvan field,
Unused to fail, foredoomed to yield:
For in the groins of branches, lo!
The cancers of the orchid grow.

Silent as in the listed ring
Two chartered wrestlers strain and cling;
Dumb as by yellow Hooghly's side
The suffocating captives died;
So hushed the woodland warfare goes
Unceasing; and the silent foes
Grapple and smother, strain and clasp
Without a cry, without a gasp.
Here also sound thy fans, O God,
Here too thy banners move abroad:
Forest and city, sea and shore,
And the whole earth, thy threshing-floor!
The drums of war, the drums of peace,
Roll through our cities without cease,
And all the iron halls of life
Ring with the unremitting strife.

The common lot we scarce perceive.
Crowds perish, we nor mark nor grieve:
The bugle calls—we mourn a few!
What corporal's guard at Waterloo?
What scanty hundreds more or less
In the man-devouring Wilderness?

What handful bled on Delhi ridge?
—See, rather, London, on thy bridge
The pale battalions trample by,
Resolved to slay, resigned to die.
Count, rather, all the maimed and dead
In the unbrotherly war of bread.
See, rather, under sultrier skies
What vegetable Londons rise,
And teem, and suffer without sound:
Or in your tranquil garden ground,
Contented, in the falling gloom,
Saunter and see the roses bloom.
That these might live, what thousands died!
All day the cruel hoe was plied;
The ambulance barrow rolled all day;
Your wife, the tender, kind, and gay,
Donned her long gauntlets, caught the spud,
And bathed in vegetable blood;
And the long massacre now at end,
See! where the lazy coils ascend,
See, where the bonfire sputters red
At even, for the innocent dead.

Why prate of peace? when, warriors all,

We clank in harness into hall,
And ever bare upon the board
Lies the necessary sword.
In the green field or quiet street,
Besieged we sleep, beleaguered eat;
Labour by day and wake o' nights,
In war with rival appetites.
The rose on roses feeds; the lark
On larks. The sedentary clerk
All morning with a diligent pen
Murders the babes of other men;
And like the beasts of wood and park,
Protects his whelps, defends his den.

Unshamed the narrow aim I hold;
I feed my sheep, patrol my fold;
Breathe war on wolves and rival flocks,
A pious outlaw on the rocks
Of God and morning; and when time
Shall bow, or rivals break me, climb
Where no undubbed civilian dares,
In my war harness, the loud stairs
Of honour; and my conqueror

Hail me a warrior fallen in war.

Vailima.

XXXIX—TROPIC RAIN

As the single pang of the blow, when the metal is mingled well,
Rings and lives and resounds in all the bounds of the bell,
So the thunder above spoke with a single tongue,
So in the heart of the mountain the sound of it rumbled and clung.

Sudden the thunder was drowned—quenched was the levin light—
And the angel-spirit of rain laughed out loud in the night.
Loud as the maddened river raves in the cloven glen,
Angel of rain! you laughed and leaped on the roofs of men;

And the sleepers sprang in their beds, and joyed and feared as you fell.
You struck, and my cabin quailed; the roof of it roared like a bell.
You spoke, and at once the mountain shouted and shook with brooks.
You ceased, and the day returned, rosy, with virgin looks.

And methought that beauty and terror are only one, not two;
And the world has room for love, and death, and thunder, and dew;
And all the sinews of hell slumber in summer air;
And the face of God is a rock, but the face of the rock is fair.
Beneficent streams of tears flow at the finger of pain;

And out of the cloud that smites, beneficent rivers of rain.

Vailima.

XL—AN END OF TRAVEL

Let now your soul in this substantial world
Some anchor strike. Be here the body moored;—
This spectacle immutably from now
The picture in your eye; and when time strikes,
And the green scene goes on the instant blind—
The ultimate helpers, where your horse to-day
Conveyed you dreaming, bear your body dead.

Vailima.

XLI

We uncommiserate pass into the night
From the loud banquet, and departing leave
A tremor in men's memories, faint and sweet
And frail as music. Features of our face,
The tones of the voice, the touch of the loved hand,
Perish and vanish, one by one, from earth:
Meanwhile, in the hall of song, the multitude
Applauds the new performer. One, perchance,
One ultimate survivor lingers on,
And smiles, and to his ancient heart recalls

The long forgotten. Ere the morrow die,
He too, returning, through the curtain comes,
And the new age forgets us and goes on.

XLII

Sing me a song of a lad that is gone,
  Say, could that lad be I?
Merry of soul he sailed on a day
  Over the sea to Skye.

Mull was astern, Rum on the port,
  Eigg on the starboard bow;
Glory of youth glowed in his soul:
  Where is that glory now?

Sing me a song of a lad that is gone,
  Say, could that lad be I?
Merry of soul he sailed on a day
  Over the sea to Skye.

Give me again all that was there,
  Give me the sun that shone!
Give me the eyes, give me the soul,
  Give me the lad that's gone!

Sing me a song of a lad that is gone,
  Say, could that lad be I?
Merry of soul he sailed on a day
  Over the sea to Skye.

Billow and breeze, islands and seas,
  Mountains of rain and sun,
All that was good, all that was fair,
  All that was me is gone.

XLIII—TO S. R. CROCKETT

(On receiving a Dedication)

Blows the wind to-day, and the sun and the rain are flying,
  Blows the wind on the moors to-day and now,
Where about the graves of the martyrs the whaups are crying,
  My heart remembers how!

Grey recumbent tombs of the dead in desert places,
  Standing stones on the vacant wine-red moor,
Hills of sheep, and the howes of the silent vanished races,
  And winds, austere and pure:

Be it granted me to behold you again in dying,

Hills of home! and to hear again the call;
Hear about the graves of the martyrs the peewees crying,
And hear no more at all.

Vailima.

XLIV—EVENSONG

The embers of the day are red
Beyond the murky hill.
The kitchen smokes: the bed
In the darkling house is spread:
The great sky darkens overhead,
And the great woods are shrill.
So far have I been led,
Lord, by Thy will:
So far I have followed, Lord, and wondered still.

The breeze from the enbalmèd land
Blows sudden toward the shore,
And claps my cottage door.
I hear the signal, Lord—I understand.
The night at Thy command
Comes. I will eat and sleep and will not question more.

Vailima.

Footnotes

[44] This is the same Princess Moë whose charms of person and disposition have been recorded by the late Lord Pembroke in South Sea Bubbles, and by M. Pierre Loti in the Mariage de Loti.

[45] The yacht Casco had been so called by the people of Fakarava in the Paumotus.

EDINBURGH: PICTURESQUE NOTES

CHAPTER I. INTRODUCTORY.

The ancient and famous metropolis of the North sits overlooking a windy estuary from the slope and summit of three hills. No situation could be more commanding for the head city of a kingdom; none better chosen for noble prospects. From her tall precipice and terraced gardens she looks far and wide on the sea and broad champaigns. To the east you may catch at sunset the spark of the May lighthouse, where the Firth expands into the German Ocean; and away to the west, over all the carse of Stirling, you can see the first snows upon Ben Ledi.

But Edinburgh pays cruelly for her high seat in one of the vilest climates under heaven. She is liable to be beaten upon by all the winds that blow, to be drenched with rain, to be buried in cold sea fogs out of the east, and powdered with the snow as it comes flying southward from the Highland hills. The weather is raw and boisterous in winter, shifty and ungenial in summer, and a downright meteorological purgatory in the spring. The delicate die early, and I, as a survivor, among bleak winds and plumping rain, have been sometimes tempted to envy them their fate. For all who love shelter and the blessings of the sun, who hate dark weather and perpetual tilting against squalls, there could scarcely be found a more unhomely and harassing place of residence. Many such aspire angrily after that Somewhere-else of the imagination, where all troubles are supposed to end. They lean over the great bridge which joins the New Town with the Old—that windiest spot, or high altar, in this northern temple of the winds—and watch the trains smoking out from under them and vanishing into the tunnel on a voyage to brighter skies. Happy the passengers who shake off the dust of Edinburgh, and have heard for the last time the cry of the east wind among her chimney-tops! And yet the place establishes an interest in people's hearts; go where they will, they find no city of the same distinction; go where they will, they take a pride in their old home.

Venice, it has been said, differs from another cities in the sentiment which she inspires. The rest may have admirers; she only, a famous fair one, counts lovers in her train. And, indeed, even by her kindest friends, Edinburgh is not considered in a similar sense. These like her for many reasons, not any one of which is satisfactory in itself. They like her whimsically, if you will, and somewhat as a virtuoso dotes upon his cabinet. Her attraction is romantic in the narrowest meaning of the term. Beautiful as she is, she is not so much beautiful as interesting. She is pre-eminently Gothic, and all the more so since she has set herself off with some Greek airs, and erected classic temples on her crags. In a word, and above all, she is a curiosity. The Palace of Holyrood has been left aside in the growth of Edinburgh, and stands grey and silent in a workman's quarter and among breweries and gas works. It is a house of many memories. Great people of yore, kings and queens, buffoons and grave ambassadors, played their stately farce for centuries in Holyrood. Wars have been plotted, dancing has lasted deep into the night,—murder has been done in its chambers. There Prince Charlie held his phantom levees, and in a very gallant manner represented a fallen dynasty for some hours. Now, all these things of clay are mingled with the dust, the king's crown itself is shown for sixpence to the vulgar; but the stone palace has outlived these charges. For fifty weeks together, it is no more than a show for tourists and a museum of old furniture; but on the fifty-first, behold the palace reawakened and mimicking its past. The Lord Commissioner, a kind of stage sovereign, sits among stage courtiers; a coach and six and clattering escort come and go before the gate; at night, the windows are lighted up, and its near neighbours, the workmen, may dance in their own houses to the palace music. And in this the palace is typical. There is a spark among the embers; from time to time the old volcano smokes. Edinburgh has but partly abdicated, and still wears, in parody, her metropolitan trappings. Half a capital and half a country town, the whole city leads a double existence; it has long trances of the one and flashes of the other; like the king of the Black Isles, it is half alive and half a monumental marble. There are armed men and cannon in the citadel overhead; you may see the troops marshalled on the high parade; and at night after the early winter even-fall, and in the morning before the laggard winter dawn, the wind carries abroad over Edinburgh the sound of drums and bugles. Grave judges sit bewigged in what was once the scene of imperial deliberations. Close by in the High Street perhaps the trumpets may sound about the stroke of noon; and you see a troop of citizens in tawdry masquerade; tabard above, heather-mixture trowser below, and the men themselves trudging in the mud among unsympathetic by-standers. The grooms of a well-appointed circus tread the streets with a better presence. And yet these are the Heralds and Pursuivants of Scotland, who are about to proclaim a new law of the United Kingdom before two-score boys, and thieves, and hackney-coachmen. Meanwhile every hour the bell of the University rings out over the hum of the streets, and every hour a double tide of students, coming and going, fills the deep archways. And lastly, one night in the springtime—or say one morning rather, at the peep of day—late folk may hear voices of many men singing a psalm in unison from a church on one side of the old High Street; and a little after, or perhaps a little before, the sound of many men singing a psalm in unison from another church on the opposite side of the way. There will be something in the words above the dew of Hermon, and how goodly it is to see brethren dwelling together in unity. And the late folk will tell themselves that all this singing denotes the conclusion of two yearly ecclesiastical parliaments—the parliaments of Churches which are brothers in many admirable virtues, but not specially like brothers in this particular of a tolerant and peaceful life.

Again, meditative people will find a charm in a certain consonancy between the aspect of the city and its odd and stirring history. Few places, if any, offer a more barbaric display of contrasts to the eye. In the very midst stands one of the most satisfactory crags in nature—a Bass Rock upon dry land, rooted in a garden shaken by passing trains, carrying a crown of battlements and turrets, and describing its war-like shadow over the liveliest and brightest thoroughfare of the new town. From their smoky beehives, ten stories high, the unwashed look down upon the open squares and gardens of the wealthy; and gay people sunning themselves along Princes Street, with its mile of commercial palaces all beflagged upon some great occasion, see, across a gardened valley set with statues, where the washings of the Old

Town flutter in the breeze at its high windows. And then, upon all sides, what a clashing of architecture! In this one valley, where the life of the town goes most busily forward, there may be seen, shown one above and behind another by the accidents of the ground, buildings in almost every style upon the globe. Egyptian and Greek temples, Venetian palaces and Gothic spires, are huddled one over another in a most admired disorder; while, above all, the brute mass of the Castle and the summit of Arthur's Seat look down upon these imitations with a becoming dignity, as the works of Nature may look down the monuments of Art. But Nature is a more indiscriminate patroness than we imagine, and in no way frightened of a strong effect. The birds roost as willingly among the Corinthian capitals as in the crannies of the crag; the same atmosphere and daylight clothe the eternal rock and yesterday's imitation portico; and as the soft northern sunshine throws out everything into a glorified distinctness—or easterly mists, coming up with the blue evening, fuse all these incongruous features into one, and the lamps begin to glitter along the street, and faint lights to burn in the high windows across the valley—the feeling grows upon you that this also is a piece of nature in the most intimate sense; that this profusion of eccentricities, this dream in masonry and living rock, is not a drop-scene in a theatre, but a city in the world of every-day reality, connected by railway and telegraph-wire with all the capitals of Europe, and inhabited by citizens of the familiar type, who keep ledgers, and attend church, and have sold their immortal portion to a daily paper. By all the canons of romance, the place demands to be half deserted and leaning towards decay; birds we might admit in profusion, the play of the sun and winds, and a few gipsies encamped in the chief thoroughfare; but these citizens with their cabs and tramways, their trains and posters, are altogether out of key. Chartered tourists, they make free with historic localities, and rear their young among the most picturesque sites with a grand human indifference. To see them thronging by, in their neat clothes and conscious moral rectitude, and with a little air of possession that verges on the absurd, is not the least striking feature of the place. [10]

And the story of the town is as eccentric as its appearance. For centuries it was a capital thatched with heather, and more than once, in the evil days of English invasion, it has gone up in flame to heaven, a beacon to ships at sea.

It was the jousting-ground of jealous nobles, not only on Greenside, or by the King's Stables, where set tournaments were fought to the sound of trumpets and under the authority of the royal presence, but in every alley where there was room to cross swords, and in the main street, where popular tumult under the Blue Blanket alternated with the brawls of outlandish clansmen and retainers. Down in the palace John Knox reproved his queen in the accents of modern democracy. In the town, in one of those little shops plastered like so many swallows' nests among the buttresses of the old Cathedral, that familiar autocrat, James VI., would gladly share a bottle of wine with George Heriot the goldsmith. Up on the Pentland Hills, that so quietly look down on the Castle with the city lying in waves around it, those mad and dismal fanatics, the Sweet Singers, haggard from long exposure on the moors, sat day and night with 'tearful psalmns' to see Edinburgh consumed with fire from heaven, like another Sodom or Gomorrah. There, in the Grass-market, stiff-necked, covenanting heroes, offered up the often unnecessary, but not less honourable, sacrifice of their lives, and bade eloquent farewell to sun, moon, and stars, and earthly friendships, or died silent to the roll of drums. Down by yon outlet rode Grahame of Claverhouse and his thirty dragoons, with the town beating to arms behind their horses' tails—a sorry handful thus riding for their lives, but with a man at the head who was to return in a different temper, make a dash that staggered Scotland to the heart, and die happily in the thick of fight. There Aikenhead was hanged for a piece of boyish incredulity; there, a few years afterwards, David Hume ruined Philosophy and Faith, an undisturbed and well-reputed citizen; and thither, in yet a few years more, Burns came from the plough-tail, as to an academy of gilt unbelief and artificial letters. There, when the great exodus was made across the valley, and the New Town began to spread abroad its draughty parallelograms, and rear its long frontage on the opposing hill, there was such a flitting, such a change of domicile and dweller, as was never excelled in the history of cities: the cobbler succeeded the earl; the beggar ensconced himself by the judge's chimney; what had been a palace was used as a pauper refuge; and great mansions were so parcelled out among the least and lowest in society, that the hearthstone of the old proprietor was thought large enough to be partitioned off into a bedroom by the new.

CHAPTER II. OLD TOWN—THE LANDS.

The Old Town, it is pretended, is the chief characteristic, and, from a picturesque point of view, the liver-wing of Edinburgh. It is one of the most common forms of depreciation to throw cold water on the whole by adroit over-commendation of a part, since everything worth judging, whether it be a man, a work of art, or only a fine city, must be judged upon its merits as a whole. The Old Town depends for much of its effect on the new quarters that lie around it, on the sufficiency of its situation, and on the hills that back it up. If you were to set it somewhere else by itself, it would look remarkably like Stirling in a bolder and loftier edition. The point is to see this embellished Stirling planted in the midst of a large, active, and fantastic modern city; for there the two re-act in a picturesque sense, and the one is the making of the other.

The Old Town occupies a sloping ridge or tail of diluvial matter, protected, in some subsidence of the waters, by the Castle cliffs which fortify it to the west. On the one side of it and the other the new towns of the south and of the north occupy their lower, broader, and more gentle hill-tops. Thus, the quarter of the Castle over-tops the whole city and keeps an open view to sea and land. It dominates for miles on every side; and people on the decks of ships, or ploughing in quiet country places over in Fife, can see the banner on the Castle battlements, and the smoke of the Old Town blowing abroad over the subjacent country. A city that is set upon a hill. It was, I suppose, from this distant aspect that she got her nickname of Auld Reekie. Perhaps it was given her by people who had never crossed her doors: day after day, from their various rustic Pisgahs, they had seen the pile of building on the hill-top, and the long plume of smoke over the plain; so it appeared to them; so it had appeared to their fathers tilling the same field; and as that was all they knew of the place, it could be all expressed in these two words.

Indeed, even on a nearer view, the Old Town is properly smoked; and though it is well washed with rain all the year round, it has a grim and sooty aspect among its younger suburbs. It grew, under the law that regulates the growth of walled cities in precarious situations, not in extent, but in height and density. Public buildings were forced, wherever there was room for them, into the midst of thoroughfares; thorough—fares were diminished into lanes; houses sprang up story after story, neighbour mounting upon neighbour's shoulder, as in some Black Hole of Calcutta, until the population slept fourteen or fifteen deep in a vertical direction. The tallest of these lands, as they are locally termed, have long since been burnt out; but to this day it is not uncommon to see eight or ten windows at a flight; and the cliff of building which hangs imminent over Waverley Bridge would still put many natural precipices to shame. The cellars are already high above the gazer's head, planted on the steep hill-side; as for the garret, all the furniture may be in the pawn-shop, but it commands a famous prospect to the Highland hills. The poor man may roost up there in the centre of Edinburgh, and yet have a peep of the green country from his window; he shall see the quarters of the well-to-do fathoms underneath, with their broad squares and gardens; he shall have nothing overhead but a few spires, the stone top-gallants of the city; and perhaps the wind may reach him with a rustic pureness, and bring a smack of the sea or of flowering lilacs in the spring.

It is almost the correct literary sentiment to deplore the revolutionary improvements of Mr. Chambers and his following. It is easy to be a conservator of the discomforts of others; indeed, it is only our good qualities we find it irksome to conserve. Assuredly, in driving streets through the black labyrinth, a few curious old corners have been swept away, and some associations turned out of house and home. But what slices of sunlight, what breaths of clean air, have been let in! And what a picturesque world remains untouched! You go under dark arches, and down dark stairs and alleys. The way is so narrow that you can lay a hand on either wall; so steep that, in greasy winter weather, the pavement is almost as treacherous as ice. Washing dangles above washing from the windows; the houses bulge outwards upon flimsy brackets; you see a bit of sculpture in a dark corner; at the top of all, a gable and a few crowsteps are printed on the sky. Here, you come into a court where the children are at play and the grown people sit upon their doorsteps, and perhaps a church spire shows itself above the roofs. Here, in the narrowest of the entry, you find a great old mansion still erect, with some insignia of its former state—some scutcheon, some holy or courageous motto, on the lintel. The local antiquary points out where famous and well-born people had their lodging; and as you look up, out pops the head of a slatternly woman from the countess's window. The Bedouins camp within Pharaoh's palace walls, and the old war-ship is given over to the rats. We are already a far way from the days when powdered heads were plentiful in these alleys, with jolly, port-wine faces underneath. Even in the chief thoroughfares Irish washings flutter at the windows, and the pavements are encumbered with loiterers.

These loiterers are a true character of the scene. Some shrewd Scotch workmen may have paused on their way to a job, debating Church affairs and politics with their tools upon their arm. But the most part are of a different order—skulking jail-birds; unkempt, bare-foot children; big-mouthed, robust women, in a sort of uniform of striped flannel petticoat and short tartan shawl; among these, a few surpervising constables and a dismal sprinkling of mutineers and broken men from higher ranks in society, with some mark of better days upon them, like a brand. In a place no larger than Edinburgh, and where the traffic is mostly centred in five or six chief streets, the same face comes often under the notice of an idle stroller. In fact, from this point of view, Edinburgh is not so much a small city as the largest of small towns. It is scarce possible to avoid observing your neighbours; and I never yet heard of any one who tried. It has been my fortune, in this anonymous accidental way, to watch more than one of these downward travellers for some stages on the road to ruin. One man must have been upwards of sixty before I first observed him, and he made then a decent, personable figure in broad-cloth of the best. For three years he kept falling—grease coming and buttons going from the square-skirted coat, the face puffing and pimpling, the shoulders growing bowed, the hair falling scant and grey upon his head; and the last that ever I saw of him, he was standing at the mouth of an entry with several men in moleskin, three parts drunk, and his old black raiment daubed with mud. I fancy that I still can hear him laugh. There was something heart-breaking in this gradual declension at so advanced an age; you would have thought a man of sixty out of the reach of these calamities; you would have thought that he was niched by that time into a safe place in life, whence he could pass quietly and honourably into the grave.

One of the earliest marks of these dégringolades is, that the victim begins to disappear from the New Town thoroughfares, and takes to the High Street, like a wounded animal to the woods. And such an one is the type of the quarter. It also has fallen socially. A scutcheon over the door somewhat jars in sentiment where there is a washing at every window. The old man, when I saw him last, wore the coat in which he had played the gentleman three years before; and that was just what gave him so pre-eminent an air of wretchedness.

It is true that the over-population was at least as dense in the epoch of lords and ladies, and that now-a-days some customs which made Edinburgh notorious of yore have been fortunately pretermitted. But an aggregation of comfort is not distasteful like an aggregation of the reverse. Nobody cares how many lords and ladies, and divines and lawyers, may have been crowded into these houses in the past—perhaps the more the merrier. The glasses clink around the china punch-bowl, some one touches the virginals, there are peacocks' feathers on the chimney, and the tapers burn clear and pale in the red firelight. That is not an ugly picture in itself, nor will it become ugly upon repetition. All the better if the like were going on in every second room; the land would only look the more inviting. Times are changed. In one house, perhaps, two-score families herd together; and, perhaps, not one of them is wholly out of the reach of want. The great hotel is given over to discomfort from the foundation to the chimney-tops; everywhere a pinching, narrow habit, scanty meals, and an air of sluttishness and dirt. In the first room there is a birth, in another a death, in a third a sordid drinking-bout, and the detective and the Bible-reader cross upon the stairs. High words are audible from dwelling to dwelling, and children have a strange experience from the first; only a robust soul, you would think, could grow up in such conditions without hurt. And even if God tempers His dispensations to the young, and all the ill does not arise that our apprehensions may forecast, the sight of such a way of living is disquieting to people who are more happily circumstanced. Social inequality is nowhere more ostentatious than at Edinburgh. I have mentioned already how, to the stroller along Princes Street, the High Street callously exhibits its back garrets. It is true, there is a garden between. And although nothing could be more glaring by way of contrast, sometimes the opposition is more immediate; sometimes the thing lies in a nutshell, and there is not so much as a blade of grass between the rich and poor. To look over the South Bridge and see the Cowgate below full of crying hawkers, is to view one rank of society from another in the twinkling of an eye.

One night I went along the Cowgate after every one was a-bed but the policeman, and stopped by hazard before a tall land. The moon touched upon its chimneys, and shone blankly on the upper windows; there was no light anywhere in the great bulk of building; but as I stood there it seemed to me that I could hear quite a body of quiet sounds from the interior; doubtless there were many clocks ticking, and people snoring on their backs. And thus, as I fancied, the dense life within made itself faintly audible in my ears, family after family contributing its quota to the general hum, and the whole pile beating in tune to its timepieces, like a great disordered heart. Perhaps it was little more than a fancy altogether, but it was strangely impressive at the time, and gave me an imaginative measure of the disproportion between the quantity of living flesh and the trifling walls that separated and contained it.

There was nothing fanciful, at least, but every circumstance of terror and reality, in the fall of the land in the High Street. The building had grown rotten to the core; the entry underneath had suddenly closed up so that the scavenger's barrow could not pass; cracks and reverberations sounded through the house at night; the inhabitants of the huge old human bee-hive discussed their peril when they encountered on the stair; some had even left their dwellings in a panic of fear, and returned to them again in a fit of economy or self-respect; when, in the black hours of a Sunday morning, the whole structure ran together with a hideous uproar and tumbled story upon story to the ground. The physical shock was felt far and near; and the moral shock travelled with the morning milkmaid into all the suburbs. The church-bells never sounded more dismally over Edinburgh than that grey forenoon. Death had made a brave harvest, and, like Samson, by pulling down one roof, destroyed many a home. None who saw it can have forgotten the aspect of the gable; here it was plastered, there papered, according to the rooms; here the kettle still stood on the hob, high overhead; and there a cheap picture of the Queen was pasted over the chimney. So, by this disaster, you had a glimpse into the life of thirty families, all suddenly cut off from the revolving years. The land had fallen; and with the land how much! Far in the country, people saw a gap in the city ranks, and the sun looked through between the chimneys in an unwonted place. And all over the world, in London, in Canada, in New Zealand, fancy what a multitude of people could exclaim with truth: 'The house that I was born in fell last night!'

CHAPTER III. THE PARLIAMENT CLOSE.

Time has wrought its changes most notably around the precincts of St. Giles's Church. The church itself, if it were not for the spire, would be unrecognisable; the Krames are all gone, not a shop is left to shelter in its buttresses; and zealous magistrates and a misguided architect have shorn the design of manhood, and left it poor, naked, and pitifully pretentious. As St. Giles's must have had in former days a rich and quaint appearance now forgotten, so the neighbourhood was bustling, sunless, and romantic. It was here that the town was most overbuilt; but the overbuilding has been all rooted out, and not only a free fair-way left along the High Street with an open space on either side of the church, but a great porthole, knocked in the main line of the lands, gives an outlook to the north and the New Town.

There is a silly story of a subterranean passage between the Castle and Holyrood, and a bold Highland piper who volunteered to explore its windings. He made his entrance by the upper end, playing a strathspey; the curious footed it after him down the street, following his descent by the sound of the chanter from below; until all of a sudden, about the level of St. Giles's, the music came abruptly to an end, and the people in the street stood at fault with hands uplifted. Whether he was choked with gases, or perished in a quag, or was removed bodily by the Evil One, remains a point of doubt; but the piper has never again been seen or heard of from that day to this. Perhaps he wandered down into the land of Thomas the Rhymer, and some day, when it is least expected, may take a thought to revisit the sunlit upper world. That will be a strange moment for the cabmen on the stance besides St. Giles's, when they hear the drone of his pipes reascending from the bowels of the earth below their horses' feet.

But it is not only pipers who have vanished, many a solid bulk of masonry has been likewise spirited into the air. Here, for example, is the shape of a heart let into the causeway. This was the site of the Tolbooth, the Heart of Midlothian, a place old in story and namefather to a noble book. The walls are now down in the dust; there is no more squalor carceris for merry debtors, no more cage for the old, acknowledged prison-breaker; but the sun and the wind play freely over the foundations of the jail. Nor is this the only memorial that the pavement keeps of former days. The ancient burying-ground of Edinburgh lay behind St. Giles's Church, running downhill to the Cowgate and covering the site of the present Parliament House. It has disappeared as utterly as the prison or the Luckenbooths; and for those ignorant of its history, I know only one token that remains. In the Parliament Close, trodden daily underfoot by advocates, two letters and a date mark the resting-place of the man who made Scotland over again in his own image, the indefatigable, undissuadable John Knox. He sleeps within call of the church that so often echoed to his preaching.

Hard by the reformer, a bandy-legged and garlanded Charles Second, made of lead, bestrides a tun-bellied charger. The King has his backed turned, and, as you look, seems to be trotting clumsily away from such a dangerous neighbour. Often, for hours together, these two will be alone in the Close, for it lies out of the way of all but legal traffic. On one side the south wall of the church, on the other the arcades of the Parliament House, enclose this irregular bight of causeway and describe their shadows on it in the sun. At either end, from round St. Giles's buttresses, you command a look into the High Street with its motley passengers; but the stream goes by, east and west, and leaves the Parliament Close to Charles the Second and the birds. Once in a while, a patient crowd may be seen loitering there all day, some eating fruit, some reading a newspaper; and to judge by their quiet demeanour, you would think they were waiting for a distribution of soup-tickets. The fact is far otherwise; within in the Justiciary Court a man is upon trial for his life, and these are some of the curious for whom the gallery was found too narrow. Towards afternoon, if the prisoner is unpopular, there will be a round of hisses when he is brought forth. Once in a while, too, an advocate in wig and gown, hand upon mouth, full of pregnant nods, sweeps to and fro in the arcade listening to an agent; and at certain regular hours a whole tide of lawyers hurries across the space.

The Parliament Close has been the scene of marking incidents in

Scottish history. Thus, when the Bishops were ejected from the Convention in 1688, 'all fourteen of them gathered together with pale faces and stood in a cloud in the Parliament Close:' poor episcopal personages who were done with fair weather for life! Some of the west-country Societarians standing by, who would have 'rejoiced more than in great sums' to be at their hanging, hustled them so rudely that they knocked their heads together. It was not magnanimous behaviour to dethroned enemies; but one, at least, of the Societarians had groaned in the boots, and they had all seen their dear friends upon the scaffold. Again, at the 'woeful Union,' it was here that people crowded to escort their favourite from the last of Scottish parliaments: people flushed with nationality, as Boswell would have said, ready for riotous acts, and fresh from throwing stones at the author of 'Robinson Crusoe' as he looked out of window.

One of the pious in the seventeenth century, going to pass his trials (examinations as we now say) for the Scottish Bar, beheld the Parliament Close open and had a vision of the mouth of Hell. This, and small wonder, was the means of his conversion. Nor was the vision unsuitable to the locality; for after an hospital, what uglier piece is there in civilisation than a court of law? Hither come envy, malice, and all uncharitableness to wrestle it out in public tourney; crimes, broken fortunes, severed households, the knave and his victim, gravitate to this low building with the arcade. To how many has not St. Giles's bell told the first hour after ruin? I think I see them pause to count the strokes, and wander on again into the moving High Street, stunned and sick at heart.

A pair of swing doors gives admittance to a hall with a carved roof, hung with legal portraits, adorned with legal statuary, lighted by windows of painted glass, and warmed by three vast fires. This is the Salle des pas perdus of the Scottish Bar. Here, by a ferocious custom, idle youths must promenade from ten till two. From end to end, singly or in pairs or trios, the gowns and wigs go back and forward. Through a hum of talk and footfalls, the piping tones of a Macer announce a fresh cause and call upon the names of those concerned. Intelligent men have been walking here daily for ten or twenty years without a rag of business or a shilling of reward. In process of time, they may perhaps be made the Sheriff-Substitute and Fountain of Justice at Lerwick or Tobermory. There is nothing required, you would say, but a little patience and a taste for exercise and bad air. To breathe dust and bombazine, to feed the mind on cackling gossip, to hear three parts of a case and drink a glass of sherry, to long with indescribable longings for the hour when a man may slip out of his travesty and devote himself to golf for the rest of the afternoon, and to do this day by day and year after year, may seem so small a thing to the inexperienced! But those who have made the experiment are of a different way of thinking, and count it the most arduous form of idleness.

More swing doors open into pigeon-holes where judges of the First Appeal sit singly, and halls of audience where the supreme Lords sit by three or four. Here, you may see Scott's place within the bar, where he wrote many a page of Waverley novels to the drone of judicial proceeding. You will hear a good deal of shrewdness, and, as their Lordships do not altogether disdain pleasantry, a fair proportion of dry fun. The broadest of broad Scotch is now banished from the bench; but the courts still retain a certain national flavour. We have a solemn enjoyable way of lingering on a case. We treat law as a fine art, and relish and digest a good distinction. There is no hurry: point after point must be rightly examined and reduced to principle; judge after judge must utter forth his obiter dicta to delighted brethren.

Besides the courts, there are installed under the same roof no less than three libraries: two of no mean order; confused and semi-subterranean, full of stairs and galleries; where you may see the most studious-looking wigs fishing out novels by lanthorn light, in the very place where the old Privy Council tortured Covenanters. As the Parliament House is built upon a slope, although it presents only one story to the north, it measures half-a-dozen at least upon the south; and range after range of vaults extend below the libraries. Few places are more characteristic of this hilly capital. You descend one stone stair after another, and wander, by the flicker of a match, in a labyrinth of stone cellars. Now, you pass below the Outer Hall and hear overhead, brisk but ghostly, the interminable pattering of legal feet. Now, you come upon a strong door with a wicket: on the other side are the cells of the police office and the trap-stair that gives admittance to the dock in the

Justiciary Court. Many a foot that has gone up there lightly enough, has been dead-heavy in the descent. Many a man's life has been argued away from him during long hours in the court above. But just now that tragic stage is empty and silent like a church on a week-day, with the bench all sheeted up and nothing moving but the sunbeams on the wall. A little farther and you strike upon a room, not empty like the rest, but crowded with productions from bygone criminal cases: a grim lumber: lethal weapons, poisoned organs in a jar, a door with a shot-hole through the panel, behind which a man fell dead. I cannot fancy why they should preserve them unless it were against the Judgment Day. At length, as you continue to descend, you see a peep of yellow gaslight and hear a jostling, whispering noise ahead; next moment you turn a corner, and there, in a whitewashed passage, is a machinery belt industriously turning on its wheels. You would think the engine had grown there of its own accord, like a cellar fungus, and would soon spin itself out and fill the vaults from end to end with its mysterious labours. In truth, it is only some gear of the steam ventilator; and you will find the engineers at hand, and may step out of their door into the sunlight. For all this while, you have not been descending towards the earth's centre, but only to the bottom of the hill and the foundations of the Parliament House; low down, to be sure, but still under the open heaven and in a field of grass. The daylight shines garishly on the back windows of the Irish quarter; on broken shutters, wry gables, old palsied houses on the brink of ruin, a crumbling human pig-sty fit for human pigs. There are few signs of life, besides a scanty washing or a face at a window: the dwellers are abroad, but they will return at night and stagger to their pallets.

CHAPTER IV. LEGENDS.

The character of a place is often most perfectly expressed in its associations. An event strikes root and grows into a legend, when it has happened amongst congenial surroundings. Ugly actions, above all in ugly places, have the true romantic quality, and become an undying property of their scene. To a man like Scott, the different appearances of nature seemed each to contain its own legend ready made, which it was his to call forth: in such or such a place, only such or such events ought with propriety to happen; and in this spirit he made the Lady of the Lake for Ben Venue, the Heart of Midlothian for Edinburgh, and the Pirate, so indifferently written but so romantically conceived, for the desolate islands and roaring tideways of the North. The common run of mankind have, from generation to generation, an instinct almost as delicate as that of Scott; but where he created new things, they only forget what is unsuitable among the old; and by survival of the fittest, a body of tradition becomes a work of art. So, in the low dens and high-flying garrets of Edinburgh, people may go back upon dark passages in the town's adventures, and chill their marrow with winter's tales about the fire: tales that are singularly apposite and characteristic, not only of the old life, but of the very constitution of built nature in that part, and singularly well qualified to add horror to horror, when the wind pipes around the tall lands, and hoots adown arched passages, and the far-spread wilderness of city lamps keeps quavering and flaring in the gusts.

Here, it is the tale of Begbie the bank-porter, stricken to the heart at a blow and left in his blood within a step or two of the crowded High Street. There, people hush their voices over Burke and Hare; over drugs and violated graves, and the resurrection-men smothering their victims with their knees. Here, again, the fame of Deacon Brodie is kept piously fresh. A great man in his day was the Deacon; well seen in good society, crafty with his hands as a cabinet-maker, and one who could sing a song with taste. Many a citizen was proud to welcome the Deacon to supper, and dismissed him with regret at a timeous hour, who would have been vastly disconcerted had he known how soon, and in what guise, his visitor returned. Many stories are told of this redoubtable Edinburgh burglar, but the one I have in my mind most vividly gives the key of all the rest. A friend of Brodie's, nested some way towards heaven in one of these great lands, had told him of a projected visit to the country, and afterwards, detained by some affairs, put it off and stayed the night in town. The good man had lain some time awake; it was far on in the small hours by the Tron bell; when suddenly there came a creak, a jar, a faint light. Softly he clambered out of bed and up to a false window which looked upon another room, and there, by the glimmer of a thieves' lantern, was his good friend the Deacon in a mask. It is characteristic of the town and the town's manners that this little episode should have been quietly tided over, and quite a good time elapsed before a great robbery, an escape, a Bow Street runner, a cock-fight, an apprehension in a cupboard in Amsterdam, and a last step into the air off his own greatly-improved gallows drop, brought the career of Deacon William Brodie to an end. But still, by the mind's eye, he may be seen, a man harassed below a mountain of duplicity, slinking from a magistrate's supper-room to a thieves' ken, and pickeering among the closes by the flicker of a dark lamp.

Or where the Deacon is out of favour, perhaps some memory lingers of the great plagues, and of fatal houses still unsafe to enter within the memory of man. For in time of pestilence the discipline had been sharp and sudden, and what we now call 'stamping out contagion' was carried on with deadly rigour. The officials, in their gowns of grey, with a white St. Andrew's cross on back and breast, and a white cloth carried before them on a staff, perambulated the city, adding the terror of man's justice to the fear of God's visitation. The dead they buried on the Borough Muir; the living who had concealed the sickness were drowned, if they were women, in the Quarry Holes, and if they were men, were hanged and gibbeted at their own doors; and wherever the evil had passed, furniture was destroyed and houses closed. And the most bogeyish part of the story is about such houses. Two generations back they still stood dark and empty; people avoided them as they passed by; the boldest schoolboy only shouted through the keyhole and made off; for within, it was supposed, the plague lay ambushed like a basilisk, ready to flow forth and spread blain and pustule through the city. What a terrible next-door neighbour for superstitious citizens! A rat scampering within would send a shudder through the stoutest heart. Here, if you like, was a sanitary parable, addressed by our uncleanly forefathers to their own neglect.

And then we have Major Weir; for although even his house is now demolished, old Edinburgh cannot clear herself of his unholy memory. He and his sister lived together in an odour of sour piety. She was a marvellous spinster; he had a rare gift of supplication, and was known among devout admirers by the name of Angelical Thomas. 'He was a tall, black man, and ordinarily looked down to the ground; a grim countenance, and a big nose. His garb was still a cloak, and somewhat dark, and he never went without his staff.' How it came about that Angelical Thomas was burned in company with his staff, and his sister in gentler manner hanged, and whether these two were simply religious maniacs of the more furious order, or had real as well as imaginary sins upon their old-world shoulders, are points happily beyond the reach of our intention. At least, it is suitable enough that out of this superstitious city some such example should have been put forth: the outcome and fine flower of dark and vehement religion. And at least the facts struck the public fancy and brought forth a remarkable family of myths. It would appear that the Major's staff went upon his errands, and even ran before him with a lantern on dark nights. Gigantic females, 'stentoriously laughing and gaping with tehees of laughter' at unseasonable hours of night and morning, haunted the purlieus of his abode. His house fell under such a load of infamy that no one dared to sleep in it, until municipal improvement levelled the structure to the ground. And my father has often been told in the nursery how the devil's coach, drawn by six coal-black horses with fiery eyes, would drive at night into the West Bow, and belated people might see the dead Major through the glasses.

Another legend is that of the two maiden sisters. A legend I am afraid it may be, in the most discreditable meaning of the term; or perhaps something worse—a mere yesterday's fiction. But it is a story of some vitality, and is worthy of a place in the Edinburgh kalendar. This pair inhabited a single room; from the facts, it must have been double-bedded; and it may have been of some dimensions: but when all is said, it was a single room. Here our two spinsters fell out—on some point of controversial divinity belike: but fell out so bitterly that there was never a word spoken between them, black or white, from that day forward. You would have thought they would separate: but no; whether from lack of means, or the Scottish fear of scandal, they continued to keep house together where they were. A chalk line drawn upon the floor separated their two domains; it bisected the doorway and the fireplace, so that each could go out and in, and do her cooking, without violating the territory of the other. So, for years, they coexisted in a hateful silence; their meals, their ablutions, their friendly visitors, exposed to an unfriendly scrutiny; and at night, in the dark watches, each could hear the breathing of her enemy. Never did four walls look down upon an uglier spectacle than these sisters rivalling in unsisterliness. Here is a canvas for Hawthorne to have turned into a cabinet picture—he had a Puritanic vein, which would have fitted him to treat this Puritanic horror; he could have shown them to us in their sicknesses and at their hideous twin devotions, thumbing a pair of great Bibles, or praying aloud for each other's penitence with marrowy emphasis; now each, with kilted petticoat, at her own corner of the fire on some tempestuous evening; now sitting each at her window, looking out upon the summer landscape sloping far below them towards the firth, and the field-paths where they had wandered hand in hand; or, as age and infirmity grew upon them and prolonged their toilettes, and their hands began to tremble and their heads to nod involuntarily, growing only the more steeled in enmity with years; until one fine day, at a word, a look, a visit, or the approach of death, their hearts would melt and the chalk boundary be overstepped for ever.

Alas! to those who know the ecclesiastical history of the race—the most perverse and melancholy in man's annals—this will seem only a figure of much that is typical of Scotland and her high-seated capital above the Forth—a figure so grimly realistic that it may pass with strangers for a caricature. We are wonderful patient haters for conscience sake up here in the North. I spoke, in the first of these papers, of the Parliaments of the Established and Free Churches, and how they can hear each other singing psalms across the street. There is but a street between them in space, but a shadow between them in principle; and yet there they sit, enchanted, and in damnatory accents pray for each other's growth in grace. It would be well if there were no more than two; but the sects in Scotland form a large family of sisters, and the chalk lines are thickly drawn, and run through the midst of many private homes. Edinburgh is a city of churches, as though it were a place of pilgrimage. You will see four within a stone-cast at the head of the West Bow. Some are crowded to the doors; some are empty like monuments; and yet you will ever find new ones in the building. Hence that surprising clamour of church bells that suddenly breaks out upon the Sabbath morning from Trinity and the sea-skirts to Morningside on the borders of the hills. I have heard the chimes of Oxford playing their symphony in a golden autumn morning, and beautiful it was to hear. But in Edinburgh all manner of loud bells join, or rather disjoin, in one swelling, brutal babblement of noise. Now one overtakes another, and now lags behind it; now five or six all strike on the pained tympanum at the same punctual instant of time, and make together a dismal chord of discord; and now for a second all seem to have conspired to hold their peace. Indeed, there are not many uproars in this world more dismal than that of the Sabbath bells in Edinburgh: a harsh ecclesiastical tocsin; the outcry of incongruous orthodoxies, calling on every separate conventicler to put up a protest, each in his own synagogue, against 'right-hand extremes and left-hand defections.' And surely there are few worse extremes than this extremity of zeal; and few more deplorable defections than this disloyalty to Christian love. Shakespeare wrote a comedy of 'Much Ado about Nothing.' The Scottish nation made a fantastic tragedy on the same subject. And it is for the success of this remarkable piece that these bells are sounded every Sabbath morning on the hills above the Forth. How many of them might rest silent in the steeple, how many of these ugly churches might be demolished and turned once more into useful building material, if people who think almost exactly the same thoughts about religion would condescend to worship God under the same roof! But there are the chalk lines. And which is to pocket pride, and speak the foremost word?

CHAPTER V. GREYFRIARS.

It was Queen Mary who threw open the gardens of the Grey Friars: a new and semi-rural cemetery in those days, although it has grown an antiquity in its turn and been superseded by half-a-dozen others. The Friars must have had a pleasant time on summer evenings; for their gardens were situated to a wish, with the tall castle and the tallest of the castle crags in front. Even now, it is one of our famous Edinburgh points of view; and strangers are led thither to see, by yet another instance, how strangely the city lies upon her hills. The enclosure is of an irregular shape; the double church of Old and New Greyfriars stands on the level at the top; a few thorns are dotted here and there, and the ground falls by terrace and steep slope towards the north. The open shows many slabs and table tombstones; and all round the margin, the place is girt by an array of aristocratic mausoleums appallingly adorned.

Setting aside the tombs of Roubiliac, which belong to the heroic order of graveyard art, we Scotch stand, to my fancy, highest among nations in the matter of grimly illustrating death. We seem to love for their own sake the emblems of time and the great change; and even around country churches you will find a wonderful exhibition of skulls, and crossbones, and noseless angels, and trumpets pealing for the Judgment Day. Every mason was a pedestrian Holbein: he had a deep consciousness of death, and loved to put its terrors pithily before the churchyard loiterer; he was brimful of rough hints upon mortality, and any dead farmer was seized upon to be a text. The classical examples of this art are in Greyfriars. In their time, these were doubtless costly monuments, and reckoned of a very elegant proportion by contemporaries; and now, when the elegance is not so apparent, the significance remains. You may perhaps look with a smile on the profusion of Latin mottoes—some crawling endwise up the shaft of a pillar, some issuing on a scroll from angels' trumpets—on the emblematic horrors, the figures rising headless from the grave, and all the traditional ingenuities in which it pleased our fathers to set forth their sorrow for the dead and their sense of earthly mutability. But it is not a hearty sort of mirth. Each ornament may have been executed by the merriest apprentice, whistling as he plied the mallet; but the original meaning of each, and the combined effect of so many of them in this quiet enclosure, is serious to the point of melancholy.

Round a great part of the circuit, houses of a low class present their backs to the churchyard. Only a few inches separate the living from the dead. Here, a window is partly blocked up by the pediment of a tomb; there, where the street falls far below the level of the graves, a chimney has been trained up the back of a monument, and a red pot looks vulgarly over from behind. A damp smell of the graveyard finds its way into houses where workmen sit at meat. Domestic life on a small scale goes forward visibly at the windows. The very solitude and stillness of the enclosure, which lies apart from the town's traffic, serves to accentuate the contrast. As you walk upon the graves, you see children scattering crumbs to feed the sparrows; you hear people singing or washing dishes, or the sound of tears and castigation; the linen on a clothes-pole flaps against funereal sculpture; or perhaps the cat slips over the lintel and descends on a memorial urn. And as there is nothing else astir, these incongruous sights and noises take hold on the attention and exaggerate the sadness of the place.

Greyfriars is continually overrun by cats. I have seen one afternoon, as many as thirteen of them seated on the grass beside old Milne, the Master Builder, all sleek and fat, and complacently blinking, as if they had fed upon strange meats. Old Milne was chaunting with the saints, as we may hope, and cared little for the company about his grave; but I confess the spectacle had an ugly side for me; and I was glad to step forward and raise my eyes to where the Castle and the roofs of the Old Town, and the spire of the Assembly Hall, stood deployed against the sky with the colourless precision of engraving. An open outlook is to be desired from a churchyard, and a sight of the sky and some of the world's beauty relieves a mind from morbid thoughts.

I shall never forget one visit. It was a grey, dropping day; the grass was strung with rain-drops; and the people in the houses kept hanging out their shirts and petticoats and angrily taking them in again, as the weather turned from wet to fair and back again. A grave-digger, and a friend of his, a gardener from the country, accompanied me into one after another of the cells and little courtyards in which it gratified the wealthy of old days to enclose their old bones from neighbourhood. In one, under a sort of shrine, we found a forlorn human effigy, very realistically executed down to the detail of his ribbed stockings, and holding in his hand a ticket with the date of his demise. He looked most pitiful and ridiculous, shut up by himself in his aristocratic precinct, like a bad old boy or an inferior forgotten deity under a new dispensation; the burdocks grew familiarly about his feet, the rain dripped all round him; and the world maintained the most entire indifference as to who he was or whither he had gone. In another, a vaulted tomb, handsome externally but horrible inside with damp and cobwebs, there were three mounds of black earth and an uncovered thigh bone. This was the place of interment, it appeared, of a family with whom the gardener had been long in service. He was among old acquaintances. 'This'll be Miss Marg'et's,' said he, giving the bone a friendly kick. 'The auld ---!' I have always an uncomfortable feeling in a graveyard, at sight of so many tombs to perpetuate memories best forgotten; but I never had the impression so strongly as that day. People had been at some expense in both these cases: to provoke a melancholy feeling of derision in the one, and an insulting epithet in the other. The proper inscription for the most part of mankind, I began to think, is the cynical jeer, cras tibi. That, if anything, will stop the mouth of a carper; since it both admits the worst and carries the war triumphantly into the enemy's camp.

Greyfriars is a place of many associations. There was one window in a house at the lower end, now demolished, which was pointed out to me by the gravedigger as a spot of legendary interest. Burke, the resurrection man, infamous for so many murders at five shillings a-head, used to sit thereat, with pipe and nightcap, to watch burials going forward on the green. In a tomb higher up, which must then have been but newly finished, John Knox, according to the same informant, had taken refuge in a turmoil of the Reformation. Behind the church is the haunted mausoleum of Sir George Mackenzie: Bloody Mackenzie, Lord Advocate in the Covenanting troubles and author of some pleasing sentiments on toleration. Here, in the last century, an old Heriot's Hospital boy once harboured from the pursuit of the police. The Hospital is next door to Greyfriars—a courtly building among lawns, where, on Founder's Day, you may see a multitude of children playing Kiss-in-the-Ring and Round the Mulberry-bush. Thus, when the fugitive had managed to conceal himself in the tomb, his old schoolmates had a hundred opportunities to bring him food; and there he lay in safety till a ship was found to smuggle him abroad. But his must have been indeed a heart of brass, to lie all day and night alone with the dead persecutor; and other lads were far from emulating him in courage. When a man's soul is certainly in hell, his body will scarce lie quiet in a tomb however costly; some time or other the door must open, and the reprobate come forth in the abhorred garments of the grave. It was thought a high piece of prowess to knock at the Lord Advocate's mausoleum and challenge him to appear. 'Bluidy Mackingie, come oot if ye dar'!' sang the fool-hardy urchins. But Sir George had other affairs on hand; and the author of an essay on toleration continues to sleep peacefully among the many whom he so intolerantly helped to slay.

For this infelix campus, as it is dubbed in one of its own inscriptions—an inscription over which Dr. Johnson passed a critical eye—is in many ways sacred to the memory of the men whom Mackenzie persecuted. It was here, on the flat tombstones, that the Covenant was signed by an enthusiastic people. In the long arm of the church-yard that extends to Lauriston, the prisoners from Bothwell Bridge—fed on bread and water and guarded, life for life, by vigilant marksmen—lay five months looking for the scaffold or the plantations. And while the good work was going forward in the Grassmarket, idlers in Greyfriars might have heard the throb of the military drums that drowned the voices of the martyrs. Nor is this all: for down in the corner farthest from Sir George, there stands a monument dedicated, in uncouth Covenanting verse, to all who lost their lives in that contention. There is no moorsman shot in a snow shower beside Irongray or Co'monell; there is not one of the two hundred who were drowned off the Orkneys; nor so much as a poor, over-driven, Covenanting slave in the American plantations; but can lay claim to a share in that memorial, and, if such things interest just men among the shades, can boast he has a monument on earth as well as Julius Cæsar or the Pharaohs. Where they may all lie, I know not. Far-scattered bones, indeed! But if the reader cares to learn how some of them—or some part of some of them—found their way at length to such honourable sepulture, let him listen to the words of one who was their comrade in life and their apologist when they were dead. Some of the insane controversial matter I omit, as well as some digressions, but leave the rest in Patrick Walker's language and orthography:—

> 'The never to be forgotten Mr. James Renwick told me, that he was Witness to their Public Murder at the Gallowlee, between Leith and Edinburgh, when he saw the Hangman hash and hagg off all their Five Heads, with Patrick Foreman's Right Hand: Their Bodies were all buried at the Gallows Foot; their Heads, with Patrick's Hand, were brought and put upon five Pikes on the Pleasaunce-Port. . . . Mr. Renwick told me also that it was the first public Action that his Hand was at, to conveen Friends, and lift their murthered Bodies, and carried them to the West Churchyard of Edinburgh,'—not Greyfriars, this time,—'and buried them there. Then they came about the City . . . . and took down these Five Heads and that Hand; and Day being come, they went quickly up the Pleasaunce; and when they came to Lauristoun Yards, upon the South-side of the City, they durst not venture, being so light, to go and bury their Heads with their Bodies, which they designed; it being present Death, if any of them had been found. Alexander Tweedie, a Friend, being with them, who at that Time was Gardner in these Yards, concluded to bury them in his Yard, being in a Box (wrapped in Linen), where they lay 45 Years except 3 Days, being executed upon the 10th of October 1681, and found the 7th Day of October 1726. That Piece of Ground lay for some Years unlaboured; and trenching it, the Gardner found them, which affrighted him the Box was consumed. Mr. Schaw, the Owner of these Yards, caused lift them, and lay them upon a Table in his Summer-house: Mr. Schaw's mother was so kind, as to cut out a Linen-cloth, and cover them. They lay Twelve Days there, where all had Access to see them. Alexander Tweedie, the foresaid Gardner, said, when dying, There was a Treasure hid in his Yard, but neither Gold nor Silver. Daniel Tweedie, his Son, came along with me to that Yard, and told me that his Father planted a white Rose-bush above them, and farther down the Yard a red Rose-bush, which were more fruitful than any other Bush in the Yard. . . . Many came'—to see the heads—'out of Curiosity; yet I rejoiced to see so many concerned grave Men and Women favouring the Dust of our Martyrs. There were Six of us

concluded to bury them upon the Nineteenth Day of October 1726, and every One of us to acquaint Friends of the Day and Hour, being Wednesday, the Day of the Week on which most of them were executed, and at 4 of the Clock at Night, being the Hour that most of them went to their resting Graves. We caused make a compleat Coffin for them in Black, with four Yards of fine Linen, the way that our Martyrs Corps were managed. . . . Accordingly we kept the aforesaid Day and Hour, and doubled the Linen, and laid the Half of it below them, their nether jaws being parted from their Heads; but being young Men, their Teeth remained. All were Witness to the Holes in each of their Heads, which the Hangman broke with his Hammer; and according to the Bigness of their Sculls, we laid the Jaws to them, and drew the other Half of the Linen above them, and stufft the Coffin with Shavings. Some prest hard to go thorow the chief Parts of the City as was done at the Revolution; but this we refused, considering that it looked airy and frothy, to make such Show of them, and inconsistent with the solid serious Observing of such an affecting, surprizing unheard-of Dispensation: But took the ordinary Way of other Burials from that Place, to wit, we went east the Back of the Wall, and in at Bristo-Port, and down the Way to the Head of the Cowgate, and turned up to the Church-yard, where they were interred closs to the Martyrs Tomb, with the greatest Multitude of People Old and Young, Men and Women, Ministers and others, that ever I saw together.'

And so there they were at last, in 'their resting graves.' So long as men do their duty, even if it be greatly in a misapprehension, they will be leading pattern lives; and whether or not they come to lie beside a martyrs' monument, we may be sure they will find a safe haven somewhere in the providence of God. It is not well to think of death, unless we temper the thought with that of heroes who despised it. Upon what ground, is of small account; if it be only the bishop who was burned for his faith in the antipodes, his memory lightens the heart and makes us walk undisturbed among graves. And so the martyrs' monument is a wholesome, heartsome spot in the field of the dead; and as we look upon it, a brave influence comes to us from the land of those who have won their discharge and, in another phrase of Patrick Walker's, got 'cleanly off the stage.'

CHAPTER VI. NEW TOWN—TOWN AND COUNTRY.

It is as much a matter of course to decry the New Town as to exalt the Old; and the most celebrated authorities have picked out this quarter as the very emblem of what is condemnable in architecture. Much may be said, much indeed has been said, upon the text; but to the unsophisticated, who call anything pleasing if it only pleases them, the New Town of Edinburgh seems, in itself, not only gay and airy, but highly picturesque. An old skipper, invincibly ignorant of all theories of the sublime and beautiful, once propounded as his most radiant notion for Paradise: 'The new town of Edinburgh, with the wind a matter of a point free.' He has now gone to that sphere where all good tars are promised pleasant weather in the song, and perhaps his thoughts fly somewhat higher. But there are bright and temperate days—with soft air coming from the inland hills, military music sounding bravely from the hollow of the gardens, the flags all waving on the palaces of Princes Street—when I have seen the town through a sort of glory, and shaken hands in sentiment with the old sailor. And indeed, for a man who has been much tumbled round Orcadian skerries, what scene could be more agreeable to witness? On such a day, the valley wears a surprising air of festival. It seems (I do not know how else to put my meaning) as if it were a trifle too good to be true. It is what Paris ought to be. It has the scenic quality that would best set off a life of unthinking, open-air diversion. It was meant by nature for the realisation of the society of comic operas. And you can imagine, if the climate were but towardly, how all the world and his wife would flock into these gardens in the cool of the evening, to hear cheerful music, to sip pleasant drinks, to see the moon rise from behind Arthur's Seat and shine upon the spires and monuments and the green tree-tops in the valley. Alas! and the next morning the rain is splashing on the windows, and the passengers flee along Princes Street before the galloping squalls.

It cannot be denied that the original design was faulty and short-sighted, and did not fully profit by the capabilities of the situation. The architect was essentially a town bird, and he laid out the modern city with a view to street scenery, and to street scenery alone. The country did not enter into his plan; he had never lifted his eyes to the hills. If he had so chosen, every street upon the northern slope might have been a noble terrace and commanded an extensive and beautiful view. But the space has been too closely built; many of the houses front the wrong way, intent, like the Man with the Muck-Rake, on what is not worth observation, and standing discourteously back-foremost in the ranks; and, in a word, it is too often only from attic-windows, or here and there at a crossing, that you can get a look beyond the city upon its diversified surroundings. But perhaps it is all the more surprising, to come suddenly on a corner, and see a perspective of a mile or more of falling street, and beyond that woods and villas, and a blue arm of sea, and the hills upon the farther side.

Fergusson, our Edinburgh poet, Burns's model, once saw a butterfly at the Town Cross; and the sight inspired him with a worthless little ode. This painted country man, the dandy of the rose garden, looked far abroad in such a humming neighbourhood; and you can fancy what moral considerations a youthful poet would supply. But the incident, in a fanciful sort of way, is characteristic of the place. Into no other city does the sight of the country enter so far; if you do not meet a butterfly, you shall certainly catch a glimpse of far-away trees upon your walk; and the place is full of theatre tricks in the way of scenery. You peep under an arch, you descend stairs that look as if they would land you in a cellar, you turn to the back-window of a grimy tenement in a lane:—and behold! you are face-to-face with distant and bright prospects. You turn a corner, and there is the sun going down into the Highland hills. You look down an alley, and see ships tacking for the Baltic.

For the country people to see Edinburgh on her hill-tops, is one thing; it is another for the citizen, from the thick of his affairs, to overlook the country. It should be a genial and ameliorating influence in life; it should prompt good thoughts and remind him of Nature's unconcern: that he can watch from day to day, as he trots officeward, how the Spring green brightens in the wood or the field grows black under a moving ploughshare. I have been tempted, in this connexion, to deplore the slender faculties of the human race, with its penny-whistle of a voice, its dull cars, and its narrow range of sight. If you could see as people are to see in heaven, if you had eyes such as you can fancy for a superior race, if you could take clear note of the objects of vision, not only a few yards, but a few miles from where you stand:—think how agreeably your sight would be entertained, how pleasantly your thoughts would be diversified, as you walked the Edinburgh streets! For you might pause, in some business perplexity, in the midst of the city traffic, and perhaps catch the eye of a shepherd as he sat down to breathe upon a heathery shoulder of the Pentlands; or perhaps some urchin, clambering in a country elm, would put aside the leaves and show you his flushed and rustic visage; or a fisher racing seawards, with the tiller under his elbow, and the sail sounding in the wind, would fling you a salutation from between Anst'er and the May.

To be old is not the same thing as to be picturesque; nor because the Old Town bears a strange physiognomy, does it at all follow that the New Town shall look commonplace. Indeed, apart from antique houses, it is curious how much description would apply commonly to either. The same sudden accidents of ground, a similar dominating site above the plain, and the same superposition of one rank of society over another, are to be observed in both. Thus, the broad and comely approach to Princes Street from the east, lined with hotels and public offices, makes a leap over the gorge of the Low Calton; if you cast a glance over the parapet, you look direct into that sunless and disreputable confluent of Leith Street; and the same tall houses open upon both thoroughfares. This is only the New Town passing overhead above its own cellars; walking, so to speak, over its own children, as is the way of cities and the human race. But at the Dean Bridge, you may behold a spectacle of a more novel order. The river runs at the bottom of a deep valley, among rocks and between gardens; the crest of either bank is occupied by some of the most commodious streets and crescents in the modern city; and a handsome bridge unites the two summits. Over this, every afternoon, private carriages go spinning by, and ladies with card-cases pass to and fro about the duties of society. And yet down below, you may still see, with its mills and foaming weir, the little rural village of Dean. Modern improvement has gone overhead on its high-level viaduct; and the extended city has cleanly overleapt, and left unaltered, what was once the summer retreat of its comfortable citizens. Every town embraces hamlets in its growth; Edinburgh herself has embraced a good few; but it is strange to see one still surviving—and to see it some hundreds of feet below your path. Is it Torre del Greco that is built above buried Herculaneum? Herculaneum was dead at least; but the sun still shines upon the roofs of Dean; the smoke still rises thriftily from its chimneys; the dusty miller comes to his door, looks at the gurgling water, hearkens to the turning wheel and the birds about the shed, and perhaps whistles an air of his own to enrich the symphony—for all the world as if Edinburgh were still the old Edinburgh on the Castle Hill, and Dean were still the quietest of hamlets buried a mile or so in the green country.

It is not so long ago since magisterial David Hume lent the authority of his example to the exodus from the Old Town, and took up his new abode in a street which is still (so oddly may a jest become perpetuated) known as Saint David Street. Nor is the town so large but a holiday schoolboy may harry a bird's nest within half a mile of his own door. There are places that still smell of the plough in memory's nostrils. Here, one had heard a blackbird on a hawthorn; there, another was taken on summer evenings to eat strawberries and cream; and you have seen a waving wheatfield on the site of your present residence. The memories of an Edinburgh boy are but partly memories of the town. I look back with delight on many an escalade of garden walls; many a ramble among lilacs full of piping birds; many an exploration in obscure quarters that were neither town nor country; and I think that both for my companions and myself, there was a special interest, a point of romance, and a sentiment as of foreign travel, when we hit in our excursions on the butt-end of some former hamlet, and found a few rustic cottages embedded among streets and squares. The tunnel to the Scotland Street Station, the sight of the trains shooting out of its dark maw with the two guards upon the brake, the thought of its length and the many ponderous edifices and open thoroughfares above, were certainly things of paramount impressiveness to a young mind. It was a subterranean passage, although of a larger bore than we were accustomed to in Ainsworth's novels; and these two words, 'subterreanean passage,' were in themselves an irresistible attraction, and seemed to bring us nearer in spirit to the heroes we loved and the black rascals we secretly aspired to imitate. To scale the Castle Rock from West Princes Street Gardens, and lay a triumphal hand against the rampart itself, was to taste a high order of romantic pleasure. And there are other sights and exploits which crowd back upon my mind under a very strong illumination of remembered pleasure. But the effect of not one of them all will compare with the discoverer's joy, and the sense of old Time and his slow changes on the face of this earth, with which I explored such corners as Cannonmills or Water Lane, or the nugget of cottages at Broughton Market. They were more rural than the open country, and gave a greater impression of antiquity than the oldest land upon the High Street. They too, like Fergusson's butterfly, had a quaint air of having wandered far from their own place; they looked abashed and homely, with their gables and their creeping plants, their outside stairs and running mill-streams; there were corners that smelt like the end of the country garden where I spent my Aprils; and the people stood to gossip at their doors, as they might have done in Colinton or Cramond.

In a great measure we may, and shall, eradicate this haunting flavour of the country. The last elm is dead in Elm Row; and the villas and the workmen's quarters spread apace on all the borders of the city. We can cut down the trees; we can bury the grass under dead paving-stones; we can drive brisk streets through all our sleepy quarters; and we may forget the stories and the playgrounds of our boyhood. But we have some possessions that not even the infuriate zeal of builders can utterly abolish and destroy. Nothing can abolish the hills, unless it be a cataclysm of nature which shall subvert Edinburgh Castle itself and lay all her florid structures in the dust. And as long as we have the hills and the Firth, we have a famous heritage to leave our children. Our windows, at no expense to us, are most artfully stained to represent a landscape. And when the Spring comes round, and the hawthorns begin to flower, and the meadows to smell of young grass, even in the thickest of our streets, the country hilltops find out a young man's eyes, and set his heart beating for travel and pure air.

CHAPTER VII. THE VILLA QUARTERS.

Mr. Ruskin's denunciation of the New Town of Edinburgh includes, as I have heard it repeated, nearly all the stone and lime we have to show. Many however find a grand air and something settled and imposing in the better parts; and upon many, as I have said, the confusion of styles induces an agreeable stimulation of the mind. But upon the subject of our recent villa architecture, I am frankly ready to mingle my tears with Mr. Ruskin's, and it is a subject which makes one envious of his large declamatory and controversial eloquence.

Day by day, one new villa, one new object of offence, is added to another; all around Newington and Morningside, the dismallest structures keep springing up like mushrooms; the pleasant hills are loaded with them, each impudently squatted in its garden, each roofed and carrying chimneys like a house. And yet a glance of an eye discovers their true character. They are not houses; for they were not designed with a view to human habitation, and the internal arrangements are, as they tell me, fantastically unsuited to the needs of man. They are not buildings; for you can scarcely say a thing is built where every measurement is in clamant disproportion with its neighbour. They belong to no style of art, only to a form of business much to be regretted.

Why should it be cheaper to erect a structure where the size of the windows bears no rational relation to the size of the front? Is there any profit in a misplaced chimney-stalk? Does a hard-working, greedy builder gain more on a monstrosity than on a decent cottage of equal plainness? Frankly, we should say, No. Bricks may be omitted, and green timber employed, in the construction of even a very elegant design; and there is no reason why a chimney should be made to vent, because it is so situated as to look comely from without. On the other hand, there is a noble way of being ugly: a high-aspiring fiasco like the fall of Lucifer. There are daring and gaudy buildings that manage to be offensive, without being contemptible; and we know that 'fools rush in where angels fear to tread.' But to aim at making a commonplace villa, and to make it insufferably ugly in each particular; to attempt the homeliest achievement, and to attain the bottom of derided failure; not to have any theory but profit and yet, at an equal expense, to outstrip all competitors in the art of conceiving and rendering permanent deformity; and to do all this in what is, by nature, one of the most agreeable neighbourhoods in Britain:—what are we to say, but that this also is a distinction, hard to earn although not greatly worshipful?

Indifferent buildings give pain to the sensitive; but these things offend the plainest taste. It is a danger which threatens the amenity of the town; and as this eruption keeps spreading on our borders, we have ever the farther to walk among unpleasant sights, before we gain the country air. If the population of Edinburgh were a living, autonomous body, it would arise like one man and make night hideous with arson; the builders and their accomplices would be driven to work, like the Jews of yore, with the trowel in one hand and the defensive cutlass in the other; and as soon as one of these masonic wonders had been consummated, right-minded iconoclasts should fall thereon and make an end of it at once.

Possibly these words may meet the eye of a builder or two. It is no use asking them to employ an architect; for that would be to touch them in a delicate quarter, and its use would largely depend on what architect they were minded to call in. But let them get any architect in the world to point out any reasonably well-proportioned villa, not his own design; and let them reproduce that model to satiety.

CHAPTER VIII. THE CALTON HILL.

The east of new Edinburgh is guarded by a craggy hill, of no great elevation, which the town embraces. The old London road runs on one side of it; while the New Approach, leaving it on the other hand, completes the circuit. You mount by stairs in a cutting of the rock to find yourself in a field of monuments. Dugald Stewart has the honours of situation and architecture; Burns is memorialised lower down upon a spur; Lord Nelson, as befits a sailor, gives his name to the top-gallant of the Calton Hill. This latter erection has been differently and yet, in both cases, aptly compared to a telescope and a butter-churn; comparisons apart, it ranks among the vilest of men's handiworks. But the chief feature is an unfinished range of columns, 'the Modern Ruin' as it has been called, an imposing object from far and near, and giving Edinburgh, even from the sea, that false air; of a Modern Athens which has earned for her so many slighting speeches. It was meant to be a National Monument; and its present state is a very suitable monument to certain national characteristics. The old Observatory—a quaint brown building on the edge of the steep—and the new Observatory—a classical edifice with a dome—occupy the central portion of the summit. All these are scattered on a green turf, browsed over by some sheep.

The scene suggests reflections on fame and on man's injustice to the dead. You see Dugald Stewart rather more handsomely commemorated than Burns. Immediately below, in the Canongate churchyard, lies Robert Fergusson, Burns's master in his art, who died insane while yet a stripling; and if Dugald Stewart has been somewhat too boisterously acclaimed, the Edinburgh poet, on the other hand, is most unrighteously forgotten. The votaries of Burns, a crew too common in all ranks in Scotland and more remarkable for number than discretion, eagerly suppress all mention of the lad who handed to him the poetic impulse and, up to the time when he grew famous, continued to influence him in his manner and the choice of subjects. Burns himself not only acknowledged his debt in a fragment of autobiography, but erected a tomb over the grave in Canongate churchyard. This was worthy of an artist, but it was done in vain; and although I think I have read nearly all the biographies of Burns, I cannot remember one in which the modesty of nature was not violated, or where Fergusson was not sacrificed to the credit of his follower's originality. There is a kind of gaping admiration that would fain roll Shakespeare and Bacon into one, to have a bigger thing to gape at; and a class of men who cannot edit one author without disparaging all others. They are indeed mistaken if they think to please the great originals; and whoever puts Fergusson right with fame, cannot do better than dedicate his labours to the memory of Burns, who will be the best delighted of the dead.

Of all places for a view, this Calton Hill is perhaps the best; since you can see the Castle, which you lose from the Castle, and Arthur's Seat, which you cannot see from Arthur's Seat. It is the place to stroll on one of those days of sunshine and east wind which are so common in our more than temperate summer. The breeze comes off the sea, with a little of the freshness, and that touch of chill, peculiar to the quarter, which is delightful to certain very ruddy organizations and greatly the reverse to the majority of mankind. It brings with it a faint, floating haze, a cunning decolourizer, although not thick enough to obscure outlines near at hand. But the haze lies more thickly to windward at the far end of Musselburgh Bay; and over the Links of Aberlady and Berwick Law and the hump of the Bass Rock it assumes the aspect of a bank of thin sea fog.

Immediately underneath upon the south, you command the yards of the High School, and the towers and courts of the new Jail—a large place, castellated to the extent of folly, standing by itself on the edge of a steep cliff, and often joyfully hailed by tourists as the Castle. In the one, you may perhaps see female prisoners taking exercise like a string of nuns; in the other, schoolboys running at play and their shadows keeping step with them. From the bottom of the valley, a gigantic chimney rises almost to the level of the eye, a taller and a shapelier edifice than Nelson's Monument. Look a little farther, and there is Holyrood Palace, with its Gothic frontal and ruined abbey, and the red sentry pacing smartly too and fro before the door like a mechanical figure in a panorama. By way of an outpost, you can single out the little peak-roofed lodge, over which Rizzio's murderers made their escape and where

Queen Mary herself, according to gossip, bathed in white wine to entertain her loveliness. Behind and overhead, lie the Queen's Park, from Muschat's Cairn to Dumbiedykes, St. Margaret's Loch, and the long wall of Salisbury Crags: and thence, by knoll and rocky bulwark and precipitous slope, the eye rises to the top of Arthur's Seat, a hill for magnitude, a mountain in virtue of its bold design. This upon your left. Upon the right, the roofs and spires of the Old Town climb one above another to where the citadel prints its broad bulk and jagged crown of bastions on the western sky.—Perhaps it is now one in the afternoon; and at the same instant of time, a ball rises to the summit of Nelson's flagstaff close at hand, and, far away, a puff of smoke followed by a report bursts from the half-moon battery at the Castle. This is the time-gun by which people set their watches, as far as the sea coast or in hill farms upon the Pentlands.—To complete the view, the eye enfilades Princes Street, black with traffic, and has a broad look over the valley between the Old Town and the New: here, full of railway trains and stepped over by the high North Bridge upon its many columns, and there, green with trees and gardens.

On the north, the Calton Hill is neither so abrupt in itself nor has it so exceptional an outlook; and yet even here it commands a striking prospect. A gully separates it from the New Town. This is Greenside, where witches were burned and tournaments held in former days. Down that almost precipitous bank, Bothwell launched his horse, and so first, as they say, attracted the bright eyes of Mary. It is now tesselated with sheets and blankets out to dry, and the sound of people beating carpets is rarely absent. Beyond all this, the suburbs run out to Leith; Leith camps on the seaside with her forest of masts; Leith roads are full of ships at anchor; the sun picks out the white pharos upon Inchkeith Island; the Firth extends on either hand from the Ferry to the May; the towns of Fifeshire sit, each in its bank of blowing smoke, along the opposite coast; and the hills enclose the view, except to the farthest east, where the haze of the horizon rests upon the open sea. There lies the road to Norway: a dear road for Sir Patrick Spens and his Scots Lords; and yonder smoke on the hither side of Largo Law is Aberdour, from whence they sailed to seek a queen for Scotland.

'O lang, lang, may the ladies sit,

Wi' their fans into their hand,
Or ere they see Sir Patrick Spens
Come sailing to the land!'

The sight of the sea, even from a city, will bring thoughts of storm and sea disaster. The sailors' wives of Leith and the fisherwomen of Cockenzie, not sitting languorously with fans, but crowding to the tail of the harbour with a shawl about their ears, may still look vainly for brave Scotsmen who will return no more, or boats that have gone on their last fishing. Since Sir Patrick sailed from Aberdour, what a multitude have gone down in the North Sea! Yonder is Auldhame, where the London smack went ashore and wreckers cut the rings from ladies' fingers; and a few miles round Fife Ness is the fatal Inchcape, now a star of guidance; and the lee shore to the east of the Inchcape, is that Forfarshire coast where Mucklebackit sorrowed for his son.

These are the main features of the scene roughly sketched. How they are all tilted by the inclination of the ground, how each stands out in delicate relief against the rest, what manifold detail, and play of sun and shadow, animate and accentuate the picture, is a matter for a person on the spot, and turning swiftly on his heels, to grasp and bind together in one comprehensive look. It is the character of such a prospect, to be full of change and of things moving. The multiplicity embarrasses the eye; and the mind, among so much, suffers itself to grow absorbed with single points. You remark a tree in a hedgerow, or follow a cart along a country road. You turn to the city, and see children, dwarfed by distance into pigmies, at play about suburban doorsteps; you have a glimpse upon a thoroughfare where people are densely moving; you note ridge after ridge of chimney-stacks running downhill one behind another, and church spires rising bravely from the sea of roofs. At one of the innumerable windows, you watch a figure moving; on one of the multitude of roofs, you watch clambering chimney-sweeps. The wind takes a run and scatters the smoke; bells are heard, far and near, faint and loud, to tell the hour; or perhaps a bird goes dipping evenly over the housetops, like a gull across the waves. And here you are in the meantime, on this pastoral hillside, among nibbling sheep and looked upon by monumental buildings.

Return thither on some clear, dark, moonless night, with a ring of frost in the air, and only a star or two set sparsedly in the vault of heaven; and you will find a sight as stimulating as the hoariest summit of the Alps. The solitude seems perfect; the patient astronomer, flat on his back under the Observatory dome and spying heaven's secrets, is your only neighbour; and yet from all round you there come up the dull hum of the city, the tramp of countless people marching out of time, the rattle of carriages and the continuous keen jingle of the tramway bells. An hour or so before, the gas was turned on; lamplighters scoured the city; in every house, from kitchen to attic, the windows kindled and gleamed forth into the dusk. And so now, although the town lies blue and darkling on her hills, innumerable spots of the bright element shine far and near along the pavements and upon the high facades. Moving lights of the railway pass and repass below the stationary lights upon the bridge. Lights burn in the jail. Lights burn high up in the tall lands and on the Castle turrets, they burn low down in Greenside or along the Park. They run out one beyond the other into the dark country. They walk in a procession down to Leith, and shine singly far along Leith Pier. Thus, the plan of the city and her suburbs is mapped out upon the ground of blackness, as when a child pricks a drawing full of pinholes and exposes it before a candle; not the darkest night of winter can conceal her high station and fanciful design; every evening in the year she proceeds to illuminate herself in honour of her own beauty; and as if to complete the scheme—or rather as if some prodigal Pharaoh were beginning to extend to the adjacent sea and country—half-way over to Fife, there is an outpost of light upon Inchkeith, and far to seaward, yet another on the May.

And while you are looking, across upon the Castle Hill, the drums and bugles begin to recall the scattered garrison; the air thrills with the sound; the bugles sing aloud; and the last rising flourish mounts and melts into the darkness like a star: a martial swan-song, fitly rounding in the labours of the day.

CHAPTER IX. WINTER AND NEW YEAR.

The Scotch dialect is singularly rich in terms of reproach against the winter wind. Snell, blae, nirly, and scowthering, are four of these significant vocables; they are all words that carry a shiver with them; and for my part, as I see them aligned before me on the page, I am persuaded that a big wind comes tearing over the Firth from Burntisland and the northern hills; I think I can hear it howl in the chimney, and as I set my face northwards, feel its smarting kisses on my cheek. Even in the names of places there is often a desolate, inhospitable sound; and I remember two from the near neighbourhood of Edinburgh, Cauldhame and Blaw-weary, that would promise but starving comfort to their inhabitants. The inclemency of heaven, which has thus endowed the language of Scotland with words, has also largely modified the spirit of its poetry. Both poverty and a northern climate teach men the love of the hearth and the sentiment of the family; and the latter, in its own right, inclines a poet to the praise of strong waters. In Scotland, all our singers have a stave or two for blazing fires and stout potations:—to get indoors out of the wind and to swallow something hot to the stomach, are benefits so easily appreciated where they dwelt!

And this is not only so in country districts where the shepherd must wade in the snow all day after his flock, but in Edinburgh itself, and nowhere more apparently stated than in the works of our Edinburgh poet, Fergusson. He was a delicate youth, I take it, and willingly slunk from the robustious winter to an inn fire-side. Love was absent from his life, or only present, if you prefer, in such a form that even the least serious of Burns's amourettes was ennobling by comparison; and so there is nothing to temper the sentiment of indoor revelry which pervades the poor boy's verses. Although it is characteristic of his native town, and the manners of its youth to the present day, this spirit has perhaps done something to restrict his popularity. He recalls a supper-party pleasantry with something akin to tenderness; and sounds the praises of the act of drinking as if it were virtuous, or at least witty, in itself. The kindly jar, the warm atmosphere of tavern parlours, and the revelry of lawyers' clerks, do not offer by themselves the materials of a rich existence. It was not choice, so much as an external fate, that kept Fergusson in this round of sordid pleasures. A Scot of poetic temperament, and without religious exaltation, drops as if by nature into the public-house. The picture may not be pleasing; but what else is a man to do in this dog's weather?

To none but those who have themselves suffered the thing in the body, can the gloom and depression of our Edinburgh winter be brought home. For some constitutions there is something almost physically disgusting in the bleak ugliness of easterly weather; the wind wearies, the sickly sky depresses them; and they turn back from their walk to avoid the aspect of the unrefulgent sun going down among perturbed and pallid mists. The days are so short that a man does much of his business, and certainly all his pleasure, by the haggard glare of gas lamps. The roads are as heavy as a fallow. People go by, so drenched and draggle-tailed that I have often wondered how they found the heart to undress. And meantime the wind whistles through the town as if it were an open meadow; and if you lie awake all night, you hear it shrieking and raving overhead with a noise of shipwrecks and of falling houses. In a word, life is so unsightly that there are times when the heart turns sick in a man's inside; and the look of a tavern, or the thought of the warm, fire-lit study, is like the touch of land to one who has been long struggling with the seas.

As the weather hardens towards frost, the world begins to improve for Edinburgh people. We enjoy superb, sub-arctic sunsets, with the profile of the city stamped in indigo upon a sky of luminous green. The wind may still be cold, but there is a briskness in the air that stirs good blood. People do not all look equally sour and downcast. They fall into two divisions: one, the knight of the blue face and hollow paunch, whom Winter has gotten by the vitals; the other well lined with New-year's fare, conscious of the touch of cold on his periphery, but stepping through it by the glow of his internal fires. Such an one I remember, triply cased in grease, whom no extremity of temperature could vanquish. 'Well,' would be his jovial salutation, 'here's a sneezer!' And the look of these warm fellows is tonic, and upholds their drooping fellow-townsmen. There is yet another class who do not depend on corporal advantages, but support the winter in virtue of a brave and merry heart. One shivering evening, cold enough for frost but with too high a wind, and a little past sundown, when the lamps were beginning to enlarge their circles in the growing dusk, a brace of barefoot lassies were seen coming eastward in the teeth of the wind. If the one was as much as nine, the other was certainly not more than seven. They were miserably clad; and the pavement was so cold, you would have thought no one could lay a naked foot on it unflinching. Yet they came along waltzing, if you please, while the elder sang a tune to give them music. The person who saw this, and whose heart was full of bitterness at the moment, pocketed a reproof which has been of use to him ever since, and which he now hands on, with his good wishes, to the reader.

At length, Edinburgh, with her satellite hills and all the sloping country, are sheeted up in white. If it has happened in the dark hours, nurses pluck their children out of bed and run with them to some commanding window, whence they may see the change that has been worked upon earth's face. 'A' the hills are covered wi' snaw,' they sing, 'and Winter's noo come fairly!' And the children, marvelling at the silence and the white landscape, find a spell appropriate to the season in the words. The reverberation of the snow increases the pale daylight, and brings all objects nearer the eye. The Pentlands are smooth and glittering, with here and there the black ribbon of a dry-stone dyke, and here and there, if there be wind, a cloud of blowing snow upon a shoulder. The Firth seems a leaden creek, that a man might almost jump across, between well-powdered Lothian and well-powdered Fife. And the effect is not, as in other cities, a thing of half a day; the streets are soon trodden black, but the country keeps its virgin white; and you have only to lift your eyes and look over miles of country snow. An indescribable cheerfulness breathes about the city; and the well-fed heart sits lightly and beats gaily in the—bosom. It is New-year's weather.

New-year's Day, the great national festival, is a time of family expansions and of deep carousal. Sometimes, by a sore stoke of fate for this Calvinistic people, the year's anniversary fails upon a Sunday, when the public-houses are inexorably closed, when singing and even whistling is banished from our homes and highways, and the oldest toper feels called upon to go to church.

Thus pulled about, as if between two loyalties, the Scotch have to decide many nice cases of conscience, and ride the marches narrowly between the weekly and the annual observance. A party of convivial musicians, next door to a friend of mine, hung suspended in this manner on the brink of their diversions. From ten o'clock on Sunday night, my friend heard them tuning their instruments: and as the hour of liberty drew near, each must have had his music open, his bow in readiness across the fiddle, his foot already raised to mark the time, and his nerves braced for execution; for hardly had the twelfth stroke sounded from the earliest steeple, before they had launced forth into a secular bravura.

Currant-loaf is now popular eating in all house-holds. For weeks before the great morning, confectioners display stacks of Scotch bun—a dense, black substance, inimical to life—and full moons of shortbread adorned with mottoes of peel or sugar-plum, in honour of the season and the family affections. 'Frae Auld Reekie,' 'A guid New Year to ye a',' 'For the Auld Folk at Hame,' are among the most favoured of these devices. Can you not see the carrier, after half-a-day's journey on pinching hill-roads, draw up before a cottage in Teviotdale, or perhaps in Manor Glen among the rowans, and the old people receiving the parcel with moist eyes and a prayer for Jock or Jean in the city? For at this season, on the threshold of another year of calamity and stubborn conflict, men feel a need to draw closer the links that unite them; they reckon the number of their friends, like allies before a war; and the prayers grow longer in the morning as the absent are recommended by name into God's keeping.

On the day itself, the shops are all shut as on a Sunday; only taverns, toyshops, and other holiday magazines, keep open doors. Every one looks for his handsel. The postman and the lamplighters have left, at every house in their districts, a copy of vernacular verses, asking and thanking in a breath; and it is characteristic of Scotland that these verses may have sometimes a touch of reality in detail or sentiment and a measure of strength in the handling. All over the town, you may see comforter'd schoolboys hasting to squander their half-crowns. There are an infinity of visits to be paid; all the world is in the street, except the daintier classes; the sacramental greeting is heard upon all sides; Auld Lang Syne is much in people's mouths; and whisky and shortbread are staple articles of consumption. From an early hour a stranger will be impressed by the number of drunken men; and by afternoon drunkenness has spread to the women. With some classes of society, it is as much a matter of duty to drink hard on New-year's Day as to go to church on Sunday. Some have been saving their wages for perhaps a month to do the season honour. Many carry a whisky-bottle in their pocket, which they will press with embarrassing effusion on a perfect stranger. It is inexpedient to risk one's body in a cab, or not, at least, until after a prolonged study of the driver. The streets, which are thronged from end to end, become a place for delicate pilotage. Singly or arm-in-arm, some speechless, others noisy and quarrelsome, the votaries of the New Year go meandering in and out and cannoning one against another; and now and again, one falls and lies as he has fallen. Before night, so many have gone to bed or the police office, that the streets seem almost clearer. And as guisards and first-footers are now not much seen except in country places, when once the New Year has been rung in and proclaimed at the Tron railings, the festivities begin to find their way indoors and something like quiet returns upon the town. But think, in these piled lands, of all the senseless snorers, all the broken heads and empty pockets!

Of old, Edinburgh University was the scene of heroic snowballing; and one riot obtained the epic honours of military intervention. But the great generation, I am afraid, is at an end; and even during my own college days, the spirit appreciably declined. Skating and sliding, on the other hand, are honoured more and more; and curling, being a creature of the national genius, is little likely to be disregarded. The patriotism that leads a man to eat Scotch bun will scarce desert him at the curling-pond. Edinburgh, with its long, steep pavements, is the proper home of sliders; many a happy urchin can slide the whole way to school; and the profession of errand-boy is transformed into a holiday amusement. As for skating, there is scarce any city so handsomely provided. Duddingstone Loch lies under the abrupt southern side of Arthur's Seat; in summer a shield of blue, with swans sailing from the reeds; in winter, a field of ringing ice. The village church sits above it on a green promontory; and the village smoke rises from among goodly trees. At the church gates, is the historical joug; a place of penance for the neck of detected sinners, and the historical louping-on stane, from which Dutch-built lairds and farmers climbed into the saddle. Here Prince Charlie slept before the battle of Prestonpans; and here Deacon Brodie, or one of his gang, stole a plough coulter before the burglary in Chessel's Court. On the opposite side of the loch, the ground rises to Craigmillar Castle, a place friendly to Stuart Mariolaters. It is worth a climb, even in summer, to look down upon the loch from Arthur's Seat; but it is tenfold more so on a day of skating. The surface is thick with people moving easily and swiftly and leaning over at a thousand graceful inclinations; the crowd opens and closes, and keeps moving through itself like water; and the ice rings to half a mile away, with the flying steel. As night draws on, the single figures melt into the dusk, until only an obscure stir, and coming and going of black clusters, is visible upon the loch. A little longer, and the first torch is kindled and begins to flit rapidly across the ice in a ring of yellow reflection, and this is followed by another and another, until the whole field is full of skimming lights.

CHAPTER X. TO THE PENTLAND HILLS.

On three sides of Edinburgh, the country slopes downward from the city, here to the sea, there to the fat farms of Haddington, there to the mineral fields of Linlithgow. On the south alone, it keeps rising until it not only out-tops the Castle but looks down on Arthur's Seat. The character of the neighbourhood is pretty strongly marked by a scarcity of hedges; by many stone walls of varying height; by a fair amount of timber, some of it well grown, but apt to be of a bushy, northern profile and poor in foliage; by here and there a little river, Esk or Leith or Almond, busily journeying in the bottom of its glen; and from almost every point, by a peep of the sea or the hills. There is no lack of variety, and yet most of the elements are common to all parts; and the southern district is alone distinguished by considerable summits and a wide view.

From Boroughmuirhead, where the Scottish army encamped before Flodden, the road descends a long hill, at the bottom of which and just as it is preparing to mount upon the other side, it passes a toll-bar and issues at once into the open country. Even as I write these words, they are being antiquated in the progress of events, and the chisels are tinkling on a new row of houses. The builders have at length adventured beyond the toll which held them in respect so long, and proceed to career in these fresh pastures like a herd of colts turned loose. As Lord Beaconsfield proposed to hang an architect by way of stimulation, a man, looking on these doomed meads, imagines a similar example to deter the builders; for it seems as if it must come to an open fight at last to preserve a corner of green country unbedevilled. And here, appropriately enough, there stood in old days a crow-haunted gibbet, with two bodies hanged in chains. I used to be shown, when a child, a flat stone in the roadway to which the gibbet had been fixed. People of a willing fancy were persuaded, and sought to persuade others, that this stone was never dry. And no wonder, they would add, for the two men had only stolen fourpence between them.

For about two miles the road climbs upwards, a long hot walk in summer time. You reach the summit at a place where four ways meet, beside the toll of Fairmilehead. The spot is breezy and agreeable both in name and aspect. The hills are close by across a valley: Kirk Yetton, with its long, upright scars visible as far as Fife, and Allermuir the tallest on this side with wood and tilled field running high upon their borders, and haunches all moulded into innumerable glens and shelvings and variegated with heather and fern. The air comes briskly and sweetly off the hills, pure from the elevation and rustically scented by the upland plants; and even at the toll, you may hear the curlew calling on its mate. At certain seasons, when the gulls desert their surfy forelands, the birds of sea and mountain hunt and scream together in the same field by Fairmilehead. The winged, wild things intermix their wheelings, the sea-birds skim the tree-tops and fish among the furrows of the plough. These little craft of air are at home in all the world, so long as they cruise in their own element; and, like sailors, ask but food and water from the shores they coast.

Below, over a stream, the road passes Bow Bridge, now a dairy-farm, but once a distillery of whisky. It chanced, some time in the past century, that the distiller was on terms of good-fellowship with the visiting officer of excise. The latter was of an easy, friendly disposition, and a master of convivial arts. Now and again, he had to walk out of Edinburgh to measure the distiller's stock; and although it was agreeable to find his business lead him in a friend's direction, it was unfortunate that the friend should be a loser by his visits. Accordingly, when he got about the level of Fairmilehead, the gauger would take his flute, without which he never travelled, from his pocket, fit it together, and set manfully to playing, as if for his own delectation and inspired by the beauty of the scene. His favourite air, it seems, was 'Over the hills and far away.' At the first note, the distiller pricked his ears. A flute at Fairmilehead? and playing 'Over the hills and far away?' This must be his friendly enemy, the gauger. Instantly horses were harnessed, and sundry barrels of whisky were got upon a cart, driven at a gallop round Hill End, and buried in the mossy glen behind Kirk Yetton. In the same breath, you may be sure, a fat fowl was put to the fire, and the whitest napery prepared for the back parlour. A little after, the gauger, having had his fill of music for the moment, came strolling down with the most innocent air imaginable, and found the good people at Bow Bridge taken entirely unawares by his arrival, but none the less glad to see him. The distiller's liquor and the gauger's flute would combine to speed the moments of digestion; and when both were somewhat mellow, they would wind up the evening with 'Over the hills and far away' to an accompaniment of knowing glances. And at least, there is a smuggling story, with original and half-idyllic features.

A little further, the road to the right passes an upright stone in a field. The country people call it General Kay's monument. According to them, an officer of that name had perished there in battle at some indistinct period before the beginning of history. The date is reassuring; for I think cautious writers are silent on the General's exploits. But the stone is connected with one of those remarkable tenures of land which linger on into the modern world from Feudalism. Whenever the reigning sovereign passes by, a certain landed proprietor is held bound to climb on to the top, trumpet in hand, and sound a flourish according to the measure of his knowledge in that art. Happily for a respectable family, crowned heads have no great business in the Pentland Hills. But the story lends a character of comicality to the stone; and the passer-by will sometimes chuckle to himself.

The district is dear to the superstitious. Hard by, at the back-gate of Comiston, a belated carter beheld a lady in white, 'with the most beautiful, clear shoes upon her feet,' who looked upon him in a very ghastly manner and then vanished; and just in front is the Hunters' Tryst, once a roadside inn, and not so long ago haunted by the devil in person. Satan led the inhabitants a pitiful existence. He shook the four corners of the building with lamentable outcries, beat at the doors and windows, overthrew crockery in the dead hours of the morning, and danced unholy dances on the roof. Every kind of spiritual disinfectant was put in requisition; chosen ministers were summoned out of Edinburgh and prayed by the hour; pious neighbours sat up all night making a noise of psalmody; but Satan minded them no more than the wind about the hill-tops; and it was only after years of persecution, that he left the Hunters' Tryst in peace to occupy himself with the remainder of mankind. What with General Kay, and the white lady, and this singular visitation, the neighbourhood offers great facilities to the makers of sun-myths; and without exactly casting in one's lot with that disenchanting school of writers, one cannot help hearing a good deal of the winter wind in the last story. 'That nicht,' says Burns, in one of his happiest moments,—

'That nicht a child might understand

The deil had business on his hand.'

And if people sit up all night in lone places on the hills, with Bibles and tremulous psalms, they will be apt to hear some of the most fiendish noises in the world; the wind will beat on doors and dance upon roofs for them, and make the hills howl around their cottage with a clamour like the judgment-day.

The road goes down through another valley, and then finally begins to scale the main slope of the Pentlands. A bouquet of old trees stands round a white farmhouse; and from a neighbouring dell, you can see smoke rising and leaves ruffling in the breeze. Straight above, the hills climb a thousand feet into the air. The neighbourhood, about the time of lambs, is clamorous with the bleating of flocks; and you will be awakened, in the grey of early summer mornings, by the barking of a dog or the voice of a shepherd shouting to the echoes. This, with the hamlet lying behind unseen, is Swanston.

The place in the dell is immediately connected with the city. Long ago, this sheltered field was purchased by the Edinburgh magistrates for the sake of the springs that rise or gather there. After they had built their water-house and laid their pipes, it occurred to them that the place was suitable for junketing. Once entertained, with jovial magistrates and public funds, the idea led speedily to accomplishment; and Edinburgh could soon boast of a municipal Pleasure House. The dell was turned into a garden; and on the knoll that shelters it from the plain and the sea winds, they built a cottage looking to the hills. They brought crockets and gargoyles from old St. Giles's which they were then restoring, and disposed them on the gables and over the door and about the garden; and the quarry which had supplied them with building material, they draped with clematis and carpeted with beds of roses. So much for the pleasure of the eye; for creature comfort, they made a capacious cellar in the hillside and fitted it with bins of the hewn stone.

In process of time, the trees grew higher and gave shade to the cottage, and the evergreens sprang up and turned the dell into a thicket. There, purple magistrates relaxed themselves from the pursuit of municipal ambition; cocked hats paraded soberly about the garden and in and out among the hollies; authoritative canes drew ciphering upon the path; and at night, from high upon the hills, a shepherd saw lighted windows through the foliage and heard the voice of city dignitaries raised in song.

The farm is older. It was first a grange of Whitekirk Abbey, tilled and inhabited by rosy friars. Thence, after the Reformation, it passed into the hands of a true-blue Protestant family. During the covenanting troubles, when a night conventicle was held upon the Pentlands, the farm doors stood hospitably open till the morning; the dresser was laden with cheese and bannocks, milk and brandy; and the worshippers kept slipping down from the hill between two exercises, as couples visit the supper-room between two dances of a modern ball. In the Forty-Five, some foraging Highlanders from Prince Charlie's army fell upon Swanston in the dawn. The great-grandfather of the late farmer was then a little child; him they awakened by plucking the blankets from his bed, and he remembered, when he was an old man, their truculent looks and uncouth speech. The churn stood full of cream in the dairy, and with this they made their brose in high delight. 'It was braw brose,' said one of them. At last they made off, laden like camels with their booty; and Swanston Farm has lain out of the way of history from that time forward. I do not know what may be yet in store for it. On dark days, when the mist runs low upon the hill, the house has a gloomy air as if suitable for private tragedy. But in hot July, you can fancy nothing more perfect than the garden, laid out in alleys and arbours and bright, old-fashioned flower-plots, and ending in a miniature ravine, all trellis-work and moss and tinkling waterfall, and housed from the sun under fathoms of broad foliage.

The hamlet behind is one of the least considerable of hamlets, and consists of a few cottages on a green beside a burn. Some of them (a strange thing in Scotland) are models of internal neatness; the beds adorned with patchwork, the shelves arrayed with willow-pattern plates, the floors and tables bright with scrubbing or pipe-clay, and the very kettle polished like silver. It is the sign of a contented old age in country places, where there is little matter for gossip and no street sights. Housework becomes an art; and at evening, when the cottage interior shines and twinkles in the glow of the fire, the housewife folds her hands and contemplates her finished picture; the snow and the wind may do their worst, she has made herself a pleasant corner in the world. The city might be a thousand miles away, and yet it was from close by that Mr. Bough painted the distant view of Edinburgh which has been engraved for this collection; and you have only to look at the etching, to see how near it is at hand. But hills and hill people are not easily sophisticated; and if you walk out here on a summer Sunday, it is as like as not the shepherd may set his dogs upon you. But keep an unmoved countenance; they look formidable at the charge, but their hearts are in the right place, and they will only bark and sprawl about you on the grass, unmindful of their master's excitations.

Kirk Yetton forms the north-eastern angle of the range; thence, the Pentlands trend off to south and west. From the summit you look over a great expanse of champaign sloping to the sea, and behold a large variety of distant hills. There are the hills of Fife, the hills of Peebles, the Lammermoors and the Ochils, more or less mountainous in outline, more or less blue with distance. Of the Pentlands themselves, you see a field of wild heathery peaks with a pond gleaming in the midst; and to that side the view is as desolate as if you were looking into Galloway or Applecross. To turn to the other is like a piece of travel. Far out in the lowlands Edinburgh shows herself, making a great smoke on clear days and spreading her suburbs about her for miles; the Castle rises darkly in the midst, and close by, Arthur's Seat makes a bold figure in the landscape. All around, cultivated fields, and woods, and smoking villages, and white country roads, diversify the uneven surface of the land. Trains crawl slowly abroad upon the railway lines; little ships are tacking in the Firth; the shadow of a mountainous cloud, as large as a parish, travels before the wind; the wind itself ruffles the wood and standing corn, and sends pulses of varying colour across the landscape. So you sit, like Jupiter upon Olympus, and look down from afar upon men's life. The city is as silent as a city of the dead: from all its humming thoroughfares, not a voice, not a footfall, reaches you upon the hill. The sea-surf, the cries of ploughmen, the streams and the mill-wheels, the birds and the wind, keep up an animated concert through the plain; from farm to farm, dogs and crowing cocks contend together in defiance; and yet from this Olympian station, except for the whispering rumour of a train, the world has fallen into a dead silence, and the business of town and country grown voiceless in your ears. A crying hill-bird, the bleat of a sheep, a wind singing in the dry grass, seem not so much to interrupt, as to accompany, the stillness; but to the spiritual ear, the whole scene makes a music at once human and rural, and discourses pleasant reflections on the destiny of man. The spiry habitable city, ships, the divided fields, and browsing herds, and the straight highways, tell visibly of man's active and comfortable ways; and you may be never so laggard and never so unimpressionable, but there is something in the view that spirits up your blood and puts you in the vein for cheerful labour.

Immediately below is Fairmilehead, a spot of roof and a smoking chimney, where two roads, no thicker than packthread, intersect beside a hanging wood. If you are fanciful, you will be reminded of the gauger in the story. And the thought of this old exciseman, who once lipped and fingered on his pipe and uttered clear notes from it in the mountain air, and the words of the song he affected, carry your mind 'Over the hills and far away' to distant countries; and you have a vision of Edinburgh not, as you see her, in the midst of a little neighbourhood, but as a boss upon the round world with all Europe and the deep sea for her surroundings. For every place is a centre to the earth, whence highways radiate or ships set sail for foreign ports; the limit of a parish is not more imaginary than the frontier of an empire; and as a man sitting at home in his cabinet and swiftly writing books, so a city sends abroad an influence and a portrait of herself. There is no Edinburgh emigrant, far or near, from China to Peru, but he or she carries some lively pictures of the mind, some sunset behind the Castle cliffs, some snow scene, some maze of city lamps, indelible in the memory and delightful to study in the intervals of toil. For any such, if this book fall in their way, here are a few more home pictures. It would be pleasant, if they should recognise a house where they had dwelt, or a walk that they had taken.

Footnotes:

[10] These sentences have, I hear, given offence in my native town, and a proportionable pleasure to our rivals of Glasgow. I confess the news caused me both pain and merriment. May I remark, as a balm for wounded fellow-townsmen, that there is nothing deadly in my accusations? Small blame to them if they keep ledgers: 'tis an excellent business habit. Churchgoing is not, that ever I heard, a subject of reproach; decency of linen is a mark of prosperous affairs, and conscious moral rectitude one of the tokens of good living. It is not their fault it the city calls for something more specious by way of inhabitants. A man in a frock-coat looks out of place upon an Alp or Pyramid, although he has the virtues of a Peabody and the talents of a Bentham. And let them console themselves—they do as well as anybody else; the population of (let us say) Chicago would cut quite as rueful a figure on the same romantic stage. To the Glasgow people I would say only one word, but that is of gold; I have not yet written a book about Glasgow.

About Author

Childhood and youth

Stevenson was born at 8 Howard Place, Edinburgh, Scotland on 13 November 1850 to Thomas Stevenson (1818–87), a leading lighthouse engineer, and his wife Margaret Isabella (born Balfour, 1829–97). He was christened Robert Lewis Balfour Stevenson. At about age 18, he changed the spelling of "Lewis" to "Louis", and he dropped "Balfour" in 1873.

Lighthouse design was the family's profession; Thomas's father (Robert's grandfather) was civil engineer Robert Stevenson, and Thomas's brothers (Robert's uncles) Alan and David were in the same field. Thomas's maternal grandfather Thomas Smith had been in the same profession. However, Robert's mother's family were gentry, tracing their lineage back to Alexander Balfour who had held the lands of Inchyra in Fife in the fifteenth century. His mother's father Lewis Balfour (1777–1860) was a minister of the Church of Scotland at nearby Colinton, and her siblings included physician George William Balfour and marine engineer James Balfour. Stevenson spent the greater part of his boyhood holidays in his maternal grandfather's house. "Now I often wonder what I inherited from this old minister," Stevenson wrote. "I must suppose, indeed, that he was fond of preaching sermons, and so am I, though I never heard it maintained that either of us loved to hear them."

Lewis Balfour and his daughter both had weak chests, so they often needed to stay in warmer climates for their health. Stevenson inherited a tendency to coughs and fevers, exacerbated when the family moved to a damp, chilly house at 1 Inverleith Terrace in 1851. The family moved again to the sunnier 17 Heriot Row when Stevenson was six years old, but the tendency to extreme sickness in winter remained with him until he was 11. Illness was a recurrent feature of his adult life and left him extraordinarily thin. Contemporaneous views were that he had tuberculosis, but more recent views are that it was bronchiectasis or even sarcoidosis.

Stevenson's parents were both devout Presbyterians, but the household was not strict in its adherence to Calvinist principles. His nurse Alison Cunningham (known as Cummy) was more fervently religious. Her mix of Calvinism and folk beliefs were an early source of nightmares for the child, and he showed a precocious concern for religion. But she also cared for him tenderly in illness, reading to him from John Bunyan and the Bible as he lay sick in bed and telling tales of the Covenanters. Stevenson recalled this time of sickness in "The Land of Counterpane" in A Child's Garden of Verses (1885), dedicating the book to his nurse.

Stevenson was an only child, both strange-looking and eccentric, and he found it hard to fit in when he was sent to a nearby school at age 6, a problem repeated at age 11 when he went on to the Edinburgh Academy; but he mixed well in lively games with his cousins in summer holidays at Colinton. His frequent illnesses often kept him away from his first school, so he was taught for long stretches by private tutors. He was a late reader, learning at age 7 or 8, but even before this he dictated stories to his mother and nurse, and he compulsively wrote stories throughout his childhood. His father was proud of this interest; he had also written stories in his spare time until his own father found them and told him to "give up such nonsense and mind your business." He paid for the printing of Robert's first publication at 16, entitled The Pentland Rising: A Page of History, 1666. It was an account of the Covenanters' rebellion which was published in 1866, the 200th anniversary of the event.

Education

In September 1857, Stevenson went to Mr Henderson's School in India Street, Edinburgh, but because of poor health stayed only a few weeks and did not return until October 1859. During his many absences he was taught by private tutors. In October 1861, he went to Edinburgh Academy, an independent school for boys, and stayed there sporadically for about fifteen months. In the autumn of 1863, he spent one term at an English boarding school at Spring Grove in Isleworth in Middlesex (now an urban area of West London). In October 1864, following an improvement to his health, he was sent to Robert Thomson's private school in Frederick Street, Edinburgh, where he remained until he went to university. In November 1867, Stevenson entered the University of Edinburgh to study engineering. He showed from the start no enthusiasm for his studies and devoted much energy to avoiding lectures. This time was more important for the friendships he made with other students in the Speculative Society (an exclusive debating club), particularly with Charles Baxter, who would become Stevenson's financial agent, and with a professor, Fleeming Jenkin, whose house staged amateur drama in which Stevenson took part, and whose biography he would later write. Perhaps most important at this point in his life was a cousin, Robert Alan Mowbray Stevenson (known as "Bob"), a lively and light-hearted young man who, instead of the family profession, had chosen to study art. Each year during vacations, Stevenson travelled to inspect the family's engineering works—to Anstruther and Wick in 1868, with his father on his official tour of Orkney and Shetland islands lighthouses in 1869, and for three weeks to the island of Erraid in 1870. He enjoyed the travels more for the material they gave for his writing than for any engineering interest. The voyage with his father pleased him because a similar journey of Walter Scott with Robert Stevenson had provided the inspiration for Scott's 1822 novel The Pirate. In April 1871, Stevenson notified his father of his decision to pursue a life of letters. Though the elder Stevenson was naturally disappointed, the surprise cannot have been great, and Stevenson's mother reported that he was "wonderfully resigned" to his son's choice. To provide some security, it was agreed that Stevenson should read Law (again at Edinburgh University) and be called to the Scottish bar. In his 1887 poetry collection Underwoods, Stevenson muses on his having turned from the family profession:

Say not of me that weakly I declined

The labours of my sires, and fled the sea,

The towers we founded and the lamps we lit,

To play at home with paper like a child.

But rather say: In the afternoon of time

A strenuous family dusted from its hands

The sand of granite, and beholding far

Along the sounding coast its pyramids

And tall memorials catch the dying sun,

Smiled well content, and to this childish task

Around the fire addressed its evening hours.

In other respects too, Stevenson was moving away from his upbringing. His dress became more Bohemian; he already wore his hair long, but he now took to wearing a velveteen jacket and rarely attended parties in conventional evening dress. Within the limits of a strict allowance, he visited cheap pubs and brothels. More importantly, he had come to reject Christianity and declared himself an atheist. In January 1873, his father came across the constitution of the LJR (Liberty, Justice, Reverence) Club, of which Stevenson and his cousin Bob were members, which began: "Disregard everything our parents have taught us". Questioning his son about his beliefs, he discovered the truth, leading to a long period of dissension with both parents:

What a damned curse I am to my parents! As my father said "You have rendered my whole life a failure". As my mother said "This is the heaviest affliction that has ever befallen me". O Lord, what a pleasant thing it is to have damned the happiness of (probably) the only two people who care a damn about you in the world.

Early writing and travels

Stevenson was visiting a cousin in England in late 1873 when he met two people who became very important to him: Sidney Colvin and Fanny (Frances Jane) Sitwell. Sitwell was a 34-year-old woman with a son, who was separated from her husband. She attracted the devotion of many who met her, including Colvin, who married her in 1901. Stevenson was also drawn to her, and they kept up a warm correspondence over several years in which he wavered between the role of a suitor and a son (he addressed her as "Madonna"). Colvin became Stevenson's literary adviser and was the first editor of his letters after his death. He placed Stevenson's first paid contribution in The Portfolio, an essay entitled "Roads".

Stevenson was soon active in London literary life, becoming acquainted with many of the writers of the time, including Andrew Lang, Edmund Gosse, and Leslie Stephen, the editor of the Cornhill Magazine who took an interest in Stevenson's work. Stephen took Stevenson to visit a patient at the Edinburgh Infirmary named William Ernest Henley, an energetic and talkative man with a wooden leg. Henley became a close friend and occasional literary collaborator, until a quarrel broke up the friendship in 1888, and he is often considered to be the model for Long John Silver in Treasure Island.

Stevenson was sent to Menton on the French Riviera in November 1873 to recuperate after his health failed. He returned in better health in April 1874 and settled down to his studies, but he returned to France several times after that. He made long and frequent trips to the neighborhood of the Forest of Fontainebleau, staying at Barbizon, Grez-sur-Loing, and Nemours and becoming a member of the artists' colonies there. He also traveled to Paris to visit galleries and the theatres. He qualified for the Scottish bar in July 1875, and his father added a brass plate to the Heriot Row house reading "R.L. Stevenson, Advocate". His law studies did influence his books, but he never practised law; all his energies were spent in travel and writing. One of his journeys was a canoe voyage in Belgium and France with Sir Walter Simpson, a friend from the Speculative Society, a frequent travel companion, and the author of The Art of Golf (1887). This trip was the basis of his first travel book An Inland Voyage (1878).

Marriage

The canoe voyage with Simpson brought Stevenson to Grez in September 1876 where he met Fanny Van de Grift Osbourne (1840–1914), born in Indianapolis. She had married at age 17 and moved to Nevada to rejoin husband Samuel after his participation in the American Civil War. Their children were Isobel (or "Belle"), Lloyd, and Hervey (who died in 1875). But anger over her husband's infidelities led to a number of separations. In 1875, she had taken her children to France where she and Isobel studied art.

Stevenson returned to Britain shortly after this first meeting, but Fanny apparently remained in his thoughts, and he wrote the essay "On falling in love" for the Cornhill Magazine. They met again early in 1877 and became lovers. Stevenson spent much of the following year with her and her children in France. In August 1878, she returned to San Francisco and Stevenson remained in Europe, making the walking trip that formed the basis for Travels with a Donkey in the Cévennes (1879). But he set off to join her in August 1879, against the advice of his friends and without notifying his parents. He took second-class passage on the steamship Devonia, in part to save money but also to learn how others traveled and to increase the adventure of the journey. He then traveled overland by train from New York City to California. He later wrote about the experience in The Amateur Emigrant. It was good experience for his writing, but it broke his health.

He was near death when he arrived in Monterey, California, where some local ranchers nursed him back to health. He stayed for a time at the French Hotel located at 530 Houston Street, now a museum dedicated to his memory called the "Stevenson House". While there, he often dined "on the cuff," as he said, at a nearby restaurant run by Frenchman Jules Simoneau which stood at what is now Simoneau Plaza; several years later, he sent Simoneau an inscribed copy of his novel Strange Case of Dr Jekyll and Mr Hyde (1886), writing that it would be a stranger case still if Robert Louis Stevenson ever forgot Jules Simoneau. While in Monterey, he wrote an evocative article about "the Old Pacific Capital" of Monterey.

By December 1879, Stevenson had recovered his health enough to continue to San Francisco where he struggled "all alone on forty-five cents a day, and sometimes less, with quantities of hard work and many heavy thoughts," in an effort to support himself through his writing. But by the end of the winter, his health was broken again and he found himself at death's door. Fanny was now divorced and recovered from her own illness, and she came to his bedside and nursed him to recovery. "After a while," he wrote, "my spirit got up again in a divine frenzy, and has since kicked and spurred my vile body forward with great emphasis and success." When his father heard of his condition, he cabled him money to help him through this period.

Fanny and Robert were married in May 1880, although he said that he was "a mere complication of cough and bones, much fitter for an emblem of mortality than a bridegroom." He travelled with his new wife and her son Lloyd north of San Francisco to Napa Valley and spent a summer honeymoon at an abandoned mining camp on Mount Saint Helena. He wrote about this experience in The Silverado Squatters. He met Charles Warren Stoddard, co-editor of the Overland Monthly and author of South Sea Idylls, who urged Stevenson to travel to the South Pacific, an idea which returned to him many years later. In August 1880, he sailed with Fanny and Lloyd from New York to Britain and found his parents and his friend Sidney Colvin on the wharf at Liverpool, happy to see him return home. Gradually, his wife was able to patch up differences between father and son and make herself a part of the family through her charm and wit.

Attempted settlement in Europe and the US

Stevenson searched in vain between 1880 and 1887 for a residence suitable to his health. He spent his summers at various places in Scotland and England, including Westbourne, Dorset, a residential area in Bournemouth. It was during his time in Bournemouth that he wrote the story Strange Case of Dr Jekyll and Mr Hyde, naming the character Mr. Poole after the town of Poole which is situated next to Bournemouth. In Westbourne, he named his house Skerryvore after the tallest lighthouse in Scotland, which his uncle Alan had built (1838–44). In the wintertime, Stevenson travelled to France and lived at Davos Platz and the Chalet de Solitude at Hyères, where he was very happy for a time. "I have so many things to make life sweet for me," he wrote, "it seems a pity I cannot have that other one thing—health. But though you will be angry to hear it, I believe, for myself at least, what is is best." In spite of his ill health, he produced the bulk of his best-known work during these years. Treasure Island was published under the pseudonym "Captain George North" and became his first widely popular book; he wrote it during this time, along with Kidnapped, Strange Case of Dr Jekyll and Mr Hyde (which established his wider reputation), The Black Arrow: A Tale of the Two Roses, A Child's Garden of Verses, and Underwoods. He gave a copy of Kidnapped to his friend and frequent Skerryvore visitor Henry James.

His father died in 1887 and Stevenson felt free to follow the advice of his physician to try a complete change of climate, so he headed for Colorado with his mother and family. But after landing in New York, they decided to spend the winter in the Adirondacks at a cure cottage now known as Stevenson Cottage at Saranac Lake, New York. During the intensely cold winter, Stevenson wrote some of his best essays, including Pulvis et Umbra. He also began The Master of Ballantrae and lightheartedly planned a cruise to the southern Pacific Ocean for the following summer.

Politics

Stevenson believed in Conservatism for most of his life. His cousin and biographer Sir Graham Balfour said that "he probably throughout life would, if compelled to vote, have always supported the Conservative candidate." In 1866, Stevenson voted for Benjamin Disraeli, future Conservative Prime Minister of the United Kingdom, over Thomas Carlyle for the Lord Rectorship of the University of Edinburgh. During his college years, he briefly identified himself as a "red-hot socialist". He wrote at age 26: "I look back to the time when I was a Socialist with something like regret.... Now I know that in thus turning Conservative with years, I am going through the normal cycle of change and travelling in the common orbit of men's opinions."

Journey to the Pacific

In June 1888, Stevenson chartered the yacht Casco and set sail with his family from San Francisco. The vessel "plowed her path of snow across the empty deep, far from all track of commerce, far from any hand of help." The sea air and thrill of adventure for a time restored his health, and for nearly three years he wandered the eastern and central Pacific, stopping for extended stays at the Hawaiian Islands where he became a good friend of King Kalākaua. He befriended the king's niece Princess Victoria Kaiulani, who also had Scottish heritage. He spent time at the Gilbert Islands, Tahiti, New Zealand, and the Samoan Islands. During this period, he completed The Master of Ballantrae, composed two ballads based on the legends of the islanders, and wrote The Bottle Imp. He preserved the experience of these years in his various letters and in his In the South Seas (which was published posthumously). He made a voyage in 1889 with Lloyd on the trading schooner Equator, visiting Butaritari, Mariki, Apaiang, and Abemama in the Gilbert Islands. They spent several months on Abemama with tyrant-chief Tem Binoka, whom Stevenson described in In the South Seas.

Stevenson left Sydney on the Janet Nicoll in April 1890 for his third and final voyage among the South Seas islands. He intended to produce another book of travel writing to follow his earlier book In the South Seas, but it was his wife who eventually published her journal of their third voyage. (Fanny misnames the ship in her account The Cruise of the Janet Nichol.) A fellow passenger was Jack Buckland, whose stories of life as an island trader became the inspiration for the character of Tommy Hadden in The Wrecker (1892), which Stevenson and Lloyd Osbourne wrote together. Buckland visited the Stevensons at Vailima in 1894.

Last years

In 1890, Stevenson purchased a tract of about 400 acres (1.6 km^2) in Upolu, an island in Samoa where he established himself on his estate in the village of Vailima after two aborted attempts to visit Scotland. He took the native name Tusitala (Samoan for "Teller of Tales"). His influence spread among the Samoans, who consulted him for advice, and he soon became involved in local politics. He was convinced that the European officials who had been appointed to rule the Samoans were incompetent, and he published A Footnote to History after many futile attempts to resolve the matter. This was such a stinging protest against existing conditions that it resulted in the recall of two officials, and Stevenson feared for a time that it would result in his own deportation. He wrote to Colvin, "I used to think meanly of the plumber; but how he shines beside the politician!"

He also found time to work at his writing, although he felt that "there was never any man had so many irons in the fire". He wrote The Beach of Falesa, Catriona (titled David Balfour in the US), The Ebb-Tide, and the Vailima Letters during this period.

Stevenson grew depressed and wondered if he had exhausted his creative vein, as he had been "overworked bitterly" and that the best he could write was "ditch-water". He even feared that he might again become a helpless invalid. He rebelled against this idea: "I wish to die in my boots; no more Land of Counterpane for me. To be drowned, to be shot, to be thrown from a horse — ay, to be hanged, rather than pass again through that slow dissolution." He then suddenly had a return of energy and he began work on Weir of Hermiston. "It's so good that it frightens me," he is reported to have exclaimed. He felt that this was the best work he had done.

On 3 December 1894, Stevenson was talking to his wife and straining to open a bottle of wine when he suddenly exclaimed, "What's that?", asked his wife "does my face look strange?", and collapsed. He died within a few hours, probably of a cerebral haemorrhage. He was 44 years old. The Samoans insisted on surrounding his body with a watch-guard during the night and on bearing him on their shoulders to nearby Mount Vaea, where they buried him on a spot overlooking the sea on land donated by British Acting Vice Consul Thomas Trood. Stevenson had always wanted his Requiem inscribed on his tomb:

Under the wide and starry sky,

Dig the grave and let me lie.

Glad did I live and gladly die,

And I laid me down with a will.

This be the verse you grave for me:

Here he lies where he longed to be;

Home is the sailor, home from sea,

And the hunter home from the hill.

Stevenson was loved by the Samoans, and his tombstone epigraph was translated to a Samoan song of grief. (Source: Wikipedia)

CPSIA information can be obtained
at www.ICGtesting.com
Printed in the USA
LVHW051339251119
638400LV00005B/831/P

9 789353 8395